J.T. ELLISON

TEAR ME APART

mira

mira

Recycling programs for this product may not exist in your area.

ISBN-13: 978-0-7783-3000-4
ISBN-13: 978-0-7783-0826-3 (Library Hardcover Edition)

Tear Me Apart

For questions and comments about the quality of this book, please contact us at CustomerService@Harlequin.com.

BookClubbish.com

Printed in U.S.A.

To Margaret Marbury and Nicole Brebner,
for helping me find the darkness within.

And, as always, to Randy, who keeps the darkness at bay.

TEAR ME APART

"Man is least himself when he talks in his own person. Give him a mask and he will tell you the truth."

—OSCAR WILDE

PROLOGUE

VIVIAN

I remember the day she arrived so clearly. What quirk of fate led her to me? I wondered about this for years. If only I had stepped right instead of left at the corner, or taken the stairs instead of the elevator at the hospital, perhaps ordered chicken instead of steak for my last meal with my father before his death, the principles of chaos—the butterfly effect—would have altered the course of my life enough that she wouldn't have appeared. But I did step right, and I took the elevator, and I had the steak, and she did appear, and I will never recover from her.

★ ★ ★

It's my eighth Turkey Tetrazzini Tuesday. I push the food around on my tray, not hungry. The meds they give me make me in turns nauseous and lacking in appetite and dinner is at five, anyway, only a few hours away. If I feel better then, I'll eat.

Everyone else is happily communing with the glob of gray matter on their plates. They don't know any better. Half are drooling in their trays, the other half are tracing the voyage of little green men through the gravy or wadding the tinfoil wrapping from their rolls into bouquets they hang on their bedsteads to keep away the government spies. Suffice it to say we don't have anything common. I have no exciting diagnosis. I haven't committed a crime. I'm just depressed. Like, suicidal ideation with three attempts under my belt depressed. Yes, it's the bad kind.

I wander back to my room, glancing in the open doors of the ward. Occasionally, the occupants leave out fun things to play with. Magazines. String. Cards. I'm not picky, anything to break the tedium. I'm out of luck today. The rooms are spotless. Beds are made, towels hang straight and even, the whole ward smells of Pine-Sol. The janitors have been through. They will have pocketed anything of worth.

I bail on the reconnaissance mission and swing by my small hole for my cigarettes. Four times a day, I am allowed to stand in a tiny six-by-six hutch off the back steps and smoke. I can see the sky and the huge brass padlock that, if opened, would give me my freedom, allow me to step into the parking lot and disappear into the world, but nothing else. Sometimes, I wonder if cigarette privileges are worth it. It must be how cows feel, penned in day after day, never able to cross to the other field.

My room, 8A, is white. White as week-old snow, the kind of white that isn't crisp and clean, but dirtied, institutional. You won't see the exact shade anywhere else. White walls, white bedding, white linoleum. White gowns. White long-sleeved jackets with shiny silver buckles if we're naughty.

Normally, we're all double-bunked, but I haven't shared in a month, not since the last roommate was sent home. As much as I hate her for getting out, I've found I enjoy the silence of having my own space. Being alone always frightened me before. I despised the dark and its creeping pulchritude. Now, I crave its simplicity. Its emptiness and solitude. Caring about fear is too hard anymore.

I stop in the doorway. There is someone in my room.

Her hair is dark and cascading, freshly washed; she reeks of the squeaky-clean scent of Johnson's Baby Shampoo. The hospital passes it out to all new inductees in their plastic "welcome" bucket.

She sits on the bed, head cocked to the side, her back to the door, staring out the four-by-two wire mesh screen window, which looks at the parking lot—bleak gray asphalt and a never-ending parade of cars. It's a strange torture, this taste of freedom they give us. We are fish in the aquarium; we can see the rest of the world passing by, disinterested people living uninteresting lives.

This intrusion into my private space infuriates me, and I slam back out to the nurses' station. There is a nurse named Eleanor Snow who runs the ward, but we all call her Ratchet because she is a bitch. No one said we had to be original.

Ratchet is calmly doing an intake form. Probably for my new roommate. Her serenity infuriates me further. I don't get serenity. My mind never quiets and allows me to sit, smiling, as I fill in forms.

I snarl at her, "Who is in my room?"

"Your new roommate. I suggest you go introduce yourself. And keep your hands to yourself. You don't want me to cut your nails again."

I shudder. I don't, and she knows it.

"You didn't ask my permission to move someone in."

"We don't have to. Now scat. I have work to do. And eat your dinner, or I'll talk with Dr. Freeman about your lack of proper nutrition."

"Be sure to tell him the meds he gives me make me puke."

I storm off. It's the only power I have, not eating. They force the drugs in me; tell me when to sleep, shower, and shit; make me sit in a circle with the other drooling idiots to share my story—*You'll feel so much better after you've talked it out, dear.* No. No!

To hell with the cigarette break. I head back to 8A. The girl is still sitting in the same spot, her head cocked the same way. She has long hands, set to the sides of her hips. They prop her up as if they are grounding her to the world.

I make noise, and she doesn't turn. I step in front of the window, looming over her so she'll look at me. I snap my fingers under her nose, and she barely flinches.

Oh.

It doesn't take a brain surgeon to diagnose her silence and lack of movement. She's riding with King Thor. Thorazine for the uninitiated. A strong antipsychotic agent overused in mental facilities to keep rowdy, disturbed, or otherwise uncooperative patients calm.

I like riding with the King even less than having Ratchet snip my nails, so I cut the stranger some slack. I rifle through her things. Her few street clothes are wadded in the bottom of the laundry bag, and she wears the same baggy sweats and sweatshirt I currently model because my civvies are in the laundry. The rest of the bag has small toiletries, a hospital-issued toothbrush and toothpaste, a comb. She isn't a voluntary.

Voluntary commitment, when the patient agrees to come in for a certain amount of time to get their head shrunk. Technically, I am a voluntary, which is why I have a few more privileges than most. I've also been here for a little over two months, and I am ready as fuck to get out of here. What they don't like to tell you is when you go in *voluntarily*, you don't get the choice to *voluntarily* leave. No, that's up to them, to Dr. Freakazoid and Ratchet and the "treatment team."

Bastards.

I quickly search the rest of the room and see she only has the clothes on her back and in her bag. Interesting. A non-voluntary could be a nice diversion. When she comes back from her ride, I might find she's a mumbling, drooling idiot, or a tinfoil baby, or a suicide, or even a criminal. We're all mixed in, the permanent residents and the temporary, the clinically insane and the criminally. The latter makes for fascinating conversation. The thick white bandage on her arm tells me the rest of the story. Someone was a bad girl. I like her already.

I pick up her comb. Mine is missing several teeth. I need a brush—my hair is too thick for this tiny piece of plastic crap—but a fresh comb is better than what I have. I switch them out, then get to work on my hair.

Without moving, in a voice low and melodious and laden with the sharpness of a thousand razors, she says, "Touch my things again, and I'll kill you."

"Right."

I continue with the comb. She turns, and when I look up, I am startled. The hatred in her eyes is so intense it's like a demon from hell is suddenly perched on the bed. Her hair floats around her head like a dark storm cloud, and I can practically smell the thunder coming off her. I take a step back and toss the comb on her bed.

At this movement, she smiles and turns back toward the window.

PART ONE

1

"Now coming to the gates, last year's junior Alpine Downhill champion, Mindy Wright."

Mindy hears her name called, and her heart pounds in her throat. She knows what they are saying in the booth. They are discussing her leap into the majors. A year ago she was the Junior World Champion in three disciplines and the overall. She is special. Unique. Now, barely one year into her adult career, she is killing it. They are comparing her to her heroes, Lindsey Vonn and Mikaela Shiffrin, speculating that with this final run, she can overtake their records and become the new youngest Alpine Downhill champion. They are talking about her parents, their sacrifices, and Mindy's grueling training, the intense life she's led, uncomplaining, with a smile on her face all the time. Sunny. They call her the girl with the sunny disposition.

This sunny girl is going to become the world's fastest female downhill skier in less than two minutes, and then what will they call her?

Mindy can feel the energy in the air; the tension is palpable. She has a good chance, she knows it. Her practice run was at a record-breaking pace. She is going to blow this run away. The mountain is hers for the taking.

Everyone wants her to win this race and take the trophy. Trophy be damned; if she hits her points, she will automatically qualify for the US Olympic team. No pressure or anything.

She takes the little burst of adrenaline from that thought, lets it get her moving. The snow started falling intensely about ten minutes earlier. She'd heard the officials discussing whether to hold the skiers on the hill until it passed, but now their radios crackle with assurances that the blizzard is only at the very top and the course clears after the first turn.

Mindy readies herself, visualizes the course, her body bending and weaving as her mind takes her through every turn one last time.

A buzzer pulls her to the surface. There are no shouts and screams as Mindy slides into place in the starting house; the crowds are at the bottom of the mountain, less than ninety seconds away. Up here, she's surrounded by coaches and officials and other competitors; it is not a friendly place.

It's snowing hard, not gentle whispers of white drifting down, but tiny flakes wedged together in the sky creating a perpetual wall of white. The eerie silence, the loneliness of it, makes her heart pump harder. She often feels like this when she takes her place at the gate. Beat, *alone*. Beat, *alone*. Beat, *alone*. It feels good. It feels right.

She adjusts her goggles against the blinding white and slaps her skis against the icy snow, digging in her poles, making sure her ankles are seated and her boots tightly clipped. In response, the snow seems to come down even faster; the first section of the course is completely obscured from her vantage point above the gates. She has to have faith that they won't send her down if it is too dangerous, that the reports saying it clears after the first turn hold true. Anyway, Mindy knows this course like the back of her hand. She has raced here many times. Considering the awful weather, it is a blessing that the championship is being held in Vail. She has the home-field advantage.

Kill it, Mindy!

It is her mom's voice, spectral and distant. It happens every race, and it's strange because she knows her mom and dad are at the bottom of the mountain, waiting for her to slide to a stop in front of them, her skis shuddering on the snow, her fist in the air, pumping hard because she's won.

Once, she'd told her mom how cool it was, standing up there alone, hearing her voice cheer her on. It had become the talisman, the good luck charm. Her mom smoothed down her hair with a quizzical smile and said, "I'm always with you, Mindy. No matter what."

Not for the first time, Mindy wishes her mom had ridden up the mountain in the gondola with her. She can imagine her perfectly: starkly beautiful, not speaking, her mouth tight, her blond hair mussed and sticking out from under her red snowflake hat, holding her daughter's gloved hand tightly. It isn't allowed, but it would be nice. Then again, maybe it wouldn't. Mindy sometimes wonders if her mom is more nervous than she is when it comes to the final run. She wouldn't want that negative energy seeping into her psyche.

Let's go, let's go, let's go.

Finally, the official signals. It's time. She slaps her skis against the ice again. Tight, a little grainy, and she can barely see the track now because the snow is coming down so hard. But she knows it's there, a long, invisible line flowing out from the tips of her skis downward. Without another thought, she leans forward, into the mountain, feels the hard bar across her shins. Sets her poles again. Takes a deep breath. Her coach's voice now. *Visualize it. Visualize winning.*

The beep sounds three times and she's off, bursting out of the gate, poling hard, gaining speed quickly. She slices through the first turn, a hard bank left, her downhill edge rattling against the ice. It feels good, so good, and she tucks her poles against her body and lets the skis take her through the first flat. The skies do clear; she can finally see the blue lanes of the race course. Into the second turn, she starts gaining speed, feels the total thrill when she accelerates to eighty-five, ninety, ninety-five miles per hour. She is a rocket, a cheetah, the fastest girl on earth.

Left, right, left, right, poles stuck to her body, over the jump, airborne, arms windmilling slightly, but she stays tucked perfectly, totally in control. She has it; she has it, she is flying down the slope. She can hear the screams and cheers as she zooms past. She knows with the assurance of years of skiing that she is in the zone, is going faster than she ever has. All the hard work, the ski camps, the weight training, it is all coming together.

Left. Right. Left. Tuck.

The burst of swirling snow comes from nowhere. It catches her full in the face just as she makes the last gate. Her skis slip out of the ruts. The tip of her left ski hits the plastic guard of the flag, and she is in midair, flying for real this time.

Everything is silent. She doesn't hear the gasps, the screams, just focuses on relaxing, like she's always been taught. Though she is airborne, if she isn't too far off, she can still make it if she keeps her tuck, lands correctly, gets the damn right ski down, and makes the next turn... The flag slaps her in the face, and she goes down in a flurry of skis and poles and snow.

She doesn't know how long she lies there before it registers she has crashed. Her champion's body resists the idea, continues to make the last turns, her torso writhing in the snow.

The snow is cold.

My face hurts.

My leg *hurts.*

Her eyes are closed. She opens them to whiteness. *I'm blind, oh my God*, then realizes her face is freezing. She is facedown. She plants her arms in the snow and tries to rise. The pain in her leg is white-hot, and she cries out. Seconds later, she is surrounded. Ski patrols, red jackets, white crosses. The first touch is from a woman, her face deeply tanned, her goggles opaque.

"Your leg's broken, sweetie, try not to move. I know it's cold. Hang tight. We'll get you splinted and get you on the sled."

"My leg? It's broken? How do you know? Did I make it all the way down?"

"Tough girl, you didn't. You tagged that last flag, and it knocked you upside down. You did a backflip, came down hard. You've been out for a few minutes. Pretty spectacular crash. And your leg…trust me, honey, it's broken. No, no, don't look."

Mindy ignores the admonition, wishes she hadn't. There is a large jag of white sticking out of her shin. Her blood looks like rubies against the icy slush. She fights back the urge to scream. "But my time…if I don't finish, I'm DQd from the event. I have to get down. You've gotta let me up."

The patrol's voice is sympathetic. "You're out of it now, sweetie, I'm sorry. Maybe you have enough points to qualify from your other races. But you can't go anywhere, this leg's pretty gnarly. Okay, here's the splint, hang tight, this is going to hurt like a bitch."

Mindy grits her teeth as they start pumping up the air cast. Fights back the tears, focuses on the voice that keeps saying, *You didn't make it, you didn't make it.* She stops fighting, tries to relax as they lift her into the sled and start down the remainder of the mountain. She tries to be a good sport about it, as she's been taught, raises a fist toward the worried faces, and the crowd goes absolutely wild, cheering for their girl, but inside she is wailing.

She wanted this so badly. It's all she's ever wanted. And she's blown it.

What happened? She runs the course again in her mind, realizes there is a big blank. She doesn't remember how she went down. She knows this isn't entirely unusual; she's heard about it happening to other racers. She's been so blessed, so lucky, never to have had a major injury. Granted, she's seventeen, and she's only been on the circuit at this level for a year. But still.

What if I can never ski again?

This spike to her heart is too much to bear. She wipes away tears as they reach the bottom. Her dad is waiting; she can see his bright red North Face jacket, concern etched on his handsome face. He pushes aside two ski patrols and kneels beside her.

"Poor baby. Does it hurt?"

"Daddy, I didn't make it."

"Let's worry about your leg first, peanut, then we'll worry about the rest."

"I don't remember falling. What happened?"

"Microburst of snow. Came out of nowhere." As if to prove his point a swirl of snow surrounds them. Her father says, "They really should close the course, it's too dangerous now." He pats her hand. Mindy can only feel pressure through the glove, not the warm reassurance of her father's hand.

"Where's Mom?"

"I'm right here, honey. Right here. You're okay. I'm here."

Mindy hears the calm concern of her mother's voice and takes a deep breath. If her mom isn't frantic, it isn't too bad.

"Mom will meet us at the hospital, honey. They won't let us both ride with you. She's going to drive the car—"

"No!"

Her dad's face registers a tiny bit of shock. "Okay, no worries. Mom will ride with you, and I'll bring the car."

"No, it's fine. I don't care who rides with me. But we can't leave. I need to find out who wins." As she speaks, she hears them blow the horn. The course is being closed.

Her dad's smile warms her. He leans close, whispers, "Maybe we'll get lucky. You're still in first place overall."

The EMT isn't quite glaring at them but is clearly anxious to get moving. "We have to take her now, folks. Who's riding with us?"

Her mom presses her palm against Mindy's cheek, unstraps her helmet. "Hang tight, baby. I'll meet you at the hospital. We'll get you fixed up. Be strong."

Mindy grits her teeth again when they put her into the ambulance; the jostling makes red-hot pokers shoot through her leg. Her mother's face disappears as the doors slam closed, the worry etched as deep as a fissure in granite.

Her dad takes a seat on the bench, trying to stay out of the way. The paramedic leans over her, takes her blood pressure and pulse. She tries to stay calm, not cry, not fall apart. All she can think about is her coach's disappointment that someone else will be standing on the podium because she got too aggressive toward the bottom and let her ski get caught in that rut. He's always told her aggressive equals arrogance, and arrogance equals crash.

"Mindy, I'm Todd. I'm going to start an IV and give you some pain meds so that leg doesn't hurt so bad. Okay? A little pinch here, hang tight…that's a brave girl, well done."

Within moments, the horrible pain in her leg is gone. Her thoughts become disjointed.

Arrogant Crash. That's a good band name. I wonder if they'll let me have the gate I hit. Would it be arrogant to ask? The snow was so cold.

I didn't make it.

Mindy doesn't care, which surprises her. She feels sleepy and warm, hears her dad and Todd talking. And then there is nothing.

2

VAIL HEALTH HOSPITAL

Lauren Wright bursts through the Emergency Room doors exactly ten seconds behind the stretcher carrying her broken daughter. The paramedics wheel Mindy into a treatment room. Jasper is holding Mindy's hand, even though she's asleep. When he sees Lauren, his eyes close in relief. He reaches out his free arm and she snuggles in, letting him hold her while he also holds their daughter's hand. Mindy looks dead. Gray, pained, lifeless.

"Is she okay?" Lauren asks, her voice barely a whisper.

"Yeah. They gave her some morphine so she wouldn't hurt so badly. She was mumbling about a band named Arrogant Crash before she went out like a light. Todd here thinks it's a punk rock band from Aspen who played Coachella last spring, but who knows?" Jasper grins, and Lauren manages a breath.

"Hope she's okay. She's an amazing skier," Todd the EMT says, and Lauren nods her thanks to him.

"We appreciate you taking care of her."

"Sure thing." He hands off the chart to a petite redheaded nurse in blue scrubs. "Fingers crossed."

The nurses are sweet and smiley, and Lauren's blood pressure ticks down another notch. They bustle around, adjusting the IV tubing, attaching leads, turning Mindy from skier to patient. It makes Lauren uneasy to see her daughter tethered to the beeping machines. One of the nurses lifts the white-and-red towel covering Mindy's leg, and Lauren gets her first good look at the severity of the injury. The lower half of Mindy's leg is a tangle of hamburger with a large white bone sticking out. Lauren feels an odd tingle run through her body. Gooseflesh raises on her arms.

Jasper sees her blanch. "What's wrong? What is it?"

She points at Mindy's leg, whispers, "That. Oh God, Jasper, what if—"

He grabs her hand tightly, tips up her chin so she has to look into his eyes. They are good eyes. Exceptional eyes. Light blue centers with a dark blue ring. Add in the sandy hair and athletic frame, and Jasper is a man to be noticed. A man who, to her never-ending relief, only notices Lauren.

"No, no, no. Do not say it. Don't even think it. She's going to be fine. She's young and healthy. The leg is badly broken, but it's fixable. Everything is fixable."

Fixable.

Lauren feels the wail begin inside her. Her lip wobbles. She cried in the car all the way to the hospital, tears of fear, tears of anger, tears of frustration for her only child. Jasper was right to separate them, if only for ten minutes. He'd given her a gift, moments alone to come to grips with the situation. It was kind, and necessary.

When she arrived at the hospital and put the car in Park, the tears ended. She'd wiped her face, fixed her hair. Vowed to be strong for Mindy. And for Jasper. And for everyone. Because that's what mothers do. And Lauren is great in a crisis. Ask anyone.

Now, she is doing everything she can to stay calm and in control. Mindy is so strong, so driven, so determined—*so perfect*—and seeing her daughter broken and bleeding in the snow, and now unconscious on this impersonal bed, breaks something inside her. She doesn't want to be overly emotional in front of Mindy, who hates scenes. Keeps Lauren at arm's length when she makes a fuss. Mindy has a cold, calculating streak in her—which is why she is such a brilliant athlete and competitor. She can turn the emotions *off* and *on* at will. It is a trait Lauren continually worries about. Did Mindy get it from her? From Jasper? They are both excellent compartmentalizers. Have they done their only child a disservice by being overly rational?

Oh, her leg…it looks hideous. Lauren doesn't want to think about what this accident might mean. Lesser injuries end careers. And she doesn't know what will happen to her little girl if she can no longer ski.

A burly dark-haired man comes into the room. "I'm Joe, from radiology. I'm going to take her to X-ray now. You guys stay here. We'll be back in fifteen."

"Can't we come?" Lauren asks.

"We're going three doors down. You can come if you want, but trust me, I've got her."

She gives the boy her best *mother* look, a steely-eyed glance that usually makes even the strongest young people quake in their boots. He smiles. "Come on then, let's go."

The X-rays are quick. Lauren has a hard time watching. The radiographs pop up on the screen, one after another. The angles of Mindy's bones are so wrong, and the very thought that she is seeing under Mindy's skin makes her stomach queasy. It's too intimate. At least Mindy is still out cold from the morphine and doesn't feel the chilly steel of the plate beneath her, doesn't hear the snick and whir of the X-ray camera, doesn't hear her father peppering the tech with questions. She lies inert under a thick lead apron to protect her as Joe from radiology takes shot after shot. Lauren knows Mindy will be furious when she finds out. She is private, her daughter. Aloof. Protective of her personal space, even from her parents.

The tech won't answer Jasper's questions, and Lauren can see them both getting frustrated. "We aren't allowed to give opinions," Joe says for the third time, but mutters under his breath so that they overhear the dreaded words: "Compound fracture of tibia and fibula."

The rest are denials.

"Can't say for sure."

"The surgeon will talk to you."

"Bad break, yes."

True to his promise, they are back in the room in fifteen minutes flat.

Jasper begins his research into Mindy's injury, fingers flying on his phone. Lauren fusses with the pillow, trying and failing to get her daughter's head to stay in a spot that looks comfortable. A tall blonde, all messy ponytail and shiny engagement ring, walks in, glances at the chart, lifts the medicated towel and looks at Mindy's leg, then faces Lauren and Jasper.

"Hey, Mom and Dad. Got yourself a tough girl here. We saw the crash. We're lucky she only broke her leg."

"You were watching?" Jasper asks, and despite himself, his face glows with the praise and attention. He's a stage mother of the worst sort when it comes to Mindy's talent. It makes Lauren happy. It is the only way they can manage the pressure of having an athlete of this caliber. He is in charge of Pride; Lauren is responsible for Humility. They needn't worry—Mindy's charm belays all. She is what they call the real deal—a tough, hardworking athlete who recognizes her gifts but doesn't let them go to her head. She has no close friends, but she has the respect of the skiing world, and that is more important to her than sleepovers and proms and whispered secrets in the night.

They've done well with her. Yes, perhaps Lauren too has a dash of pride for producing this remarkable creature.

"Watching our hometown girl? You betcha. It was a horrible crash, and too bad, she totally had the best run going." She crosses her arms over her chest, the ring winking in the light, and is suddenly forbidding, like an angel of wrath descending on the room. "So, brass tacks. We've already called Dr. Stuart. He's our best orthopedic surgeon. We sent an SUV to get him here safely. The storm's getting worse, but he's coming in to work on Mindy. We're going to take her straight to the OR and see what's what."

Taking possession of their daughter, like she's a car being repossessed. Lauren steps in front of the bed, effectively blocking Mindy from view. "I'm sorry, but who are you again?"

"Oh, sorry, Mom. I'm Dani, Dr. Stuart's PA. I'll be assisting Dr. Stuart in the surgery."

"Surgery?" they say in unison, concern bleeding through. They can't help it, they're parents, after all.

"It's the only way to put these bones back together. Dr. Stuart will come in and explain everything to you afterward, but we have to get the wound cleaned out before a bacterial infection starts. These open fractures can get nasty. He'll most likely need to put in a rod to stabilize things. It's going to be rough for Mindy for the next few weeks, but you've raised a seriously tough girl, and she's in great physical shape. She'll be back on the slopes in no time."

Abhorrent visions dance through Lauren's head: her girl limping around, her leg permanently scarred. What will she think of this mar on her otherwise smooth and perfect beauty? Lauren has no idea how Mindy will react. She has no scars on her lean body, a miracle, considering. Will she freak out, beg for plastic surgery? Be stoic, wear it like a badge of honor? If Lauren is honest with herself, she thinks it will be the latter. Mindy is so tough, so unlike other girls her age. No, a scar won't faze her.

Movement, a whispered gasp from the bed. "Mom?"

Lauren grabs Mindy's hand. She is groggy and pale, and Lauren's heart constricts. *Oh God. My baby. I don't know if I can handle this. Why can't I be the one who's hurt? Why can't I shoulder this pain?*

"Don't move, sweetie. Your leg is broken. You need surgery." She can't help it; tears roll down her cheek.

"I know. Don't cry, Mom. It will be okay. This happens. They'll fix me."

Brave, so brave. Comforting *Lauren*. At the sting of the role reversal, Lauren sniffs and smiles, pulls herself together.

"Yes, tough girl, they will. You're going to be just fine. Dr. Stuart is the best orthopedic surgeon on staff."

The PA slaps the chart back into place. "That's right, Mindy, we're going to fix you right up. So kisses and hugs, family, it's time to put this little egg back together again."

As instructed, they kiss and hug their drawn, pale daughter. They stay strong. They assure and pet. There are no more tears, no more weaknesses allowed. If Mindy is going to be strong, then damn it, so will they.

Yet, as they wheel her away, Lauren has a moment of sheer panic. A premonition of sorts. Something is not right with their world. Little does she know, this is only the beginning.

★ ★ ★

The surgery is estimated to take just under an hour. They are in an impersonal, yellow-walled room with brown couches covered in industrial-strength faux leather, the kind that looks like it will withstand a knife attack or a pack of rabid dogs.

Lauren can't sit. How can she sit? Her daughter is anesthetized, effectively dead, having a metal rod screwed into the fragile bones of her leg. Jasper doesn't seem nearly as concerned. After looking up the doctor and seeing that he is the number one orthopod for local skiers and sanctioned by the Vail Ski Club, he's settled in, drinking coffee and making phone calls, updating friends to Mindy's status, talking to her coach, Steve Hakuri, who is stuck on the mountain in the blizzard, waiting to find out if they are going to keep running the race when the storm clears. The speaker is on so Lauren can hear both ends of Jasper's conversation—Steve seems to think they are going to call the whole event, which means Mindy will still have the overall lead, and almost more importantly, enough World Cup points to qualify for the Olympic team.

Lauren doesn't know if they'll get that lucky. Jasper gives her a *chin-up* motion from five feet away. The room—the disgusting yellow-and-brown room—is small, but she doesn't think she's ever felt farther away from him than she does right now.

There is a chasm. It has been widening all day. As if this is her fault. As if Lauren is the one who's flung her child down the mountain and slammed her into a flag, snapping her leg in two.

He might say that. It is true, in a sense. Lauren has pushed Mindy. But she wanted to be pushed. She is naturally driven. Naturally talented. She likes the workouts, the running, the weights, the yoga to keep her young body supple and mind clear, the ultra-clean food. And she loves the mountain. It is her favorite place to be, leaning into that hill, feeling the wind whip past, defying gravity, space, time. Truly, Mindy loves it more than she loves them.

Lauren does her best not to be jealous. She doesn't want to lose Mindy to her life's joy. She wants to be a part of it, to participate, to support and help. To push, when needed.

The way Mindy describes skiing, it is holy, sacred. A sacrament between her and the gods who created the mountain in the first place. Lauren and Jasper love to ski, but the connection Mindy has with the snow and ice is corporeal. Anyone who watches her knows this. She's meant to be a skier.

Lauren can't help the thought: *What are we going to do if this ends her career?*

She watches Jasper, wondering how he can be so cheerful. She knows he's trying to keep her spirits up—he's naturally a happy kind of guy—an eternal optimist. They've been married for a long time now, almost eighteen years of ups and downs, of Mindy's crazy training schedules, late nights and early mornings, homeschooling, tutors, days spent cold and frozen at the bottom of too many mountains, sleeping rough on transatlantic flights, and through it all, he has been a wonderful father and husband.

She resents his forced cheer, which is completely unfair. The stress of the day is catching up to her. There's only so much coffee can do. They need real food, real rest.

Her Apple watch shows she's paced two miles before the doctor finally comes out, his face drawn and tired. He is a large man, balding, with small round glasses like a schoolteacher of old. He radiates intelligence and warmth. She trusts him immediately.

But when he says, "Mom, Dad," Lauren can't help being annoyed. Why won't they use their names? Why must they be reduced to the roles of parents instead of being acknowledged as people, living, breathing human beings?

Regardless, they gather at his feet, supplicants.

"We've put her back together, and she's going to be just fine. We'll have to watch carefully for infection, but we've loaded her up with all the best antibiotics. One concern is I don't know that she's done growing, so there may be some surgeries in the future to lengthen this bone to match her right side, but that's something we'll know more about later on."

"This is good, though, right? She'll heal and be able to ski again?" Jasper's face lights up with hope. Lauren still feels no relief. There is something else. Something is coming.

"Sure thing. It looked pretty bad, but once I got in there and cleaned things up, turns out it was a good break, no splintering, no leftover shards of bone. Her leg's in a halo, which looks pretty gruesome, but that's only to keep things stable while the wound heals. Crutches for six weeks, minimum, and lots of rehab, but she'll come out of it okay." The frown deepens, the lines of his forehead collapsing in on themselves so he looks like a Shar-Pei puppy. "There is one complication."

When he says this, another doctor enters the room, as if he's been waiting in the wings for his cue. Spotlight, stage right, please, and follow.

Lauren resists that urge to say, *I told you so.* Instead, her muscles tighten.

"This is Dr. Oliver. He's with oncology."

"Oncology? What?" Jasper grabs Lauren's hand. He is crushing her bones, and she wants to pull away, but she clings as hard as he, and at the doctor's next words, the world bottoms out around them.

3

There are so many words Lauren doesn't understand. But somewhere in them, a bone-deep terror starts. She ignores the terminology, the foreign, frightening words, and focuses on the face of the doctor as he explains their new normal.

Their daughter has cancer.

Leukemia.

She needs immediate treatment.

Jasper asks all the right questions. He is still holding on to Lauren's hand, but she gets the sense she is the one holding him upright.

She lets them talk until she can't stand it anymore.

"How could we not have known she was sick?" she blurts.

The doctor smiles kindly, perfectly square Chiclet teeth that are surely veneers shining in the fluorescent light. "A very good question, Mom. We—"

"Lauren."

"Excuse me?"

"My name is Lauren. Not Mom. His name is Jasper. Not Dad. Please stop it."

"Yes, ma'am. Of course." He regroups, then begins again, with a long emphasis on their names that is almost as infuriating to her as the parental nomenclature.

"Lauren. Jasper. Mindy is an athlete, used to pushing herself. If I were to guess, she's always tired, always sore, and that's been going on for several months, am I right? My bet is she's been running ragged competing this winter, and it was easily missed, blamed on her training regime."

Easily missed. Lauren's daughter has a disease that might kill her, and it was *easily missed* by those closest to her.

Dear God. How will they live with themselves if Mindy dies, and they chalked up her symptoms to aggressive training?

The surgeon's beeper squawks. He reaches down, frowning at his belt. "I need to go, we have another emergency surgery. I'll leave you in Dr. Oliver's care, and I'll see Mindy tomorrow morning during rounds. She's a tough girl. Don't worry yourselves too much. The leg will heal."

And he bustles away, a flurry of blue scrubs and white coat. Lauren senses relief in the lines of his retreating shoulders—his job is finished, and Dr. Oliver's, and Mindy's, is just beginning.

Dr. Oliver gestures to the couch.

"Let me tell you where we go from here."

The names of the tests are lengthy and confusing. He hands over a pamphlet with a smiling bald blue-eyed wraith on it— *Dealing with Your Child's Cancer Diagnosis*. Lauren's stomach flips. She wants to see Mindy, right now, wants to see her so badly it's like a hole is being seared into her heart.

But she sits still as the grave, and pretends to listen, to comprehend; holds Jasper's hand and leans into his warm body and prays they aren't already at the end, when this morning, she'd awakened thinking they were at the beginning.

There is a plan, a "protocol," that Dr. Oliver is going to follow. It involves aggressive chemotherapy—the induction period—followed by more treatment. Mindy will be moved from the surgical floor to oncology for more testing.

She cannot go home. She cannot pass Go. She cannot collect two hundred dollars. She is going to be stuck in this small hospital for the next few days, and they are welcome to stay with her. Many parents do, especially the first night.

Dr. Oliver is still talking, but Lauren tunes him out. She watches his mouth move. She watches Jasper's eyes track over the man's face, looking desperately for something positive to take away from this speech.

There is nothing more to glean, and Jasper is shivering when they stand and allow themselves to be escorted to a room two floors up. It is small but sunny, with the same oddly industrial yellow walls. Lauren does her best not to see any of the other patients as they pass rooms bedecked in personal items, afghans and photographs, ignores the small, bald children in wheelchairs staring into the hallways, ignores the chills creeping down her spine.

Dr. Oliver's nurse gets them settled. Her name is Hazel, and she seems very kind—they are all so very kind, so kind it sets Lauren's teeth on edge.

"Is there someone we can call, any family you'd like us to reach out to?"

Who would she call?

Her phone hasn't rung since the accident, has it?

She digs into her bag, only to find the phone's battery has died. Lauren doesn't ever allow that to happen, but since her entire world is right here in this hospital room, there is no one she wants to talk to, so she's left the phone in her purse, zipped tidily away so it won't fall out, and it's dead.

Stop thinking that word, Lauren.

Like Mindy, Lauren doesn't have any close friends. With Mindy's activities, it's always been hard to establish friendships with the mothers of other girls her age. Either they were busy with their own extracurriculars, or too competitive to allow their daughters to spend time with Lauren's. They are a solid, happy threesome, Jasper, Mindy, and Lauren. Truthfully, Lauren prefers it this way. Their solitude is a comfort to her. She was never much for large groups anyway.

"We should call Juliet," Jasper says, and Lauren nods. Oh, of course. Juliet. Her little sister. Mindy's favorite—only—aunt. She must be told. Jasper steps out to make the call.

Lauren is beginning to think she must be in shock. She is not thinking clearly. She watches the blizzard outside the window. The fluorescent lights and kindly nurses are making her so claustrophobic she wants to scream. Her instinct to flee is strong, to run into the snow and go back up the mountain to their house and wake up again and do this day over.

Of course, she can't. She must stay together for Jasper. She must stay tethered to the real world for Mindy's sake.

There is a small commotion in the hall. Mindy is arriving.

The techs wheel in the bed. Mindy's leg is suspended, thin metal pieces disappearing into the bandages like the legs on a butterfly into its thorax. Her foot is half-casted, her toes peeking from their nest, black and blue and a strange orange-yellow—Betadine, from being sanitized before the surgery. She is still deeply asleep, her mouth slightly open. The painkillers must be tremendous to knock her out; her metabolism is Thoroughbred quick, and Lauren hasn't ever seen anything touch it. She's never seen her daughter asleep like this, either, unnaturally still, and the word prances in again—*dead, dead, dead.*

How will Lauren tell her how sick she is? How is this even happening? Mindy has been pale, yes, and she's been tired, but Mindy thought—Lauren thought?—they all thought Mindy was simply training hard.

Oliver's nurse watches these proceedings, then straightens a pillow and smiles at them again.

"Mrs. Wright? Ma'am? Is there someone we can call?"

"No, thank you. I'll charge my phone and make a few calls myself. Thank you. You're very kind."

Lauren makes a mental note to send flowers to the nurses' station. Something cheery, bright. They probably aren't thanked enough. They work so hard.

Jasper comes back in the room wearing a tight smile, which

makes the grooves around his mouth deepen. They are growing older, he and Lauren, but this fact often catches her by surprise. She still sees the young lawyer she married all those years ago. The strands of gray at his temples, the deepening lines—he's aging very well. Lauren, on the other hand, worries she's not. Too much sun as a child, too many cigarettes, too much booze in school. Soon enough she will be haggard and drawn, her skin wrinkled and gray.

Is Mindy going to age at all?

At the thought, she has to brace herself not to burst into tears and run screaming from the hospital.

Jasper glances at the metal halo holding Mindy's leg in place, pales. He licks his chapped lips. "She's in."

"What do you mean, she's in?"

"They called the race. Her points stand. She's in."

Lauren laughs, worthless and cold. She can't help herself. All the work, all the sleepless nights and long, cold days, and the triumph her girl has been working toward is going to be snatched away by a chance encounter with a set of rogue blood cells.

Again, the thought: *She is going to be so furious when she wakes.*

Mindy caught a terrible cold once, right before a race. They couldn't give her any medication because of the drug standards for the competition, and she was downright miserable, but she decided she was going to race anyway. She couldn't breathe, her nose was running, and yet she turned in a personal best time, qualifying for junior nationals, did three TV interviews, and *then* let her mother coddle her with hot chocolate and chicken soup.

Nothing comes between Mindy and the mountain.

Now, a broken leg and leukemia might.

"They're playing favorites," Lauren says. "Won't everyone complain?"

"Everyone wants Mindy on Team USA. You know how much they all love her."

This is true. Even the dreaded Janice Cuthbert, a year younger and nearly as good, loves Mindy. Follows her around like a puppy, happy to be anywhere near her hero. Janice won't make the team now. Lauren is not a vindictive woman, but she is glad, for the moment, that the accolades still belong to Mindy. Though she can't imagine how her girl will be able to train and go to the Olympics if she is as sick as they say, not to mention heal from the broken leg quickly enough.

For the first time, she prays for a miracle.

★ ★ ★

The treatment plan is set by the next afternoon.

They took bone marrow and spinal fluid while Mindy was out from the anesthesia, so they have a jump start on her status. The cancer is identified as AML—acute myeloid leukemia. Not nearly as common as its sister ALL, it is tougher to cure, which means more aggressive treatment from the get-go. Lauren listens and takes notes, Jasper types on his phone. They will stay up all night reading horror stories, and by morning, will convince themselves that nothing will stop their daughter's survival. Nothing.

The surgery will complicate the induction period, but they have no choice now. The doctors are very clear. They have to kill the cancer cells in Mindy's blood, and they have to do it quickly. Or else.

4

Dr. Juliet Ryder hates the smell of hospitals. Ironic, considering she spends her days in a lab. The Queen of Pipettes, that's what her coworkers call her. As lead DNA tech and lab manager for the Colorado Bureau of Investigation, she accepts the title with grace and aplomb.

She pops a piece of spearmint gum in her mouth to mask the industrial scent and takes the elevator to the third floor. When she exits, she is confused: The walls state she is in the oncology ward. She inquires at the nurses' station, and is even more surprised when they point her down the hall to a private room.

There must be an explanation.

She hurries down the hall, pausing for a moment outside the room. She hears the television inside, but no voices. She knocks gently and sticks her head in.

Mindy lies on the bed, eyes glazed over, staring dully at the screen on the opposite wall. She is alone.

"Hey, kiddo."

Mindy turns her head, then brightens and straightens a bit. "Aunt J! How are you?"

"How am I? How are you, kiddo?"

"Stuck here. Bored out of my skull. The blizzard finally let up?"

"Yes. They opened the pass about two hours ago, and I got here as fast as I could."

"Mom will be glad. She needs you."

Juliet doubts this will be the case. Lauren hasn't needed her, ever. She is older. Accomplished. An artist. A mother. Successful, happy.

"What's going on, sweetie? Your leg giving you problems?"

"Oh, Mom didn't tell you? Apparently, I have cancer."

Juliet's stomach drops. "What?"

"They found it when they were doing blood work for the surgery. Leukemia. I have to do chemo. My hair's going to fall out."

Mindy sounds old, so old, worn and tired. Juliet sits on the edge of the bed and grabs her niece's hand. It is freezing; she rubs it hard between hers.

"Where are your parents?"

"I kicked them out. Mom needed a good cry. Dad needed to comfort her. They couldn't fall apart in front of me, so I begged for some soup, and sent them both down to get it. They're in the cafeteria, or the chapel, somewhere where I won't know they're freaking out."

"How did you get so cynical, child?"

"Gee, I wonder…"

"I am not a cynic."

"No, but you're a scientist. You are rational, cool, and effortlessly calm."

"Kid, I think you're a little stoned. They have you on the wacky juice for the leg, don't they?"

It works. Mindy smiles. Juliet stuffs away the fear and pain.

"Now, tell me more. What kind of cancer? There are a lot of different kinds of leukemia."

"AML. They're doing more tests, but they ran the spinal fluid. Aunt J?"

"Yes, baby?"

"I don't want to die." The voice is so small, so quiet, Juliet's heart breaks.

"You aren't going to. I won't allow it."

"My hair is going to fall out. I have to have chemo, and other awful drugs and I have to come back to this godforsaken hospital constantly. How am I going to train? How am I going to make the rest of the season?"

Juliet gestures to Mindy's leg. "Hate to break it to you, kid, but you're going to be off your skis for the foreseeable future. I mean, look at that leg. You have rods screwed into the bone. You can't put weight on that, I presume?"

"No, not for at least six weeks. But…" She shakes her head. "This is *stupid*. Who breaks their leg and finds out they have cancer?"

"You, apparently. You've always been precocious."

Silence. Juliet lifts the mass of black hair off the pillow, stroking through its gorgeous thick length.

"You know, kiddo, I think you'd look adorable with a pixie cut. If it's going to fall out anyway, maybe we should take you total punk rock for a few weeks instead of mourning it as it goes."

"Mom will kill me." But her eyes brighten, and she grins.

"Really? Word choice, child."

Mindy giggles and a small weight lifts off Juliet's chest.

"I hate to say it, but who the hell cares what your mom thinks? If you're going to lose it anyway, let's have some fun. I could cut it for you now."

She moves the thick hair to and fro, arranging, and Mindy looks alive with the idea of doing something naughty.

"Oh, my God. I've always wanted short hair. It's just too damn cold on the mountain. Go find some scissors before she comes back."

"You're serious?"

"Aren't you?"

A dare. Juliet finds a pair of scissors at the nurses' station but realizes there is no way she'll be able to get them through Mindy's thick hair. It is so unlike her own fuzzy blond, even

Lauren's sleekly perfect highlights. No, not highlights. *Balay-age*. Even how she colors her hair must be unique and special.

A nurse sees Juliet rummaging, approaches with a raised brow. "Excuse me. Can I help you?"

Juliet jerks away from the desk. "I'm sorry. I'm looking for scissors. My niece—"

"Oh. You want these," the nurse says, reaching into her desk drawer. Out comes a pair of professional offset hair shears.

"I can't believe you have them," Juliet says, then it hits her. "Oh, wow, of course you do. Sorry about this. I just found out. I haven't quite wrapped my head around it."

"You're...?"

"Mindy's aunt. Juliet."

"Ah. I'm Hazel. Nice to meet you. Mindy's a doll. She'll look adorable with short hair. Do you have a ponytail holder? It's a lot easier to cut if you put it in a pony on top of her head first."

At the direction, a wellspring of sorrow bubbles inside her. How many little girls' hair has Hazel cut off for them? Juliet shuts her heart against it. Later, she can be upset later. She has to be strong and cool for Mindy now.

"Bring them back when you're done," Hazel calls after her. "They're expensive."

Mindy has raised the head of her bed. She is still in an awkward position because of her leg, and Juliet feels badly when she sees her niece wincing at the movement.

"Hurts?"

"Yes, sometimes the pain breaks through the meds. I don't know if it's the cancer, or the surgery. I feel weird. I've felt weird for a while, but I figured it was just overtraining."

"The drugs aren't helping your weirdness, kiddo. You're on some pretty hefty painkillers." She brandishes the shears. "I mean you're under the influence and can't make a rational decision."

Mindy laughs. "I'm plenty rational. Cut it."

"As you wish." Juliet gathers her niece's hair into a ponytail on top of her head, then brutally slices through the hair. She tosses the pony on the table, and Mindy shakes her head. The hair falls around her ears. She looks like a pixie.

"Holy cow. You look different."

"Cut the rest. I want the bangs longer on the right side, okay? So they sweep over my eye. Gotta say, Aunt J. Grandma K was right, you have the touch. How did you end up a scientist instead of a hairdresser?"

"Your grandma insisted I learn a skill. I wanted to go to Space Camp because I was harboring ideas of going into astrophysics. I wanted to work at NASA, to be an astronaut. Your grandma thought my plans were ridiculous, and gave me a choice—slinging pizza for the summer, or beauty school. She said, 'Learn a skill, Juliet. Space Camp might be fun, but you need a contingency plan if things go south.'"

Juliet gets to work, shaping and shearing, for once mentally thanking her mother, gone five years now, for forcing her into the summer beautician program when she was seventeen.

"I was so furious at the time. I mean, I understand why she made me do it, but I didn't speak to her for weeks. I ended up studying genetics instead of astrophysics, and I applied to the astronaut program at NASA to be a payload specialist. Made it to the final round before I got cut, too. I had a bunch of job offers, though, and I took the position with the Colorado Bureau of Investigation forensics lab."

"Was she proud of you? I mean, the CBI lab is a big deal."

Juliet laughed. "She said how nice it was that I'd have a steady paycheck, but to always keep my beautician license up to date because you never knew when I'd need a fallback position."

"Ouch."

"No kidding."

Juliet snipped some more. She hadn't been close to her mother. Kathleen Ryder had raised two girls on her own with no help from their biological father, who Kathleen divorced when Juliet was a baby. Juliet had looked him up once. He lived in Oregon, was married to a dental hygienist who'd produced three strapping sons, and seemed to have conveniently forgotten his first family existed.

When Juliet was two and Lauren thirteen, Kathleen remarried, but their stepfather was killed in a mugging a couple of years later. From then on, Kathleen remained a staunch, strict, outspoken single mother, always on the edge of bitter. Juliet always felt like Kathleen blamed her for their life, somehow.

Juliet didn't remember either father figure, and her mother told her time and again that she hadn't missed anything. Juliet didn't fully believe that. Having a father would have been nice.

Lauren, though, had always been their mother's favorite. The two were thick as thieves, and Juliet had always felt left out. It was Lauren who complied with their mother's wishes, kept her heart tethered to home. Juliet, the outsider, always dreamed of more and got out the first chance she had.

When a stroke took Kathleen, Juliet was filled with grief, but a part of her, the dark part she didn't like to acknowledge, was relieved. She would never live down to her mother's expectations. Her mom wanted her to have a small life. Like hers ended up being.

No reason to share all that with Mindy, though.

Besides, the CBI has been good to her. She is a star in her field. She's been developing new DNA sequencing methods that are changing how the CBI investigates crimes and increasing their success rates, and that is good enough for her, for the time being. Not that she doesn't stand on her deck at night with a glass of wine and her telescope, staring at what might have been... But on the bright side, she has the forever bonus of being able to cut her own hair, saving her money in the lean times.

And she's just whacked off a foot of her niece's hair on a whim. Mindy is sliding her hands over her head, utterly delighted. Even

Juliet has to admit, it looks cute. She pulls one last strand into place, then hands Mindy the mirror from her purse.

"Oh, Aunt J, it's perfect!"

And of course, at that moment, Lauren comes back to the room.

"What in the name of God are you doing?"

Juliet tries not to tuck her imaginary tail between her legs at Lauren's disapproving voice. It's hard; the shock and outrage have slipped past her sister's perfectly cool veneer, making her sound almost exactly like their mother.

Instead, Juliet squares her shoulders. "Styling your daughter's new haircut."

Lauren looks exactly like hell. She hasn't properly bathed, her eyeliner is smudged and her lipstick chewed off. Her clothes are rumpled and her cheekbones stand out like she's been starving herself. Juliet hasn't seen her in a few months, but she's lost weight before the events of the past day. Lauren is as focused on Mindy winning as Mindy is, to the detriment of all those around her. Juliet almost feels sorry for her. She pushes herself to smile, to open her arms for a hug.

"Hi, Lauren."

Lauren casts her one last vicious glance and makes a beeline for the bed. "Melinda Eliza Wright. What on earth have you let her do to you?"

Mindy is grinning, puts a hand behind her head to show it off. "Don't you like it, Mom?"

"No, I do not like it one bit. What in the world were you thinking?" She rounds on Juliet. "What were *you* thinking? You're the adult here. Or so we're supposed to believe. I leave you alone for five minutes and—"

"Relax, sis. This is what aunties are for, totally corrupting our nieces."

"You…you…"

Mindy sputters out a laugh. The sound makes Lauren whirl

back to the bed, a finger raised, getting ready to scold. But the sight of her newly shorn daughter giggling her head off is enough to defuse things.

"What's so damn funny?"

"I told Aunt J you'd be furious." She holds out a hand, the smile on her wan face warm. "Thank you for losing it."

"What? What do you mean?"

But Juliet knows exactly what is going on. Mindy, clever girl, didn't give a hang about her hair. She'd wanted to get her mother to treat her like a human being again, like her little girl, instead of like a possibly dying patient.

Mindy offers an olive branch. She swipes the hair off her face. "Aunt J could cut the bangs so it isn't so punk rock."

Lauren brushes the hair back down over Mindy's right eye. "No. It's cute. You look cute."

The *my daughter is about to die* tone is back, and Mindy pulls away.

Juliet winks at her niece. "Hey, Lauren, let's get some coffee. I haven't seen you forever, and I think Miss MEW here needs a nap."

"I do not." But her eyes are drooping. While they argued, the morphine pump gave her a shot, and she isn't long for the world.

Lauren fluffs her pillows and kisses her on the forehead. "We're going to have a talk about your wild ways, young lady, but for now, take a little snooze while I go beat up your aunt."

"Give it to her good, Mom," Mindy says as she drifts off, one hand in her short hair, a smile still on her face.

Lauren crooks her finger in a *follow me* gesture. It's time for Juliet to take her lumps. Hazel isn't at her desk, so Juliet puts the scissors in her top drawer as they walk past.

Lauren leads her to a small room at the end of the hall. Juliet looks around and realizes it's soundproofed. A place for parents to scream their agonies to the universe, perhaps?

When the door closes with a meaty click, Lauren rounds on Juliet.

"I disappear for five minutes and you're already causing trouble." But there is no heat in the recrimination. Instead, she sags against the wall, puts her face in her hands, and grinds her fists into her eyes.

Juliet touches her on the shoulder, but Lauren hunches and brushes her off.

"I'm so sorry."

"For messing up her hair or for the fact that she's dying?"

"She's not dying. Not yet, anyway. They've just diagnosed her. You have to give it some time. The advances they've made are incredible. The—"

"All well and good for you to say. She's not your daughter."

Juliet flinches. "No need to attack me, Lauren. I'm here to offer support. Mindy needs you to be a human being now, not an overbearing mother. You're going to drown her in your sorrow."

"What are you talking about?"

"She wanted me to cut her hair because it's going to fall out anyway."

"You don't know that."

"Mindy does. She's putting on a brave face for you, and you're acting like she's already in the grave."

"You have no idea—"

"Yes, I do. I saw the look on your face when you came through the door. You were doe-eyed, tiptoeing around. She needs you to be brave and to treat her like the competitor she is. Nothing will stop Mindy, not even cancer. Quit acting like she's been given a death sentence."

And with that, she starts for the door.

"Wait," Lauren commands. Juliet stops.

"I'm sorry. I'm stressed out. I know you were only trying to help."

"That's better," Juliet says. "It's nice to see you, too."

Juliet accepts the contrite hug. Lauren's bones feel hollow and insubstantial beneath her turtleneck like she's empty inside her clothes.

"Work going well?" Lauren asks.

"As well as can be expected. I'm happy, if that's what you're asking."

"Do you have a fellow yet?"

"A fellow? Are you from the '40s? Are we going to wash our hair and put it up in pin curls now?"

The look Lauren gives is so patently big sister that Juliet starts to laugh. "No, I don't have a *fellow*. I've been much too busy. I don't have time to meet anyone."

"You should think about it. You're not getting any younger, and…"

"No. We are not doing this. I took enough judgment from Mom. How's Jasper holding up?"

Lauren's face lights up. Juliet loves Jasper like a brother; seeing Lauren still happy with him after all these years is a balm to her soul.

"He's fine. We're struggling, trying to figure out how to balance his work with the hospital. They're letting him take time off as he needs, but he has so much on his plate he can't be away indefinitely. He's heading there now, giving away some cases to the junior associates."

"I meant, how is he? Really?"

"Terrified," Lauren whispers, sinking down into the brown leather couch. "How else could he be?"

"I understand. Mindy seems to be handling things well."

"She was fascinated by the details of the surgery, by the incisions, by the halo, for exactly five minutes. She made me take pictures of it from every angle and show her. She said, 'Wow, that's gnarly.'"

"Sounds like her."

"And then she said, 'Tell me the truth. I can see something's wrong. Am I crippled for life or something?'"

Lauren sniffs. "We told her the truth. God, Juliet, she is so strong. Such a champion. 'I'm going to fight, I'm going to win, I'm going to be back on the slopes in time for the Olympics.' We didn't tell her she couldn't—"

"Good, because you don't know that. She is a champion, Lauren. She has the heart of ten kids, and the strength of a thousand. She might beat this in one blow."

Lauren's eyes close. A tear leaks out.

"I hope you're right."

"At the very least, Lauren, you have to let her try. I'm here for you guys. And for Mindy. Anything you need."

"We appreciate that."

Lauren's gone wooden again, formal. She stands, briskly rubbing her hands down her pant legs. "Now, let's go talk to my willful daughter."

"Seriously, Lauren, anything I can do."

"I know. Thank you." And she bustles out the door, completely composed, together again.

Juliet follows, shaking her head. Her sister is not fine. And neither is her niece.

5

THE WRIGHTS' HOUSE
THREE WEEKS LATER

Mindy watches the FIS coverage of the World Cup event in Lake Louise with professional detachment. Shiffrin looks sharp as ever and takes the downhill by over a second, and Mindy bites back the jealousy. Mindy should be in that spot. She can taste the Canadian snow, feel the bone-deep cold, the chattering of her skis on the ice. Except she's stuck in Vail, cozy warm in her bedroom, not out there with her teammates. It sucks.

At least they let her out of the hospital. She was going mad in there. The constant noise and the bright lights and the needles at all hours… Home is better.

Mindy switches off the television, sends a text of congratulations, ignoring the knot in her stomach. It's bad enough she's out for the season, that her chances to be included on Team USA are questionable. She is sick of it all. The coddling. The lack of movement. The pain that sits deep in her bones, like the worst workout hangover she's ever had, but the pain isn't the good kind, when you're sore from overexertion. This is wrong. Alien. She's felt it for a while, for at least a couple of months before the trials, but having a name on it makes it so much worse.

Cancer.

She is pissed. She is pissed at the world. Pissed at her parents, and the doctor, and the damn rod in her leg, and the therapists who won't let her do anything more than gently ride the bike with her good leg only and stretch her arms over her head. Pissed at the idea of an unseen creature eating her from the inside out, at the underlying nausea that persists no matter what antiemetics they give her, at the strange hollowness she feels when she wakes every morning, like she's slowly emptying inside.

Thank God for Aunt Juliet. At least someone treats her normally.

Her parents are acting stupidly protective. Something has shifted between them, subtle but insidious. Every look her mother gives is couched in the throes of *it might be the last*. Her dad has always been the cautious one, but even he hasn't ever held her back.

Until now. They are both stifling her with their well-meaning love and attention.

Which is strange, because Mindy has faced much more dangerous situations and her mom has never had anything but fire in her eyes. She's sent her off to fly down the hill without a moment's admonition of *be careful, don't go too fast*. Mindy has a better chance of dying in the ninety seconds she spends hurtling upwards of eighty-five miles per hour down a mountain of ice.

She understands their worry, of course she does, but she wants to see the fire in her mother's eyes again, not this mealy, moony crap. She wants her dad to argue with her, not acquiesce to her every wish.

Maybe now is the time to ask for that little BMW convertible she saw pull into the parking lot of the hospital while she was having her first chemo treatment.

God, was she ever sick. She'd never felt anything like it. It took a couple of days for them to find the right combination of anti-nausea meds so she didn't hurl all over the place. Even now, the memory of the past two treatments, knowing she has to go back tomorrow and do it again, and again the following week, and the next, makes her want to scream.

No, Mindy must accept this new reality. There will be no World Cup celebrations for her. She is Ill, capital *I*, and she has no choice but to hold their hands and let them all doctor and parent and aunt her to death.

She wishes her mom would leave her alone for a day. Just a day. Just so she could have a chance to catch her breath. She hasn't been properly alone since she took off down the mountain three weeks ago, has been under constant, vigilant supervision by her parents, her aunt, the nurses and doctors, and she is slowly going mad for lack of privacy and silence.

She could ask her parents to leave, ask them to go to dinner and a movie, but she can't handle the idea of her mother's hurt eyes, welling with tears at the thought of being parted.

She shifts uncomfortably, folding her right leg underneath her like a flamingo. The cast is heavy, ungainly, banging into her ankle and shin at night. The stabilization halo is gone but her skin smells oily and rank under the cast, and the incision, though healing, itches like fire. She needs to wash her hair, stand in the hot water, let it run over her aching bones, but she can't even do that properly; the cast isn't meant to get wet.

God, she has to get out. She has to live, too, but she needs to get out of this bed, her room, her house. She has to move.

She can do some modified yoga. She hasn't been given permission, but Mindy isn't the type of girl to ask permission. At least yoga will be movement. She searches her drawers, but her favorite top isn't there. Her mom probably washed it and it's in the laundry.

She swings down the hall on her crutches, into her parents' room.

She loves it in here. The whole house, really, but this room is sheer perfection. Mindy shares her mother's minimalist taste. It's done in creams and pale sage greens, the cedar ceiling vaulted, the view off the side of the mountain panoramic, the green of the trees, now covered in white, postcard perfect. The view is lovely in the summer, too, and the fall, when the aspens turn, but the winterscape is Mindy's second heart. Their house is built to take advantage of the views, with its floor-to-ceiling windows, and Mindy has spent the week cuddled in front of the fire, watching the snow billow to the ground, missing its taste, its texture, the way her skis slide through it like a lover's embrace.

Mindy is surprised to see her mother standing in front of her dresser, holding something in her hands that looks like spiral notebook paper, crying.

"Mom? What's wrong?"

Lauren wipes her eyes and shoves the paper into the open dresser drawer, whips around to face Mindy, all in one motion. The smile is painted on. Her mother looks so tired.

"Honey! What are you doing up? I thought you were napping. You need your rest."

"I'm bored out of my skull and thought I'd do some yoga. Don't worry, just stretching. Where's my yellow top?"

"Oh, it's on the line. Why don't I pop it in the dryer and warm it up for you?"

Lauren bustles into the adjoining laundry room and sets about the task, then starts folding towels as the dryer runs. Mindy, perched on the edge of her mother's bed, glances at the dresser out of the corner of her eye. What was she reading? Did it have something to do with her diagnosis?

Her mother's back is turned. She could look. But the dryer buzzer goes off, and her mom is suddenly there. "Here you go, sweetheart." She holds out the top, then yanks it back. "Do not do anything that could hurt, okay? No pushing."

Mindy takes the top and threads it through her left crutch. "I won't."

She clumps away. Her mother moves in the opposite direction, toward the living room. Mindy doesn't think twice. As quietly as she can, she goes back to the bedroom and straight to the dresser. She deserves to know the truth, the whole truth, about her diagnosis.

But that isn't what she finds.

The notepaper is old, the edges ripped and soft, like a hand has stroked them over and over as the words were read. The handwriting is juvenile, girlish and round, completely unfamiliar.

December 14, 1993

My dearest Liesel,

I was so happy to get your letter. We didn't really have a proper goodbye. Man, do I miss you. It's dreadfully dull here. Ratchet et al. are especially surly without your sunny disposition. They miss you, too, I think. I hope they didn't let me out too soon. I've been so worried about you. Are you well? Still no cuts?

We had crafts today—guess what day it is? Yes, it's Tuesday, give that girl a prize!—and I swear if I see one more stupid painted doormat I am going to jump off the roof. I told them that, then fainted spectacularly, in a dead heap, right at their feet, which is why I'm writing you instead of sitting in group. They locked me away again, five hours in the box, and only let me out if I promised to stop being so dramatic.

Isn't that why we're stuck in here in the first place? Because we're overly dramatic? Except for you. I mean, you had cause.

I'm supposed to be sans roommate for a while. We'll see how long that lasts.

What are you doing out there in the big wide world? Is the sky bluer when you're free? Does the sun shine brighter? God knows they've pumped you full of every imaginable drug, so maybe you're just asleep. Which I'm going to do. Maybe I'll dream of my mom again. That was cool. Write me!

Love and stitches,

V

Mindy is confused. Who is Liesel? And who is the writer of this strange letter, this anonymous "V"? 1993? That was way before Mindy was born. She does the math—her mom is forty-one now, she would have been sixteen in 1993.

Just a year younger than Mindy is now.

Her mom calls, "Mindy, hon? Where are you?" which sends her heart into frantic mode. She scrabbles the letter back into the drawer, plops some underwear on top of it, and makes a break for it. She gets to the laundry room just as her mom appears in the doorway.

"What are you doing?"

"Forgot a towel," Mindy says nonchalantly, grabbing one off the top of the fluffy pile.

Her mother's face stretches into a grin. "You should have called me, silly, I would have brought you one. Want some company while you stretch? Maybe I can spot you if you need help."

Mindy stifles a groan. "Sure, Mom. That'd be nice."

Love and stitches. What in the world does that mean?

6

VAIL HEALTH HOSPITAL

They arrive at the hospital at 7:00 a.m., complete with a blanket, headphones, fuzzy slippers, and a soft pillow, and Mindy hasn't said much. She is being stoic, but Lauren can tell she's not feeling well. What will she be like after weeks of this? Will she continue to be sick?

Lauren feels so useless, so incapable of doing anything to help. She can feed, clean, and love her daughter, but she can't kill the thing growing inside of her. It's making her bitchy; she knows she's riding the edge. Old urges sweep through her, and she fights them down like dogs growling at a fence. *Never again.*

Soon enough, they are settled. The bag of evil medicine is attached to the pole, a tube snaking into Mindy's arm. Lauren straightens the sheet and thin blanket, pats Mindy's forehead with a cool cloth.

Jasper spends the first hour with them, then has to go back to work. Thankfully, Lauren's art means she can stay and no one will be upset or mad. For the past few weeks she's canceled all her appointments and showings. She hasn't painted. She hasn't contacted her clients. She's refused visitors. She has been there nonstop for Mindy. It's what a mother does. The idea of deserting her daughter even for a moment is too much to bear. As if death will slip in and take Mindy from her the moment Lauren turns her cheek.

Irrational, yes, but she can't help herself. Every drumbeat of her heart screams *live, live, live*. She's lost weight, along with Mindy. They've grown matching black circles under their eyes. But they are fighting. Together, they are fighting.

Mindy shifts, and lets out a tiny gasp. She looks at Lauren with pain in her eyes, apologetic. Lauren has to force herself not to run into the hall, screaming for painkillers. They weaned Mindy off the morphine quickly, but the chemo causes her pain too, just like the surgery. Every eight hours, she is allowed one Lortab. Just one. Just in case they need to ramp things up again. It takes most of the edge off, but sometimes, she has breakthrough pain, and they have to gut it out.

Pain makes Mindy looks like a five-year-old child instead of an accomplished young woman. The effect is startling. As if the chemo is leaching years from her baby.

"Oh, sweetie. Do you want your headphones? Or shall I tell you a story, take your mind off things?"

"Yeah. A story would be okay."

"Once there was a young girl who lived in a forest."

Mindy rolls her eyes dramatically. "Mom. Seriously? Fairy tales?"

Lauren adjusts herself on the thin mattress. "Fairy tales are good for the soul."

"Can we just watch *The Sound of Music* again?"

Still in love with the movie, as she has been since she saw it the first time when she was six. It is the one childish thing about this girl, her obsession with Julie Andrews spinning in circles high atop a mountain, singing about hills.

"You need a healthy dose of fantasy right now."

"I'm seventeen, not seven. What about Sarah J. Maas? You could read some of that."

"You are seventeen, going on eighteen," Lauren sings. She has a lovely soprano, and Mindy laughs, but it is strained, weak. She is so diminished. The chemo has already stripped her of muscle, of energy, of vitality. It is slowly killing her, and they both know it. The poison runs through her veins like a raging river down a hill—unyielding, unending, without thought or remorse for its consequence.

"Maas has too much raunchy sex. Oh, don't roll your eyes at me, little girl. What, you think I'm going to read you an adult story? How embarrassing would that be, for both of us? That's what television is for. Your choice—*Days of Our Lives* or Mom tells you *Sleeping Beauty*."

"Ugh. I'm sick of soap operas. *Sleeping Beauty*."

"Gotcha. Now, as I was saying—"

A knock at the door interrupts them. Dr. Oliver enters, and it is clear by the grave look on his face the news isn't good.

"Do I need to get Jasper on the phone?" Lauren asks immediately, and Dr. Oliver nods.

She is grateful for his honesty, at least. Mindy made them all agree at the beginning there would be no holds barred, no sneaking off into corners to share news and updates. Everyone gets the information at the same time. It is the only control Mindy has over the process. She doesn't want parents and doctors talking about her in the hallways, then sugarcoating the truth.

Lauren dials and Jasper answers right away.

"Everything okay?"

"Dr. Oliver has news, I'm putting you on Speaker." She presses the button, then holds out the phone to the doctor and takes Mindy's hand.

"I'm sorry to be the bearer of bad tidings, but the tests are back, and the cancer is more aggressive than we realized. We want to move ahead to a stem cell transplant, and we need to do it quickly."

"At least it won't hurt," Mindy says with a watery grin.

They've already discussed all the science about this possibility. She is right, it won't hurt her. But it could kill her.

"Take mine," Lauren says. "Let's go. Now."

Dr. Oliver smiles. "We'll test you both right away. Jasper, how quickly can you get here?"

"I'm on my way. Be there in fifteen."

He clicks off, and Dr. Oliver hands the phone back to Lauren. He goes to the other side of the bed and addresses Mindy directly.

"We talked about this possibility. Happens a lot in these cases. AML is a bitch, and she doesn't like to give up her hold of the body. I've already talked to a colleague of mine from Boston. He's going to oversee the transplant, make sure we have exactly the right stem cells to work with. We are going to lick this, missy. You just keep fighting your tail off."

He passes a hand over her balding head. Mindy's eyes are huge in her thinned-out face, but they are clear, no tears, nothing but fire.

"Yes, sir. Go get me some decent blood cells and let's kick this bitch's ass."

"Mindy," Lauren scolds, but Dr. Oliver nods, clearly pleased.

"That's my girl. You're going to win this battle, Mindy. You're a winner. I know it in my heart. Now, I'm going to get things moving on our end. You rest. Big days ahead!"

He nods at Lauren, who, despite a nasty look from Mindy, follows him out into the hall.

He shakes his head immediately, speaks loudly so Mindy can hear. "There's nothing more to say, Lauren. We're on it. But you'll want to assemble as many close family relations as you can so we can test everyone for a match. Aunts, uncles, cousins, the works."

"We don't have many. Jasper's an only child, and I just have my sister. We have no other family to speak of."

"Well then, with any luck, between the three of you, we'll find a good match. I just want the closest possible familial connection. Gives us a better chance of avoiding rejection."

Lauren drops her voice. "Dr. Oliver? I need you to be honest with me. What are her chances?"

He smiles and rubs her shoulder. "They're really good. My colleague from Boston is the best in the business. He's created the most advanced protocols, and his success rate for ameliorating AML with stem cell regeneration is off the charts. She's in the best hands."

Lauren nods, unconvinced.

"Better get back in there. That's a heavy burden for her to carry alone, even if she is our superstar. Page me when Jasper arrives. And you'll want to get your sister here, too."

"I will. Thank you."

His clogs squeak as he walks away, and Lauren feels like every eye is on her, all the children, the nurses, the other doctors strolling around. Another storm is brewing; the winter has been hard this year, as if in mourning for its lost playmate, and the sun disappears, leaving her in shadow.

Her worst fears have come to pass. Oh, God.

She realizes she is running her thumbnail over the skin of her forearm, hard enough to leave a long, deep red scratch.

Stop that. For heaven's sake, stop.

She pulls down her sleeve and licks her lips, takes a deep breath in through her nose, then goes back to her daughter's side. As she walks the long hallway, she calls Juliet.

★ ★ ★

Mindy watches her mother come back in the room, eyes red and frightened, and something clicks.

Liesel.

L.

Lauren.

The Sound of Music has always been their thing. Liesel is the name of the eldest daughter, the one who is having a secret affair with the young soldier who is her unknown enemy.

Perhaps there was a reason why her mother has the letter, after all.

7

CBI LAB
DENVER, COLORADO

Juliet is deep into a DNA run, the lab clicking and whirring around her, when her assistant, Bai, shouts that her sister is on the phone. Without missing a step, she tells him to transfer the call to the lab and put it on Speaker. She doesn't want to contaminate herself and have to start from scratch; she is in a delicate portion of her process.

Lauren is breathless, and Juliet can tell she's been crying. Her voice is thick and she sounds stuffy.

She halts her machine. "Lauren? What's wrong?"

"How quickly can you get here?"

"What's happened?"

"The cancer is getting worse. The doctor just came to see us. They have to move forward with a stem cell transplant right away. He asked for you to come. They want to get as close a match as they can."

"Do you or Jasper match?"

"I don't know yet. Insurance wouldn't let them test us until it was necessary. Dr. Oliver's been optimistic, and she's been responding, but the latest tests aren't good. They're moving so quickly. A specialist is flying in from Boston—thank goodness for Dr. Oliver, he's a skier too, and such a fan, I think if we didn't have him we wouldn't have had a chance to—"

"Slow down. Take a breath."

A ragged, tear-filled sigh. "Please, Juliet."

The longing, the fear, in her sister's voice about kills her. Lauren has never shown an ounce of vulnerability to Juliet. Even when they were children, Lauren was always together. The strong one. The focused one. The perfect one. The private one. For her to be asking for help, allowing those walls to come down, to let her sister hear the anguish she is feeling, is huge.

Juliet puts down her pipette. "I'll be there as soon as I can. We're supposed to get another foot of snow tonight. If I get going now, hopefully I can beat the storm."

"Thank you," Lauren breathes, and hangs up the phone.

Thirty minutes later, Juliet is on I-70, climbing through Georgetown. It will take another two hours to get to Vail in the afternoon traffic, and the storm is bearing down. She is pushing it, speeding when she can. If she gets pulled over, she can flash her credentials, explain the situation, and get off with a stern warning.

She doesn't want to think the worst, but she has to be the rational one. Stem cell transplants are tricky. Just like any organ transplant, the match needs to be as close to perfect as possible in order to prevent rejection. Siblings are often the best chance, but with Mindy, they have to hope for a match within the family. Juliet quails at the thought of the donor database. It could be months before a good match is found, months a child with aggressive AML doesn't have.

She's never heard this kind of pain from her sister. Even when Lauren's first marriage fell apart, when her husband Kyle took off and left her alone, pregnant and unemployed, she hadn't reached out, hadn't asked for help.

Truthfully, Juliet wasn't at all surprised to see their union fail—she'd never liked Kyle, felt he wasn't right for Lauren from the start; he was a blustery, booming kind of man, a braggart of the worst sort, the kind who didn't know his own shortcomings—but she hadn't heard a word about the split until well after Mindy was born. All she knew was he hadn't wanted a child and had gotten mad when Lauren found out she was pregnant, so they divorced and he moved to California.

What a jerk he'd been. Rotten and self-involved. What kind of man leaves when he finds out his wife is pregnant?

Juliet likes Jasper much, much better. He is kind, and smart, and loves Lauren beyond reason, and Mindy, too. That is good enough for her.

She feels guilty for even thinking of Kyle right now. The topic is verboten, and for good reason. Mindy has no idea Jasper isn't her biological father. It is an agreement they'd all made soon after Lauren and Jasper married. Kyle didn't want Mindy, Jasper did. That, in Lauren's eyes, made him her real father. Honestly, sometimes Juliet forgets that he isn't.

But in a situation like this...if there isn't a match, will Kyle have to be brought back into the picture? That could get very ugly.

Don't put the cart before the horse. Of course one of us will be a match.

She drives in the near dark grimly, watching the first flakes of the storm in her headlights, wondering what the next few days hold for them.

★ ★ ★

VAIL HEALTH HOSPITAL

Lauren is frantic waiting for Juliet to arrive, and not hiding it well. She's been tearing at her hair; a glance in the bathroom mirror shows it standing on end, but she doesn't care, doesn't bother to smooth it down. Mindy is calm and collected, handling this new setback with typical stoicism, but after Lauren has her cheek swabbed, she leaves her daughter alone with Jasper and walks the halls of the hospital, praying.

I will do anything. I will do anything. Please. Please.

She walks to the front doors of the hospital, stations herself to watch for her sister. The storm is on them, the snow coming down in true blizzard style, tiny stinging flakes spaced so closely together the parking lot has become a blur. Just when she starts to get worried, she sees a sweep of headlights and starts to breathe again.

Get her swabbed, get the results. That's all she can think of. Surely the odds will be in their favor, and one of the three of them will be a close enough match they will be able to save Mindy's life.

Juliet waves as she walks toward the doors. *Hurry, hurry,* Lauren thinks, knowing she's being unreasonable; the DNA results will take hours to be returned. She curses herself, why hadn't they done this before? Why hadn't they been ready? Anticipated the worst?

Because the insurance won't pay for what if *tests,* Jasper's voice echoes in her head, and she cringes at the thought of what this is going to cost them, the first time she's really allowed herself to have the thought. Mindy has tried to talk to them about it, but they've brushed it off. Even with their excellent insurance, the finances are going to be an issue now that they have to move into a whole different stage of treatment. It takes money to raise an athlete of Mindy's caliber. Jasper's lawyering pays well, and Lauren's art makes up the difference. But adding hundreds of thousands in hospital bills and medications and new treatment protocols is going to strain them. And if they need to do experimental treatments, apply for studies...

It won't happen. This is going to work. It has to work.

"Aren't you freezing?" Juliet asks when she reaches her, shaking her hair, snow slipping to the ground.

"No," Lauren answers, though she is, she is frozen to her core, to the bone. Everything rides on one of the three of them being a match. Everything.

"Let's go. They're ready for you upstairs."

She pretends not to see Juliet's lips compress at not being properly greeted or welcomed, just marches away into the hospital, knowing her sister will follow. Later, she'll apologize. Later, when things aren't so murky and scary.

Lauren hasn't ever needed Juliet before, not like this, and it makes her terribly uncomfortable. They are so dissimilar, the two of them. One a scientist, one an artist. One a loner, the other a mother, a wife, a coach. Lauren sometimes feels badly about the distance between them, but then she looks at Mindy, at her accomplishments, and knows she's done right to be 100 percent present for her daughter, even if it means she's isolated herself from the only family she has. Mindy is the only one who's ever truly mattered to Lauren, then, and now.

In the elevator, she offers the finest olive branch she can think of. "I wish you were running the tests. At least I'd know they were right."

Juliet looks surprised, then shyly pleased. "They'll be right. I'm sure we'll find a match. Dr. Oliver knows what he's doing."

"I'd have believed you without a second thought if the chemo was working. She's so weak, Juliet. It's made her so sick. And the cancer is still eating her alive, despite all he's done."

"That happens sometimes. Hang tight, okay? Have faith."

"Easy for you to say."

"Knock it off, Lauren. I'm as upset about this as you are."

"Are you?" The elevator dings and Lauren's hand goes to her throat. "God, Juliet, I'm sorry. I haven't slept, I'm worried, I'm—"

"I know. I *know*. So stop, okay? Stop snapping, stop apologizing. It is what it is. Let's go see Mindy, let me give her a hug, then I'll take the test."

8

That evening, Juliet sends Lauren and Jasper to the cafeteria for food before it shuts down. They are haggard, both of them, pale and gray-skinned. She instructs them to eat a decent, hot meal and take a break. She's happy to watch over Mindy for a while.

Lauren begins to protest, but Jasper grabs her hand and gives Juliet a grateful smile.

"We'll see you in an hour."

"Take two. I'm not going anywhere."

Mindy sleeps through it all. The emotions of the day have been grueling, and she's finally crashed.

Standing at the end of the bed, watching her, Juliet is filled with love. What a magnificent creature her sister has created. What a wonderful young woman they've raised.

Juliet sees a red light out of the corner of her eye. The electronic chart on the screen across the room has an update. The system is state of the art—the lab tests show up the moment they're finalized. She can't help herself, she moves closer. It has to be the DNA results. It has to. The timing is impeccable.

Any minute now, the doctor will come into the room and tell them who is a match.

Or she can look herself…

She's been around the hospital long enough to see the password to the system. The nurses don't try to hide it—who would want to log in and look at the charts, most of which are in gibberish scientific code so dense most laypeople can't understand them?

But Juliet isn't a layperson.

She glances once over her shoulder at the door, which is cracked but almost closed. No one will know.

She crosses to the computer and types in the password she'd seen the nurse use earlier in the evening. The system is tied directly to the lab, and the email is bolded.

Case #867745453 Results Ready

Juliet clicks on the file and begins to read.

Confusion fills her.

There is no DNA match. The results from the three of them— well, Juliet knew it was a long shot for Jasper to be even a peripheral match, but Lauren and Juliet should at least share a few markers with Mindy. Maybe not enough for a stem cell transplant, but as mother and aunt, the mitochondria should match.

She runs through the screens again. It isn't possible. They don't match Mindy at all.

How can this be? She shakes her head. The lab has made a mistake.

She checks the name of the lab. It is a private firm out of Denver that is incredibly well respected. She knows the head of the lab, Cameron Longer. The odds of his people making a mistake of this magnitude...no, they must have been given the wrong sample for Mindy. It will be a huge fuss; they will have to retest her. It could cost the lab the contract with the hospital.

Perhaps Juliet can help a different way. She can call Cameron and tell him they need to redo things, and quickly. Help them avoid a costly and embarrassing mistake.

"Ma'am? Excuse me, what exactly are you doing?"

Juliet jumps away from the computer, smack into Mindy's tray, which tips over, spilling everything from water and Kleenex to ChapStick on the floor with a clatter. Mindy jerks awake.

"Aunt J? What's the matter?"

"Ma'am, what do you think you're doing?"

"Mindy, it's fine." And to the nurse, "I'm sorry, I'm sorry. I was just checking to see if I could access the internet off this thing."

The nurse slaps the keyboard up into place, effectively shutting off the machine. "You can't. It's an intra-hospital system. No outside internet."

"I see that. Sorry, just wanted to check the storm, my phone battery is dead and the charger is out in the car."

The nurse isn't buying it, but Juliet ignores her stares and goes to Mindy's side. "Hey, kiddo, it's all good. Just your clumsy aunt knocking everything off your tray."

She bends and picks everything up, mind whirling. She needs to move fast if she is going to get in touch with Cameron.

"Don't let me catch you messing with the computer again, ma'am."

"Of course not. It's of no use to me, I couldn't get in. You have a password on that thing, you know."

The nurse glares at her once more, then leaves the room, probably to report the incident and get the passwords changed. The system is secure, yes, but this is a hospital, one of the most insecure environments in the world. Anyone can walk in, take an elevator up to any floor, and walk into a room. Who's to say they couldn't pick up a password or two, dive right into the patient files? Records can be hacked, altered, stolen. It's a nightmare for security, both in person and online.

Mindy rubs her eyes. "What's wrong? You look like you saw a ghost."

"That chick scared the you-know-what out of me, that's all."

"Why were you snooping in my chart?"

Oh, precocious child. She hadn't been asleep the whole time.

"Don't tell on me."

"I won't."

"I was looking to see if the DNA results were back yet. Which they weren't. It was all a waste of my oh-so-excellent covert ninja skills."

She spies the ChapStick across the room, picks it up.

Mindy giggles. "Yes, you're a ninja all right. Where's Mom?"

Eating her dinner in happy ignorance.

"I sent them to the local broom closet for a date. Figured they could use some alone time."

"Eww, Aunt J! Gross."

Perfect, she's distracted her. "How do you think you came to be, child?"

Mindy obligingly sticks her finger in her mouth and makes gagging noises.

"Hey, want some tea?"

"Yes, please. Peppermint."

"I'll be right back."

9

Mindy wants to know what Aunt J was looking at on the computer. Clearly, something was wrong; Aunt J went white as snow and jumped like a rabbit when the nurse caught her snooping.

Probably there isn't a match, and they are going to have to go out of the family to the donor database. Mindy doesn't like the idea of a stranger's DNA floating around inside her, though the idea of being a chimera is pretty cool. She could be two people at once. She should start looking at images of chimeras online, a tattoo of one would be awesome. She'll do it on her left shoulder blade, intricate and coiled, like a snake about to strike.

As she is playing with this idea, Aunt Juliet comes back to the room with her tea. Her aunt is so pretty when she's not worried. Now she is still white-faced but tosses Mindy a box of Hot Tamales candy with a grin. For some reason, the spicy cinnamon candy helps settle her stomach as well, or better, than the tea, but Lauren doesn't like her to have them.

Mindy wants to be more like Aunt J. Carefree, smart, not constrained by whatever weirdness her mother has. Lauren and Juliet are nothing alike. How did two people from the same parents who grew up in the same household turn into such different people? Mindy catches Juliet's eye, points at the computer, and raises an eyebrow. She could swear Juliet blanches again before she bites her lip, then shakes her head slowly.

No match, then.

Mindy lets out her breath, slow and controlled. It is good of Juliet to let her know. Now she can better school herself and be prepared while everyone freaks out about how to tell her.

Juliet sits on the edge of the bed. "You look distracted. Are you worried? I'm sure we'll find a match."

"Well, yeah, sure I'm worried. But it's not that. Do you remember anyone ever calling my mom Liesel?"

"Liesel? Like the kid in *The Sound of Music*? No. Why do you ask?"

Mindy feels her face turn red, and Aunt J's right brow hikes. "What did you do?"

"Nothing. I didn't do anything, I swear. Mom has this weird letter in her underwear drawer from 1993. Whoever wrote it must have been a good friend, it said she missed her, and there was some other stuff. Mom was crying when she read it. You were, what, five, six in 1993? Do you remember anything strange?"

"I barely remember anything before we moved here in 1994. I was in first grade, and that's when I got into the idea of going to space. With all the aerospace companies here, lots of parents worked at a firm called Martin Marietta, now Lockheed Martin, that made the rocket boosters. They were all into space stuff. We used to watch every launch—they'd bring all the grades into the cafeteria. For a little girl, it was almost like going to the movies, but it was real. The space bug bit me, and from then on, I wanted to be an astronaut. But I don't remember much before that."

"But Mom?"

"Your mom was away at boarding school. I barely saw her." She is playing with Mindy's ChapStick, turning it over and over as if remembering the weird dislocation of not having a sister around outside of photos and phone calls.

"I didn't know she went to boarding school."

"God, what was it called… Kent Country Day, something like that. Really elite school. Mom had to work two jobs to keep her there. Lauren worked, too, she was on scholarship, didn't get to come home on breaks or anything. Then she went to college and studied art and met your dad and you came along. You know we weren't super close. She was so much older than me."

"Do you remember anything else?"

"Nope. Sorry, kiddo. We just weren't the kind of sisters who confided in one another. I could ask about it for you."

"No. No way. She'll know I was snooping."

"I'm sure she'd forgive you. You are practically under house arrest, after all. Hey, tell me about the new skis you're getting for Christmas."

"What?"

"I thought I overheard someone talking about a sponsorship? K2, was it?"

Mindy squeals, all thoughts of Lauren and the mystery letter gone.

10

Juliet is rattled by Mindy's line of questioning but tries to stay cool.

There's an explanation. It's a mistake. There's a completely rational reason why the labs don't match up.

Mindy is so overjoyed at the thought of the K2 sponsorship that she takes the explanation at face value and doesn't ask again. They goof around for another twenty minutes until Lauren and Jasper come back, not exactly smiling, but looking a little less peaked.

"Hey, sis. They have meat loaf and mashed potatoes. Why don't you go down and grab some?"

"I think I will. I skipped lunch. Mindy, you want anything?"

"More Hot Tamales. They have the boxes by the register."

"Your wish is my command, princess. Back in a few."

Juliet leaves them to adore their daughter. The nurse who busted her is nowhere to be seen, but she waits until she gets to the elevator to call Cameron.

He answers on the first ring in his crisp British accent.

"Juliet Ryder, please tell me you've decided to chuck that nasty job chasing criminals and come to work for me."

"Hey, Cameron. No, sadly, I'm still a slave to the CBI. It's that whole getting justice for the underrepresented thing. Call me crazy."

"You're crazy."

She laughs. "Hey, listen. I actually called to ask a favor. It's a bit of a delicate situation."

"Shoot."

"You ran some DNA on a case I'm…involved with."

"You know I can't discuss our cases, Juliet."

"I do know that, but the DNA you ran was mine, so I'm giving you permission to look at the results and talk to me about them."

"Ah. Juliet, darling, I don't know that I can do it. Especially since I know you, it's a total conflict of interest, and—"

"It's life and death, Cam. My niece has cancer. You tested us all for a match to do a stem cell transplant. I've already seen the results. Something is wrong, and I'm trying to help you save your lab because if it gets out you're making mistakes, it will sink you, and fast."

His voice cools. "That sounds suspiciously like a threat, madam."

"It's not, but, Cameron, seriously, someone in your lab screwed up. Pull the case. Look at it yourself. Run the test again. You don't want to look bad. This is enough of a high-profile situation without an error muddying the waters."

"Your niece—you're talking about Mindy Wright, the skier?"

"Yes. I wouldn't normally ask, but as I said, the test had an obvious issue, so you're going to want to run it again and get it right. Something might have been contaminated in the process, who knows. But there's a problem."

"Well, if you tell me, it might give me a leg up."

"According to the DNA results I saw, I'm not related to her, and neither is her mother. Which would be a miracle of epic proportions, as I met the child before and after she came into the world."

"Oh," he says, a new tone in his voice. "Yes, that might be an issue. It won't be under your names, though, you know we double-blind everything. What's that case number?"

She lists it off, thankful as always for her facility with numbers. "I'll be back to you as soon as I can."

"Thanks, Cameron. I owe you one."

Juliet buys herself some dinner, scarfs it down, and sits for a while in the cafeteria, thinking.

Surely there is a mistake. It happens more than people know. Even the best labs have issues.

She should be ashamed of herself, snooping like that, but thank heavens she did. She is going to save her friend's reputation, and they'll find a match for Mindy on the second round, and all will be well.

11

Juliet's phone rings a little past six in the morning, waking her from a deep but uncomfortable sleep in which she is dreaming about squirrels taking over her yard after eating mutant superhero-inducing black-oil sunflower seeds. Two of them have just roared and dumped out the biggest feeder when the chirping begins. It sounds like a cricket, so she rolls with it as part of the dream, but finally drags herself to the surface.

Chair. Legs under a coat. Hospital.

That's right. She opted to stay at the hospital with everyone, instead of trying to make her way to the house. The storm was terrible when she'd curled up in here, but she can tell it has stopped; the room is quiet and light gray, the dawn beginning.

She stretches and answers the call with a groggy hello.

"It's Cameron. And you, my friend, are a bitch. I've been up all night trying to prove your theory."

Juliet unfolds herself from the chair.

"Yeah, well I slept in a chair and dreamed of mutant squirrels. What's up?"

"The tests are correct. I ran a clean sample from scratch myself. There's not a genetic match between you and your sister and your niece. Nor her dad, by the way. I'm sorry."

"Well, that's freaking confusing."

"It is. I'd start looking at the hospital records from the day of her birth if I were you."

"What?"

"If she's not a biological match to your sister, then who is she a match to? I'm just saying, there might be a chance there was a screwup at the hospital. It happens."

"You mean, like, she was switched with another kid?"

"You say you knew her before and after birth…then yes, it's the only explanation."

How? How can this be happening? But she bites back her reply. Cameron is good at what he does, and if he says there is no match, then she needs to start looking at the alternatives.

"I'll get on it. Jeez. How in the world do I break this news?"

"Let the doctors handle it. They'll have seen the results by now and will be coming to say something. I sent them the final reports a few minutes ago."

"But this is my sister we're talking about. My family. I have to give her a heads-up. I don't want her freaking out in front of Mindy."

Cameron answers with a long yawn. "Your call. Let me know what happens, will you? I admit I'm intrigued. It's not often that we have switched-at-birth cases. If you find the parents, we could publish together. And now I'm going home for a few hours' rest."

"Thanks a lot, Cam. I appreciate it. I owe you one."

His laugh is a comforting rumble. "Come work for me, and all will be forgotten and forgiven."

"We'll see… Sleep well. Thanks again."

She sits in silence for a few moments, trying to absorb what she already knew, but hasn't wanted to believe. There is only one answer possible here, and Juliet does not relish sharing it with her sister.

Somehow, someway, seventeen years ago, the hospital made a horrible mistake and sent Lauren home with the wrong child.

★ ★ ★

The doctors come at 7:00 a.m., their faces calm masks. They talk. They are upbeat. This happens sometimes. The donor database is being contacted as they speak. They are sure there will be several matches. And, the doctor from Boston adds, he's developed a new system that helps alleviate GvHD, graft-versus-host disease, which means he can fine-tune the matches to the point where it is virtually impossible for Mindy's body to reject the donor cells. New system, highly sophisticated, blah, blah blah. Her chances are even better than before.

Juliet's gaze swings from Mindy, who doesn't look surprised by the news there isn't a match, to Jasper and Lauren, who look terrified. Juliet feels horrible. She should have warned them; she should have given them a chance to process the information. Carrying secrets has never been her forte, and holding back something this huge from her sister is overwhelming.

She wonders which doctor is going to break the rest of the news and spare her the agony. She puts her bet on the new guy, the tall, handsome fellow with the Boston accent who gave her a very appreciative glance when he came into the room, thank you very much.

She missed his name, something like Berger or Barger, so she is mentally calling him Dr. Braveheart. He has that classic nose and lots of long brown hair. He looks like a rebel. He looks like he has nothing to lose.

She is surprised when the two men simply nod at her and leave without saying a word.

What's she supposed to do now? Call them out? Then she'll have to admit she's been spying in the files, and that won't go over well.

Crap.

She can't just let this go. It is too big, too important. Not find-

ing a match is one thing. But the fact that Mindy is not genetically related to her own family? That is a disaster in the making.

Lauren starts to cry. Juliet spares her a quick glance. Jasper is
attending to her, so she follows the doctors into the hall to see
if she can glean something off of them. But they are hurrying
away, heads down, talking low to each other.

Gee thanks, guys.

Back inside the room, Mindy is now holding her mother, trying to calm the flood of tears, while Jasper looks on miserably.
Mindy catches her eye, and Juliet sees the fierce pain in them.

They've already given up, her look screams. *Don't you dare give
up on me, too.*

"Lauren. Lauren, honey. Come here." Juliet pulls Lauren from
Mindy's bed and marches her out into the hall. Lauren is like
Jell-O, legs wobbling, body malleable, going wherever Juliet
leads her, which is right down the hall into the private, quiet
room.

She pushes Lauren inside, shuts the door, leans against it, and
crosses her arms.

"Scream."

"What?"

"Scream. Do it here, do it now. You can't fall apart in front
of her like that. She needs you to fight with her. Not to give
up, not to give in."

"The odds—"

"Fuck the odds. This kid is more than the odds. She always
has been."

"Don't talk to me like that. You have no idea what it's been
like. What it's like to lose your heart, your soul. If she dies—"

"She's not yours."

Lauren stops dead, mouth open in a small little O, a silent
scream.

"What did you just say?"

Shit.

"I'm sorry. I didn't mean to blurt it out like that."

"What in the name of God are you talking about?"

"The reason there isn't a match. She's not your child. Not only isn't there a match for the stem cells, but there's not a genetic match at all."

"There must be some mistake."

"That's what I thought, too. I saw the file yesterday, and I thought they'd done something wrong, so I called the lab—I know the head of it—and had him redo the tests himself. She's not your child. The hospital must have made a horrible mistake, and they switched her with another baby. I have no idea how that happened, but it was seventeen years ago. The security and standards have changed dramatically. I bet the other family has no idea, either."

"Juliet Ryder, you are out of your mind."

Lauren tries to push past her, heading for the door, but Juliet is taller and heavier, and simply stands in the way.

"I'm not. It's science. It's a terrible thing, but this is real, it's happening, and you have to listen to me. We're going to have to open an investigation, the CBI will handle it, and of course we'll be discreet with it, but you know I can't stay quiet about this. It's going to get out."

"An investigation?" Lauren manages to sound fearful and furious at the same time. "There will be no such thing. This is a mistake. If it were true, the doctors would have said something. You've dreamed up all this because you aren't the center of attention, for once. You are welcome to leave. Leave, now, and don't come back, and we'll forget this entire conversation ever happened."

"Lauren. You know I can't do that. It's not a mistake. Blood doesn't lie."

Lauren looks wild, completely out of control. She wrenches Juliet's arm away from the door, throws it open and stalks off. Juliet lets her go. Denial. She is in denial. Understandable. It is too much to process. She shouldn't have blurted it out like that. She handled it poorly. She doesn't blame Lauren a bit for being pissed off.

But the truth is the truth, and sooner or later, they are all going to have to face it. Mindy is not a blood relation to them. Who does she belong to?

12

Lauren's heart is in her throat. This can't be happening. This cannot be happening!

She wants to scream; she wants to run. She can't face them, not like this, when she is torn apart, her heart in a million pieces.

She takes a lap around the hospital—the way she's gotten the bulk of her exercise lately. She usually works out with Mindy; though she can't keep up with everything her daughter does, Lauren can hold her own. Without the work, her muscles are atrophying, and she's lost weight. She can feel her skin loose on her bones.

Damn Juliet, and her prying, meddling nature. Lauren hadn't even thought to ask how her sister managed to see the records before anyone else. And to go straight to the lab—that means how many people know about this? The doctors, surely, the lab owner, plus Juliet. It is only a matter of time before someone talks, someone remarks on it, and then they will all be trotted out in front of the media. What a story. Olympic hopeful Mindy Wright in a scandal. Switched at birth. Not her mother's daughter.

Lauren sits down hard on a bench in the first-floor atrium. The snow has stopped, the glass roof is covered. Tiny gleams of sun break through as the melt begins.

She thinks of Mindy's adorable, scrunched face, the tiny cries and wagging hands—even as an infant, unable to keep herself still, always wanting to go, to move, to explore. How Lauren learned to swaddle her tight to keep her quiet, how she slept with her in the bed, how she put the baby naked on her chest to bond.

And then Jasper, and falling in love with him, especially because of his utter and complete devotion to the babe he called his own. The screaming freak girl child he carried around the apartment to let Lauren get a few hours of rest, the two of them doing lap after lap until Mindy no longer yelled, and instead cooed and gurgled into his hair while he talked to her in a language neither of them understood.

Their baby. They'd been with her almost every day for the past seventeen years. Every bump and bruise, every nightmare. Lauren is assailed by the memories: the look on Mindy's face when she'd touched snow the first time, three-year-old Mindy on short skis and no poles, coming down the bunny hill at speed with her mouth open in a silent scream of pleasure. They'd taken her up and down that hill fifty times at least, watching in fascination as she became more coordinated, more flexible, how she leaned forward into the hill to allow herself to go faster.

They'd taken her on a green slope that first afternoon, trying to keep her hands in theirs, but she'd darted away and slid down the hill, already mimicking the side-to-side motion she saw from the other skiers. They'd caught up to her at the base of the slope, where she sat on her bottom with her mittens off, her hands in the icy slush, making tiny snowballs. She'd looked at them like, *hey, what took you so long?* and gave them a baby-toothed smile.

Gen, Mama.

Even as a baby, Mindy had been at one with the mountain. Even when fun became training, training, training, and the enthusiasm the tiny girl had for the mountain was dimmed by the enforced discipline of her mother and coach, and days went by when she narrowed her eyes and didn't speak to Lauren because she didn't want to put on her skis, didn't want to go out in the blizzard, didn't want to have another meal of chicken and rice and spinach, didn't want to do the leg press and ballet, and Lauren would remind her what was at stake, that she wasn't a quitter, even then, she'd find abandon on the slopes.

Of course, she is theirs. Of course, she is Lauren's.

Blood doesn't lie.

Her cell phone rings. Jasper. She wipes her eyes, sniffs. Forces some cheer into her tone.

"Hey, babe. I'm just, uh, taking a walk."

"Mindy's asking for you. She's asking questions."

Panic floods her system. "Questions? About what?"

There is uncharacteristic stress in Jasper's voice. "What do you think, Lauren? She wants to know what her chances are. She wants to get an idea of what's ahead. Not what the doctors are saying, but what you think. She wants reassurance she isn't going to die. She wants her mother. She wants you."

He manages to sound bitter and terrified at the same time.

"I'm coming. I'm right downstairs. I'll bring us all some cocoa, and we can talk."

"Bring four. Juliet is still here."

Lauren bites back the response she wants to give. "Sure. Be right there."

Juliet. Always the fly in the ointment. From the moment she arrived on the scene and cut Mindy's hair, Lauren has wanted to force her away. She loves her sister; she just doesn't have the bond she knows some people do with their siblings. From birth, Juliet was obstinate and difficult. A finicky eater, never getting along with anyone, always fighting with her sister, her friends, their mother. And as she grew up, always having to be the smartest one in the room, the little budding scientist. A brainy loner, relentless and intractable.

A problem.

Lauren rises, turns toward the cafeteria. She will bring the cocoa, let Juliet drink it, then escort her out herself and make sure Juliet keeps her big mouth shut. She refuses—refuses!—to put Mindy through the ignominy of the idea that she isn't their child, not for a second. Mindy doesn't need any more pressure on her than she already has. Her leg is just beginning to heal properly, and the stem cell transplant means all new protocols, new medications, and new stress. Lauren will be damned if she allows the mental stress of this clear mistake to weigh on Mindy, to in any way affect her treatment and its efficacy.

★ ★ ★

Juliet watches as Lauren comes into the room, a forced smile on her face. Lauren sends her a mental *do not dare speak* glare and hands her the cocoa.

"You have to get on the road early to get to work on time, won't you?"

"Oh, you're leaving?" Mindy asks, taking the proffered cup. "I thought we could play *Trivial Pursuit*. I schooled you last time."

Juliet rolls her eyes. "You schooled me last time because you were studying for AP history and the categories were all historical. I'm up for a rematch. Bring it, sister." And she looks at Lauren with that gleam in her eye that says, *I dare you to stop me*.

Lauren wants to scratch her nails down her sister's smug face, leave runnels of red, then force her into the snow to freeze to death. Maybe she'll get lucky, and a wolf will smell the blood and come eat her.

Instead, she hands Jasper his cup, and takes her own, dropping the Styrofoam tray into the trash, and smiles. "Of course we can play, Mindy dear. But your aunt has to go back to Denver and to work. Don't you, Juliet? We wouldn't want you to get fired from a job you love."

Mindy's frown is unreadable, but Jasper's head swings toward Lauren's in an instant. She blinks at him, and he straightens. The advantage of a long marriage, the marital glance. Words unspoken but messages sent.

Jasper edges around to the other side of the bed. "Yeah, Mindy, we don't want Juliet to get busted by her boss. Besides, I think it's my turn to play hooky. I haven't gotten nearly enough time with *ma leetle babushka*."

At his horrendously ridiculous Russian accent, Mindy starts to giggle, and he advances on her, opening and closing his fingers like he is going to pinch her cheeks, which sends her squealing under the bedclothes.

Lauren takes advantage to steer Juliet into the hall.

"Say your goodbyes, and get out of here."

"Lauren, you can send me away, but it's not going to change facts. This is going to come out."

Lauren speaks in a furious whisper. "It won't if you keep your mouth shut. Now leave, and I don't want to hear you speak of this again. And if you let this slip, if you tell anyone your outlandish theory, I will make sure your bosses know you were interfering with the files here at the hospital. How do you think that will go over? I don't think the CBI would take kindly to the news one of their employees was breaking into secure medical documents. Are we clear? Do you understand what I'm saying?"

They face off for a moment, then Juliet exhales a heavy breath out of her nose and sticks her head back into the room. She blows Mindy a kiss. "I'll be back this weekend, peanut. Try not to beat your parents too badly. Especially go easy on your mother. You know what a sore loser she can be."

"Bye, Aunt J," Mindy calls, still under a puppy pile of pillows and blankets and dad. "Thanks for the candy, and the talk."

Lauren's eyes narrow, but Juliet tosses her a crisp salute and saunters off down the hall.

Lauren sags a little inside but doesn't move an inch until she sees the elevator doors close behind her sister.

This is a problem. A very big problem.

Juliet is always a problem.

Later. She'll deal with it later.

Pasting a smile on her face, she goes back into her daughter's room to join her family.

13

UNIVERSITY HOSPITAL

NASHVILLE, TENNESSEE

1993

VIVIAN

The new roommate doesn't talk to me for the first week. She doesn't talk to anyone, really, though she's relatively polite to Ratchet, as if recognizing a kindred spirit straight from hell.

I'm in the art room, painting a seascape copied from a book, when I realize I'm not alone and look up to see my phantom roommate standing to the left of my easel, a thoughtful look on her face.

"You're good. But you might want to mix in some vermilion. Your greens are all off. They lack depth."

"Red won't work."

"It will tone your blue. Add it to the blue, then redo that line, right there."

I bite back the response I prefer to give—*fuck off, psycho*—and try it. All part of my new life plan to be cooperative so I can get the hell out of here.

Damn if it doesn't work.

The crests of the waves are suddenly alive, and the froth they churn now looks like proper seafoam instead of dead gray ice.

"How did you know to do that?"

"I paint, too."

"Are you ever going to tell me your name?"

"What's in a name? Names are stupid."

"Or is it you don't want me to ask for a newspaper so I find out what you did to land in here?"

She stares, and I mentally give myself a point. She's afraid of what I might think.

The painting is done. There's nothing more I can do with it. I step back and admire the new *depth*.

"I killed someone," she says, softly, her voice barely a whisper.

I don't look away from the painting, but a chill crawls down my spine. "How?"

"With a knife."

"Why?"

"Because she didn't clean her brushes right." She grins and rushes out of the room.

I do a good job on my brushes, just in case. The last name on our door now reads *Thompson, L.*

Inside, I lean against the wall. *Thompson, L* is fussily making her bed.

"What's the *L* stand for?"

"Liesel."

"What kind of a name is Liesel?"

"German."

"You're American. Thompson isn't a German name."

"So?"

"Who did you kill?"

"No one of consequence."

"Then why are you here?"

She stares at me for a brief moment, then she leaves the room. I don't doubt she's telling me the truth about what she's done. Who is my new roommate?

* * *

Now that I know I'm sleeping next to a murderer, I am desperate to find out what's happening. I ask at the desk for the newspaper and am rewarded, but can't find anything about someone named Liesel Thompson. I ask for the past week and am denied. Perhaps there is something in them they don't want me to see.

I wait until shift change, when Ratchet heads home. Roger is on tonight, and he likes me. He gives me Marlboros and lets me smoke in their lounge instead of out in the hutch.

Once the first bed check is done, and Liesel is snoring, I head down the dark hallway to the nurses' station. I jerk my head toward the lounge. Roger, thin, blond, wispy mustache and ropy arms, unlocks the staff lounge and hands me a smoke. Once we're lit, I say, "Can I have last week's newspapers?"

"Why?"

"So I can see why my roommate is in here. She scares me. She said she…"

"Yes?" He leans forward, interested now. I take a drag, breathe in the smoke, down deep in my lungs, hold it there until I start to cough and Roger whispers, "Be quiet. You're going to get me in trouble."

I swallow the cough, choking, my eyes watering. I suddenly don't want to share my strange roommate's words.

"So? What did she say?"

"She said she would never tell. I just want to be sure I'm safe. I don't like not knowing."

Roger says, "You know what it will cost you."

I tap my fingers on the table, ash tipping off the end of my Marlboro onto the scarred wood.

"Quid pro quo, kid." He doesn't leer. This is a business transaction. I have no money to pay him, nor favors to bestow, nor property of any kind that's worth anything to him. Except me. And that I'm not willing to give. Not for this.

"I can't," I say, looking away.

"Suit yourself. One of these days, you're going to change your mind. Now finish that smoke and get to bed."

In our room, Liesel is having a nightmare. I lie on my bed, on top of the scratchy covers, and listen to her moan and pant. She murmurs "No, no, no, no" and punches in the air, and I can't help but wonder what—who—she's fighting.

14

DENVER, COLORADO

CURRENT DAY

Juliet drives back to Denver, her mind in overdrive. Lauren is hiding something. She is sure of it. Her reaction, so vehement, so visceral… Juliet hasn't seen this side of her sister since they were children. Before Lauren became a mother and her life turned into a fairy tale.

Because make no mistake about it, Lauren is living a fairy tale. Great husband, utterly devoted. Beautiful, talented daughter who is also a hardworking athlete who makes them all proud. Lauren herself, an artist who makes her own hours, does whatever she wants. Travel, money, looks. She is totally and completely free.

Juliet isn't. She has none of these things, only a career she loves.

She isn't jealous. Of course she isn't. She has plenty of time for her own happily ever after. And how could she be jealous, now, especially? Now that she knows what she knows?

As she speeds down from the mountains, the evergreens and rocky slopes covered in snow as familiar as the back of her hand, she begins to see things with new eyes. She's never noticed that sheer drop-off. She's never seen that frozen waterfall. When did they put up that netting so the rockslides wouldn't make it across the entire highway?

She is so used to the drive, so used to—so desensitized to—the reality in which she is living, she's been in a fugue state. If all of these things along her path are new and different, what does this mean? Is it possible that Mindy too is simply new and different? Or has she been a wolf in sheep's clothing her whole life, seventeen years a stranger in their midst, and none of them knew it?

It makes her uncomfortable, at best. The idea that their family is an outlier, suddenly different, being unmade, rocks her to the core. Juliet likes the known. The quantifiable. Theories that can be proven, not imagined.

And with that, she knows exactly what she needs to do. She isn't going to report this, not yet. She will find Kyle Noonan. Get a sample of his blood, let Cameron run it. If he isn't Mindy's father, then she can go to Lauren with empirical evidence and make her see sense, make her see reason. It is the only way.

★ ★ ★

Back in the lab, she answers some email, forwards two mitochondrial profiles to the team of agents she's been working with who are on a unique manhunt, looking for a suspect of both Asian and Scottish descent, then shelves all her projects. She gives herself an hour. She is law enforcement. She has access to all the databases. If anyone asks what she is doing, she'll chalk it up to research.

Juliet has more leeway than most simply because she is breaking new ground with her techniques. Entranced with the idea of familial DNA to solve crimes, she set out over a year earlier to perfect the method known as DNA phenotyping. Instead of searching for an exact match in CODIS—the combined DNA index used to identify and match a criminal's DNA with crime scene evidence—phenotyping is a more organic, environmental approach: decoding the DNA source sample itself.

The idea is simple. As Juliet told Lauren, blood doesn't lie. Blood is its own witness. A tech can take a blood sample and within twenty-four hours have a full-blown profile of who it belongs to: white, black, blue eyes, green, blonde, brunette, red, male, female. In theory, if a witness says she was raped by a man of African descent, yet the DNA sample belongs to a white male of European descent, the police will know immediately a mistake has been made; that the witness is wrong, her memory fuzzy, or she has an agenda.

Juliet's phenotyping method is gaining traction, too, turning profiling on its ear. It is becoming exceptionally useful in murder cases. If law enforcement officials are looking into a serial killer, and all the signs pointed to a specific type of person, the phenotype DNA can help prove or disprove their theory.

Which is all well and good, but Juliet wants to take it further. She is working on a new kind of phenotypic analysis, looking for facial features and familial traits, and applying them to the possible perpetrators of the crimes committed. She's been matching DNA samples with the FBI's NGI facial recognition system. So far, she's helped the CBI close twenty cold-case murders, and she has another massive stack in her to-do pile.

She is an unconventional leader in her field. Not to mention the program she has written allows her to input DNA material into a 3-D printer and have it spit out a face. Completely unusable in court, for now, but she's been using it to double-check her work once a suspect is caught. A third control, as it were.

Thinking of this, the idea glimmers in the back of her mind, there but not acknowledged. It is this phenotypic method she can use to narrow down Mindy's true biological parents, should it come to that. But she can't do it without permission from all involved, including her bosses. Working on the project behind everyone's backs is unethical, at best; illegal at worst, and quite possibly a waste of time. There are better ways to prove her theories.

Lauren and Kyle didn't part on good terms, but her famously private sister never let any other news leak. All Juliet knows is he was furious about the pregnancy, filed for divorce, and re-

quested a transfer to another office, preferably as far away from
Lauren as he could get. How he ended up in California was beyond her, but it worked to get him away as well as if he'd decided to join the space program and go to the moon.

Kyle wasn't smart enough for that.

Catty, Juliet.

She racks her brain—what firm did he work for before he
took off? Spencer something... Spencer Landry. That's it. She
grabs the phone and looks up the number on the web, dials it.
The receptionist answers, her long vowels a dead giveaway that
she's from the north.

"Good morning, Spencer Landry and Associates. How may
I direct your call?"

"I need to speak with your HR department, please."

"Oh, I don't think we're hiring right now—"

"This is Juliet Ryder, CBI."

"Oh! Well, certainly, ma'am, hold one moment."

She bites back a laugh. Sometimes it is good to be with the
CBI, even if she is using the title for nefarious purposes.

A moment later, a man's voice comes through the phone.
"This is Eres Patrone. How can I help you, Agent Ryder?"

She doesn't disabuse him of the title. She holds a Ph.D. in
microbiology and genetics and is not an agent pro forma. But
Agent Ryder will get farther than Dr. Ryder.

"Good morning, Mr. Patrone. I'm looking for some information on a former employee of yours, a Kyle Noonan. I have
a record of him leaving the firm in 2000 to take a position else-
where. I was hoping you had the name of the firm he went to
so I can reach out to him."

"Wow, 2000. I wasn't here then, but let me look into the archives and I can give you a call back. Will that work?"

"I'm in a bit of a hurry, actually. Can you put me on hold
while you look? Surely a firm as advanced as Spencer Landry
is all online."

"We are, but…um, this is personal information, and I think I may need to talk to my supervisor—"

"Really, there's no need for that," she says, warmly now, conspiratorial. "I'm just looking for the forwarding address. You would have to send the man a final W-2. I could get a warrant, but that's going to waste everyone's time."

"You do know we are a law firm, right?"

She laughs and hopes it doesn't sound as stilted as it feels.

"All right, I was hoping not to have to do this, but here's what's going on. He's my brother-in-law. He and my sister are divorced, but she's sick, and I need to get in touch with him right away. She's in the hospital, and I'm in charge of getting in touch with everyone. Please. I wouldn't normally throw my title around, but I thought it was the most expedient way."

"Oh, wow. That's terrible. I'm sorry to hear it. But I'm afraid I can't help you."

"Okay, then, I'll go get the warrant—"

"No, I mean, I can't help you, because there's nothing here. He transferred to our San Diego office, then he must have left the firm because his records with Spencer Landry end in 2000. I'm so sorry I can't be more help. And I'm sorry about your sister. I hope she gets better soon."

"Thank you, Mr. Patrone. You've been a great help. Have a good day."

She hangs up the phone, mouth slightly agape. What has she just done? She's just tried to extort personal information, without a warrant, without any probable cause, only to further her own goals. And has hit a brick wall to boot.

Serves you right for meddling, Lauren's voice rings clear in her head. *I warned you. Stay away from this.*

God, now she is hearing voices. She needs sleep. She needs to take three weeks off, find a warm beach somewhere, drink fruity drinks and crisp herself in the equatorial sun, but this isn't an option. Mindy isn't resting; she is getting sicker and sicker.

And if Lauren won't do the right thing, damn it, Juliet will figure out a way.

She googles Kyle Noonan again, adding Spencer Landry and San Diego in the search box.

She finds nothing. But this isn't unusual. She's searching for information from seventeen years ago. Not everything was as plugged in then as it is now. Not every thought, word, and deed that happened every moment of every day made it onto the web back then.

Maybe she needs to do this the modern way. Social media holds all truths. She can troll Facebook for a while, see if anything pops. Lauren doesn't have an account, but maybe Kyle does.

Like all CBI employees, she has a public server and a private server—the private clearly marked so they can exchange sensitive information and case-specific files without worrying about external hacking. The government has no quibble with her going online during work hours, but they frown on mixing the outside world with their internal confidential information. She opens her personal server and pulls up Facebook, logs in under a false name she often uses to look at people's private accounts. It wouldn't do to have her real name out there. *Hi, I'm with the CBI, wanna be friends?* doesn't always go over well.

Once she's become Jessica Baker—busty and icy blonde, exactly Juliet's opposite—she searches Kyle's name.

She scrolls through several Kyle Noonans, frustrated that none look familiar. But there is an entry for the Douglas County High School Alumni Group. Perfect. His high school is a great jumping off point.

It is an open group, meaning all she has to do is join and then she becomes a part of the page. No one has to approve her. A stroke of luck. Closed groups are harder to infiltrate. Not impossible, but harder.

She searches through the page a bit, doesn't see him listed. Undeterred, she reads through the page, gets a sense for the language and approach people use when trying to hook up with their long-lost friends, then posts a status update.

JESSICA BAKER: Hey '87! What's up? I'm looking for Kyle Noonan. Anyone got the 411 on him?

She feels like an idiot, but it is her only shot.

She stretches again, refills her coffee mug, and sits back down only to see she's already gotten an answer.

MO CABOT: Hey, weren't you in Mr. Williamson's science class? I totally remember you. Looking good!

Oh, no. Has she picked the name of someone already in the group? She does a quick Control-F and searches the name Jessica Baker, finds nothing. Eight Jessicas but no Baker. Two of the Jessicas can be mistaken for her, and since it's so many years later…married name…

Before she can respond, a few more people pop onto the thread.

OSCAR FIELDING: Hey, Jess, welcome. Noonan, haven't heard his name in a while. I thought he moved overseas or something. Haven't seen him around here. What are you up to now?

WILL LINDSY: Hate to be the bearer of bad tidings, but I think Noonan is no longer with us. I remember hearing something about a diving accident years ago.

CAROL CHILDS: That wasn't Noonan, that was Robert Sanford. Remember?

WILL LINDSY: No, you're not remembering correctly. Sanford got caught in an avalanche somewhere in the Alps. Remember he was always talking about summiting K2? He died on a climb.

ELIZABETH FLYNN: Man, we've lost a lot of friends over the years.

OSCAR FIELDING: I just did a search of the archives we posted in the group section and found this from 2000.

Sad to report the news that Kyle Noonan, class of '87, died in a scuba accident off the coast of Baja, Mexico. He will be remembered fondly by all who knew him.

Juliet is floored. Kyle, dead? Why hadn't Lauren told her?

15

Juliet types in another question.

JESSICA BAKER: Who reported that? Do you know?

ELIZABETH FLYNN: I don't remember you, Jessica. What class were you in again?

JESSICA BAKER: '87, but I moved right at the beginning of sophomore year. I was going through my yearbook and saw Kyle's name. I hadn't talked to him in a long time and wanted to say hi. I can't believe he's gone.

ELIZABETH FLYNN: Oh. Yes, it's very sad.

OSCAR FIELDING: I can't find who posted this, but I'm sure you'll be able to Google his obit or something. So where'd you move when you left?

JESSICA BAKER: California. Very different from home. Gotta go, my lunch is over. Thanks for the info you guys. Go Huskies!

She closes the page and sighs. If it's true, this is terrible news—she doesn't feel so bad about the loss of Kyle, he was a boozy, arrogant jerk—but the chance to prove to Lauren once and for all Mindy was switched at birth is gone.

She needs confirmation, so moves on to the Mexican news-papers and does a character search for the names Kyle, Noonan, American, drowning, and scuba.

While she finds plenty of entries that match the American, drowning, and scuba entries, they all scratch out the name Kyle Noonan.

Okay, Juliet, think this through.

Kyle Noonan disappeared off the radar in 2000. A snippet on an alumni board claims he's died. Maybe he's changed his name. Which isn't out of bounds, he was a jerk and hadn't wanted Mindy anyway. A new identity would be a good ruse to avoid paying child support to Lauren.

"What a dick," she says to herself.

Bai stops a foot from her desk. "I'll just…go away then."

"No, no, no, come here. I need you."

"I need you, too. We got a match on the Crusie case. They want you in the conference room to go over the DNA with the investigators."

Juliet tucks her hair behind her ears and stands. "Right. While I'm gone, can you do me a favor? Look into a guy named Kyle Noonan. He used to live here in Denver, moved to San Diego circa 2000, and I have an unsubstantiated report he died in Baja, Mexico. He was a lawyer with Spencer Landry. Be discreet, okay?"

"You mean don't tell anyone what I'm doing?"

"Yes. I mean that exactly."

Bai gives her a crooked smile. "I always love it when you rebel, Juliet."

She pulls the Crusie file off her stack. "Yes, well, let's not get fired over this, okay?"

* * *

Two hours later, on total meeting fatigue, Juliet staggers back to her office. Bai is gone for the day but has left a note on her desk, folded in thirds, with TOP SECRET written on it in his perfect architectural-plan block lettering.

Mighty subtle there, buddy.

She opens the note.

You know the weirdest people. See your personal email for info.

She practically throws herself at the desk. As she did when she went on Facebook, she switches to her personal server and opens her email. There is a note from Bai.

Looks like your dude is dead. All I could find was this. Sorry. Hope the meeting went well. See you in the morning.

Attached is another obituary report, this time a small news article from the *Denver Post*. It is dated August 31, 2000. For some reason, she hadn't been able to find it in her searches.

Kyle Noonan, 32, a Highlands Ranch, Colorado, native, was killed last week in a diving accident off the coast of Baja, Mexico. Noonan, a member of the Colorado and California Bar, was an associate at Spencer Landry in San Diego at the time of his death. Noonan was known for his blustery court appearances. As a public defender, he had a record number of cases seen in the Arapahoe County court system. He went to Douglas County High School in Castle Rock and was briefly married to local artist Lauren Ryder. In lieu of flowers, the family requests donations to Noonan's favorite charity.

There is no byline, which means this could have been written by a family member. She wracks her brain, thinking about Kyle's family. He was an only child, and there was a great-aunt. Juliet remembers Lauren being excited they'd gotten some money when the woman passed away.

She sinks back into the chair. At some point, she is going to have to admit this is a dead end.

Still, she can't believe Lauren has never seen fit to tell her Kyle is dead. She's going to have to ask her about it, but at this moment, she is too tired to do anything but go home and crash. No matter what, Kyle is not going to be Mindy's savior.

She calls her niece's cell phone but gets voice mail. She debates trying Lauren but decides against it. Lauren will just ignore her anyway. When Lauren gets angry like this, it could be days before she'll cool off enough to answer a call. Juliet will have to wait until the weekend, when she goes back to Vail, and talk to her then. In person.

Switched at birth.

So where is her real niece?

She has no choice. If they can find Mindy's birth parents, there will be a better chance of saving her life. She must talk to someone about this, even if it costs her Lauren and Mindy. Mindy's life is worth more.

Juliet knows there is only one way to investigate without anyone knowing. She picks up her phone and calls Cameron.

"Two calls in a week? Whatever have I done now?"

"I need your help. Some advice. I have a problem."

"Want to meet for a drink and talk about it?"

"Can I come to your office instead? I need…privacy."

His tone changes. He must hear the worry in hers. "I'm here. I'll wait for you. Buzz when you're at the door."

"Thanks, Cam."

16

Juliet navigates the streets carefully. The gentle snow from this afternoon is driving hard now. What normally takes five minutes is instead a white-knuckled thirty, the truck slipping and sliding all the way despite her excellent four-wheel drive and snow tires.

Shaking the snow out of her hair, she buzzes, and the door obligingly buzzes back. At the click of the lock, she enters. Cameron's offices are clean and bright: floor-to-ceiling windows in the reception area, the lab itself spotless, stainless and white machines gleaming. He runs a clean shop. She trusts him implicitly.

He meets her in the hall. Cameron is a handsome man, of this there is no doubt. A solid six feet tall, hair prematurely gray, he has a black goatee, always wears black turtlenecks, a gray half-zip, faded jeans and black high-top Converse—his uniform. Tonight he's wearing his glasses instead of contacts, and she has to admit, he looks good. A handsome nerd. He was born in London but has lived in Colorado since he was ten. He still has some British phrases and the slightest accent on some words, which makes him sound mysterious and interesting. Women flirt with him constantly.

In another life, she might even think he'd be a good match for her. But something has always held her back, though Cameron has made it very clear he'd be more than happy to take things further. That *something* is his prodigious mind. She would hate to lose him because he is one of the most challenging, intelligent, interesting people she's ever met. His intellect, and his biting sarcasm, aren't for the weak of heart. She adores that about him.

"Come on, then. Let's get you something hot to drink, and you can tell Uncle Cameron what's wrong."

"Uncle Cameron? Creepy, dude."

He throws a rakish grin over his shoulder, and she laughs.

In his office, he hands her a cup of tea, then leans on his desk, arms crossed.

"It's my sister. She told me that the labs are wrong. We both know that's not the case. And I think Lauren is hiding something. I mean, wouldn't you want to know why the test results don't match? There's only one logical conclusion, right?"

"That the baby isn't hers? That it looks like Mindy was switched at birth?"

"Yes. And since the baby is someone else's, that would mean Lauren's real child is living with strangers. And if that's the case, the biological family could be a transplant match. There could be siblings."

"This is juicy. Do go on."

"Don't make fun. I'm serious. I want to open an investigation."

"So do it."

"Lauren practically begged me not to, then shoved me out the door, insisting I'm crazy as she did. But, Cameron, blood doesn't lie."

"No, it doesn't." Cameron takes a sip of tea, and she senses there is more coming.

"But?"

"Juliet, your sister is going through a horrible trauma. Her wunderkind is sick, and her sister is telling her that the child she's loved, raised, trained to be an elite athlete is not hers. I might not react well to the situation, either."

"Which is all fine, except Mindy needs a stem cell transplant, STAT. We have to put aside our feelings."

"Let them take her out onto the donor database."

"Well, they are. But in the meantime…"

"Oh. You don't need my permission to tell your bosses if that's what you're thinking. I will release the information if there's an investigation, no problem. I'll tell them I ran the samples twice just to be sure, because of Mindy's stature. Since a subpoena will show we did just that."

She doesn't say anything. She can feel Cameron watching her. Finally, he sets down his tea.

"What's wrong, Juliet? Why are you here?"

She takes a deep breath, blows it out hard. "I'm only wondering… There is a way to investigate this without going the official route."

Cameron pulls off his glasses, scratches the side of his nose. "Ah."

"Yes, ah."

He puts the glasses back on. "I'm surprised at you, Juliet. It goes against everything you believe in. You know the consequences if we do that and we're found out. Every case you've ever worked could be reopened. Criminals you've put behind bars could have their verdicts vacated, be granted new trials, and justice might not be served the second time around. Plus, you'll get fired, be in disgrace, and be forced to live out your days eating potted meat sandwiches. Isn't it easier to have it out with your sister than risk your career? If that's not enough to freak you out, the idea of perpetually stale bread and mystery meat should scare the bejesus out of you. Not to mention the fact I could lose the lab."

"Cam, I know the consequences. But something about this feels all wrong to me. If it were me, I'd be banging down the hospital's doors, threatening a lawsuit if they don't explain how my kid went home with someone else."

"But it's not you. Lauren is trying to protect Mindy. Can you imagine how that girl's going to feel when the truth comes out, that she's not Lauren and Jasper's kid?"

"Only part of that is relevant. She's actually not Jasper's kid."

"What?"

"Lauren's first husband left when she got pregnant. She met Jasper when Mindy was a newborn, only a few weeks old. Mindy doesn't know that, either."

"Where's the ex?"

"Dead. Diving accident in Mexico."

She slumps in her chair.

Cameron kneels next to her. "Juliet, I understand why you want to do this. But if you're found out, you lose everything. How do you explain a sudden genetic match? If you come blazing in with a solution to a problem that has only one answer, you're going to come under scrutiny. You don't need your sister's permission to open an investigation. You're CBI. Woody will be discreet, I'm sure, under the circumstances. You can search to your heart's content if this is official. Make your fun little 3-D images of possible family members, maybe even get some press for your new techniques. No disgrace, or potted meat, in sight."

She knows he's right. "Of course we have to do this by the book. I'm not going to risk everything for Lauren. God knows she wouldn't do that for me. I don't know what I was thinking. Forget I came by, all right? I'm embarrassed to have even brought it up."

He smiles. "Come now. You love your sister and your niece, and you don't want to cause them any more pain. I admire you, Juliet. You love deeply, and you're loyal, and that's rare nowadays. If there's anything I can do, you let me know. I'm always willing and able. How about some dinner? Steak?"

"Rain check, Cam? I need to talk to Lauren before I talk to Woody."

★ ★ ★

Juliet calls Lauren when she gets home and is surprised when Lauren answers.

"It's late, Juliet. What's wrong?"

"I wanted you to know I'm going to talk to my boss tomorrow. We need to find out what happened to your biological child. I will be discreet, and we will do everything we can to keep names out of the record. I'm going to label Mindy as a Jane Doe. It will be safe, I swear it."

"What? What are you talking about? You're opening a case with the CBI?"

"I am. We need—"

"No, no, no. Absolutely not."

"Lauren. Listen to me—"

The vitriol in her sister's voice astounds Juliet. "You listen to *me*, little sister. If you do this, I will never speak to you again. Ever. And I will make sure Mindy doesn't see you. I will cut you from our lives."

"You're overreacting, Lauren. Then again, I don't know why I'm surprised. You didn't even tell me Kyle was dead."

Lauren doesn't miss a beat. "His death is hardly relevant."

"You don't know that. We could have tested him...my God, Lauren, don't you want to know where your real daughter is?"

Lauren starts to cry, softly. "Please, I'm begging you, leave this alone."

"I can't. I'm sorry. A law has been broken, and I am a law enforcement officer."

"You're a fucking lab rat. You aren't even an agent."

"And on that sisterly note—"

"Wait. Wait. I'm sorry." Lauren blows out a heavy breath. "Can you come up here tomorrow?"

"I have to work. I need to file the paperwork with the hospital."

"I will tell you everything, okay? But I want to do it in person, not on the phone."

"Is there something you're not telling me?"

"No. Just…for Christ's sake, Juliet, cut me some slack. Come here tomorrow, and let's talk."

The uncharacteristic vulgarity surprises Juliet. Lauren doesn't curse. She doesn't lose her temper like this. She doesn't threaten, and she doesn't speak harshly. The past few weeks are taking their toll.

"On one condition," Juliet says.

"Fine. What?"

"After you finish explaining, you let me take your deposition that you didn't know Mindy wasn't yours. It will help you in the long run, Lauren. You don't want the investigators looking at this the wrong way."

Another sigh. "You won't leave this alone, will you? Trust me. After we talk, there won't be any need for depositions or investigations. I'll see you tomorrow."

She hangs up, and Juliet is stunned.

What in the hell is going on?

17

VAIL HEALTH HOSPITAL

Lauren hangs up the phone, trying to quell the growing panic that threatens to engulf her. Juliet is going to use her rapier mind to reopen the deepest wound Lauren has, whether Lauren wants her to or not. Her whole world is going to collapse.

She can't let it happen. She has to stop her sister.

Lauren can hardly believe how much their lives have changed. It is like a waking nightmare, every day pushing them deeper into a labyrinth that has no path out. And now Juliet is going to ruin everything.

Again.

Think. Think!

Lauren returns to Mindy's room, to the big lounge chair under the cozy blanket, the book she hasn't read a page of nestled beside her. Her hair is in a messy bun on the top of her head; she is wearing thick shearling Uggs on her feet. There was a time when Lauren wouldn't leave the house without a shower and full face. Now, she barely manages to drag a brush through her hair. She knows how she looks. Like an unkempt, worn woman. She doesn't even care.

Mindy sleeps beside her, exhausted, thin, her hair sparse, her collarbones jutting out.

Lauren strokes Mindy's forearm, rebuilds her child into the girl she remembers.

How her dark lashes used to lie across her cheek—when she had any, that is.

How her muscles gleamed, defined and taut.

How her skin turns the color of warm tea in the summer.

How when Mindy was little, she couldn't wait for the weekend, because that meant they'd be packing up the car and heading somewhere fabulous to spend the weekend together. They'd ski all the mountains, drink cocoa by the fire, sit in hot tubs to ease sore muscles. Those days were golden. They were perfection.

How her daughter used to want nothing more than to spend all her time with her parents, in their pockets, to the point where they used to take her to her room and hand her a book so she could learn how to have quiet alone time.

Now, the arriving weekend has them back in the hospital overnight because Mindy's pain was off the charts this afternoon. While her daughter sleeps, drugged and incoherent, Lauren is met with a sleepless night of endless beeping, coughing, cries, fluorescent lights. Snow, too, gray icy snow that batters the windows and leaves them all chilled. Lauren can't believe they used to spend all their time in it. She never wants to see snow again. If Mindy survives...her mind chokes on that thought, the wail building inside her.

She has to survive.

We have to survive this.

A soft voice interrupts her thoughts. "Mrs. Wright?" The nurse smiles timidly. She is a CA—clinician's assistant—a new girl, quiet and sweet, with squeaky clean blond hair in a bouncy ponytail.

"I was wondering if you have a minute. Not me, um, Dr. Oliver."

A trill of panic spreads through Lauren's chest, almost blinding in its intensity.

"What is it? Is something wrong?"

"No, he's in his office and asked me to grab you. I'll stay with her while you go. In case she wakes up. I know Mr. Wright isn't here."

Lauren nods and stands, carefully folding the blanket and setting the book on top of it. She doesn't bother to mark her page.

"What's your name again?"

"Oh, I'm Lolly," the girl says, her dimples practically boring holes in her cheeks. "I'm doing my oncology rotation. I've heard so many good things about Mindy. I can't wait to meet her."

Lauren bites back the tears, the snappish comment. This girl looks barely old enough to have an after-school job, much less be training at this level. She forces herself to smile.

"Well, don't wake her, but if she does, talk to her about anything you want. She's terribly bored. Most of her teammates, friends, are out on the slopes, and she's stuck in here."

"I bet. You go on. Dr. Oliver is waiting."

Lauren puts her phone in her back pocket and dutifully follows the hallway down to Oliver's office. He is behind the big desk, the room a warm jumble of photos and books and lamplight. No fluorescents. She closes her eyes and opens them again, realizing the strain she's been under in Mindy's all-fluorescent room.

He looks up, his eyes kind, and smiles, gesturing her to a seat across from him.

"What's going on?"

"Hi, Lauren. I wanted to see how you were holding up."

"Oh. Well, as good as can be expected. Mindy is such a champion. She's being so strong, and—"

"But how are *you*, Lauren? You and Jasper."

She is silent for a moment. "Considering we might lose our daughter? Pretty shitty. Excuse my French."

Dr. Oliver looks delighted. "No excuses necessary. I'm glad to see you still have some fire left. I know it's hard. For the record, you've been amazing. You both have. But I think you need to get yourself together. Go on home. You can come back and get her tomorrow."

"No, thanks." She knows she sounded mulish, but what is she supposed to do? Abandon her sick daughter? Never.

The doctor steeples his fingers. "Listen to me. You're no good to her like this. You are holding up well, considering. But you're as diminished as she is. She's watching you fade into nothingness, and it's hurting her, badly. You're hurting yourself, too."

"Did she tell you this? What do you mean?"

"Lauren, the girl's face is glass. She's trying to hide it so hard. But yes, she did mention it to me. She's worried about you."

"You talked to her? What else did she say?"

"Yes, I talked to her. When I was adjusting her port in our appointment yesterday. I'm not only about the science, Lauren. The psychology of her illness is important to me, too." His smile moves to something warmer. "She's so feisty. She wanted to know why you and Jasper weren't a match. She made me explain the science behind DNA."

Lauren's heart skips a beat, then rushes back to life, flooding her with adrenaline.

"You aren't supposed to speak to her without us."

"Lauren—"

"And what did you tell her, exactly? What did you explain?"

She sounds harsh and paranoid. She doesn't care. Oliver frowns briefly.

"We talked about how the DNA match works. You want a rundown? I'd expect you to have already done all your research on it."

"I have, but—"

He waits.

Lauren takes a deep breath. "We aren't matched for a reason."

He nods as if he's been waiting for her to bring it up all along.

"I just… I didn't… You didn't tell Mindy, did you?"

"Of course not. I emphasized it's often difficult to find a match with parents, which is why we have a donor database. And, Lauren, you don't owe me any explanations. You're that girl's mother, and that's all I need to know. But I'm glad you've mentioned it, because this is what I wanted to talk to you about. It would be good for us to get in contact with the biological family. There may be a match there, save us the trouble of going wide."

But she is already shaking her head, so he holds up his hands.

"You don't know where they are? It was a closed adoption?"

"Yes."

"I understand. Just curious, why didn't you tell me to begin with?"

"I didn't know it was going to matter. I thought between the three of us, someone would match. I guess I'm not as schooled in the finer points of science as my sister."

"I see. Well, we've loaded Mindy's profile into the system and put out an urgent request for donors. We'll find someone soon, I hope."

"Dr. Oliver, what happens if we don't?"

He smiles again, and this time, it is sad.

"I won't lie to you, Lauren. Her numbers aren't improving. But let's not think that way, okay? Now, I want you to pack it in for the night. Go home. Spend some time there. Give Mindy a little space. She's tired of being brave and is putting up as good a front as you are. Oh, and, Lauren?"

"Yes?"

"Your arm is bleeding. I noticed you scratching at it. I can give you some Ativan if you think it will help."

She looks down at her arm, aghast to see blood on her shirt. Her nail is rimed with red. She was dragging it across her skin without realizing it while they talked, and she's opened a wound.

"I'm fine," she says sharply. "Thank you for pointing it out. I'll get a Band-Aid from the nurses' station."

Lauren leaves the office angry. Angry at God, at Dr. Oliver—who doesn't deserve it, the man is a saint—angry at herself, for her incredible lack of discipline. Scratching open her arm like a common dog. She has to get herself together.

18

Juliet shows up midmorning, looks Lauren up and down and shakes her head.

"My God, you've lost even more weight since I was here. When's the last time you had a decent meal—not from the hospital kitchens? Hey, are you bleeding?"

Lauren glances down at her arm. The Band-Aid needs changing. She has gone too deep. So much for getting herself together.

"I'm fine. Mindy—"

"Needs her mother, yes. But she needs you whole and healthy, not a shadow of yourself. Come on. We're going to go get a gigantic cheeseburger, and ten orders of fries, and you're going to creak when you're finished. And you can tell me what the hell is going on."

"Junk food is not—"

"Since when is a cheeseburger junk food? For heaven's sake, I remember—"

Lauren holds up a hand.

"Onion rings. I want onion rings, too."

"You're on, sister."

"Let me get my purse."

Juliet walks with her to Mindy's room. Mindy is still asleep. The CA is sitting quietly, reading Lauren's book. She smiles and motions toward Mindy with a thumbs-up. Lauren nods, whispers, "We're going to get some food, can you stay?"

"I'm here for the next couple of hours. You go on."

And Lauren realizes Dr. Oliver has given her Lolly as a gift. He really is a good man. They are so lucky.

Juliet drives, her Xterra plowing through the icy streets. They don't talk. Lauren isn't ready. It feels so wrong to be gone but also so freeing, like she can do anything. She can bail, run to Mexico and never come back. *Do it. Run, now!* She tells that ridiculous voice to shut up. She dabs at her arm with a tissue. The bleeding has stopped. It's long sleeves for her for the next week until it heals.

"We could go to the Little Diner—" Juliet starts, but Lauren knows what she wants.

"Why don't we go to the Arapahoe Cafe."

"In Dillon? Seriously?"

"Forty-five minutes to heaven. If you're up for it."

"Absolutely. Let's do it. I haven't eaten there in forever."

Juliet whips the truck around and gets onto I-70 heading east toward Denver.

"Please tell me what's going on," she says quietly, and Lauren rests her head against the window. This isn't going to be avoidable, she knows, and she doesn't want to keep fighting everyone.

"Juliet—"

"Why didn't you tell me Kyle died? I know I'm not your confidant, but he was part of the family."

Lauren doesn't move but cuts her eyes toward her sister. "Because he was out of our lives and I didn't feel like dragging him back in."

"Hard to drag him in from the grave. I just thought you would have told me. He had a diving accident?"

"Yes, somewhere off some reef. Baja, I think, something like that."

"I didn't know he was into scuba."

Lauren shrugs. "He was into a lot of things you didn't know about."

"Don't do that. Don't shut me out."

"What do you want me to say?"

"I want you to tell me what the hell is going on. Mindy doesn't register as a blood relation to us, the man I thought was her biological father is dead, and you're acting like the fucking sphinx over there, all mysterious and weird. I want you to tell me what's going on. I want you to tell me the truth. If I have the truth, I might be able to help you."

Lauren laughs, harsh and bitter. "There's no helping this situation. You couldn't possibly understand."

"Try me."

Should she? Could she? It's all she's been thinking about. What difference does it make at this point what Juliet knows? Surely she can be trusted. She is Lauren's sister, not some nurse or doctor or coach. Her flesh and blood.

"No matter what I tell you, I need your word it will not leave this car. You cannot mention this to Mindy, the doctors, or Jasper. Especially Jasper."

Juliet drags her finger across her chest. "Cross my heart and hope to die."

"This is my story. No one else's. You have to promise you're not going to run off to your bosses when I finish."

"Well, it's Mindy's story, too, but that's between you and her. I swear, if you've done nothing wrong, then tell me already, and I promise I won't interfere."

"I had a miscarriage."

Juliet's face is neutral, though she touches Lauren's hand gently. "I'm so sorry. Was this recent?"

"No. It happened when I was six months along. After Kyle left." She ignores the shocked gaze of her little sister.

"Why you didn't tell any of us?"

"You have to understand where I was at that time. Kyle was a raging asshole. I wanted a baby so badly, and he didn't. I thought for sure once he got used to the idea, he would be thrilled, but I was wrong. I waited until I was really showing, until all the checks and tests were clear and there was no chance of the baby having any issues, and when I told him, he lost his mind. Punched me, punched my stomach, beat me up. And then he said he was filing for divorce and was thinking about taking a job at some bookstore in California. He was going to write, he claimed. He'd sold a short story to some little podunk magazine, and it sparked his creative streak. He'd always wanted to write novels and live at the beach, that I do know. But I thought for sure he'd want a family along with that dream. I was wrong."

"So you miscarried when he beat you up? If he weren't already dead, I'd kill him myself."

"No, it was later, almost two months. Though I'm sure that's what caused it. Something went wrong at that point. I never felt quite the same after. And when the blood started...he was long gone by then."

Juliet is silent, her hands gripping the steering wheel so hard her knuckles are white.

"God, Lauren. I am so sorry. That couldn't have been easy."

Lauren nods. "It was a long time ago."

"But Mindy?"

"When I was in the hospital, the doctor I saw was very sympathetic. She said I had a severe clotting disorder, that it was a miracle the baby made it as long as she had. She mentioned that the odds of me ever carrying to term were very, very low." The words start to come faster and faster until they are a torrent. So many lies, mistruths, omissions—years of hiding the whole story. It pours out of her like a tsunami.

"It was devastating, and I probably wasn't thinking as clearly as I should have been. I'd miscarried before, you see, a couple of times, but early, when I was only a few weeks along. I read up on multiple miscarriages, saw that the doctors were starting to recommend baby aspirin, took it for a couple of months, and voilà, got pregnant again. That time, it stuck.

"Then Kyle was a shithead, and I lost the baby, and this doc-tor was so kind, and she made it so clear I couldn't have another. She said she had a patient, a teenager, who was going to have a baby right when mine had been due, who wanted to put it up for adoption. A little girl, just like mine.

"She set everything up for us. It was a closed adoption. The mother didn't ever want to be contacted. I suspect she had been raped or something because she was so adamant about giving up the baby and moving on. I met her once, two days later. She was pretty. Haggard, too haggard to be that young. She took one look at me and hugged me, said, 'Thank you, take care of her,' and then I didn't hear or see anything until the baby was born. The doctor called, I went to the hospital, and took her home."

Juliet is shaking her head.

"But your party, your stomach… I mean, I saw you in the last couple of months. You weren't huge, but you looked pregnant. You never said you weren't pregnant."

"I was ashamed. Miscarriage wasn't as out in the open as it is now. I didn't want to talk to anyone about it. And I knew this was going to be a perfect solution. I wanted the baby. She was mine, and we agreed, and the doctor helped everything go smoothly, I didn't see any reason to say anything."

Juliet steers the truck off I-70 onto the Dillon exit.

"You've been lying for more than seventeen years," she says, turning into the parking lot of the restaurant.

"I haven't. Mindy is my daughter. She has been since before she was born."

"It's still a lie of omission. My God, Lauren."

"You don't get to judge me, Juliet. You don't know the things I've been through. You don't know me at all. You were just a child. What was I supposed to do, confide in you? You were worried about school, a science fair if I recall. This was way above your pay grade."

"I'm not judging. I'm just saying, I'm family. You could have told me. Did Mom know?"

"No one knew."

Juliet puts the truck into Park, turns in her seat. The light is dim in the car; they are parked in the shadow of the restaurant, and though the sun is glowing on the frozen lake, this small corner of the lot is steeped in shadows.

"Tell me the rest, Lauren. Why am I not supposed to talk to Jasper?" Juliet asks, her teeth clenched.

Lauren blows out a breath. "Because he doesn't know. I've never told him I'm not Mindy's biological mother."

19

The silence in the truck is overwhelming. The enormity of what Lauren has just confided hits Juliet, hard. Lauren closes her eyes as if she realizes it's too late; she can't take it back. That everything is going to come out now, and she is powerless against it. She begins to worry at her stained sleeve. Juliet lays her hand on Lauren's, and she stills.

Juliet starts to speak and stops a few times. She has to admit, the relief she feels is overwhelming. The idea of a baby switched at birth was almost too much to bear. This—adoption—will tear Mindy apart, but at least she'll know she was raised with Lauren and Jasper because she was wanted, not because of a fluke mistake. And another family won't be dragged into the judicial morass, either.

When she finally finds words, her tone is curious, detached. Not at all the judgmental little sister, but the rational scientist solving a puzzle.

"How could you not tell Jasper?"

"Because he didn't care. When I met him, Mindy was a tiny, squalling, milk-sucking beastie. That's all he knew. He was madly in love with her from day one, bless him. What did it matter?"

"I don't know—he might think differently about her, about you?"

"She wasn't his, and he loved her anyway. It wouldn't have

made a difference to him if he'd known I adopted her. He wouldn't have cared. It didn't matter," she emphasizes again. "She's mine. She is *mine*."

"I understand how you feel. No one could have been a better mother to Mindy, Lauren. You're an incredible mother. But she's *not* biologically yours. And she's sick. And we need to find a donor. Which means you need to 'fess up, big sister, to all of it, so we can go find Mindy's birth mother and get her tested, right away."

Lauren shakes her head. "It's impossible."

"I work for the CBI. Trust me when I say nothing is impossible."

"But this is. I don't know who the biological mother is. I don't have an address. I don't even remember the girl's name, if I ever knew her real one, which I seriously doubt. She was a sweet, mixed-up Hispanic teenager who barely spoke English and was thrilled to be rid of the baby. Trust me, I doubt she's ever looked back. I know I haven't."

"You paid her money. There will be a record—"

"Cash. Up front. No receipt. All that paperwork made me feel like I was buying a child, so I—we—agreed not to have any. There are no records to find."

"Give me the doctor's name, then."

"I don't have it."

"Now you're being stubborn."

Lauren slams her fist into the dashboard. "You don't understand."

"I do understand. You're trying to save your own skin because you're worried Jasper is going to boot you out the door when he finds out you've been lying to him all these years."

"No, you don't understand. It's impossible. The doctor has absolutely no information on the girl, no records, nothing. It was a closed, private adoption, with legal guarantees that I will never try to contact the birth mother."

"In other words, it was an illegal adoption."

"No. Not…illegal. I guaranteed I would never try to find her, that's all."

"Well, now you're going to break that vow."

"No, I'm not."

"Yes, you are. Because if you don't, I will."

Lauren stares at her little sister. "What do you mean, you will? You will do nothing of the sort. This is my family, my decision. You don't have a say."

"I don't have a say? She's my niece. And I won't let her die if there's a way to save her life. You can't possibly think you're going to be able to keep this secret, do you? The doctors know she's not your biological child. How long will it be before they slip in front of Jasper? He's not stupid. He knows something's wrong."

"That's not true."

"You really do have blinders on, big sister. Everyone knows something's up with you. Look at you. You're disintegrating before our eyes. Look at your arm."

Lauren glances down. She is bleeding again, has been clawing at her skin while Juliet confronts her. Juliet feels a strange recognition with this gesture, something long hidden rearing up. A fragment from the past, barely even a memory. Lauren across from her at the big round wooden table, the red checked tablecloth—*it was Colorado, we got that at Target*—playing with a bandage on her arm, fraying the edges, and their mother smacking Lauren's hand away, yelling, "Stop doing that!"

Juliet doesn't recall seeing Lauren do it ever again. Until now.

"Juliet, if Mindy dies—"

"If she dies, *then* you'll tell? You think that will make this all right? This lie? This epic, world-changing lie?"

"Stop screaming at me. This is my life. My choice. I won't break the rules that I set out for myself."

"The rules you set out for yourself? Fuck *yourself*. This is

Mindy's life. Who cares what you think about the way things ought to have been done? This is what has to happen. And trust me, if you don't step up, I will do it without you."

"Do that, and I will never speak to you again, Juliet Ryder. I swear it."

"Empty threats. You don't speak to me now, Lauren. What difference would it make?"

The bitter words hang in the air between them.

"I'm not hungry anymore," Lauren says, looking out the window.

"Neither am I," Juliet replies. "This whole charade makes me sick. But we're going to go inside and eat a proper meal because you are out of your mind, and maybe some food will help you think with clarity."

She pulls the keys from the ignition and opens her door, then sticks her head back inside.

"And, Lauren, when we get back to Vail, you have to tell Jasper."

"He'll never forgive me."

"You should have thought about that before you decided to base your entire life with him on a lie." Juliet slams the door hard enough to rock the truck and stalks into the restaurant.

20

The sun is bright on the fresh powder, shimmering off the frozen lake twenty yards from the truck. Lauren pulls a fresh tissue from her purse, dabs at her arm, then applies a new Band-Aid. She didn't realize she'd pulled the other one off, finds it crumpled under her left heel.

The bones in her wrist are sharp; buff-colored skeleton's hands on her wasted, skinny thighs. Juliet is right, there's not much of her left. She has shrunk over the past month.

The well of fear threatens to drown her. Juliet isn't kidding. She is going to force Lauren's hand. Another wave of panic hits.

Lauren can feel the edges of her world unraveling. Images she forced away long ago come back to her—Kyle's hateful, sneering face, the wrenching pain in her abdomen, the blood on her hands. The small ball of warmth with wisps of black hair and translucent skin, silent, so silent, so still. The healthy cries from Mindy's crib, the sleepless few weeks before she'd met Jasper, when she thought she might die of exhaustion and frustration.

That familiar tug of desperation fills her now, the sense of being out of control, of not having any recourse, of the world spinning too fast for her feet to move on the earth.

What is she willing to lose to save Mindy's life? What cost will the truth bring?

Juliet is right, damn her. She is going to have to talk about this with Jasper. She is going to have to admit the truth, that Mindy isn't hers. And suffer the consequences.

She has to do it now, get out ahead of this. She can't let Juliet be the one to tell him. Jasper will never forgive Lauren, but maybe, for Mindy's sake, he can learn to live with her deception. She alone can frame the situation. Make him understand.

She marches inside where Juliet has already taken a table by the window that looks out onto the lake. There are two glasses of iced tea on the table. Lauren assiduously avoids her sister's gaze when she sits down, as if she can see right through her sister's body. Like she's a ghost. Like she doesn't exist.

"Juliet."

At last, Juliet's head turns, and Lauren is shocked to see her sister's red-rimmed eyes, her nose rabbit-pink. Juliet Ryder doesn't cry at anything. She didn't cry when she broke her wrist in fifth grade, when her steady boyfriend broke it off the weekend before they left for college, when she missed the astronaut program by a fraction of a point. Juliet Ryder doesn't cry, ever, period, yet here she is, struggling for control, in public, no less.

Lauren covers her sister's hand in hers. "I'll tell him tonight. Then I'll go back through my files and see if I can find the doctor's name. I don't remember her name, only that she was Hispanic, that's all I recall. You're right, we need to find Mindy's birth mother and try to find a match among her family."

"Thank you," Juliet manages, but Lauren grips her hand harder until she feels a knuckle pop under the pressure, and Juliet's eyes grow wary at the pain.

"But *I* will handle this, Juliet. This is my family, my mistake, and it's my responsibility. Not yours. You stay out of it from now on, you hear me? I will take care of things."

Juliet simply nods.

"Good. Now, do you still want onion rings?"

21

UNIVERSITY HOSPITAL

NASHVILLE, TENNESSEE

1993

VIVIAN

Liesel has been a silent member of the ward for two weeks. She won't participate in group, she won't participate in one-on-one, she certainly won't participate with me more than the perfunctory. She seems to like art, though, paints with abandon during arts and crafts, but as for the rest, she is mute.

After art, when we're cleaning our brushes—me extra thoroughly—I finally decide to go for it.

"You were crying in your sleep last night. Again. Want to talk about it?"

There is a long, pungent silence, before a small, quiet "Maybe."

"We could go smoke."

"I don't smoke anymore."

"Then our room."

"Fine. I guess."

Twenty minutes later, after I smuggle us in sodas and the sandwich crackers with sour cream and chive cheese I know she likes, I shut the door almost all the way and we have a small party, sitting on the floor in between the beds, our blankets as a combo picnic blanket and cushion.

Munching her crackers, she finally tosses an opening salvo. "Do I say anything, in my sleep?"

"You keep saying 'no.' Over and over. And punching the sky."

She nods, calmly, as if she was expecting this. "That's all?"

"Yes. But you seem…upset. Scared. It's freaky."

"Why do you sneak out at night? What are you doing?"

A test. I decide I have nothing to lose. "One of the night guys lets me smoke in the lounge."

"What's he want in return?"

"For smokes, nothing. But for information—everything has its price." I shrug. "I haven't paid it."

"Would you?"

"Fuck an orderly for information? If I had to. If it was important enough."

I sound braver than I feel.

"You'd do that to find out about me?"

"He offered. I said no. I would much rather hear it from you."

"Don't ever trade yourself for information. You're better than that. Swear to me you'll never do it."

"I swear. Okay? I swear. Now, what's the story?"

"I tried to kill myself. That's why I'm here." She pushes up her left sleeve, and I have to admire the vertical slice that starts at her palm and heads toward her elbow. It is straight, uniform, still red against her pale skin, but clean and healing well. In the light, I can also see multiple scars, two inches long, straight across the soft flesh of her inner forearm. Only two of the horizontal lines intersect the newer slice. They are much older, a perpendicular railway built over a long time.

"That's pretty work."

She slides the sleeve down. "Thank you. Precision is important to me."

"When did you start cutting?"

"A few years ago." She shrugs. "It's no big deal."

"I tried it once. It freaked me out."

"It makes me feel good. Dr. Freakazoid says I'm looking for an unhealthy release for my psychic pain, but really, it just feels good."

"I have a tattoo. I liked how that felt. The needle going in and out—it hurt, but there was something good in the pain, too."

"Serotonin rush. It's addictive. Let me see."

I slide down the shoulder of my shirt. The tattoo is small, a butterfly, on my shoulder blade. It is yellow with blue spots. I dig it.

"I had to use a fake ID, and the tattoo guy didn't buy it for a second, but he was an anarchist and loved the idea of sticking it to the man, so he did it anyway, for half price."

"It's very pretty. Maybe I'll get one. See how it feels."

I pull up my shirt. "I have my belly button pierced, too. Obviously, my nose, too. They won't let me have my jewelry, think I'm going to use it to stab out my eyes or something."

She touches the hole in my stomach. Her fingers are soft, her nails chewed down, and it feels good. Strange, but good. I realize no one has voluntarily touched me without anger in months.

I yank down my shirt. "You said you killed someone."

Her face shutters. She shifts on the blanket, staring over my shoulder now, at nothing. "I did."

"Liesel, tell me. You'll feel better. I swear I'll never say a word."

With a deep, racking sigh, a girl old beyond her years, she begins to speak.

"I told the police what I'm telling you."

"Which means it's the truth, or it's the story your lawyer told you to stick to?"

"Is there a difference?"

★ ★ ★

She tells me everything. In detail. Enough that my stomach turns and I look at her in a new light. She has been through hell, my roommate. More hell than me, that's for sure. She almost makes me feel like my depression isn't important. That I'm being selfish by not being happy.

"So that's how I ended up here. That's how I ended up with this miserable life. Do you feel sorry for me?"

I know I am looking at her with a combination of horror and sympathy on my face. I shut my eyes briefly, take a breath.

"No. You did what you had to do. I'm sorry you're being punished, but I don't feel sorry for you."

"What about now?"

She takes my hand and puts it on her stomach. The uniform sweats they provided the night she was brought in have hidden the pregnancy so well.

22

THE WRIGHTS' HOUSE
CURRENT DAY

Shaken by her confrontation with Juliet, Lauren pulls into the cobbled driveway of their house, seeing it with fresh eyes. It looks deserted. Not like they have been on vacation, but that they have decamped without warning. The rose trellis by the garage has cracked, a large, packed snowbank leans against the house where Jasper hasn't bothered to shovel it away. Their windows are grimy, the curtains pulled. There is snow on the balconies, piled up high. Lauren cringes to think what the stone beneath is experiencing; they'll have to regrout the entire lower level come spring. A mountain house needs regular upkeep, lots of tender loving care, and they have fallen down on the job.

The house is too big for them, but cozy, nonetheless. They bought it thirteen years ago, the second they realized Mindy was going to be tethered to the ski slopes and had come to the attention of the Vail Ski Club, one of the best paths to becoming a world champion skier in the country. Designed to look like a European ski lodge, with vaulted wood ceilings and balconies, it was overpriced then, but the views are incredible, and from the moment Lauren entered the living space, all she wanted to do was grab a brush and paint the scape in front of her. That feeling has never changed. The second floor is almost all windows; they can see three separate mountain peaks, plus have a clear view of Vail's back bowl ski runs.

The way the prices have risen in this area, they could sell it for ten times what they paid, or more, but that is little comfort. Even with the rising costs of Mindy's treatments, Lauren has no desire to sell her life. She's poured body and soul into making the house a home. Every room has been ministered to; she's marked them all like a cat leaving its scent behind. She loves it with abandon, like she does Mindy. It is as much a part of her as her arms and legs. She will never willingly give it up.

She pulls into the garage, noting Jasper's Audi isn't inside. Good. She needs some time to figure out exactly how she is going to handle things. What to say. How to manage the situation.

The situation. *Hello, darling. How was your day? Make you a martini? By the way, our whole life is a lie.*

The living room is dusty and cold. She lights a fire in the oversized potbellied stove and cranks open the vent. The air begins to warm immediately. She throws in more wood until the stove roars with happiness, then climbs the stairs to the master, desperate for a long, hot shower and change of clothes.

The bedroom is a mess. Jasper is a naturally tidy man, Lauren is a neat freak, and Mindy is a minimalist, which means the house is designer showcase ready at all times, but she finds their bed unmade, the sheets stale and crumpled, magazines and books spilling from the side table onto the floor.

An unreasonable anger seizes her. Damn Jasper for leaving her this mess. Damn Juliet. Damn Mindy for crashing into that gate. Damn the cancer eating her alive. Damn the doctors and the DNA and the needles and tests. Damn it all.

She sweeps the books and magazines to the floor with a crash. Rips the sheets off the bed, throws them on the floor, too. The fury grips her and she takes it out on every available thing that is light enough to move, then collapses onto the bed in a puddle of frustrated tears.

She hears the gentle chime of the alarm system indicating a door has opened. Jasper is home. Damn that, too.

"Honey?" he calls. She hears him on the stairs but doesn't move. She can't do this. Not anymore.

"Dear God, Lauren, what's going on? What are you doing?"

"Grieving," she manages, throwing herself facedown so she won't have to see his pity.

Jasper begins to laugh. It is the nervous laughter of someone trapped too long in solitary confinement. Lauren rolls onto her back and looks at him incredulously, which makes him laugh harder.

"Look at this mess. You trashed the bedroom."

"You come home to find your wife in tears, and you laugh? What kind of sicko are you?"

He laughs harder. "The kind that gets his kicks from coming home to a bedroom that looks like a drunken rock star threw a three-day bender in it, apparently. Come here."

He gathers her in his arms. The tears have stopped; Lauren has never been much of a crier. Even now, even faced with Mindy's possible death, with her world falling apart, the possibility that she will lose everything looming large, crying feels like a useless waste of time.

Jasper has stopped murmuring nonsense meant to soothe and is softly kissing her neck. She lets him. She needs a shower, needs to straighten up, but she needs this more. It will make what she has to tell him easier.

She turns to face him, straddling his legs, pulling off his glasses and tossing them to the nightstand, then proceeds to get his pants open enough to take advantage of the position. He helps, dragging off her leggings as she smothers him with kisses, his mouth, his neck, his chest, sliding farther and farther down until she has him in her mouth and he is moaning her name.

They've always been good at this.

Always been good at everything.

He pulls her back up, and her legs naturally wind around his waist. He holds her tight in his arms, moving into her, and she grinds against him, losing herself in the rhythm, in the exquisite feeling of being alive, of feeling him inside her, his arms around her, his head thrown back. They go faster, then he stands and turns around, lays her on the bed, but not gently, she doesn't want it gentle, she wants to know she's alive. He senses this and moves hard into her. She bites him on the shoulder and bucks against him, and he loses all control, his movement inevitable and unstoppable now. She goes right over the edge with him, trembling and shaking and calling his name.

When she comes back to herself, she opens her eyes to see his sheepish face hovering above hers.

"I am so—"

She puts her finger on his lips. "No. Don't apologize. I needed it, too."

"But you were crying."

"And now I'm not. Mission accomplished, wouldn't you say?"

He kisses her deeply then, slowly, and she relaxes into the bed, savoring him, allowing the connection between them to cement itself.

Together, it whispers. *You're in this together.*

23

They shower, taking advantage of the double heads, and dress, speaking of nothing important, marriage talk, assiduously avoiding all mention of Mindy and the hospital and why Lauren is home instead of there.

When her hair is dry and tied back in a ponytail, Jasper helps her change the sheets and put the room back into place.

"Sorry it was such a mess. I rushed to the office this morning."

"It's fine, babe. Don't worry. I wasn't mad at the mess. I'm mad at the whole situation."

"That's good. I'm glad to see you feeling something. You've been on autopilot for a while now. What happened to your arm?"

The bandage is secure, thank heavens. "Just a scratch. Nothing to worry about."

"You'd tell me…"

"Of course. It's all good. I'm hungry, how about you?"

They've been married long enough for Jasper to know when to back off.

They make dinner, still not speaking of Mindy, of her absence at their family meal, of their absence at her bedside. It is strange and feels wrong, but something tells her she needs this. Needs the space. She'll be a much better mother and wife if she takes care of herself, even if she only indulges in a long shower and sex and a good night's sleep.

She is pleased to see the kitchen is provisioned well enough and sets about making French onion soup. She caramelizes the onions, the fragrant scents of butter and sherry making her mouth water. When the onions are done, she adds the stock and sets it to simmer, then pulls a baguette out of the freezer and puts it in the oven. Shredding the Gruyère, she goes slower than normal, being careful, cautious. Lets the slow scrape of the fragrant cheese against the metal teeth soothe her.

She still has no idea how she is going to explain things. But food and sex are a good buffer. She'll tell him after dinner. Wine, she should open wine, too. French, one of the burgundies, maybe splurge with a Pomerol?

"So what's the big secret you need to tell me?" Jasper plops down on one of the kitchen stools, facing her. It brings them to eye level; he is much taller than she is. She stops grating.

"Here, give me that. Go stir the soup."

She hands over the cheese and shredder, using the moment to school her face. When she turns back, she takes a deep breath.

"Why do you think I have a secret?"

He gives her that lopsided smile she loves so much. "Babe, we've been married for a very, very long time. I can tell when you need to tell me something. Spit it out, you'll feel much better."

She takes the cheese from him and sets it aside.

"Please don't hate me for not telling you this sooner."

"I could never hate you, Lauren. I love you. Now, what's going on?"

She chews on her lip briefly, then blurts it out. "I adopted Mindy before she was born."

There are many reactions she expects from him, but cool acceptance isn't one of them. "Is that why neither you nor Juliet was a match?"

"Yes."

"Why didn't you tell me when we met? Do you think it would have made a difference to me?"

"Well, yes, actually, I did. It's one thing to be with a woman who has a child, but if that woman has chosen to bring the child into her life, and it's not hers…"

"That is the dumbest logic I think I've ever heard."

"You are taking this very well."

"No, I'm really not. Inside I'm screaming at you." Jasper scrubs his hand across his face, his stubble rasping. "That girl is my greatest gift. I knew it from the moment I met you and met her. It makes no difference to me who birthed her. Though I am hurt—hurt as hell—that you didn't trust me enough to tell me."

"I am so sorry."

"So am I. You've broken the trust between us. Just when we need it the most."

He sounds so sad, it makes her want to weep. He is trying to look into her eyes as if seeing into her soul will help him understand, but she averts her gaze. It hurts too much, seeing the pain she's caused. She is a coward. Such a coward.

"I never meant to hurt you. I never meant to hold this back. It was personal. It was a decision I made when I might not have been entirely in my best mind, and once I made it, I couldn't—wouldn't—walk away."

"Tell me."

So she does. Tells him the whole story, from beginning to end, from Kyle's hateful indifference and the pregnancies and the miscarriage to the doctor, as dispassionately as she can.

When she finishes, he sighs. "We'll deal with my hurt feelings soon, but for right now, I agree with Juliet. We have to find Mindy's real mother."

"I *am* her real mother." The words rip out of her in a snarl, and Jasper holds up a hand.

"Biological, babe. That's all I meant. You're not in a position to attack me, you know. I'm behaving very rationally for a man who's just found out his wife's been lying to him for seventeen years."

"You are, and I'm sorry." The timer dings, the bread is done. "Let's eat. Then—"

"Then we will look for this woman, whether you like it or not." She starts to interrupt, but he shakes his head. "Lauren, you don't have a choice anymore. This is bigger than you, your feelings, your pride. We must do whatever it takes to save Mindy's life."

"You can't tell her. You can never tell her."

He shakes his head again. "The time for secrets is over. We are going to tell her. She loves you. No one could ever take your place."

"Are you thinking clearly, Jasper? Because I don't think you are. If we tell Mindy I adopted her, we'll also have to tell her you're not her real father. Are you ready for that? We've always promised not to share that with her, and now you want to drop the biggest bombshell of her life on top of a potentially fatal disease. She's seventeen, for heaven's sake. Even though you think she's Supergirl, she's just a seventeen-year-old child who is sick, and might die."

Genuine pain crosses his face as if her words have been attached to an anvil smashing into his stomach. "Honey, listen to me. This couldn't have happened in a worse way, I'll grant you that, but Mindy isn't stupid. I think she already suspects. She asked me for a book on DNA. She said it was because she was thinking about following Juliet's steps into the CBI, but I think she wants to understand what her charts are saying. Maybe she senses this, maybe she's always wondered. Who knows? But she has the right to know her true heritage. And she has the right to the hope that we can find her a match. It's our duty now. We must put our personal stakes aside and do what's right by our daughter."

"You've changed your tune. You always said—"

"Circumstances have changed, Lauren. I can't save my daughter's life with my blood, and now I know why you can't, either. So yes, I've changed my tune. She's old enough to know the truth. And we are going to tell her."

Lauren serves their meal stiffly, silently furious. She can't let Mindy know. She just can't. She will do anything she has to, anything, to keep the truth from her.

24

Lauren finds sleep impossible. The bed is too comfortable, the room too dark and quiet. Jasper's gentle snores and the roaring wind in the trees outside feel like a jackhammer to her brain.

She gets up slowly so as not to wake her sainted husband, wraps herself in his discarded sweater, and steals to her office on the first floor. It is chilly but she welcomes the discomfort, it helps her relax a bit.

He took it so well, the news she wasn't Mindy's biological mother. Outside of his desire to tell Mindy the whole truth, he's handled the revelation better than expected. Oh, she could tell he was furious, ready to burst into screams, but he'd kept himself under control. They sniped at each other the rest of the evening until she locked herself in the bath and he stomped off to clear the snow from the decks. But that was to be expected.

The problem is Jasper's planned next steps. He doesn't understand her reluctance to share the news with Mindy. She has to make him see the light.

Lauren will not—cannot—run the risk of losing her daughter to a technicality.

She peels the bandage away from her arm. The cut is ragged, nonuniform. It bisects the other scars, long faded, scars few people outside the family know are there. Everyone who's ever seen them has been told they occurred in a car accident when she was young. Arm through the glass windshield. Tons of tiny little cuts. The scars so pale now that no one but Lauren can see them.

The scratch has crusted over. She runs the pad of her finger over it, feels the bumpy line. Pulls at the edge of the scab until a bead of bright red blood appears. She touches the tip of her finger to it, brings the smear of red to her tongue. Takes a deep breath and puts the bandage back into place.

Her laptop is completely out of battery. She plugs it in and gives it a few minutes to charge, then opens her email. It has been piling up. Even though she's looked at the account occasionally on her phone, she's let it grow wild, and now it needs to be pruned back.

Fifteen minutes later, after ruthlessly deleting every email from a stranger or a store, she is left with five. Two are from friends checking in on Mindy, asking if they can bring dinners by, or help in any way. The other three are nothing of note, class schedules for an art program she is involved with, a home-school standardized test notice. She answers them all quickly and efficiently, then turns her browser to private so the internet's bots won't track her. In Google, she types in a name she hasn't thought about in a very, very long time.

She types and searches and clicks and reads until she is satisfied.

Her secret is safe. She lets out the breath she's been holding all day.

"Babe, what are you doing? It's three in the morning."

Lauren jumps in her seat and slaps the lid of the laptop down. Jasper stands in the doorway to her office, rumpled, yawning, his face a mask of confusion.

"My God, you scared me. I'm sorry, did I wake you?"

"I heard a noise, realized you weren't in bed. It's freezing in here. Seriously, what are you doing?"

"I couldn't sleep, so I thought I'd tend my email. It's gotten out of control."

She stands, surreptitiously pulling the power cord out of the laptop. "But I'm done. I was wasting time surfing. I'm finally tired." She yawns for effect. "I'm sorry I woke you. I'm sorry about tonight, too. About everything. I don't want to fight. I know you're right. We have to tell her."

She goes to him, presses her cheek against his chest, her arms sliding around his waist as if they've been born for that purpose alone.

"Let's go back to bed," she says, allowing her voice to go husky, and he doesn't resist, just switches off the light and starts down the hall, his arm solid around her shoulders. They are a few steps away when she says, "Oh, crap, I forgot to plug in my laptop. I'll be right there. Start without me."

He stiffens but nods, letting himself be lied to. Is this how things will be between them, lies and mistruths and sneaking around? She hopes not. She wants to put this whole story to bed once and for all.

She fumbles with the cord long enough to open the lid of the computer, log in one-handed, close the private browser and reopen it in her normal mode. On the surface, it will do, and tomorrow she'll go in and purge the history, make sure everything has been deleted.

Jasper is waiting for her, eyes cool in the darkness. She slides into the bed and shimmies off her clothes, nestles against him, toying with the waistband of his boxers. Says a small prayer as she kisses him.

So many secrets. So many lies.

Let them be enough.

25

DENVER, COLORADO

Juliet knows she should leave things well enough alone, but that isn't who she is. She can't just sit back and wait to see what Lauren cooks up, as much as she promised she would. She stares at the slowly rotating ceiling fan, the minutes and hours ticking off, thinking, *Why? Why in the world would she lie about this?*

Finally, recognizing sleep is going to be elusive, she goes to the kitchen and makes a cup of tea. As the water heats, she wonders again—what is Lauren hiding? The whole story rings of half-truths. Juliet knows her sister well enough to recognize when she's lying. She is terrible at it, always has been.

But a lie of omission, that is different than an outright falsehood, right?

As far as Juliet can tell, Lauren has never given anyone any reason to doubt Mindy is hers, but she certainly never claimed it. She's allowed everyone to assume, and there was no reason to question her about it. Is that truly lying?

Juliet thinks back to her sister's pregnancy. The only time she saw Lauren between the divorce and Mindy's birth was at her baby shower.

There was an ultrasound on the refrigerator, Juliet remembers that. She tries to remember the women who'd attended, their names, faces, and comes up blank. Truthfully, she hadn't paid much attention. Juliet was a teenager at the time, involved in her own world.

It wasn't until after Kathleen passed away that Juliet got back into their lives on a more regular basis, so yes, Juliet can understand why Lauren hasn't confided in her. They weren't close then, and they certainly aren't close now.

But something is wrong with all of this, and as much as Juliet wants to walk away, she can't.

The tea is ready. She sits at her desk, blowing on the edge of the cup to cool the scalding liquid. She touches the mouse and her iMac is up in an instant. She starts with the easy part—looking up doctors who practiced obstetrics at the hospital where Mindy was born. She gives a range of eighteen to sixteen years ago, just in case, and gets a list of names that is workable, only ten. Not surprisingly, seven were men, so they are eliminated immediately. That leaves her with three doctors, only one of whom's name is remotely Hispanic.

Dr. Soledad Castillo. Educated at the Colorado School of Mines for undergrad, medical school at the University of Colorado, did her postdoc specialization in obstetrics and gynecology, worked at Swedish Medical from 1998–2000 as a staff OB/GYN instead of going into private practice. Which helps make sense of the situation Lauren explained—if Castillo worked the emergency room and was in the general physician pool, she would come across all sorts of people who might want a shortcut.

In other words, jackpot.

She checks her watch, surprised to find it's already 8:00 a.m. Why not? A little fishing expidition won't hurt. She dials the hospital.

"Hello, Swedish Medical Center. I'm Jasmina, your red stripe volunteer today. How many I direct your call?"

"Could you transfer me to Dr. Castillo? She should be in obstetrics."

The woman on the other end of the line hums a little tune while she looks.

"I'm sorry, dear, there's no Castillo in obstetrics."

"Perhaps she's left the hospital. Can you forward me to HR?"

"Certainly, dear. I don't know if anyone's in this early, but you can leave a message if they don't answer. Have a blessed day." There is a long beep, then an elevator version of a Britney Spears tune with a sweeping clarinet solo. Just as Juliet begins to worry she's contracted an earworm, another voice comes on, this one harried.

"What can I help you with?"

"I'm sorry to bother you so early. I'm looking for information on Dr. Soledad Castillo. She was an OB there in 2000."

"Who's this again?"

"My name is Juliet Ryder, CBI."

"Well, ma'am, I'm sorry to tell you this. Dr. Castillo is no longer with us."

"Do you have any forwarding information?"

"You might try Fairmount Cemetery."

Juliet groans. "Seriously? She's dead?"

"Yes, ma'am. Dr. Castillo passed away...gosh, it must have been in 2000. Yes, that's right. I remember because it was my first year here. It was a big deal at the time. She was a kind woman."

"Tell me, are her records still in the hospital archives?"

"I'm sure they would be, but—" his voice takes on a peculiar tone. "I'm afraid I won't be able to access them without a court order. Sorry I can't be more help."

"Thanks anyway."

She hangs up and runs her fingers along her forehead, tapping against her temple to unseat the light ache that has taken hold there.

Dr. Castillo is dead. Damn. That will make things much more difficult. Exhuming a living doctor's patient file is hard enough, but one who's been dead for so long? The guy in HR isn't wrong; she'll have to get a court order, without a doubt. Even if the doctor's files at Swedish were easily searchable, assuming Castillo was doing things off the books, as Lauren claims, then she's out of luck, again.

Her tea is cold. She pops it into the microwave, taps her fingers along the counter ledge, thinking.

How to find a teenager who gave birth around the time of Mindy's birthday—August 3, 2000—who doesn't want to be found.

A teenager who was desperate to give up a baby.

She probably used a false name; she could be anyone, anywhere.

The odds of Juliet finding her are slim to none. Without DNA, that is.

Surely, though, there has to have been a lawyer involved. Lauren said she agreed not to contact the mother, ever. That the adoption was closed. The doctor couldn't have been facilitating private adoptions without a lawyer, could she?

Oh, this is ridiculous. There is a simple way to handle this, the shortcut of all shortcuts. It is illegal, unethical, and if anyone ever finds out, she'll absolutely lose her job, but there is a way.

Cameron said he was willing to help. He has Mindy's DNA coded already. If Juliet asks—begs, pleads, promises her firstborn?— he can upload it into CODIS and see if there is any kind of match, familial or direct. Not to be a jerk about it, but she knows the life of a teenager who got pregnant and gave up her kid could have led somewhere dark instead of being a way out. She sees it all the time. All the time.

And if there is a match in the system, direct, or even a brother, a father, a cousin, then they'll have that shortcut they need to get Mindy a donor.

She sits at her desk and leans back in her chair. The very idea of doing this makes Juliet sick to her stomach. She flashes back to the conversation she had with Cameron, lets his voice ring in her ears.

It goes against everything you believe in…

She could lie…

"Screw it."

She picks up the phone and dials Cam's lab. He answers on the first ring.

"I got permission. Run the DNA."

"Juliet, as always, your wish is my command."

26

UNIVERSITY HOSPITAL

NASHVILLE, TENNESSEE

1993

VIVIAN

Together we watch her stomach grow. It is surreal. One day her stomach has a small pooch. A few days later, she is showing. For real. The nurses say it happens like that sometime. Zero to sixty, one of them said.

Ratchet took Liesel into her office, they talked, and now Liesel seems happy. She has stopped trying to cut herself. She is eating nutritious food. She is glowing. There are regular discussions of safe antidepressant medications for pregnancy and OB/GYN checks and special conversations. Someone is always knocking on our door frame or pulling her from our activities. The entire unit coddles and cuddles and leaves choice bits of meat and string and foil swans and sunny yellow crayons at the door to our room. Even the most insane among us is moved by the chance of a new life. Of resurrection, and redemption.

She says it's driving her up the wall, but to be honest, I can tell she enjoys it. She thrives under the constant attention, blossoming like some sort of Madonna in a field, awaiting her worshippers. She is a butterfly, escaped from a desiccated cocoon, crawling toward the sunlight. It makes me think she never got any positive reinforcement at home.

I don't like the people on the ward, and they normally give me a wide berth, too. But with Liesel as their sudden superstar, even though she coyly refuses their advances, I get their positive attention, too. We're all a bit less lonely.

She still won't talk in group, which means she gets sent back to the quiet room. I think it's her plan all along, so she can get some solitude. The ward is loud. It is bright. There is no such thing as peace when you're living among people who don't know what planet they're on, or who want to slit your throat to see what color you'll bleed. Liesel takes advantage of the white space. She says she paints in her mind while she lies on the hard bed, her child growing inside her.

It has changed her, this diagnosis. I'm not sure how I feel about the transition. She was more interesting before, I think, when she was moody and gray, closed like the first buds of spring in a flower bed that's been hit with weed killer, all gray and wizened and hurt. I didn't enjoy finding her in our bathroom, crouched down, scraping at her flesh with a plastic pen lid, but I understood and didn't tell.

How an incarcerated sixteen-year-old is going to be able to handle a child is lost on me. Liesel refuses to talk about what happens when the baby is born. She will still be in here, living out her sentence.

Personally, I would have screamed and yelled for an abortion immediately. The idea of being pregnant is abhorrent to me—the claustrophobia of not being able to escape the sentence of something growing inside you for nine months is too much for me to bear. But Liesel is surprisingly content. She says she has something to live for, now.

We reach a kind of détente when she is four months along. I stop bothering her to get rid of Satan's child; she stops throwing up in my shoes.

She goes about her days with a small smile, following the routine: wake, eat, one-on-one therapy, arts and crafts, lunch, nap, shower, dinner, television, sleep. Bed checks every fifteen minutes, then thirty, then every hour, as the nurses realize she's truly in a better place.

There's another truth I must face.

As we watch, Liesel is being cured. The insanity which drives her to cut open her skin was superseded by the murder she committed, which now everyone knows about and feels was justified, and the punishment for her actions is to bear the child of a rapist she was supposed to trust in, believe in, a man who was supposed to protect and cherish, not rip and tear. She's both a hero and a project for the doctors and nurses. She is our shooting star.

When she starts to spot, five months in, Ratchet herself escorts her to the clinic downstairs. Liesel is put on bed rest. She gets to luxuriate in our worn, thin, bleached sheets while the rest of us follow the routine.

When she starts to bleed, a week later, we can smell it from the dining room. I run to our room, find her writhing on the bed, the stain beneath her growing darker and wider. She doesn't utter a sound, is biting the pillowcase, her eyes closed tight.

In the end, there is a tiny angel to be buried somewhere, we never know where. Liesel is taken away; the mattress is taken away, the room sanitized. I have to sleep there that night, with the scent of death surrounding me.

She comes back a different girl.

She doesn't look that different, maybe not as glossy, but her eyes are dead, and her stomach has gone back to normal.

She is put back on bed checks every fifteen minutes. Ratchet asks me to keep an eye on her, too. A personal favor. She is worried about her small nestling.

Liesel doesn't speak. It is just like when she first arrived.

So I sing to her. I bring her treats. I do everything I can think of to bring her back to life.

Eventually, it works.

She smiles again.

She laughs again.

We make plans to run away, to a beach, and live in a grass hut and eat coconuts and entertain tourists. She participates in group. She teaches some of the loons how to paint—and hit the canvas, not themselves.

And then, on a freezing cold, gray morning, Ratchet knocks on the door frame. "Are you ready?" she asks Liesel, who smiles and nods. She gives me a brief, hard hug, then waves.

And she leaves the ward. She leaves me there. Alone, in our room.

Liesel gets out.

And I am stuck inside.

I hate her as much as I love her.

27

THE WRIGHTS' HOUSE
CURRENT DAY

Lauren wakes at dawn. Jasper is splayed out facedown next to her, naked, the sheet thrown off, sleeping deeply. She pulls the sheet and blanket up over his haunches. He doesn't move; his breathing doesn't change. Good. She dresses quickly, goes to the kitchen, starts the coffee, then scurries to her office to erase the history on her laptop.

Jasper is sitting naked at her desk. Her laptop is open, and he is staring at the screen.

"What are you doing?" She tries not to sound defensive or scared—but what the hell is he doing?

"Who is Zack Armstrong?"

"I, what—" she starts, but Jasper holds up a hand.

"Listen to me, and listen carefully." It is his court voice: formal, educated, remote. A chill spikes through her. He's never—never—spoken to her like that. Clients, opposing lawyers, the judge, yes. But her? Her heart flutters as it takes on a shot of pure adrenaline.

"You have put yourself in an untenable position, Lauren. I've just found out you've been lying to me for seventeen years, literally from the moment we met. Now you're sneaking around in the middle of the night doing private searches on your computer for a man I've never heard of—"

"How can you see my private searches?"

"I saw the search over your shoulder last night. I am a very patient man, and I can handle a lot, but any more lies between us will not be tolerated. Do you understand me?"

She does. She hears him loud and clear.

She turns and walks out of the room. There is no way in hell she is going to explain herself right now. She can't take that chance. And he is right; she shouldn't lie to him again.

He follows, of course, bellowing her name. She doesn't stop, doesn't hesitate. She grabs her boots and her purse, the keys to her car, and keeps on moving, straight down the back stairs into the kitchen, out to the garage. Jasper keeps on her, calling, trying to block her way, but she simply looks through him until he gets exasperated and moves, allowing her to walk out the door.

She throws herself behind the wheel and dumps her things into the passenger seat. She finally meets his eyes, forcing away the qualms she feels when she sees how truly confused and upset he is. He has his anger on a tight leash, and she knows it. She needs to be very careful; she can't afford to turn Jasper against her.

She puts down the window. "This story has nothing to do with you and is long, long past. I love you, and only you. Now, I'm going to see Mindy. I'd appreciate you not breaking into my computer again."

The window slides up with a whisper, and she backs out of the garage, her bare feet cold on the pedals.

★ ★ ★

VAIL HEALTH HOSPITAL

"Mom!"

Mindy's smile is wide and thrilled, and Lauren realizes Dr. Oliver was right. Mindy needed the break as much as she did.

"How are you, little peep?"

"I feel good today. Better. Whatever they gave me worked. I

don't hurt at all. They're going to make me stay in here another day, then I can get back home. I slept all night, and Lolly and I had fun yesterday. She likes Sarah J. Maas too, so we talked for a long time about fantasy. You know, I think I want to be a writer. I mean, when I retire from skiing."

"You do?" Lauren sits on the edge of her daughter's bed, smoothing the jumbled sheets. "What do you want to write?"

"Novels, silly. Big, sweeping fantasy novels, where I can build the world myself, and make all the rules."

"I think you'd be wonderful at it, sweetie. It's a great plan. You'll need something to do when you retire from competition. I can adjust our homeschool schedule to include a few more English modules if you'd like. Add in a creative writing class?"

"You're the best, Mom. Who knows, maybe I'll be an Olympian and World Cup champion and win the Nobel, too."

"Writers usually have a better chance at winning the Pulitzer, darling, but that's a great goal to have. I think you'd be a brilliant writer."

"I think I might, too."

This barrage of happiness, of planning for the future, rips Lauren's stomach to shreds, but she keeps the smile glued to her face and nods and coos in all the right places. The change in her daughter is startling. Overnight, she has blossomed again. There is a blush on her cheeks; her eyes are bright.

You were stifling her. She was depressed watching you suffer.

No more. Only happy and excited from now on, she swears to herself. And space. Her daughter clearly needs space. She should have known her budding Buddhist would want some meditative time. She vows to do better.

"Mom, guess what else? Aunt J called. She's coming up again today."

"That will be nice. She's fun, your aunt."

Mindy's eyes narrow only slightly at this; Lauren knows she hasn't been very enthusiastic about her sister in front of her daughter and realizes she shouldn't have done that. Especially now that Juliet knows the circumstances of Mindy's birth.

"Don't give me that look. You forget, she and I practically grew up in different decades. She was much younger, just a pest, and I had a lot on my plate."

"Like what?"

"Like you and your daddy, silly. I wanted everything to be perfect for the two of you."

"It has been, Mom. It's been so much fun."

"Well, I'm glad to hear it. Now, what should we do today? Do you want to study, do you want to go for a walk?"

"A walk. Definitely. I am shriveling up in here." She slaps her legs. "Can we do some yoga? I found a great new routine from a girl who has a broken ankle, and I can modify all the moves like she did so I don't put any pressure on the leg."

"By all means, let's do it. I'll go see where we can practice, okay?"

Mindy beams and Lauren's heart catches in her throat. She realizes she's handled Mindy so badly. Normalcy, that's what her girl needs. From now on, that's what she is going to get.

Out in the hall, Lauren talks briefly to the nurses and gets permission to use the rehab mats for an impromptu yoga session. On impulse, she sticks her head into Dr. Oliver's office. What luck, he is there.

"Lauren, come in. You're looking better this morning."

"I feel better. Thanks for sending me home. I needed the break but didn't realize it. Mindy seems much better this morning, too. We're going to do some yoga."

He nods, his face suddenly grave. "I'm glad you stopped in, I was about to call you. Her numbers fell off a cliff last night, and I felt it necessary to put some energy into the tank. We gave her a little booster shot. Some B-12, vitamins, iron. She'll burn through it in a week or so, but for the time being—"

Lauren sinks into the chair opposite the doctor's desk. "What do you mean, her numbers fell off a cliff?"

"I mean we may have to do a transplant sooner than we'd hoped, with cells that aren't the perfect match we're looking for, but as close as we can find."

"But—"

He suddenly looks so tired. Lauren often forgets she isn't the only scared mother he's dealing with. She hasn't befriended any of the other parents on the ward, has kept everyone at arm's length. She can't handle their pain on top of her own. They don't like her, but she couldn't care less. But the doctor—she isn't being fair to him.

Make that another person you've sucked dry with your worry and anger and fear.

"Lauren, listen to me. We're doing everything we can. And I know you don't want to talk about the circumstances you find yourself in, but Mindy is going to die if we don't get her a solid transplant. Maybe not tomorrow, or next week, but her time is going to run out. I hate to have to be so frank with you, but her numbers yesterday were very worrisome. There are a few things we can do, like the vitamin shot, that are temporary fixes, but without a sustainable plan…we're not finding any great matches in the database. We need someone close to her. If we don't—"

Lauren holds up a hand. "I hear you. I understand."

"I'm sorry. I've been trying to avoid this conversation, but I fear we're out of time for tact. We need the information about Mindy's biological mother."

Lauren's breath catches, and she forces herself to stay in the chair. She feels so betrayed, so wronged. This man she trusts, who's said come to him at her own pace, has just thrown the gauntlet at her. But she thinks of Mindy's face, the flush on her cheeks, the happiness, the energy, and she swallows her goddamn pride.

"I don't know who she is. It was a closed adoption. She was

a teenager, and the doctor who hooked me up with her is dead now. I don't know how we get her records, or if they even exist."

"What was the doctor's name?"

"Dr. Soledad Castillo. She died soon after Mindy was born, barely a year later. I saw her obituary in the paper."

"Can you tell me the circumstances of the adoption?"

She takes a steadying breath and tells him the story.

He sits in silence, absorbing. "You don't have the name of the mother?"

"No. She was a young, scared Hispanic teenager. She probably lied to Dr. Castillo about her identity anyway."

"Thank you for being honest with me, Lauren. At least armed with this information, we can single out the donors and try for an ancestral genetic match."

"You're going to look for Hispanic donors, you mean?"

"Correct. It might help. Now—" he steeples his fingers, and she braces herself. "Would you be willing to do a public plea?"

"A public plea?"

"Yes. Since we won't have the adopting doctor's help... A friend of mine works for Channel 9. Mindy is a local hero. It's a no-brainer local interest story. We ask for anyone who might know the birth mother to come forward—they can do it anonymously if they want—and also ask for people to submit to testing to see if they'd be a match."

She is already half out of her chair. How could he? My God, it's bad enough she is in this situation, to go on the news and talk about it?

"No. Hell no. Absolutely not."

"Lauren, it wouldn't only be Mindy we'd be helping. There are more people, more children, who need stem cell transplants. To get people to sign up for the donor registry would have lasting implications. So many lives could be changed. The Hispanic database isn't as populous—"

"We will not be an infomercial. And we have no intention of telling Mindy we are not her biological parents."

His smile is sad now, and she feels dirty somehow, that she's disappointed him.

"Lauren, it may be outside of my purview here, but is hiding the truth from her truly in her best interest?"

"It is none of your business."

"It most certainly is my business." Dr. Oliver is on his feet now, too. She's never seen him lose his cool; he is dangerously close to yelling. "My job is to provide the finest care I can to my patient. And Mindy is my patient, Lauren, not you. This situation is bigger than you or your feelings, even your privacy. Your daughter will die if we don't find her a match. Do you understand me? She will die. We have no recourse. We must go public and try to find her biological family."

This isn't happening. This isn't happening.

She feels light-headed, nauseated. Her whole world is slipping away from her, out from under her. She starts to go down, but strong, familiar arms catch her.

"Jasper. I'm so glad you're here," she hears Dr. Oliver say. "I was just explaining to Lauren an option—"

"I heard," Jasper says. "Honey, are you okay?"

Lauren shakes her head; it is buzzing, she is going to faint.

"Maybe Dr. Oliver can get you some water."

"Of course. I'll be right back."

Dr. Oliver pulls the door closed behind him, and Lauren collapses into Jasper's arms. A sob wrenches from her chest. "We can't. We can't tell her. Not now. Not yet."

He kneels on the floor in front of her. "Lauren, we have to. We have to save her life, and if that means sharing the truth, we will do it. She's not going to feel differently about you, I swear it. She adores you. She might be mad for a little while, but we'll make her see reason. I think a public plea is a good idea. We're out of options otherwise. Please, Lauren. She's my daughter, too, and I don't want to lose her."

"Jasper, I can't believe all of this is happening. I feel like our whole world is collapsing."

"It's not, but if Mindy dies, it most certainly will. Please, Lauren. See reason."

She has never felt such bone-wrenching fear before as she does when the words come out of her mouth. "You're right. I know you're right, and the doctor is right, but my God, we're going to blow up her world."

And mine.

"Her world blew up a month ago when she crashed and was diagnosed."

She sits with it for a minute, then nods, feeling Jasper relax, hearing his sigh of relief. What would he do if she said no? Tell Mindy anyway, and be damned with her? He is doing the right thing for his daughter, and to hell with his wife.

Oddly, she feels a spark of respect for him. He is always so kind and gentle and sweet; she's never seen him defiant before. She supposes that's what makes him such a good trial attorney, and he normally leaves that personality trait at work. Or maybe she just doesn't know her husband as well as she thinks she does. Perhaps he's been hiding things from her as well. She's spent their entire marriage focused on Mindy first and foremost; it's certainly possible.

"All right. If we're going to do this, we should tell her now. I can't get behind a public plea, though. I can't do it."

"But—"

"Wait, hear me out. We can ask Juliet to look for the mother. I'll give her every detail I can remember, and help her any way I can, but I can't get on television and broadcast our lives for the whole world to see. It could damage Mindy's chances of making the Olympic team when she recovers. I won't do anything that might impact her public future. Deal?"

"Deal." He pulls her into his arms. "Oh, baby, you're making the right choice here. I'll call Juliet right now, and then we'll talk to Mindy together."

He kisses her forehead and hugs her close. Cowering in his arms, she tells herself it is going to be okay. Seventeen years is a long time. She is lucky she's made it this far. She can only hope that if the whole truth comes out, Mindy won't hate her. She couldn't bear that.

And all the while, the rational, calm voice in the back of her mind, the one she avoids connecting to at all costs, laughs and laughs.

"I know we'll be able to find her, Lauren. I know it in my heart."

She nods into his hair and whispers, "The mother's name was Graciela."

28

DENVER, COLORADO

Juliet is getting out of the shower when her phone rings. She is surprised to see Jasper's number on her display. She punches the Talk button, suddenly frightened.

"Hey, is everything okay?"

"Hi, Juliet. Yes, it is. We just need your help, that's all."

"Anything."

"She told me. She told me everything. I know you know the truth."

Juliet heaves out a breath. "Oh, thank God. Now what?"

"We're telling Mindy shortly. But we need you to do something. The doctors are getting worried about finding a match. Lauren and I would like you to look for Mindy's biological family."

Juliet can't deny the charge she feels. What a relief. She will be able to cover her tracks now. But she is careful; she doesn't want Jasper knowing she's gone rogue on them already. "Without a crime involved, I can't do it through CBI, you know that."

"Right, but you're an investigator. We thought you might be able to interview some of the hospital staff, see if they'll release the doctor's files to you, that sort of thing. With a name, perhaps we can reach out to them directly and ask for them to consider donating for a possible match. Kind of like our own private eye. We'll pay you, of course."

"Oh, no you won't. I'm happy to do it. I have to admit, I've already started looking into the doctor, and unfortunately, she's been dead for a long time. But I can make some calls and see if I can shake anything loose on that front."

"Lauren told me the girl's name was Graciela. If that helps."

"Oh, wow. She told me she didn't remember."

"Honestly, I think she's been holding this information in a vault she never thought she was going to have to open. I don't think she knows more than the girl's name, or else she would have told me. Maybe it will be enough to go on. The doctors here want to go public and ask for donors of Hispanic origin, specifically from families who may know or be related to a young girl who had a baby in the right time frame, but Lauren has put her foot down. She won't allow it."

"I don't blame her. It's hard to open yourself up to public scrutiny like that, plus, we could waste a lot of time with false leads. I can work with the name. Give Mindy my love, would you? Tell her I'll be up as soon as I can, and I'm going to find a match for her if it's the last thing I do."

"She will be thrilled, I know. Thank you, Juliet."

"Of course. Good luck. And, Jasper?"

"Yes?"

"Don't worry. Mindy adores you both beyond reason, and she's a smart girl. Things might be rough for a few days, but we'll make sure she understands how very wanted she is, was, and always will be."

There is a catch in Jasper's voice. "Thank you, Juliet. That means a lot to me. To us."

"I'll call as soon as I have something. See ya."

"Oh, hey, wait a sec. Listen, this may be nothing, but one last shot in the dark. Lauren was searching for a man named Zack Armstrong last night. I saw it on her computer, and the way she reacted when I asked her about it—she got jumpy, wouldn't talk to me. I thought it might be an old boyfriend. Does that name ring a bell?"

"Zack Armstrong? No, it doesn't. But remember, she's older than me by a decade. She had all kinds of guys around, and I don't remember any of their names. I'll take a look, though chances are you're right, it's probably someone she went to school with. People react oddly to stress, Jasper. She adores you, and your life together. I don't think she'd ever willingly jeopardize that."

"No, I don't, either. But in light of all the other…issues…"

He doesn't have to finish. She knows exactly what he is saying. *In light of the lies she's been telling all of us…*

"I asked who he was and she refused to tell me."

"Sounds like it might be an old boyfriend, then. I'll look into him."

"Thanks, Juliet. And don't—"

"Don't worry, Jasper. We never talked. Got it."

He laughs quietly, says thanks again, then hangs up.

Zack Armstrong. Who the hell is he?

Juliet has a momentary longing for her mother. Kathleen would know exactly who Zack Armstrong was because Lauren would have told her everything about him, in intimate detail. She realizes Lauren even lied to their mom about Mindy. Wow.

Well, when in doubt…she doesn't have her mom's institutional knowledge anymore, but she does have the internet.

She hangs up and calls Cameron.

"Hello, beautiful."

"Any news?"

"Nothing yet."

"Damn. Listen, Jasper has asked me to look into the doctor who helped Lauren adopt Mindy. Would you help? If you want to keep playing Watson to my Sherlock, that is."

"You never mentioned you were into role-playing. I like it. Absolutely. Your place or mine? And do I get to wear the hat and carry the magnifying glass?"

She laughed. "You're a sicko. Who do you know who used to work at Swedish Medical in the early 2000s?"

"Spoilsport. I thought we were going to be—"

"Cameron. My dear. I'm dead serious. Who do we know?"

"I'll call you back."

Now it is time to talk to her boss, too. She needs to take a few days, and there are a lot of cases piling up. He answers on the first ring.

"Hi, Woody. It's Juliet."

"My brilliant one. What's happening? Are you ill? I stopped by the lab this morning, and Bai said you were out."

"I have a personal issue. You know my niece has cancer?"

"Yes, the poor thing. She's not improving, I take it?"

"No, and we've had a bit of a personal family revelation about something, and my sister has asked for my help. I have vacation days accrued—"

"Juliet, seriously, take the week. I don't know that we can spare you for more than that without advance warning, but you do what you need to, and if you need more time, just shout. We are all rooting for Mindy. She's our champion."

"You're the best, Woody. Thank you."

"No, you're the best. That sample you ran last week, from the quadruple murder in Golden? We just nailed the sucker. Can you believe it, they'd been looking at the wrong man all this time?"

"Because they were looking for a man. It's so rare for a woman to do something so heinous."

"Rare, but you never know. Women can be just as ruthless as men when they need to."

"No kidding. Thanks so much for the time off, Woody. I'll keep in touch in case something breaks and you need me immediately. Otherwise, Bai has control of the lab, and all will be well."

"Copy that. Good luck. Call if you need me for anything, I'm happy to help."

Wondering how things are going at the hospital, she thinks through her plan of action. Interview hospital staff, find out if by chance there are videotapes from the time frame, which is a long shot, but neonatal is a whole different story than the rest of the hospital. It's worth a try.

And she needs to look up everything she can find on the name Graciela. With any luck, she'll find a last name through the hospital records and the woman will be living somewhere in the Denver metropolitan area, and life will be grand.

Yeah, right. The odds of things going smoothly from here on out are astronomical, without a doubt, but it is worth being optimistic, at least until she has reason to feel otherwise.

And of course, there is the database, churning through millions of profiles, searching for the truth.

One way or the other, their mystery is about to be unraveled.

29

VAIL HEALTH HOSPITAL

Mindy is watching the downhill from Val d'Isère, fighting feeling sorry for herself that she isn't there, when her parents appear in the doorway, clutching a bag of her favorite cookies. She knows something major is up. Her mom was supposed to be finding a room to do yoga, and instead, here they are together, almost creeping into the room, eyes sliding to the side, not meeting hers at all.

She is dead. She knows it. They have some sort of test result that confirms it. She felt so awful yesterday morning, but once Dr. Oliver gave her the shot, she was better. But it wasn't enough.

Tears begin to leak immediately. She doesn't want to die. She feels the cancer moving through her, like a shadow in her blood. It has grown in the past few days, is becoming harder and harder to fight. She isn't a quitter, though, and is doing everything she can to keep it at bay. Its snapping jaws are just there, out of reach, but for how long?

So now they are going to tell her it is all over, and she has to give in gracefully, and they are prepared to let her go. It is inevitable, but it pisses her off. She wants to ski again, wants to feel the wind whip past her face. She bets they won't let her out of their sight for a minute now. They're going to condemn her to rot away in this hospital bed until she can't even move and the pain becomes so great they drug her into oblivion to make it all stop.

This is not the path she'd choose.

"You can tell me," she says, steeling herself. "I already know what you're going to say."

Her parents stare at her, and for a moment, she wavers. No, she is going to be strong, she is going to decide how things end. She read the story about the girl who moved to Washington so she could have euthanasia. Mindy doesn't think she'll have to go that far; she'll be able to convince them to get her out on the slopes once more. She'll take one run for pleasure, and the second, right off the side of the mountain. She can almost feel the thin air buffeting her as she falls...

Her dad closes the door. Her mom sits on the side of the bed, pulling the covers straight. Mindy feels claustrophobic all of a sudden and rips them back. Her mother frowns once, then puts on a perfectly blank face.

"Sweetheart, what we need to talk to you about is going to come as a shock."

"I'm dying," Mindy says, crossing her arms over her chest. "I already know. They can't find a donor, and I'm not going to make it."

Jasper pulls a chair to the bed on the other side.

"Actually, honey, no. We've certainly not come to that point, and I seriously doubt we will, especially now. Your mother..."

He looks at Lauren, who is kneading the blanket. Mindy doesn't think she's ever seen her mother so upset and reaches out a hand to still hers. Lauren smiles weakly, then nods.

"Mindy, I don't know how to say this, so I'm just going to come out with it. You're adopted. I know this comes as a huge shock, and you will have many questions. We will answer all of them, but we want you to know, that—"

"Wait, what? I'm not dying?"

The spark of hope shoots through her like a comet. She's suddenly on fire, as if everything is possible again. A small part of her is screaming, crying, throwing a tantrum, but the rest of her is flooded with relief.

"Not that we know. Nothing's changed in your diagnosis."

"But...I'm adopted? You aren't my mother, and you're not my father?"

The words are absurd. This is one of those bizarre nightmares where you're dreaming inside of a dream, and you know you're dreaming, so you tell yourself to go ahead and wake up because this isn't fun at all.

Lauren clears her throat. "I adopted you when you were a few hours old. Your father—"

"Which one? Biological or Dad?"

"Dad. He and I met when you were only a few weeks old. We fell in love, and—"

"And I've always felt you were mine, peanut. I've never had a thought otherwise." Jasper strokes her leg. "I've always loved you, from the moment you pooped on my shirt the first time."

She doesn't laugh, and his face falls. Why is she less mad at her dad than her mom? And is she really mad? Or is she so incandescently relieved that she isn't staring death in the face today that she wants to scream for joy? She is confused, she'll acknowledge that.

"Who are my real parents? My biological parents?"

"We don't know," Lauren says. "The story is very long and strange."

Mindy gestures around them. "I have time. Tell me. I want to hear it all."

They do, and Mindy listens, trying to stop her heart from fluttering every time she thinks—*Adopted. I'm adopted. I'm not yours.* The pain in her mother's voice, the guilt she is clearly feeling, Mindy doesn't know what to do with it, how to process it. Being adopted is a big deal, a huge deal, but in the face of death, in the face of her sudden plans for getting out of this life, adoption feels…dealable.

"Wait. Let me interrupt you. Can we find them?"

Jasper sits back in his chair. "We certainly hope so. Because yes, they might be a match."

"Okay. I'm pissed at you both. Really pissed that you never told me. But I'm going to put a pin in that emotion for a moment." God, she sounds like that stupid cow of a therapist. "Right now, I want you to go find them. I can feel this thing inside me, and it's like my own personal monster that won't go away. Maybe they can help fix me. I don't want to die. I want to be cured. And when that happens, then I'll have a hissy fit about you not telling me the truth."

Lauren collapses into tears then, burying her face in Mindy's lap. Mindy pets her mother's hair and gives her father a tremulous smile.

"This isn't what I thought you were going to tell me."

"I gather," Jasper says, smiling back. "You know this changes nothing about our family."

"It makes it bigger," Mindy replies. "And that seems like the stroke of luck we need very badly. You always told me life is ninety-nine percent about giving it your all, and one percent luck. Here's our one percent."

It's a brave speech. They all hug, and Lauren continues to sniff and cry, but in the end, Mindy feels almost relieved, and a little guilty. She knows her mom would prefer she have a huge meltdown to cement their love, but considering the circumstances, who is her blood and who isn't seems less important than finding the ones who might be able to save her.

She doesn't think to ask why they didn't tell her this weeks ago when it was clear she might need the transplant. That will come later.

A knock on the door and Dr. Oliver sticks his head in.

"Everything okay?"

"He knows?" Mindy asks.

"He does," Jasper answers.

This angers her to no end. "Does the whole fucking world know except for me?"

Lauren snaps up her head. "Hey. Language."

Dr. Oliver shuts the door behind him. They are their own nuclear family now.

"Who else knows? Aunt J?"

"Yes. Juliet knows," Lauren answers, cringing.

"Gee, thanks. And you too, doc."

Dr. Oliver clears his throat. "Listen, Mindy. The blood work told me the truth, and I confronted your parents. Be upset with me, not them. I'm the one who—"

"I'm furious with all of you right now. And I'm sick of this place. Can I go home?"

Lauren stands and starts to apologize for Mindy's tone, but Dr. Oliver nods. "I don't blame you a bit. Yes, you can be discharged. Take it easy, though. I'll see you back in a couple of days for a treatment, okay?"

"Thanks, doc." And to her parents who aren't her parents, "We can continue this discussion later. Get me out of here."

30

UNIVERSITY HOSPITAL

NASHVILLE, TENNESSEE

1993

VIVIAN

The first letter to arrive makes me jump with joy. It's the first truly happy moment I've had since Liesel confided in me that first time. It is almost Christmas, and Liesel has been gone for two weeks. The ward has been a horrible place without her. I'm stuck back into the daily routine with the droolers and visionaries, and I'm lonely, bone-tired, and, if I'm being honest, wondering why I'm still walking the earth when I have absolutely nothing to live for.

Ratchet brings me the letter in the music room and gives me permission to take it to my room to read. She's been trying to pull me out of my funk, but it's not working. I am funkalicious. I am the funk.

I close the door most of the way and sit on Liesel's bed with my feet drawn up. The envelope has already been opened—there is no privacy on the ward.

December 10, 1993

Dear V,

I hope you are doing well. I wanted to say thank you for all you did to help me, both before and after the miscarriage. This is a time of my life I want to put behind me. As you can imagine, the tragedy and heartbreak of the situation is overwhelming. I feel like I have paid for my sins, and now I have a chance to move forward, to experience the world in a different way.

I wasn't going to write, but then I realized so much of my recovery was because of you. So if you want to write me back, that would be okay. If you don't want to, I completely understand. We've been through a horrible thing together, you and I, and if you'd rather forget and move on, I don't blame you.

I hope you're feeling less bleak today.

Thinking of you,

Liesel

At first, I am incensed. Livid. Furious. I stomp around the room, throwing things. Here she is, with the opportunity and choice to escape this shitty life, an opportunity I fear I will never have again. Why is she looking back? I told her if she got out before me to never look back.

But the rational part of me is so fucking grateful she's reached out to me. She's given me a lifeline to the outside world. She's given me hope. It is a gift I don't know that I will ever be able to repay. I hate to be indebted to others. I hate that this small letter makes my heart burst open and gush feelings through my body.

Ours is a special friendship. We've been through too much together to let it all go.

I sit down and write back, my wrist hard against the desktop. I'm not used to writing letters, and my hand cramps so badly I have to stop and shake it out a few times.

December 14, 1993

My dearest Liesel,

I was so happy to get your letter. We didn't really have a proper goodbye. Man, do I miss you. It's dreadfully dull here. Ratchet et al. are especially surly without your sunny disposition. They miss you, too, I think. I hope they didn't let you out too soon. I've been so worried about you. Are you well? Still no cuts?

We had crafts today—guess what day it is? Yes, it's Tuesday, give that girl a prize!—and I swear if I see one more stupid painted doormat I am going to jump off the roof. I told them that, then fainted spectacularly, in a dead heap, right at their feet, which is why I'm writing you instead of sitting in group. They locked me away again, five hours in the box, and only let me out if I promised to stop being so dramatic.

Isn't that why we're stuck in here in the first place? Because we're overly dramatic? Except for you. I mean, you had cause.

I'm supposed to be sans roommate for a while. We'll see how long that lasts.

What are you doing out there in the big wide world? Is the sky bluer when you're free? Does the sun shine brighter? God knows they've pumped you full of every imaginable drug, so maybe you're just asleep. Which I'm going to do. Maybe I'll dream of my mom again. That was cool. Write me!

Love and stitches,

V

31

Mindy uses her crutches carefully as they leave the hospital. She gets in her mother's car; her dad follows in his. She puts on her headphones, and they ride in silence up the hill, lost in their own thoughts, until she finally breaks, pulls the headphones down around her neck.

"You seriously adopted me?"

"I did."

"And you have no idea who from? I find that hard to believe."

Her mom glances over, then shakes her head. "Oh, sweetheart. I know this is scary and a huge shock. It's terrible that we had to share it this way, out of desperation. But in the long run, we're going to be blessed, I can feel it. Dr. Oliver and Dr. Berger know exactly what they're doing. You're going to be fine. I promise."

"I don't feel fine, and I'm talking about your lying to me my whole life."

"I understand you're angry at me. I don't blame you." Her mom pats her arm. Her touch is foreign and unwanted.

"Stop."

"Okay. Well, I'll tell you this. Dr. Oliver is excited about the possibility of being able to find you a match in the database through something he called ancestral genetics. Your birth mother was Hispanic. Knowing that will help them narrow the choices. It was important that we be honest with him."

"But you don't know where she is?"

"Unfortunately, no, we don't. Not yet. But Aunt Juliet is looking for her right now. We're going to find a match for you, sweetheart. I promise."

"You can't know that for sure."

"I believe it, Mindy. I believe the universe is going to give us what we need right now."

"Since when are you all mystic?"

"Since when are you such a smart-ass?"

Mindy jerks her arm away. "You have no idea what this is like. I've worked my entire life to make the US team, and now that I'm there, this happens. I get cancer. I find out I'm adopted. I might die before they find a match. It's not fair. None of this is fair. Why didn't you tell them before? Why did you wait so long?"

"Because I was being a coward, Melinda. I was afraid I might lose you. Not only your life, but your heart, and your love. And I know you don't believe me, but I do know what it's like, sweet-heart. I've had unfair things happen to me, too."

Her mother sounds lost, and alone. *The letter. Ask her about the letter.*

But they are home, and the moment passes. Lauren pulls into the garage and turns off the engine. "Look at me."

Mindy glances over, then away. She feels tears threatening. She hates to cry, hates it. It's the ultimate weakness, and Mindy doesn't show weakness.

"We are going to get through this. They're going to find you a match, and you're going to get well. In time for the trials. I feel that in my heart."

Mindy can't speak without the tears falling. She nods.

"Good girl. Now, let's get you upstairs."

Mindy navigates the stairs from the garage to the main floor, noticing for the first time she is out of breath at the top. She tries not to panic. Dr. Oliver told her the chemo was going to sap all her energy and strength.

"What would you like to do, sweetheart? Are you feeling up for something to eat?"

Mindy shakes her head. She is feeling woozy and wants some time alone. She needs to adjust to this news, to the idea that she belongs to someone else. "I just want to lie down. I might watch the rest of the races. You recorded them, right?"

Lauren's face clouds, her eyebrows draw together into a single line. "Is that such a good idea, honey? You watching the team move on without you?"

Without me... "Of course it is. By the way, Coach texted me, said I have a spot as soon as I can get back on my feet. He wants to come talk to you when he gets back from France."

"I don't think we're quite ready for visitors, do you?"

"Mom, cancer isn't catching."

"But we have to keep your immune system strong, and Coach has been traveling. I think it would be best to keep you isolated, just until the transplant. Okay?"

"Is the adoption what was up between you and Aunt J?"

Lauren's eyes flash and she turns away, heads into the kitchen. "We had a disagreement, that's all. Your father will be here any minute, and he has a work call to make. If you're going to take it easy in your room for a bit, I think I'll go to King Soopers and get a few things. Low sodium broth? Sugar-free Jell-O?"

Mindy makes a face. Life-changing moments and her mom wants to go grocery shopping. "Fine. But pudding. Chocolate. Don't get the low-cal sugar-free stuff. I probably need it with sugar. I'm losing too much weight."

Lauren's face registers a moment's shock then she rearranges her features into a smile. "Of course. Real pudding it is. Anything for my sweet girl. I'll be back in an hour. Sleep some, and tonight, we'll watch a movie."

"Okay."

She waits until she sees Lauren's Lexus sweep out of the drive, then quietly edges into the master bedroom. Lauren's strong allusion in the car—unfair things have happened to me, too—might have something to do with the letter. Mindy gets the sense she still doesn't know the whole truth about her birth.

Her dad isn't here yet; she'll hear the door beep when he gets home.

The letter isn't in the drawer. It's been hidden away. Where might her mother keep it?

Mindy searches the remaining drawers, the closet, the bed, and finds nothing. The office is off-limits. Besides, her dad will need to hang there to take his call. Where else? Where does no one go, not even the maid?

The attic—but there's no chance of her making it up there with her crutches. Her mom doesn't like it either, it's cold and dark, and Mindy remembers Lauren complaining about how creepy it is once.

What if…

Back to the dresser. She pulls it from the wall—it slides easily, felt pads on the feet so as not to scratch the wood flooring— and is rewarded. There is a manila envelope taped to the back, in between the supports.

Mindy's heart is racing.

She puts the dresser back and takes the envelope to her room, and into the bathroom. She takes a book with her, too, as cover. She closes and locks the door.

She sits at her dressing table, thankful for the soft chair, and opens the envelope. There are several letters inside. All handwritten, all old and soft. They are in chronological order— and she realizes the letters are a correspondence, between this Liesel person and someone named V. Why would her mother have these?

She glances through them, confused, then starts to read.

January 1994

Dear V,

I got the tattoo! Can you believe it? It hurt so much, but just like you said, the hurt was a good kind of hurt. Of course, my mom saw the bandage and insisted I tell her why there was a butterfly outlined in blood on it. I showed her, and she promptly freaked out. She insisted I have it removed, made an appointment at this fancy dermatologist, but I said no way. Stood up for myself, like you always tell me to. She's still acting like I committed some sort of heinous crime, like she caught me plunging a knife in someone's throat. You should have seen her face, it really was priceless. I mean, you'd think I pierced my nipples or some such horror. She swore not to let me out of the house for months, and not to let me get my license. I told her should she lock me inside her dank, dreary mausoleum of a house, I would promptly slit my wrists and lie down on her precious Aubusson carpet to bleed out. (It's the pretty silver and pink one I told you about.) Heh, she didn't like that image, broke down in tears, apologized. Like I care what she thinks. She then took me for my learner's permit. I passed! I'm one step closer to freedom.

So I am now the proud owner of a tattoo that looks just like yours, (we're twinsies for real!) and a learner's permit that allows me to drive with a sanctioned adult in the car.

I don't ever want to be back in there, but I miss you. When are they going to let you out?

Love,

Liesel

Mindy sets the letter in her lap. Her mother does not have a tattoo. She cannot be this Liesel person. Mindy feels lighter already. Her mother is holding these letters for someone. A friend, perhaps someone she met in school—the boarding school Juliet said she attended. Mindy remembers when they had "the purge" and emptied out her mother's old pre-Dad boxes, the ones with photos of her with other men, other boyfriends, and Lauren had given them a single glance, then thrown them into the massive black contractor's bag with a mischievous grin. Lauren didn't have a lot of attachments to her past, preferred the now. Holding something for someone else makes the most sense. Why it would make her cry is another question, one Mindy will puzzle out later.

Wait. Maybe this is something to do with her birth mother? She turns the page to the next missive.

January 1994

Dearest Liesel,

So proud of you standing up for yourself! Your mother is a witch. She wants you to be just like her, a perfect little china doll, and you don't ever need to capitulate to her. If she was so perfect, she wouldn't have chosen that dickhead to be your stepfather. Keep working on finding yourself. You're smart, smart enough to get out of here, smart enough to be someone. You have talent, kid. You don't have to get married and produce 2.3 children and own a slobbery dog and a house in the suburbs. You want a bigger life than that, I know you do. Don't ever let her tell you otherwise.

There's big news here. Ratchet is knocked up. She refuses to say who the daddy is, but I think we all know it's Dr. Freakazoid. She's been mooning after him for months. Now she smells like vomit all the time. It's disgusting. They've been making us eat in the dining room again, no more food in our rooms because the smell "offends her sensibilities." Like we should be punished because she doesn't know how to take her birth control pills? Fucking bitch. I hate her. I hate it here without you. It's not worth it, you know? They're never going to let me out. I will die in here. Sooner, rather than later.

Sorry about the baby news. I wasn't thinking.

V

March 1994

V, where are you? I haven't heard from you and, after your last letter, I have to admit I'm worried about you. You didn't sound good. Please let me know you're okay. Mother won't let me visit, I begged and pleaded, but she refuses. I'm going to steal the car keys if I don't hear from you soonest. You promised me you wouldn't hurt yourself again. I'm holding you to it.

Love, Liesel

April 1994

Liesel,

I'm so sorry to have worried you. I know it's been weeks since my last letter. Ratchet told me you called the ward, and I appreciate it. As you probably figured out, I had an episode. I got really down. Like, really, really down. I was just so tired. I had nothing to look forward to. Nothing to be happy about. So I tried to hang myself in the closet.

It worked great, too, except Ratchet, with that fucking bizarre sixth sense she has, came by unannounced and found me. I was kept sedated for a few days while the swelling went down in my trachea, and I'm still a little hoarse. Ratchet says I sound sexy.

The good news is, I am starting to feel better. They did shock therapy, and it helped. Sort of. You know how afraid I was to try it, and I know how against it you are, but it wasn't any big deal, and after the first few treatments, I did start to feel better. I wouldn't say I'm crapping bluebirds of happiness, but I want to try to get my shit together.

Please don't be disappointed in me. I'm trying very hard. Our plans are still a priority. I want to get out, and I want to run away with you someplace warm where we can wear bikinis every day and live by the water.

And yes, I did say something nice about Ratchet. She has been really cool through all of this. She even said she knows how good you were for me, and she's going to keep a special eye out for me to make up for your absence. She's getting round as a basketball, it's hysterical. We've been doing the GED program since there's no way in hell I'm going back to school. If you can believe it, I will have my certificate by the end of the summer. They might let me out then, too.

I wish you could visit me. I miss you.

Love,

V

April 1994

V,

You could never disappoint me, not unless you weren't here at all. I'm very glad Ratchet found you in time, and that you agreed to the shock treatment, and that it's helping. The medication I'm on is helping, too. I'm actually down to only two antidepressants. Mother says my hormones are sorting themselves out~she still thinks my mood swings are just a phase that I'll grow out of~but the meds are okay. Side effects aren't too bad, and I am also pretty stable right now.

And now it's time to share my bit of bad news. We're moving. She's decided it would be better for me to be in a different environment. She hasn't told me where we're going, says she hasn't settled on a job yet, but the house is on the market. Mother still refuses to let me visit, but I'm going to do everything I can to come see you before we go. I'm just so angry at her for doing all this behind my back, but I also feel a little relieved. Like maybe I'll be able to put this whole chapter of my life behind me and start fresh with people who don't know me as "the criminal who tried to kill herself." You know?

But that means I won't be able to see you for a long time. And that's not making me happy at all. If they let you out, will you come visit me?

Love and stitches (or should we say belts?),

Liesel

May 1994

Dearest Liesel,

Oh, you make me laugh. Love and Belts! I actually did it with a sheet, which Ratchet tells me was the reason she came into the room. She thought she saw my blanket on the floor. Whoops!

I'm devastated you're going to move. Devastated. Please don't forget your friend, who loves you very much, and would like to come visit when she's deemed safe to herself and others. I had a meeting with Dr. Freakazoid today, actually, to discuss a possible transition to a halfway house. Yes. I am doing that well. So don't move before I get out!

All my love,

V

PS: Almost forgot, Ratchet had her baby! I heard the nurses talking about it after group. It's a boy. She's going to be out for a few weeks on maternity leave, so things are going to be very slow and dull around here. Write soon!!!!

August 1994

Dear Liesel,

My last few letters—

"Mindy? Where are you, honey?"

Shit, shit, shit. She turns on the water, shoves the letters under the sink.

"I'm in here, Mom. Don't worry, I'm just taking a shower."

"I got you a decadent tub of Dutch chocolate pudding. It's ready when you finish your shower."

"Thanks, I'll be out in a minute."

Mindy holds her breath. Her mom will hear her if she unlocks the door, wonder why it was locked in the first place. Lauren doesn't like locked doors. It's a thing with her. Closed is fine, and she always knocks, but locked is out of the question.

But her mom leaves, and Mindy sighs in relief. She can't return the letters, though, which is not good, but she will try later. After she's read them all. There are many more in the stack. Several years' worth of missives.

She wraps her leg in a bag and steps under the water to wash off the grime of the hospital, thinking, *Who are these girls?*

32

DENVER, COLORADO

Before Juliet can start her search, Cameron shows up at her door. He's carrying a pizza, a bunch of files, and is buzzing with suppressed energy.

"The dead doctor, Castillo? There's more to the story. Way more. She got fired back in 2000, and she committed suicide not long after."

"Come in. Suicide? What's the story? Why did they fire her?"

"Apparently, she was taking money under the table. Probably for illegal adoptions, like your sister's."

This makes Juliet's heart race. She shuts the door behind him carefully. "Illegal? Not closed?"

"Any time you have the transfer of a child, there has to be paperwork. It's illegal to give your kid away for money otherwise. Apparently, one of the services the doctor was providing was finding homes for her indigent patients' babies. She took money from the family who was adopting the child, erased the bills for the hospital records for the birth mothers, and pocketed the rest. The hospital found out and booted her. Thing is, she'd managed to place a bunch of kids."

"Wow. On one hand, I guess you could say she was doing people a service. Those babies might not have stood a chance being brought into the world by indigent teen moms. On the other hand..."

"Yeah. Baby farming. Not cool."

"Any way to find out who she worked with?"

"The files identified a couple of young women, but the majority just disappeared. But catch this. One of the women identified was named Graciela Flores. She had a baby girl and gave her up for adoption, the works."

"My God. That could be our girl."

"Except..."

"Of course it's too good to be true. Except?"

"The kid she gave up would be eighteen now, not seventeen. And you said that you saw Mindy when she was an infant—I hardly think you'd mistake an infant for a toddler."

"No, I wouldn't. Maybe she had another kid right afterward? Or they got the dates wrong."

"I don't know, Juliet. Something about this feels weird. There's more."

"What's that?"

"Castillo was fired in June 2000. Mindy was born in August."

"So she did the work behind the fence after they let her go."

"Maybe."

"Come on, a full-blown OB/GYN who'd just lost her license, and some off the path kids having babies? She'd be the ultimate midwife. She probably had a few ready to pop when she was fired, and just let them know where she'd be when their time was nigh."

He runs a hand through his silver hair, looking doubtful. "You may want to ask your sister for some more details, is all I'm saying."

"Well, I can't do that right now. They're telling Mindy the truth about her parentage as we speak. We should try to find this Graciela woman, see if she remembers Lauren at all, and see if she'd be willing to take a test. Maybe the files were wrong. We can only hope, right?" She rubs her hand across her face.

"Absolutely." He parks himself at her desk. "You have any beer to go with that pizza? Since I'm playing hooky..."

"I do. Be right back. Want a cold glass?"

"No, I can rough it."

She grabs a bottle of Yuengling, makes herself a cup of tea. Throws some pretzels into a bowl. Brings everything back to the office to find Cameron scrolling through his phone.

"What are you doing, swiping right?" Her smirk is unmistakable, but Cameron has stopped scrolling and is staring at her.

"What's wrong? You look like you've seen a ghost."

"We have a match."

Her pulse kicks up. "In CODIS? Let me see."

"Just hold on a second. I need your computer."

"Sure. Of course." She gestures toward the desktop. He opens Google, speaks quietly.

"There's a cold case, out of Nashville, Tennessee. I saw a case study of it a few years back. The man's name is Zachary Armstrong. His child was kidnapped."

"Wait, that's the same name Lauren was looking up. Jasper asked me to look into him."

He types *Zachary Armstrong baby kidnapped* into the search bar. "Look."

There are pages of hits. Her heart leaps to her throat.

"No. No, no, no. There's no way. What are you saying, that Lauren somehow bought a baby that had been stolen from a couple in Tennessee, and has raised her as her own this whole time?"

"It's so much worse than that, Juliet."

He clicks open the first of the stories. There is a photograph of a young Army officer and his very pretty wife, and at the headline, Juliet sags, her knees turning to jelly.

Fort Campbell Soldier's Baby Kidnapped, Wife Murdered

PART TWO

33

NASHVILLE, TENNESSEE

AUGUST 2000

The metal of the casket is the same color as the sky, murky gray with touches of glinting silver as the sun passes behind the clouds. The sound of sobbing, the cries of the justified, the flailing of my heart. Why did I choose such a big casket? She doesn't fit. It's the smallest adult coffin they have, but it's still too large. She is lost inside. They should have handled this. The padding needed to be expanded so her body doesn't jostle.

The body. Her body.

The words I've heard in the past few days are ones I never expected—new, untried, untested. Casket. Body. Funeral. Viewing. Embalming. Autopsy. Severed. Seven-inch non-corrosive steel blade.

Homicide.

The first responders were called in for my family. They came quickly. Only took them three minutes to arrive at the house. But it was already too late.

They were both gone.

I've forgotten where my life ends and the evening news begins. The story of my family's demise plays over and over again. The city is shocked, horrified, on red alert. Everyone is looking for my daughter. For my wife's murderer.

The sun is completely hidden now, the rain beginning to mist in the hazy air. The people in attendance, the crowd overladen with cops, look at me sympathetically, eyes hooded, shadowed. I know what they see. A tall man, dark hair cut high and tight, ribs still bandaged from a month-old gunshot wound sustained in a double-cross in Afghanistan, eyes angry and sad. A man alone. This is my second funeral this week. In the past few days, I've lost my mother, my wife, and my child.

I can't look at the casket anymore. She's wearing the blue dress I know she loves, the dark sapphire silk nearly the same color as her eyes. I had to bring her makeup bag to the funeral home intact; I didn't know what color lipstick she would want. The mascara I had down pat; I always loved to watch her put it on. It came in a red tube, and she'd get so close to the mirror, leaning until she nearly touched her reflection, swooping the black onto her lashes again and again until they fringed her perfect violet eyes in soot. But the lipstick—she wore a different color every day. I let them make the choice. It was better that way.

Umbrellas start to pop open. The priest nods and smiles sadly, a comfort to the bereaved. Arms on mine now, gentle squeezes, hugs. I don't know who anyone is. They are assigned to protect me. To keep me safe. They couldn't save my family, but by God, they will not let me die.

I nod and mimic the same sad smile the priest is wearing. It seems appropriate.

The cemetery empties. I've been left alone to grieve, to find it in my heart not to throw myself into the hole and die with her. There's only one reason why I don't. I must keep myself together in case my child is found.

My daughter. A small, sturdy flower born too early, a week ago today. Before the violence on our tiled kitchen floor. She might as well have been wrenched from my wife's womb, instead of torn from her breast.

We talked about naming her Ellie, but we ultimately decided on Violet.

V for her mother, and those violet eyes I'll never see again. V for the valiant effort she made to live despite the odds against it. V, because she is the intersection of two lines cast askew by death, not sturdy right angles, but unbalanced, falling over, not quite down.

V, for Violet.

I can only pray that she lives, and one day, I will see her again.

34

NASHVILLE, TENNESSEE
CURRENT DAY

The bottle hits the edge of the glass, the liquid sloshing into the lowball. Zack Armstrong barely notices the too-heavy clink, nor that he's missed the glass and hit the table with most of his pour. The bottle is half-empty, and he is well on his way to being trashed.

He needs the buffer. He doesn't like to make this phone call, and yet, he feels compelled. Every six months, like clockwork, he rings Detective Gorman to see where things stand with the case.

It is a pointless endeavor. Vivian's murder, Violet's kidnapping, it's old news. Seventeen-year-old cold cases aren't front and center in anyone's mind but the family left behind.

Gorman isn't even a detective anymore. He's a sergeant, runs a squad, and the last time they talked, was about to hit his retirement age, take his twenty, and bolt for greener pastures. The last thing in the world he'd do is reopen a cold case on the eve of his departure.

But Zack has to try. Every six months, he dials the number for the Nashville Metropolitan Police, asks for the homicide office, talks to Gorman, and then they both go on their way for the next six months. Fruitless, but something about it makes him function. He has Gorman's home and mobile numbers, and in the beginning, he used them frequently, but as the case ages, as the pain grows hard and deep within him, he feels the niceties should be observed. He always gives Gorman the chance not to talk to him by calling the office directly.

Not calling isn't an option, but over the years, instead of hourly, daily, weekly, he's backed it down to every six months, to show respect. Zack isn't about to let the police forget. And Gorman is the only person he can talk to. The only other one who knows the gritty details, who saw the blackened blood, who understands what it's like to have your life snatched away while your back is turned. Not only understands but sometimes even feels badly about it all.

Zack knows the detective cares, in his way. But the man can shut off his emotions with the best of them.

Yes, a little distance, a few niceties, this he can give the man who worked so hard to find his wife's killer, his daughter's kidnapper. Never mind that he failed to find the culprit. Most husbands wouldn't be so forgiving of that fact.

He takes a bracing sip of Laphroaig, then picks up the phone and dials.

"Metro Police."

"Homicide, please."

Silence, then a click. A voice he doesn't recognize answers.

"Parks here."

"I'm looking for Sergeant Gorman."

More silence. "Um, sir, I'm sorry, but Sergeant Gorman is no longer with us."

The rage blooms bright in his chest. How dare he leave without at least saying goodbye? Without warning him he was handing off the case to another detective?

He pulls himself together. "When did he retire?"

"He didn't. I'm sorry to have to tell you this, but Sergeant Gorman passed away. Is there something I can help you with? I've taken over the day shift. Sergeant Bob Parks."

"I'm Zack Armstrong."

Another brief silence. He hears papers flipping in the background, the bray of a distant laugh. He's been in that office often enough to know that the room is tiny, there is a television in the corner above the desk, and the homicide office itself is a warren of cubicle desks that house a bunch of detectives who are practically on top of one another. They are moving soon, to a new office space, one he assumes will be shiny and clean, state of the art. Maybe they already have. Maybe his image of the scene is already distorted.

"How can I help you, Mr. Armstrong?"

The tone is neutral but inquisitive. Polite. As if the man has no idea who Zack is.

"I'm calling to inquire about the status of a cold case from 2000. The murder of Vivian Armstrong. My wife."

The cop's response is automatic but sincere. "Oh. I am so sorry for your loss."

If Zack had a quarter for the number of times he's heard those words...

"Sergeant Gorman was my contact for the case. No one phoned to tell me he'd passed away."

"Sorry about that, sir. It was sudden, an accident. We're only now settling the squad's reorganization."

"What kind of accident?"

"That's...personal information I'm not authorized to release."

"Right. How did I not hear about this? I read the papers. There's been no report of the sergeant's death."

"His family didn't want a lot of attention. It's been hard for them."

"I see. Well, I am terribly sorry to hear about this, but as I said, I'm calling for an update on my wife's case."

"2000, right? Vivian Armstrong? I remember it. I was patrol back then. I didn't work the scene, but it was certainly news everywhere. Your infant daughter was kidnapped as well if I recall."

"That's right."

"Weren't you the one who found your wife? You were out of town and came home to find her dead?"

Zack grits his teeth. He hears the lingering question in the cop's tone. *Are you sure you didn't fly off the handle and murder your wife? You can tell me the truth.*

"Yes. I was in Gulf Shores. My mother was ill."

"Well, I don't have any updates for you, sir, but I'm happy to pull the case files and give it a look. Can I call you back?"

"Of course. Thank you."

"Same number and address as is in the file?"

"That's right."

"Give me a few days, okay?"

"Absolutely. Thanks."

Zack hangs up, feeling oddly elated. New eyes. He hasn't had new eyes on this case in years.

He takes the Laphroaig and steps over the dog. The stunning fawn Belgian Malinois lifts her pretty head, and he can swear she raises a furry brow.

"Sorry to disturb, Kat." Kat—short for Katerina—sighs heavily and wags her tail. "You don't need to get up, honey. I'm just going to look."

Another wag, the rug catching under her powerful tail. She understands him better than most people. She puts her head back on her paws, and Zack walks down the hall toward the guest room.

His house on Love Circle is modern, boxy, all glass and exposed brick. Impersonal, some would say. He designed it himself, placed it on the hill where he can look over the city. He can also walk or bike to work, which makes life easier. Easier? More convenient.

The cozy house where he lived with Vivian and the specter of his daughter was torn down years ago. He couldn't fathom anyone living in it, and he certainly didn't want to stay there. He'd never be able to look at the kitchen floor again without

seeing the blood. He arranged to have it dismantled, giving un-
damaged sections to Habitat for Humanity. A crane had taken
the roof off in one piece. Goodwill had taken the furniture. The
remainders: doors, windows, beams, had gone to the various
housing charities throughout Nashville. He left with nothing but
their wedding photos, a sonogram, and the clothes on his back.

He started fresh. New. But he didn't start over.

The guest room walls are plastered with news stories. Some
are yellowed and crumbling, some are more recent, printouts
from online crime websites and missing persons' networks, websites that sometimes revisit the case and speculate as to the perpe-
trator. He entertained every theory they threw out, even those
that blamed him, claiming he hired someone to kill his wife
and sell his baby into the world of traffickers.

Those people are insane, as everyone is aware. He passed a lie
detector with flying colors and was never a legitimate suspect.
Not really. Not with his alibi. No one could make the timing
work, no matter how hard they tried.

He fingers the most recent story, done three years earlier. It
is an age progression analysis of what Violet might look like as
a teenager.

He stares at the stranger's face, at his own tilted eyes, at Vivian's strong nose, the lips not thin, like his, nor full, like Viv's,
but somewhere in between, teeth an amalgamation of his and
hers based on an algorithm of age and length and root depth, and
knows it isn't even close to being right. This is not his daughter. He might not know what she looks like, but she doesn't
look like this.

Of course, he's never seen her. Never felt the warm round
of her head in his palm, saw the strong flexibility of her body,
smelled her skin. She was taken while he was burying his mother
in the quaint town of Gulf Shores, Alabama, and he never had
a chance to meet his little girl.

He's always suspected the crime wasn't committed by a

stranger. No, the villain was, is, closer to home. It has to be someone he came in contact with, someone who felt he did them wrong. Someone who wanted to punish him. His old job was in intelligence, the people he worked with were criminals of the worst sort, hidden from the world, taking money to divulge secrets. They were whores, all of them, himself included.

Of course, the police saw it differently. They'd looked at him hard from day one, but his alibi was ironclad. He'd been standing over his mother's grave, with 100 witnesses, six hours away. When he got home the next day, worried after several calls home went unanswered, the blood was dried black on the floor.

No matter, they still investigated him six ways to Sunday, took apart his finances and phone records, interviewed every person he'd come in contact with, everyone they knew in Nashville. It was Gorman who'd finally put a stop to it. Gorman knew Zack was innocent. There were no hard feelings. They were doing their jobs.

Unfortunately, after Zack, there were no other suspects.

He sits on the desk chair and stares at the walls. Kat pads in and sits by his side, putting her head under his hand. Support. She gives him unconditional love, support, and protection. Better than any person he knows.

The cut crystal glass is empty. He debates a moment—more? He hasn't eaten, and he has a mound of papers to grade. Zack always eschews the services of his TAs in favor of doing his own work. He likes to see the students' progress, detemine if they are becoming better writers under his tutelage. Another drink will send him into the stratosphere, and he won't get any more work done tonight. But it is a three-day weekend, so who the hell cares when he gets the papers graded?

"Come on, girl," he says quietly, and Kat follows him out. He stands in the doorway for a moment, staring at the detritus of his life, then closes the door with a gentle snick, goes to the kitchen, and the open bottle.

35

The hangover is bad. It is made worse by the need to rise from the rumpled bed and answer the calls of nature, for both Zack and the dog. The sun's incessant climb burns his eyes, and of course, Kat decides it is a morning to be happy, to run and frolic, tugging hard at the leash until Zack relents and guides them to the dog park. He unsnaps her lead and she takes off running, long legs loping over the dead winter grass, to the very edge of the park, the border of the woods, where she stops, on point, and stares into the darkness. The thick fur ruffles along her back, and a soft growl comes from her throat.

A deer in the woods probably, or some other creature. He whistles for her, sharply, a hand going to his head as if the pain can be contained, but she doesn't move.

He finally stalks across the park to get her, and even then she resists, looking back over her shoulder and whining as he pulls her away.

"Come on, Kat. Knock it off, and I'll go by Publix and get you a bone. Wanna bone? Wanna yummy bone?"

Kat is not in the mood for his kind of play. She wants to growl at the trees. She hangs her head and plods next to him, the very picture of dejection.

They are a pair.

Walking away, he smells hyacinth. Strange, since it is late winter, and nothing is blooming yet. Vivian wore a similar scent, but not exactly the same. His heart squeezes, as it does every time he thinks about his dead wife. He sniffs again, but the smell is gone. All in his mind. Nothing unusual there. Over the years, he's caught a perfumed whiff at the strangest times, and almost always when there are no flowers in sight. He went to a doctor once, after looking up olfactory hallucinations and finding out it could actually presage a stroke or other terrible illnesses. The doctor checked him out thoroughly, told him he was still in mourning, and reassured him there was nothing physically wrong.

Mentally, on the other hand...

Back up the hill, he unlocks the front door and practically has to push the dog inside. She finally gives in and trots to the kitchen, ears perked. He follows, slightly chagrined to see the mess. The empty bottle—no wonder he feels like hell warmed over—is sideways in the sink, the glass on the counter, a sticky pool of dried Scotch next to it.

"Impressive showing, Zack."

He cleans up, then makes himself some eggs and bacon. He scarfs them down straight out of the pan, standing over the sink, tops it with orange juice, reheated coffee from yesterday's pot, and a handful of Advil. He throws a crunchy bone to Kat, who eyes it but doesn't pounce. He heads to his office.

He boots up his computer, pulls his cell phone from the charger. He's missed a call, and there is a message. The number is one he recognizes—Metro Nashville Police.

Crap, the call came in half an hour ago, while Katerina acted up in the park. He fumbles with the phone in his hurry to return the call, not bothering to listen to the message.

"Can I speak to Bob Parks, please? Homicide."

A click, then silence, then the phone starts to ring. And ring. And ring.

Finally, a voice answers, "Homicide."

"I'm looking for Sergeant Parks."

"He's out. Leave a message?"

"I'll call back."

He clicks end, then presses the button to play his voice mail.

"Mr. Armstrong, this is Sergeant Parks. I have meetings this morning, but if you are free this afternoon, I'd like to sit down and chat about your wife's case. Please call me back and let me know if I can stop by your place. This is my cell."

Heart pounding, Zack writes the number on the flap of a torn envelope, then dials it from memory. One of his talents, long numbers stick with him as soon as he sees them written down. It makes him fun at parties, where he can recite Pi out through a hundred numbers.

When he used to be fun, that is.

"Parks."

"It's Zack Armstrong. You called?" He sounds hopeful. He can't help it; it has been so long since there's been anything from the cops.

"Right. You around after lunch? I'd like to sit down and talk."

"Have you found something?"

"Not really, I just wanted to get briefed and up to speed on the case. I work a little differently than Gorman. I like to have my hands in things. Especially cold cases."

"I'll be here."

"Great. See you in a couple of hours, then."

What exquisite torture, Zack thinks, and sets about cleaning up the house.

36

At one on the dot, the doorbell chimes. Zack practically falls over Kat trying to get to the door. The dog has decided today is the day to start barking at strangers and parks herself dead center in the foyer.

"What is wrong with you? Move."

She looks right at him, gives a final bark as if saying *screw you, buddy, I'll bark if I want*, then falls silent and sits on her haunches, elegant nose in the air.

He opens the door to a tall, dark-haired man with a thick mustache and a much smaller woman, reddish hair pulled back in a ponytail. They are both in plainclothes, though their weapons are visible on their hips. Ever the military man, even eighteen years removed, Zack identifies them by the butt, Glock 27s, and glances at their ankles, where he can see the slight bulge of ankle holsters. Four weapons, fifty-two rounds loaded between them. Bet the ranch they both have pepper spray on their belts, too. Knives, maybe. Extra magazines. On the surface, they look so benign, but he knows both are lethal.

Satisfied with his assessment, he grabs Kat's collar and gestures for them to come in.

"Mr. Armstrong, I'm Sergeant Parks, and this is Detective Brianna Starr."

"Nice to meet you. Stay still for a moment. Kat doesn't like weapons. She spent some time as a puppy training to uncover them. Don't worry if she growls, she sees it as doing her job."

Zack releases the dog's collar and Kat begins her inventory, professionally sniffing the strangers up and down, uttering short barks at waist and ankle.

"She's beautiful," the detective says, careful not to move. The cop's voice is low and smoky, not what he expects from someone so small. "What is she?"

"A Belgian Malinois. It's a herding breed."

"She was a working dog?"

"No, she failed out. Too happy."

"But a dog named Cat? That seems almost cruel."

He laughs. "Kat with a K. Short for Katerina."

"Ah."

Kat finishes her sweep, sits back, satisfied, tongue lolling. Zack pats her on the head, says, "Good job, sweet girl," then leads them to the living room.

"Can I get you anything?"

"We're fine, thanks," Parks replies.

They all sit, and silence stretches between them. Finally, Zack opens his hands expectantly. "You wanted to get updated?"

"Right." Parks smooths two fingers over his mustache, a nervous gesture that puts Zack on alert. "I took a pass through the files last night, and then I asked Detective Starr to pull everything together and get up to speed. I don't want you to get your hopes up, sir, but we wanted to give things another once-over, and I'd like to assign Detective Starr to investigate. She's had great successes with cold cases, and since there have been so many technological updates recently, she and I agree it would be wise to take fresh DNA samples and get them into the system. It's been a while, and I have to tell you when I looked last night, I didn't see a profile for you in CODIS. Your wife, yes, but not you."

Zack's entire body goes tense. "You want my DNA again? I was cleared."

"Nothing to worry about, sir," Starr says. "If I'm going to re-open a case, it's standard protocol for me to update all the files, and in this case, since you're not in the system, I'd like to get fresh DNA input. You never know what might show up."

"What, like my missing daughter is some kind of teenage criminal mastermind, and you want to see if you can find her through the system?"

She shakes her head, fighting back a smile. "Not at all, Mr. Armstrong. There's nothing villainous here. Your DNA isn't attached to the file anymore. Things get lost over time. It happens. It's a long shot we'll find a match, but I'd like to get you back into play, just in case. Okay?"

Zack crosses his arms. "Continue."

"After I update your DNA, I'm going to update CODIS—the Combined DNA Index—and put the information into ViCAP—that's our Violent Criminal Apprehension Program. These programs will look for DNA matches and any cases that are similar. I will go into deep specifics—weapon used, placement of the body, the missing infant, anything and everything I can add to the case to see if there's a chance the suspect in your wife's murder has committed another crime in the intervening years. I might even put the age progression of your daughter into the FBI's NGI facial recognition database, just for kicks."

"Back up a second. You're reopening the case?"

"Not exactly. I'm going to do some legwork and see if anything pops. If it does, then we'll reopen the case. Fair enough?"

"Yes. Quite fair."

"Good. Now. Can you run me through the whole story? I'd like to hear everything, start to finish."

"The file—"

She smiles. Her teeth are pretty. The smile makes her look

sweet and innocent, and he knows she isn't. Not by a long shot. Not after what she's seen.

"Files are what they are. I'd like to hear your point of view, verbally, instead of reading and watching the old tapes."

"Looking for inconsistencies in my answers and body language?"

"Of course. But it's better for me to understand the case from your perspective. Helps keep me from making assumptions. I know it's been a long time, but I bet you have a lot of insight to share."

She is a cool customer, he'll give her that. He looks at Parks, who nods encouragingly.

"Unfortunately, there's not much to tell. I was in lower Alabama. My mom was dying—late-stage breast cancer. Vivian wasn't due for a couple of weeks. Even though I wanted to stay close to home, she encouraged me to go down, be with my mom. She was adamant. So I went and had a chance to say goodbye, and we buried my mom the same day Vivian was murdered."

He recites these facts with as little emotion as possible, though inside his gut is churning. He wasn't expecting to reopen all his wounds this afternoon.

"And you were injured in the line of duty, yes? That's why you were home in the first place?"

"I had a meet go sideways, and was shot. They sent me home to recover. I jumped at the chance to get back stateside before the baby was born."

"According to your statement, your wife didn't call you when she went into premature labor, nor after she had the baby. Why do you think that is?"

"I don't know. She wanted a home birth, was working with University Hospital's midwife program. They delivered Violet at home with no issue, left her there with a planned follow-up OB appointment that she didn't show for.

"Trust me when I say I regret not getting in the car and driving home immediately when I couldn't reach her, but I had my hands full with my mom. It wasn't unusual for my wife not to answer. When I was overseas, I caught her only about half the time. After several missed calls, though, I finally got scared and headed home. And as we all know, after she had the baby, someone broke in and stabbed her twice, once in the stomach, once in the neck. The baby was taken. Whoever did it wore gloves, there were no fingerprints or outside DNA found, other than the midwife, who was cleared right away. And me, of course."

"You found her."

"I did. The following day. She'd been dead for a while." He looks off into the distance, out the windows, over the city. The dog sets her head on his knee. He pets her ears absently.

"I've seen the photos. It was bad," Starr says, not unsympathetically.

Bad. The understatement of the century. "Yes, it was."

"Do you have any ideas who could be responsible?"

"No. There was a thought that I got too close to discovering something in an operation, and they needed to warn me off."

"So the suspect or suspects were sending a message. But you left the Army after this incident?"

"I did. I resigned my commission and went back to school. Finished my Ph.D., landed a tenure-track position at Vanderbilt. I got lucky. They don't hand them out like jelly beans." He didn't need to add—*and with some people thinking I was a murderer...*

"You teach English, is that right?"

"Right. English Lit, creative writing, comp, the works."

"So how was your relationship with your wife?"

Zack gives her a look. "It was good, outside of the fact that I only saw her once or twice a year while I was deployed. We kept up by phone and email, some online chats when we could. It wasn't as easy as it is now. I was off the grid for a large part of my deployment."

"What did you do in the Army? I mean, counterintelligence is rather vague."

"That's classified, ma'am."

She flips a page, glances down. "You were attached to the Special Operations Aviation Unit. SOAR. First, you were a part of the Night Stalkers, flying helicopters, then you moved into Alpha Company, 902d MI Battalion, as an intelligence team leader."

"Yes, ma'am."

"You have a wad of medals, including a Bronze Star and Purple Heart, right?"

"Yes, ma'am. A wad."

"And the prevailing wisdom is someone took offense to your work, killed your wife, stole your baby."

"That's right."

"And you gave it all up to become an English teacher."

"Again…"

"I don't buy it."

"Ma'am?"

Detective Starr shifts in her seat. "It doesn't make sense. Why would they attack your wife if they wanted to send you a message? Why not kill you? Or is that what happened when you were shot? They were trying, and when they didn't succeed they came to Nashville, killed your wife and stole your child?"

"I dealt with ruthless people. They don't always think logically. They're more the *burn down the world, ask questions later* type."

"It also suggests a terror operative was in Nashville."

"It does."

"And that jibes with your experience? It's likely to be the case? It feels very convoluted to me."

"Ma'am, what the government chooses to share with local law enforcement is way above my pay grade, then, and now. Likely? I can't tell you that, but I wouldn't say it was impossible. Look at 9/11. They were here for months before they attacked, coordinating. For all I know—"

Careful...

He stops. "Sorry. I can't go there. Everything I did was highly classified, still is. Suffice it to say the scenario is not outside the realm of possibility."

"Scary," Starr says. "Still, I don't get it. Why take the baby? That in itself ruins the terror suspect profile for me."

"Punishment." Zack's voice is strained. "Sheer, unadulterated punishment."

* * *

They run through it, front and back, a couple of times. Everything that happened, everything he knows. The biggest stumbling block is, of course, Zack was the one to find Vivian. Not only that, he hadn't seen his wife for several days before she was killed, and she'd managed to deliver their child without him knowing, too.

He can see Starr draw a few conclusions.

He is an unreliable witness.

He is to blame for Vivian's death.

Simple.

An hour into the conversation, Parks checks his watch and nudges his detective, who smartly closes the files and pulls a DNA swab kit from her purse.

Zack swirls the brush around the inside of his cheek, spits into a cup, and hands them both back. He has nothing to hide.

But he has a strange sense that Parks and Starr do.

They promise to be in touch and slide out the door, leaving him no wiser as to the real reason they are interested in the case again. Oh, their claims made sense—Parks is new to the job, Starr is their—ahem—star detective for cold cases. It will be a big win for them if they solve something so heinous and so old.

And yet...

Zack walks down the hall to the guest room, sits for a few moments staring at the walls. There has been nothing new to pin up for over three years. No talk, no articles. From the beginning, no real new information has ever come out. The case is as cold as it gets.

Except there is a living, breathing child out there somewhere. His child.

And he gets the sense these detectives have a fresh lead.

Zack taps his finger along the sharp edge of the desk, then, with a deep sigh, pulls the door closed behind him and heads off to grade his papers.

37

"Well done getting him to agree to the DNA swab."

Parks and Starr are back in the unmarked, heading to their new offices on Murfreesboro Pike.

"Think he suspects anything?" Starr asks.

Parks smooths his mustache with two fingers, his left wrist draped casually on top of the steering wheel. "The man was a decorated military intelligence operative and is now a professor. Both professions rely on an ability to understand what motivates people. Yes, I'd say he was very suspicious."

"Yet he still allowed me to take his DNA. Either he's wily, or totally innocent. How long do you think you'll be able to hold him off?"

"I think he did us a professional courtesy letting us walk out of there. He smelled a rat. Over under…three days, tops. Will that be enough time?"

Starr nods. "I'll put a huge rush on it, see if I can call in some favors. It will be tight, but I'll make it happen. At least we'll be able to update everything and do a search for the girl with fresh eyes and fresh samples."

"Then what?"

"Good question. Do we sit him down and tell him what we found in Gorman's files?"

"We'll have to. He deserves to know. But Colorado… I don't know, Breezy, this doesn't feel right to me. Too much of a co-

incidence that Gorman dies while hunting down the first lead
he's had in years. Maybe it was just an accident."

"To me either, boss. That's the problem. Should we get in
touch with law enforcement out there, see if they can shed some
light?"

"What do we say? Our old boss went skiing with his family,
fell off a cliff, and we think it smells to high heaven? No, hold
off. Keep looking. Dissect everything. It's too early to bring in
outsiders."

"Roger that, sir."

"And, Breezy? Do me a favor, and check soldier boy's travel
records."

"He's an English teacher, Bob."

"Once a soldier, always a soldier. He knows how to move
without drawing attention to himself. Humor me and make
sure he hasn't been a very bad boy, okay?"

He pulls into the parking lot, and Starr gets out, then leans
in the window. "Aren't you coming in?"

"No, I think I'll take a drive."

"Where are you headed?"

"Thought I might stop by and see Andrea Austin."

"Gorman's widow? Smart idea. Check in when you get back.
I'll update you with what I know." Starr slaps the roof of the car
and walks into the building.

Parks heads to Green Hills. He doesn't bother to call ahead.
Andrea is a freelance journalist who works from home. If she
isn't around, he'll call, but chances are...

He is right. Her Prius is in the driveway.

He knocks on the door, noticing the soffit has come loose
by the porch light. He needs to come over and do some work.

It is something they do, the boys in blue. When one of their
own is widowed, they band together and try to take on some
of the weight of chores and home upkeep. And everyone liked
Gorman, and in turn, Andrea.

The bell chimes, and a few moments later, Andrea opens the door with a grin. She's lost weight but looks better than the last time Parks saw her. Her hair is in a ponytail; she is wearing yoga clothes and sneakers and a sense of impatience.

"Heading out?"

"Hey, Bob! You just caught me. Come in, come in. It's so good to see you."

She has a southern lilt, sweet as honey. He follows her to the kitchen.

The interior of the house is faring better than the outside. Seagrass green walls with white wainscoting, an updated kitchen in grays and white, creamy cabinets with a dark island. They'd just done the house in honor of Gorman's upcoming retirement. Parks knows there is a large great room off to the right done in wood paneling and leathers. A man cave, as Gorman called it. Parks wouldn't mind something like it himself, one day.

Always the hostess, Andrea has already pulled out sweet tea and ginger snaps and is arranging them on the counter.

"I don't want to put you out—"

"Oh hush, you. You need a good feeding now and then. How's Linda?"

"Somewhere in Florida, I think. We haven't spoken in a while."

She gives him a sympathetic smile. "I'm sorry to hear it. I thought you two might put things back together."

"I'd hoped to, but taking the sergeant's job shut it all down. Junior's on the street now, too, doing the family proud. I think two cops in the family is more than she can handle. It's all good. Paperwork's final next week. We've kept it civil."

"It's still a shame. But Junior, he's a good boy. Handsome in that uniform. Mine are rebels. I don't know if they'll ever grow up."

Andrea and Gorman have twin boys, and Parks knows she isn't kidding, they are both wild. Fun, and fearless, and smart. They are juniors at Sewanee now. Gorman was so proud the day they were accepted, bragging to everyone he'd come in contact with.

Andrea pushes a glass of tea toward him and gestures for him to sit at the island. She stays standing.

He takes a deep drink of the tea. "I assume you're wondering why I'm here."

"I figure it's something about a case Gorman was working on." She says her dead husband's name with barely a wince, and Parks is proud of her.

"You're right. It's the Armstrong case."

"Oh, the missing baby? Gosh, that was years ago."

"Right." More tea, a cookie nibble.

"Spit it out, Bob."

"Gorman had his own case files, yes?"

"Every homicide detective does, you know that. You need the Armstrong files? After all these years, too. Imagine that."

"It might be nothing. Zack Armstrong made a call yesterday. Apparently he called Gorman regularly, hoping for updates."

"He's not the only one. But yes, he called, on schedule, twice a year. I guess no one told him about...well, Gorman's been gone long enough, I can say it. That he died."

"Armstrong wasn't aware of the accident. He was caught off guard, for sure. It's probably nothing, but I took a look at the case files, just to familiarize myself. I hadn't seen them, figured what the heck. There was a recent notation that piqued my interest. A handwritten Post-it note. Gorman's writing. I was hoping his personal files might explain what it meant."

"What did the note say?"

"'Colorado.' It was underlined three times."

She stills, and her eyes become hooded. A hand snakes to her throat.

"Did he mention that he might be looking into anything while you were out there?"

She shakes her head, still pale. "But he wouldn't have told

me. It was a family vacation. Winter break. We'd never skied the Rockies, he thought the boys would love it. He said he wanted to experience it while his knees were still good, and while he was still fully insured with Metro, in case he broke a leg." She stares into the backyard. A squirrel is swinging wildly from a red ball feeder. "It was almost like he knew something was going to happen."

"You know how we are, Andi. Superstitious to a fault."

"I do." She meets his eyes again. Hers are misted, and she gives a weak smile. "He didn't mention anything to me that I know of, but let's go look at the files. I know where they are."

She leads him up the stairs to Gorman's office, all dark wood and heavy desk. It is immaculately polished and dusted, the bookshelves gently lit, as if their master will be home to peruse them at a moment's notice. It makes Parks's heart hurt.

"I haven't messed with anything. Haven't seen the need. I rarely came in here when he was alive. It's not like I need the space, not with the boys away at school. If one of them decides to come back home for more than a week, I'll think about it. These kids now, they have to live at home because they can't afford to buy a house and live on their own. Oh, look at me, I'm babbling. You go on in. The Armstrong files will be with the rest, in the closet. I'm just going to…" She starts to back out of the room.

"I'll be quick."

"No, no, take your time, hon. I'll make some more tea."

"Your class? I don't want to keep you if you need to go."

She stops, cocks her head to the side, purses her lips. "I think I'll skip yoga today. I was thinking about playing hooky anyway, going to Parnassus and browsing instead. I haven't read anything good lately. You take your time," she says again, and he lets her leave.

She is a tough nut, Andrea Austin.

The files are where she said, in the closet. A corrugated box, and inside, thick stacks of paper. He sets the box on the desk and digs in.

There is a skiing magazine. Photocopies of various Colorado ski areas, timetables, competition schedules. Parks is confused but keeps thumbing through.

He sees nothing that stands out. Had Gorman lost his marbles and tucked his winter break ski research into the wrong file?

Another page flip and he sees a story printed out from *Ski Magazine* stapled to the magazine's January cover. On the cover, a young woman holds a pair of skis and grins, a gold medal dangling from her right hand. Her goggles obscure her face, but it is easy to tell she is young. In red marker, the twenty-point font headline name is circled.

Mindy Wright, Skiing's Next Superstar.

"Mindy Wright?" Andi's voice startles him. She's come up the stairs again, silent and soft, and is standing behind him.

"Do you know who she is, Andi?"

"You haven't heard of her? She's one of the best young skiers out there right now. Gorman was following her career like a hawk. She was expected to get onto the Olympic team this year."

"Was? What happened to her?"

"Blew out her leg at a World Cup event last month. God, Gorman would be so disappointed if he knew. He thought she was the next Lindsey Vonn, only better. More focused, more athletic. Less likely to get injured because of how she trains. Boy, was he wrong."

"I had no idea Gorman was such a ski fanatic."

Dimples flash in Andrea's cheeks. "Oh, he loved it, though he rarely had the chance to ski himself. The boys decided they wanted to learn how to snowboard a few years back, so we took them to Snowshoe in West Virginia for winter break. They liked it well enough, but Gorman, he was hooked. Like a fish to water. I'd only ever water-skied myself, and I thought it was fun, but it was so cold, and I kept falling down because I couldn't get the hang of leaning forward instead of back.

"Gorman, he had no form, looked like a pile of sticks doing cartwheels, but the rush of flying down that hill satisfied the adrenaline junkie in him. We could barely get him off the slopes that first day. And ever since, any chance he got... He was obsessed. You know how some men watch golf on the weekends? He watched skiing. Even got an upgrade on the satellite plan so he could watch the European races. He was all FIS, all the time."

"FIS?"

"International Ski Federation. They sponsor all the World Cup events."

"Ah. And Gorman was a fan of Mindy Wright?"

"Devoted. I asked him once what the attraction was—outside of her being adorable in all the right places, of course. He said she was a huge talent, but I sometimes wondered if it was more."

"More?"

"I don't know. It wasn't like him to get so attached to a stranger, you know?"

"Did he ever meet her?"

She nods. "The weekend he...we went to Beaver Creek to see her ski. She won the race. He got her autograph. Shook her hand. I have a picture here somewhere, probably on the camera. I... I haven't looked at the photos."

"Let me do it. You don't need to."

"No," she says, voice full of steel. "It's high time I did. Come with me."

The camera is downstairs in the kitchen, shoved into the back of the junk drawer. She smiles apologetically as she moves screwdrivers and masking tape out of the way. The drawer is incongruous with the rest of the house, and it makes Parks happy to see Andrea Austin Gorman isn't utterly perfect.

The camera's battery is dead, but she has the right cord, and within minutes, it is charged enough to start looking through the photos. Outside of paling, and a few excessively loud swallows, Andrea holds it together long enough to find the shots of Gorman and his skiing celebrity crush.

She holds out the camera, and Parks looks closely.

Gorman, grinning ear-to-ear, one hand with fingers up and spread in a rock and roll sign, the other around a teenage girl with long, dark hair and dark eyes.

Parks feels his jaw drop.

"What is it?"

"Can I take this?"

"Um... I..."

"Oh hell, Andi, these are your last pictures of him. Never mind. Tell you what, can I load the pictures onto my computer?"

"That would be fine. Actually, I can dump them onto a thumb drive. Hang tight." There is a laptop on the counter, and she expertly offloads the photos and hands over the drive.

"Thank you."

"Can I ask?"

Ever the cop's wife, discretion is always paramount.

Parks gives her a long look, then gestures to the computer. "May I?"

"Sure."

He opens Google and types for a moment. A few seconds later, he turns the laptop around.

"Does she look familiar?"

"That's Mindy Wright."

He clicks again, and a photo of a young couple loads onto the screen. Side by side, the photos take his breath away.

Andi looks at the screen for a good three seconds before saying, "My God. Do you think—"

"That Gorman may have found Vivian and Zack Armstrong's kidnapped daughter? Yes. I do."

And left unsaid are the words they both think.

And it was the last thing he ever did.

★ ★ ★

Parks keeps his cool on the drive back to the office. He doesn't make any calls or set off any alarms. He has a long way to go to figure out what is going on, but his instincts have paid off.

Mindy Wright isn't a dead ringer for Vivian Armstrong. She is taller, her face leaner. But she has her father's eyes and her mother's chin. So much similarity that Parks is sure if he shows a photo of the girl to Zack Armstrong, he'll be on the first plane out of Nashville to find her.

They have to step carefully. If Gorman suspected the same and went out to Colorado to casually check things out, and something happened to him that wasn't an accident...

Parks is grasping at straws, he knows, but it all feels so strange and wrong, and he's been a cop long enough to know there is no sense ignoring a hunch.

And he has a hunch Gorman found a trail.

38

DENVER, COLORADO

Fueled by beer and pretzels, and around 2:00 a.m., delivery Chinese, Juliet and Cameron work all night, running and re-running DNA tables while researching the Armstrong murder/kidnapping. She loves Mindy heart and soul and will do anything to keep her from getting hurt. But she is becoming more and more convinced Mindy is the lost child from Nashville. The photographs of Vivian and Zack Armstrong are telling—Mindy resembles them both, especially Armstrong himself.

As horrible as the case and the situation, there is, of course, a significant upside to this discovery. Zack Armstrong, or his immediate family, might be a match for Mindy's stem cell needs.

Juliet longs for a pipette of his blood. Blood she understands. It is simple, straightforward. Hemoglobin, plasma, water. Potassium, chloride, phosphorus, sodium. Oxygen, carbon dioxide, nitrogen. It is beautiful—balanced, the perfect nutrient to keep the body moving. Until it decides to betray its host in some way, as it has Mindy.

The more she learns about the case, the stranger this all feels. She is trying to stay rational and focused but is having a hard time. She is family; these are her people. She is involved. It gives her a new appreciation for the crime victims she works with, albeit anonymously, behind the scenes.

Around four in the morning, they have the DNA profiles lined up, and Juliet goes to work. She runs the sequence one more time, bottom lip between her teeth, a pencil stuck in her hair pulling it back from her face, Cameron looking over her shoulder.

"It's a match," he says, but she shushes him and runs it again, just to be sure. Her blood is whirring in her veins, the adrenaline rush coming as the sequence lines up perfectly, again.

"Come on, Juliet. It's right. You know it's right. You've known it all night."

It is. The mitochondrial DNA doesn't lie. Mindy is Vivian Armstrong's biological daughter.

"Just…give me a second, okay?"

He rubs her shoulders, and she closes her eyes, lets him soothe her. She is having a hard time grasping what this means, and at the same time, her coolly logical side is running a situational awareness report.

Vivian Armstrong, stabbed to death. An infant daughter, stolen from the home. A doctor in Colorado, running an illegal adoption scheme.

Her sister, taking receipt of a stolen child. No teen mother named Graciela, wanting her child to have a better life. But a child ripped from her mother, who is very, very dead.

Lauren is going to freak out entirely when she finds out the whole truth behind Mindy's birth.

More importantly, how is this going to affect Mindy?

Juliet can already see the headlines. *World-Class Skier Stolen Child of Murder Victim.*

The notoriety alone will be difficult for Mindy, who only wants accolades for her hard work. She will be devastated to have her skills supplanted by what will amount to tabloid news after the initial flush.

"Okay," Juliet says, finally. "What are our next steps?"

"You have to report this to Woody, obviously. And tell your sister. As for the rest?"

She spins her chair around. "I need to get Zack Armstrong

here, immediately, is what I need to do. We need to get a blood sample. He could be a match for the transplant."

"He could. Two-pronged approach then? Find Armstrong, bring him to Colorado, and let your people start an investigation at the same time."

She leans the chair back so she can see his face. "I'm worried the investigation will take precedence. That Armstrong will say no. That the whole world is going to collapse in around us."

Cameron toys with the edge of an empty noodle container then shrugs. "Well, it might. But it all might work out for the best. It's not an optimal situation, no matter how you look at it. But you have to tell. You can't keep this a secret."

"I'm not my sister," she snaps.

"I know you're not, J. But we've made a discovery that's going to have long-term ramifications. Why don't you fill in Woody, and Lauren, then fly to Nashville and haul Armstrong's ass back here."

"I think that's my only course of action, don't you? And let the investigative chips fall where they may. I'm just… This is going to kill Lauren. She's so private, so determined to let Mindy shine. Having a spotlight on her and Jasper, her actions, it's not going to be easy on her."

"It's never easy on any victim."

"I know. At least we've helped solve part of the case."

Juliet lines up all her ducks, and Cameron helps, and when he leaves for work, bleary-eyed and rumpled, she goes through it all again.

She looks at the DNA profile as if the answers will rise from the page and give her the truth she needs. Everything she is seeing tells her the same story.

Vivian and Zack Armstrong's long-lost daughter has been found.

But the questions this raises are daunting, and as she arranges her day, she can't help letting them run through her mind.

Who killed Vivian Armstrong? And how was Mindy chosen to sell to Lauren? Was Castillo involved in more than simply helping place her indigent and illegal patients' children? Why, and how, was she trafficking in stolen babies?

These are questions for her CBI agent compatriots to answer. Juliet has to handle her family.

Juliet showers and cleans up the apartment. Despite what she told Cameron, she still doesn't know what step she wants to take first. Talk to Lauren? Talk to her boss? Get on a plane to Nashville and see if Zack Armstrong will come to Denver, no questions asked?

All of the above is the only option.

No matter what happens, this story is about to get very public, very quickly. Everyone needs to be on board because the media is going to be all over them from the moment they hear. Everyone loves a reconciliation, especially involving missing kids.

In the end, it is her sister's number she dials first.

Lauren sounds as bleary as Juliet feels.

"I'm so sorry, did I wake you?"

"Not exactly," Lauren says, the yawn imminent. "You sound like you were up all night, too."

"I was. Listen, are you alone? We need to talk."

"I am. Jasper's gone to get breakfast."

"Mindy didn't take it well?"

A ghost of a laugh. "She didn't take it well, no. She took it with hope, and grace, and excitement, and then fear and anger. If it wasn't her lifeline, I would have been insulted. She was practically vibrating with the idea that she was someone else's kid, then she attacked me for holding out on her."

"Sounds like a perfectly normal reaction, considering the situation."

"She's no dummy, Juliet. She knows a cure might be out there."

"And that's what she was excited about, Lauren. She loves you and Jasper. Nothing will change that."

"We'll see." Her sister's bitterness is surprising. *Just you wait, sister.*

Juliet takes a deep breath. "I need to talk to you about Mindy's lineage."

"You make her sound like a horse."

"Stop, okay? I think I might have found her father."

The silence from Lauren is deafening.

"Are you still there?"

Finally, "Yes. Who is it?"

"A man named Zachary Armstrong. He's from Nashville."

Her sister curses, short and mean.

"Wow, Lauren. Language."

"Where did you hear that name?"

Juliet senses this is important. That she must tread carefully. She doesn't want to start another fight between Jasper and Lauren. But she also doesn't want to tell Lauren she ran the DNA without permission, so she risks the other half of the truth.

"Jasper mentioned you'd looked him up. How do you know him, Lauren?"

"I don't know him."

"But you were looking him up the other night."

"I wasn't."

"Jasper said—"

"I wasn't looking him up personally. There's an old case—it's Castillo. I started wondering about her. I haven't thought about all of this in years, Juliet. I never thought it would come up."

"You already know Mindy is his daughter?"

"What? No. Of course not."

"But you know about the case?"

"I remembered something, that's all. About a child who was stolen. We used to live in Nashville. I look at the news from there sometimes."

"Well, when you looked, did you find him? Because I did. And Mindy is a dead ringer for him and his wife."

A little gasp of air.

Juliet tries again. "I'm sorry, I'm not trying to be confrontational. But you're not telling me everything. How do you know this man? How do you know about his missing child?"

"I told you, I don't know him. Of course I don't. And I don't know anything about the case. Like I said, I was thinking about Dr. Castillo, wondering if what she did wasn't as aboveboard as she claimed. I couldn't sleep, and I thought I'd look for missing children from the year Mindy was born, and I saw that Armstrong case. It caught my eye because of the Nashville connection. I didn't remember hearing about it. I clicked on the story, then Jasper interrupted me. I haven't even had time to look at it again." Silence. "You think Mindy is their child?"

"I know she is. After I saw the case was unsolved, I had legal leeway. I ran the DNA. It's a match. Your Dr. Castillo was in a darker business than you ever knew."

"Oh, my God. Juliet. I can't…what do we do?"

"I have to approach this Armstrong guy. I can only imagine he's gotten his hopes up a lot over the years, and this will be a huge thing for him to take in. Plus, we need to think about the long-term effects of this. Especially on Mindy's mental health. The media—"

"Go. Do it. Oh my God, Juliet, if you've found Mindy's parents, you have to tell them, and get them here, right now. We'll deal with the fallout later. Mindy is getting sicker by the day. We need a cure."

"The wife is dead."

"Oh. I'm sorry to hear that. How terrible. But if the father is alive—"

"You didn't read the whole story?"

"I told you, I'd only just started looking when Jasper interrupted me."

"The wife was murdered, and the daughter was taken from their home."

A full-blown gasp this time.

"You aren't serious."

"I am. Whoever took their baby stabbed the wife. The husband was out of town. When he got home, his wife was dead, and his baby was missing."

"My God, Juliet. That is horrible." She pauses, and the whole tenor of her voice changes. "And wonderful. This is wonderful! I don't mean to be selfish, and I am very sorry about the situation, but if there's a chance this man can help us save Mindy's life? There's no time to lose. He might have more children. He might be a match himself."

The joy in her sister's voice puts some of Juliet's worries to rest. "I agree. I wanted to get your permission to contact him."

"You have it." Lauren goes quiet again. "That poor woman, murdered."

"It's tragic. I'll be in touch. Hang in there, Lauren. We'll get this sorted out. You guys have to be prepared, though. As soon as people know Mindy is the lost Armstrong baby, it's going to be national news in an instant."

Lauren sighs heavily. "Let's cross that bridge when we get there, okay?"

39

NASHVILLE, TENNESSEE

The logistics are easy enough. There is a direct flight to Nashville leaving at 9:35 a.m. Juliet books the flight online, cringing at the last-minute full-fare price, then tosses a couple of things in a bag—toothbrush, change of clothes, brush, laptop—and opens her Uber app and orders a car. They make it to the airport in record time.

She doesn't call Woody. Not yet.

She knows it's dumb, and that she'll probably get taken to task, but there is something inside her that says, *Wait, talk to the man first, break the news gently. Get him to Colorado, and then you can tell Woody.*

Her mind is racing, but she puts the thoughts aside and takes advantage of the flight to catch some shut-eye. She is exhausted and falls asleep quickly, her head pillowed on her jacket against the hull of the plane. She wakes as they land in Nashville, the wheels screeching onto the tarmac, jolting her upright.

She has all of Armstrong's contact information, which has been easy to find with a quick database search. Climbing in another car, she tells the driver, a young woman this time, to head to Vanderbilt University.

"School's on break, so traffic is light. We'll be there in fifteen minutes."

"Wait, they're on break?"

"That's right."

"Then take me to this address instead. I might need you to stick around for a few if my meeting is canceled." She curses herself for not checking these things first. All she had thought about was getting to Armstrong immediately, assuming, because he is a professor, he could be found on campus. *You're a hell of an investigator, Juliet. This is why they keep you in the lab.*

They chat a bit, driving through the city, which is covered in cranes; there seems to be construction on every corner. Before she knows it, the driver is winding up a leafy green hill and pulling up in front of a starkly modern house, a glass rectangle perched on the side of the hill. There is a black four-door Jeep Wrangler in the driveway.

Has she just gotten lucky?

"Hang tight for a minute?" she asks the driver.

"Sure thing."

Juliet marches up the steep driveway, onto the covered porch, and rings the bell.

Nothing. Silence.

Damn.

She tries again, though she knows it's futile. Despite the car in the drive, the house feels empty.

She shifts her bag to the other shoulder, pulls out her cell phone and notebook. She waves to the driver—one finger up in a *hold on* gesture—and dials the number she wrote down.

The phone starts to ring, but as it does, she sees a tall, dark-haired man jogging up the street. He has a fawn-colored dog with a black face on a lead by his side. He takes in the car, and the woman in his driveway, and pulls up short. The dog looks interested.

The resemblance in person is much stronger than in the photos. It takes Juliet's breath away. She clicks off her phone just as Zack Armstrong reaches for the carry bag around his waist.

"Mr. Armstrong?" she calls.

He keeps his hand on his belt and mutters something to the

dog, who goes from a happy trot to alert. Slowly, they move to the base of the drive.

"Can I help you?" he asks, planted there, not moving. She doesn't move, either. She now knows this man's background. He was a serious operator in his day, though the day is long past.

"Dr. Juliet Ryder. I'm with the Colorado Bureau of Investigation." She flips open her credentials and holds them out so he can see. It feels important to her to be someone for this man, not just the sister of a grief-stricken woman and aunt to a stolen child. She needs him to take her seriously, immediately.

She doesn't understand the look that passes over his face. But some of the tension goes out of his shoulders, and the dog grins at her, and the two of them come up the drive.

Juliet nods to the driver, who's been watching, and with a little wave, the girl zooms away to get her next fare, leaving Juliet alone on Zack Armstrong's doorstep.

40

Zack lets them into the house and gives Kat a fresh bowl of water, which she laps up noisily. They did a full circuit this morning, and he took his time getting them home, stopping for a long lunch break on the way. It is a beautiful late-winter day in Nashville, crisp, cool but not cold, the edges of spring thinking about fighting their way in. Just the kind of day he likes to spend outside, and Kat does, too.

He offers the CBI agent a cold bottle of water, which she accepts. He drinks one down himself, then fills it again from the tap and sits down at the counter.

There is so much tension coming off the woman he doesn't know if she is going to last another moment without talking. She looks tired, and excited, and scared. Not the usual persona he is used to from law enforcement. And after the visit from Parks and his pet detective yesterday, Zack is paying even more attention.

"Well? What brings the CBI to Nashville?"

She breathes deeply and squares her shoulders. "This is going to come as a bit of a shock. I have a line on your daughter."

Zack stands so quickly he knocks over the water, and Kat starts to bark, low booms coming from her chest. He is at the woman's side in a heartbeat, a hand gripped like a vise around her bicep.

"What did you just say?"

"Let go of me, right now."

He realizes he has a death grip on her, lets loose his hand and steps away. "Shush," he says to Kat, who whines and sits on her haunches.

"I'm sorry. You caught me by surprise." Every word is enunciated, carefully, slowly, so there is no misunderstanding. "You think you have a line on my daughter?"

She starts for her pocket, and Zack can't help himself, he moves into a defensive position.

"Whoa," she says. "I'm getting out my phone. Calm down."

"Sorry," he repeats, simply, but keeps his hand on his waist. He has a Walther PPK in a custom-made holster tucked into his running pants, and he's kept up with his weapons practice. Old habits die hard.

Zack stands deathly still while she unlocks her phone and pulls up a photograph. When he sees it, Zack thinks his heart might burst.

"My God. She looks like Vivian. My Violet," he says, the blood rushing to his head. He feels the faint coming as it happens, goes down before a second thought comes.

★ ★ ★

Zack wakes with his head pillowed in Juliet Ryder's lap, Kat licking his face, whining and pawing at his arm.

"You fall gracefully for such a big guy," she says, a note of humor in her tone, and he realizes she has very pretty eyes, golden brown, which is hard to miss, considering how close they are to his.

He starts to sit up, and Juliet helps him. Kat is ecstatic at the change in latitudes and gives him smelly bone-breath kisses until he puts an arm around her neck and pulls her close. "Stop, you goose. I'm fine."

"You good to get up all the way?" Ryder asks.

"Yeah. Let me up."

She stands and brushes off her jeans, then holds out a hand.

Zack takes it and gets up cautiously. He hasn't fainted since his first summer in the Army, after a ten-mile run through a thick, steamy South Carolina jungle forest in full gear and one-hundred-plus temperatures. He felt foolish then, but not now. Now, fainting dead away seems like the only appropriate thing to do, considering. He steels himself, filled with dread and joy, emotions he hasn't felt in a very long time. He hasn't felt anything for so very long.

"Let me see her again."

Juliet hands over her phone. "You can just swipe around. There's a bunch of them."

He sits on the couch, staring, memorizing every image. The photos aren't in any order. Child Violet, teenage Violet, young child Violet, Violet skiing, messy Violet eating carrots with a spoon, Violet with a book, lifting weights, in a perfect backbend against a mountain sunset, laughing into the camera so hard and happy he can see her perfect molars.

Tears run freely down his cheeks. He looks at all the photos twice in utter silence, then sniffs hard, wipes his face with his sleeve. The idea that this is his daughter, his Violet, is both wrong and somehow exactly right. She doesn't look how he's always imagined; now he can't imagine her any other way. He knows her; his body reaches out to hers. His soul recognizes his baby girl.

The CBI agent is watching him with undisguised interest. It takes a few minutes before he feels able to put words together.

"Talk. Please."

"She's my niece."

"And you work for the CBI?"

"I'm a DNA analyst. I manage the lab."

"You found a match so soon? My God, they just swabbed me yesterday."

The pretty brows furrow. "What? Who swabbed you?"

"Nashville Homicide. They came yesterday, said they were considering reopening the case."

Ryder frowns deeper. He notices she's contemplatively petting Kat, who is practically floating on air with happiness at the female attention. Kat loves women. He can barely cross campus with her, she's in every girl's path, showing off, hoping for some flirting and rubbing from the fairer sex. Watching her with Ryder, he realizes maybe Kat's been trying to tell him something.

Ryder finally focuses back on him. "What are the odds? No, a colleague and I ran the DNA and found the match to your wife's case. We just found out about Mindy anyway, and blood doesn't lie, but when I learned about your case and saw the photographs, saw you…she looks so much like your—"

"Wife. Vivian. Yes."

"But you, too. She's a mix of you both, though she has your eyes. And of course, there's the blood."

Zack hands the phone back carefully as if it might explode when he releases it. "I think you need to start explaining what's going on, Agent Ryder."

"Juliet. Call me Juliet. And I will explain everything. I'm sorry, I'm getting ahead of myself. My sister, Lauren, adopted Mindy—your Violet—when she was very young. Days old. A doctor in Colorado put them together. The doctor was doing it all off-book, as we've found out, but my sister had no idea anything was wrong. She agreed to a closed adoption, paid a large sum of money to the doctor, and no one, not even me, knew Mindy wasn't hers. It's only just come to light for us in the past few days."

She stops and shakes her head slightly.

"Listen. None of this matters right now. We can figure all of it out later. What we have to talk about is Mindy. She's sick. Very, very ill. She needs a stem cell transplant, right away, to help her battle an aggressive form of leukemia that she's been fighting."

"Leukemia?"

"Yes. Mr. Armstrong, I know this is all quite a shock, and it sounds terrible, but I need you to give me a blood sample so I can test you against Mindy's DNA, just as a confirmation point that you're her father..."

"I am her father. You said the blood—"

"I have a mitochondrial match to her mother. I still need to run you. I mean, yes, we all know it, but there's still a protocol to follow, on the off chance Vivian had an affair... I'm sorry, but we need the tests. If you are a match, then we turn it over to Mindy's doctors to test as well. If you'll work for the stem cell—"

"A blood sample." *Stop repeating her words, you idiot. Wrap your head around all of this, and now.* He closes his eyes for a moment and takes a deep breath, the possibilities dancing so fast and hard he can't even focus.

Violet.

"Dr.... Juliet. Anything you need, you can have. But can I just go to Colorado and see her? I mean, I understand someone else has been raising her, and there are a lot of questions, and she might not for sure be mine and her parents... Jesus, I'm probably the last person they want to see. But if there's a chance, and I can help, you said there's no time to waste, right?"

Ryder's smile is almost blinding.

"Yes. We can fly back tonight if you can swing it. And my sister and brother-in-law will be thrilled. We all know what's at stake. Personal issues aside, Mindy is our priority. All of us."

"That's good to hear. Of course, I can go tonight. Right now. Though we should probably let the Nashville cops know what's going on. If they come knocking and I'm not here..."

"I can take care of all that. Why don't you pack, and I'll book us a flight back to Colorado. We'll talk to the police from the road."

Zack takes three steps and turns back. "How sick is she? Honestly?"

Juliet's brows touch again briefly, and she looks young and scared again. "Very. The transplant is the only chance Mindy has now. We only found out about the cancer a few weeks ago. She wrecked in the trials and broke her leg. It was a fluke. A lucky fluke."

"The trials?"

Juliet smiles, and her face shifts, at once warm and genuine, no longer scared. "Mindy is a world-class downhill skier. We're talking World Cup, Olympic level. She has a spot on the US ski team if she can beat this."

"You're sure she's ours? Neither Vivian nor I were terribly athletic. Healthy, but not competitive."

"Pretty sure," she says, with a small laugh. "Go pack."

41

Zack moves as if underwater, in a dream state. Underwear folded—*She's alive.* Toothbrush in his toiletries kit—*She might die, hurry, hurry.* Leather jacket, where the hell are my gloves—*Oh, Vivian, we might have found her at last.*

He makes a quick call to his friend Blake Malone, Kat's vet, who promises to come by in a couple of hours and take Kat to his house for a few days, then sets out her food and bones on the kitchen counter. He kisses her goodbye, promises he'll see her in a few days, then nods at Ryder.

"I'm ready."

She takes in the rucksack on his shoulder. "A man after my own heart." She shoulders her own small pack. "I travel light myself. Dog's not coming?"

"She's staying. A friend will come get her."

"Too bad you don't have one of those service dog jackets for her. She could come on the plane no questions asked."

"She does have one."

Ryder doesn't miss a beat. "Then why leave her behind?"

Kat is looking at him as if she is wondering the same thing.

"I…" Why is he? Kat serves a number of purposes for him, companionship aside. He is about to step into an emotionally fraught situation with a bunch of strangers. She is good with weapons and with words. And as he's been told over and over again, she makes him strong, not weak. Lord knows he doesn't like parading into the unknown without backup.

"Mindy loves dogs," Juliet says, scratching Kat's ears.

Zack needs no more persuading. He packages up some bones and food, and ten minutes later, they are in the back of an Uber, heading to the airport, Kat's head out the window, tongue lolling.

Zack calls his friend again and cancels the dog sitting, and then calls the airline and warns them he will be bringing an emotional support dog on the plane, and yes, he has all the paperwork.

And then he calls Parks.

"I was about to give you a shout, Mr. Armstrong. Any chance I can drop by and have another quick chat?"

"Actually, no. I'm heading to the airport. I'm going to put you on Speaker. I'm in the car with a Colorado Bureau of Investigation agent named Juliet Ryder."

"What?" Parks says, but Juliet jumps right in.

"I'm Dr. Ryder, Sergeant. Not an agent. I run the forensics lab. Sorry to be stealing your guy, but we have a lead on his daughter, and we're acting quickly because of a personal situation."

The confusion is evident in Parks's tone. "You're CBI? What's your role in this investigation?"

"Not official yet, sir, though my next call is to my boss, and I know he'll be jumping on this immediately. Mindy Wright is my niece."

"The skier Mindy Wright?"

"Yes, that's her. You're familiar with her name?"

"Um… Dr. Ryder, what time does your flight take off?"

Ryder looks at him, permission seeking, and Zack shrugs. He has nothing to hide from the detectives. "We're on the 5:45 p.m. direct to Denver. Southwest."

"I'll meet you at the gate. Don't fly off before we have a chance to talk, you hear?"

"Loud and clear."

Zack clicks off the phone and buries a hand in Kat's thick fur. "What the heck was that all about?"

"It sounded to me like your sergeant wasn't surprised by our phone call."

42

Parks pulls Starr from the meeting with a gruff wave.

In the hall, she pulls on her jacket.

"Thank you for saving me. The community alliance task force meetings are possibly the slowest, longest meetings on the planet."

"They're a ten-minute briefing."

"They used to be. Now it's an hour of lectures about how Homicide is slacking off and not doing our part."

"What's our role in the community alliance exactly?"

"That's an excellent question. Last I heard, we are responsible for exactly squat outside of our monthly weekend in uniform, yet somehow, we have the most people on the ground in this." She waves a hand. "Politics and posturing. You know how it is."

"I'll talk to the Lieutenant. See if she can't put in a word. I don't need my detectives having their time wasted."

They were in the garage now, alone, shoes echoing off the concrete.

"What's up?"

"New lead on the Armstrong case. We're heading to the airport to talk to a Colorado Bureau of Investigation DNA tech, and Zack Armstrong."

Starr waits until they are in the car to speak again.

"What kind of lead, exactly?"

"You ever heard of a skier named Mindy Wright?"

"Nope."

"I spent some time last night researching her. She's the new kid on the block. Seventeen years old, total wunderkind. Instinctual downhill skier, could be one of the greats. Unfortunately, she broke her leg at an event last month, which might hurt her chances for the Olympic team. She has a spot, but if she doesn't recover…"

"That sucks."

"Did you know Gorman was a skier?"

"I did, actually. He talked about it all the time. He was excited about the trip to Colorado. Such a shame."

"He met Mindy Wright while he was out there. And then died suddenly, in a tragic accident."

"I'm not following. What does a teenage skier have to do with the Armstrong…wait, you think this is the lost kid?"

"I think she might be. She looks a lot like Vivian Armstrong. Gorman was, by all accounts, researching her heavily. And this morning, Mindy Wright's aunt showed up at Armstrong's house."

Starr puts on a pair of Ray-Bans. "This would be the fastest cold case close in Metro history. No chance we've gotten this lucky."

"I like you, Starr. You're such an optimist."

★ ★ ★

At Nashville International, they badge the Southwest counter agents and get a gate pass. TSA doesn't put up too much of a fuss, but they do a pat-down of them both, to make sure the Nashville cops are well and truly aware who holds the power in this relationship. The manager on duty escorts them to C15, where the Denver flight is getting ready to board.

Zack Armstrong sits in a chair by the window, currents of energy coming off him like a strobe light, the elegant dog at his feet, her head up, watching, a small black badge attached to her harness that reads *Service Dog* in red stitching. Simple, straightforward. If this doesn't discourage a casual approach, the very large man sitting next to the dog who is supposed to be an English professor but instead looks like a trained operative will deter even the most curious people.

Except for the pretty woman with dark blonde hair who is talking animatedly to him, a cell phone held out for Armstrong to see. He is entranced by whatever she is showing him.

With a predator's natural ability, when Parks and Starr are ten feet away, Armstrong senses them coming and stands up. The dog's ears flick forward, but she doesn't move. The young woman—and she is young, Parks realizes, younger even than Starr—stands as well, warier now. She holds out a hand.

"Dr. Juliet Ryder, CBI."

"Sergeant Bob Parks, Detective Brianna Starr, Metro Homicide."

Pleasantries exchanged, Zack takes control of the meeting.

"We don't have much time, so cards on the table. Juliet found Violet. Her name is Mindy Wright now, and she's a skier. She's also very, very ill. Leukemia, a rare form they found during the surgery on a broken leg she sustained—"

"In a crash at a World Cup event in Vail." Parks nods. "Yeah, as of yesterday, I know all about Mindy Wright. Gorman had a note in the file—it only said Colorado. But he met Mindy the week he died. He was out there on vacation, but I think he was checking into the case."

"Bad luck he died," Zack says. "Do you have anything but gut to go on here? Seems more like a coincidence."

"There is no such thing as coincidence when you're dealing with homicide. My Spidey senses are all tingly. Something feels wrong about all this. Gorman was a good detective, solid and straightforward. He didn't tell anyone about a possible lead, so far as we know. But the timing is strange. He finally finds Violet, then dies before he can tell anyone?"

"How did he die?" Armstrong asks. "I know you're protecting the family's privacy—"

"He skied off a cliff. From what I can tell, within a day of meeting Mindy at an event."

"Accidents happen all the time," Ryder says, and it's not an unfeeling statement.

"Dr. Ryder, can you fill us in? How did you come to be here?"

"Sure. My sister, Lauren, adopted Mindy when she was only days old, but we—the family—didn't know that until a couple of days ago. Lauren never told us. She met her husband, Jasper, right after Mindy's birth but didn't tell him, either. None of us knew that Mindy wasn't her biological child."

"Big shock," Starr says.

"You have no idea."

"Why did it come out now?"

"Mindy needs a stem cell transplant, and none of us are matches. I mean, not even close genetically, which was the big clue. When we found out, Lauren admitted to us Mindy was adopted, and who she got her from. We found out the doctor in Denver was illegally selling babies. How Mindy ended up in Colorado is beyond me, I haven't had a chance to investigate any further yet. I stumbled across Zack's case yesterday, saw the pictures, tested Mindy's blood against the CODIS entry for Vivian, and found the match. I hopped on a plane immediately to see if Zack would be willing to come back and be tested. He might be able to save her life."

"Why didn't you just call?" Starr asks.

"I wanted to see him in person. This is the kind of news that should be shared gently. I also needed to beg for blood to run to see if Zack is a stem cell match. Two things at play here—reuniting a family, yes, but saving a life, too."

Parks runs his thumb and forefinger over his mustache. It helps
him think. "And solving a murder. She's that ill?"

Ryder nods. "She's very sick and getting worse. That's why
we're moving so quickly. I know it's quite unorthodox, and this
is going to be a complex investigation into how Dr. Castillo,
who's dead, by the way, could have procured the infant and
passed her along." She swallows, and suddenly there are tears
in her eyes. "But this might be our only chance to save Mindy's
life. Now that Zack knows where his daughter is, it's Mindy
first, investigation second."

The gate agent calls for the passengers to line up to board.
Parks's time is running out. "Here's what we're going to do.
You handle your end, run Armstrong's blood, and see if he can
donate to your niece. Starr or myself are on a flight to Denver
tomorrow. We're happy to work with you, or any of your colleagues, but we're going to have to be a part of the investigation."

"Absolutely. More's the merrier." Ryder holds out her phone.
"Put your number in, and the minute I have a confirmation,
you'll be my second call."

"I want to be your first."

"Sorry. The first goes to Mindy's doctor, to get Zack in line
to do the transplant."

Another boarding call comes. They all look toward the gate.

"We have to go," Armstrong says, taking the dog's lead and
shouldering his backpack. "We'll be in touch, Sergeant. I promise. I want to solve Vivian's murder as much as you do."

Parks watches until they disappear into the plane, a growing
sense of unease knotting his stomach. Starr stands next to him,
on her phone, checking flights.

"There's another flight this evening, then four nonstops tomorrow. What do you want to do?"

"Honestly? I want to get on this plane so I don't lose sight of
Armstrong, and get out to Colorado immediately. But tomorrow will be soon enough. We need to get our ducks in a row

before we jet off. And who knows? The DNA match was to Vivian, right? Once they get down to it, Armstrong might not be a match."

"You don't believe that for a second, do you?"

He shakes his head. "I believe the world is an interesting place, Starr. As for the rest, we'll see."

43

THE WRIGHTS' HOUSE

Lauren is falling asleep in her living room chair when a text dings on her phone. It's Juliet, with news.

I found Armstrong. We'll be in Vail late tonight. Can we meet you at the house?

Panic surges through her like a flame. She is scared to death—everything that happens from here on out will have severe consequences.

Mindy is asleep in her room. When Lauren checked her last, she realized how diminished her little girl is, frail and pale under the bedclothes. The temporary excitement of the news—the hope—has worn her out, and Lauren thinks she's slipped even further. She has a sudden urge to paint, to capture an image of her sleeping daughter. She'll title it, *A Sleep Before Death*.

God, Lauren. Morbid much?

How is Mindy going to handle all of this? They have to tell her what's happening, they owe her that much, but if Armstrong isn't a match, then what happens?

The idea of losing her daughter kills her. It absolutely kills her.

And losing the secret she's held for so long…having it out there, her people knowing, she feels as empty as the husk of an insect, sucked dry by a spider and left to rot on a floor behind a curtain. It has to come out, she has absolutely no other choice, but her life is going to be redefined now. She is no longer simply Lauren Wright, Mindy's mother, Jasper's wife, Juliet's sister. Now she is a woman who held back the truth. A woman with secrets. A woman who lied.

From the beginning, when she made the decision to bring Mindy home, Lauren knew there could come a time when people would find out her baby was adopted. She is lucky, in a way. Her family cares so much they've forgiven her. Haven't they? Or are they simply postponing her punishment until they see the outcome? Have her actions, her denials and secrets, cost the life of her child?

She holds no illusions. If Mindy dies, none of Lauren's actions will matter. But if Mindy lives, there is a small chance at redemption.

Another text from Juliet.

Hello?

Lauren writes back immediately.

Sorry, I was checking Mindy. That's incredible news. How quickly can you test him?

I'll stop by Cameron's and do a draw, get it into the system immediately. If it's a match, I'm sure Oliver will want to run his tests first thing. We should know by early morning.

A small gasp, she can't help it. So soon? Is that even possible?

Us science types can do amazing things if properly motivated. Just tell Mindy to hang in there.

Lauren chews her lip for a moment. Is it him, J? You can tell me.

There is a slight delay, the three dots refreshing and refreshing as if Juliet is typing a huge, long reply, until finally, only three words appear on the screen.

Without a doubt.

And then,

I know we have to have proof, but it's him. He looks just like her. She looks like him. Now we have to cross our fingers he's a close enough match for the stem cells.

I'm praying you're right.

The Nashville homicide folks were very cool. They will be heading the investigation, or a large part of it since the case originates in their jurisdiction. We'll be working closely with them.

Investigation?

Into how Dr. Castillo got Mindy in the first place. Remember, a woman was murdered. We'll have to find out what happened. But don't worry. None of that will affect Mindy. Did you tell Dr. Oliver what I was doing?

"Mom?"

Gotta go, Mindy's calling. Fly safe.

She stashes her phone in her right back pocket and hurries down the hall to Mindy's room.

"You okay, sweetie? What's wrong?"

Mindy is holding an arm across her stomach. So small, suddenly, so wasted. She looks about eight, her eyes huge in her face, her bald head shiny under the light. "I don't feel so good."

"Your tummy hurts? What do you want—ginger ale?"

"Yeah."

"Hang on, honey. I'll go get some."

Lauren's heart hurts. Her Mindy is morphing into another child, another soul. Competitive Mindy hated to ask for anything. She hit her self-reliance stage early, and never grew out of it. Until now. Lauren worries for a moment that she is giving up, that she's resigned herself, then decides no, the treatment protocol so close to a transplant is especially awful and the antiemetic needs to be adjusted. No going to the dark side, she promises herself. Not when hope incarnate is on a plane west.

She grabs a can from the refrigerator, pours it over a cup of ice, tosses the empty can into the recycling bin. Finds a bendy straw, sees a Sharpie on the counter. She carefully draws on the full cup, a goofy-eyed smiley face, eyes crossed, tongue out, a perfect rendering of an emoji she's seen Mindy use to indicate she feels silly. Anything, anything, to keep her cheered up, engaged. The drop-off from yesterday's flush of excitement is frightening. She doesn't know how to manage it, outside of continuing the daily grind of smiles and assurances.

Will these assurances still be enough if Zack Armstrong isn't a match? Or will Mindy simply wither away, let herself go, stop fighting? The patient is in control of their recovery, Dr. Oliver has said repeatedly, but at what point does the pressure to control your destiny become too much, and the patient decides to give up?

Lauren witnessed the moment her mother gave up. She died quietly twelve hours later. No fanfare. No drama. Just a small life ending.

Please, God. Please. I'll do anything if you give her strength. Give her hope. Help me fix my girl.

Back in the room, Mindy sits with her trashcan in her lap.

"Did you get sick?"

"Not yet. It was close, though." A wan smile, and Lauren hands over the silly-faced cup. Mindy takes a few sips, closes her eyes, then throws it all up neatly into the can.

44

VAIL HEALTH HOSPITAL

"Gastroenteritis," the nurse proclaims, taking Mindy's blood pressure and temperature. "There's a stomach flu making the rounds on the floor. We're going to give her fluids and some stronger antiemetics, see if we can get her through it quickly. It's been a twenty-four-hour bug."

They admit her, start an IV, hang a bag of saline, and get her settled in a room. Apparently, four kids on the floor are showing symptoms too, all of whom were attended by the same overnight nurse who called in sick for her shift this evening.

Everyone assures them it will run its course, but it is a concern. A virus in the hospital is dangerous enough. One on an oncology floor can be devastating. Lauren warns Jasper not to come, and tends to Mindy herself, praying for the best, that she'll get Mindy through it okay and won't be felled herself as well.

Hours later, Lauren has just gotten Mindy into an exhausted sleep when a shadow darkens the door.

Juliet, and by her side, a tall, solidly built dark-haired man. Lauren recognizes him from the news reports. He is a little older now, lines around his eyes, some silver threading in at the temples, but not much changed otherwise over the past seventeen years. He looks very tired, very overwhelmed.

Lauren gets to her feet, surprised by how exhausted she feels—oh, no, is she coming down with it?—and gestures for them to go silently into the hall.

Juliet steps out, but Armstrong doesn't move. He stands in the doorway, staring at the child inside the room, who sleeps fitfully, tethered to an IV. The beeps and moans and chirps and calls surround him, and Lauren watches the tears well in his eyes. She swallows hard, knowing the next few days are going to be the most trying of all their lives, and calmly waits for him to pull himself together.

This is what it's like to lose a child, she thinks, and her heart surges toward him. As if she can fix this. As if she can give him back the last seventeen years.

He finally sniffs and moves slightly, and that's when she sees the dog. A dog, in the hospital? What right does he have...and then she notices the harness. A service dog. This man, this big, strapping man, needs a service dog?

Well, he was military. Perhaps something happened on one of his postings, some sort of post-traumatic stress. She's read a number of stories about PTSD in the paper recently.

Or maybe losing his wife and daughter undid him.

She points to the hall, and he nods, and their silent dance continues until they are well away from Mindy's door, the dog padding along beside them, nails clicking on the floor.

"She has the stomach flu," Lauren says finally. "She's been sick for several hours."

"She's so small," Armstrong says.

"The last few days have been hard on her. Finding out she's adopted, now getting sick on top of the treatments. She's tough, but even the strongest can be laid low. I'm Lauren Wright. Mindy's mother." She puts out a hand. There is a touch of defiance in her tone. *She's mine, even though she's yours, too.*

"I'm Zack Armstrong. This is Kat." The dog's tail thumps against his leg.

Lauren notices Juliet hanging back, almost as if she wants to see how the two will handle things. What is she expecting, Lauren to scream and yell and clutch Mindy to her breast, not let him approach for fear of her child being stolen away? This man represents their best hope of saving Mindy's life, and at this point, Lauren has abandoned all pretense, except for the tiny voice yelling *mine mine mine* in the background.

"She's a beautiful dog," Lauren says.

"She's a beautiful child," Armstrong replies, and the raw pain in his voice almost makes her flinch.

"Let's sit down." Juliet points toward the family room at the end of the hall, but Lauren demurs.

"Mindy's asleep now, but she's been vomiting for five hours straight, and I don't want to be too far away. Let's talk here if you don't mind." That last bit is directed at Armstrong, who simply nods. "When she wakes up, we can introduce you."

"Is she ready for that? Will the stress make her sicker? I don't want to harm her in any way." His voice catches, and Lauren touches his arm gently. It feels strange to touch him. He is warm and solid, and she snatches her hand back.

"Mr. Armstrong. She knows you're out there, somewhere. I think we might be past stressing her out at this point. Besides, she has your eyes. That is going to fascinate her to no end."

"Still. And please, it's just Zack."

Juliet checks her watch. "It's nearly ten. I wish Cam would call. How long is this going to take?"

They stand awkwardly for a few moments, then Lauren smiles timidly. "Do you want to hear a story about her?"

His face transforms, forbidding to eager in a split second. "I would like to hear all her stories."

"Okay. She was—is—terribly precocious. When she was five, we caught her scaling a bookshelf because she liked the cover of one of the books on the highest shelf. It was black and had stars on the spine, and she was completely fascinated. I pulled it down and handed it to her. It was one of Juliet's astronomy texts from school that she'd left behind at our house—did Juliet tell you she wanted to go into the space program?"

Zack shakes his head. "We haven't talked about much other than Mindy, Lauren."

"Well, she did. She should have been an astronaut. She missed the cut by a fraction of a point."

"Moving on," Juliet says, blushing.

"Sorry, it still upsets me that you didn't get in. Anyway, Mindy sits down on the couch with this huge book in her lap, so big it's sticking out past her knees, and starts turning the pages. She can't read well at this point, can handle some of the kid books by herself but not this. I sit down next to her, and she looks up at me and says, 'Show me the Milky Way, Mommy. I want to see the candy bars in the sky.'"

Zack smiles, and Lauren grins at him. "She was so mad when she found out that the sky didn't have chocolate in it. Milky Ways are her favorite, but she hardly ever eats them because they're not good for her. She's a health nut, it's part of her training regimen. Nothing processed, nothing that isn't natural. She's an expensive eater."

"Then we won't talk about the things she's been eating since she's been in here," Juliet says. "I will cop to handing over another box of Hot Tamales the other day."

Zack has gone oddly quiet. Juliet notices.

"What's wrong?"

He shakes himself like he's coming awake. Maybe for the first time in years, he is, she thinks.

"Oh. It's nothing. Milky Ways are my favorite candy, too. What else does she love?"

"Dogs, for one. She's going to go mad for Kat. Sunflower seeds. She eats them from the bag like a baseball player, putting in a handful and spitting out the shells. Avocados, she puts them on everything. She hates watermelon, though. We can't figure that one out."

He looks stunned. "Vivian was allergic to watermelon."

"I suppose that answers that."

"What else?"

"She writes poetry, but won't show anyone. And skiing. You should see her on the slopes. That kid and her fall line. It's incredible. It's her one true love."

"I'd like to see that. I'd like to talk to her. I...you've done such a good job with her, I can tell." His voice cracks.

"Except for this. The cancer. I don't know where it came from, or why. Does it run in your family?"

"Yes. My mother had breast cancer. She died..." His eyes are filming over with tears. "She died right before Vivian... When the baby was born."

"I'm so sorry," Lauren says. "It's hard to lose your parents."

Juliet's phone rings, startling them all.

45

Juliet sees the matching looks of hope and fear on her sister's and Zack's faces and turns her back on them to answer the phone.

"It's Cameron. I came across something you might want to hear."

"I'm all ears. Hang on." To Zack and Lauren, whose eyes are following her every move, she shakes her head. "This is business. I'll be back in a few minutes."

She returns to the call. "Talk to me, Cam. You have the results?"

"Not yet. It's running now. Here's what I called about. Castillo had a partner."

"What?"

"I managed to track down the woman your sister mentioned, Graciela Flores? She lives in Alamosa, and agreed to talk to me when I told her we were looking at all the patients Dr. Castillo had worked with, and by worked, I mean that loosely. Long story short, she told me Castillo had a partner, a man who delivered the money. It was an installment plan—you got the first $2000 up front, and the second $2000 a few weeks later, after delivery, and once the baby was placed."

"Four thousand? Lauren said she paid ten."

"Tidy profit, $6000 a kid, right?"

"Definitely. What's this partner's name?"

"Carlos Fuentes. According to the papers, he's currently doing a nickel in Englewood Federal Correctional for mail fraud."

"No kidding? That's convenient."

"Totally. Listen, Juliet. I think it's time to push this up the chain, you know?"

"I do know, and you're right. I've already spoken to the Nashville police, and they'll probably be here tomorrow. As soon as we have the results from the test, see whether Zack is enough of a match, God willing, and get the ball rolling here for the transplant, I'll turn my attention to the criminal side of this case. You can retire your investigative hat, Cam. I can't thank you enough for all your help on this."

"You'll repay me. Maybe I'll entice you away from the CBI one of these days."

"I won't say no, how's that? I'll be in touch."

She clicks off, thinking for a moment. *He's right. It's time.*

To Zack and Lauren, who are waiting impatiently, "More news, some new info on Dr. Castillo. Lauren, do you remember her having a partner named Carlos? Carlos Fuentes?"

"No, I don't. I only ever spoke with her. Who's this Carlos person?"

"Sounds like the bagman. He ran the money to the mothers she helped."

"This is all so convoluted." Lauren touches her forehead as if a small headache has started. "If it's okay with you, I'd like to go back to Mindy now. I'm feeling a bit light-headed myself. Let's hope I don't come down with this bug, too. Zack, you and Juliet are welcome to stay with us. She has a key. Why don't you go there, drop your bags, and grab some dinner? I'm sure Kat needs to be fed as well. Give us a few hours to kick this nasty bug."

"That's very kind of you, but I don't want to impose. I can get a hotel room."

"I insist. Jasper will be home soon if he's not there already.

I told him not to come here because of the bug going around. He'll get you settled in."

"Don't bother fighting her, Zack. Lauren is the consummate cruise director. I'm a little beat myself, it's been a long day, and we have no idea when Mindy might wake up. Let's get some food and rest, what do you say?"

He still doesn't move.

"I understand the urge to watch her sleep, and to be near her," Lauren says. "I understand completely. But trust me when I say you don't need your first interaction with her to be on the wrong end of a green bag. It's not pretty, and it will stress you both out. Go. I'll call if there are any changes."

Juliet tugs on Zack's arm. Kat stands up, head cocked to one side. A flow of nurses parade past, sparing them barely a glance; it is time for a shift change, she knows from experience this means all kinds of chaos while the new shift gets up to speed on the day's goings-on among their patients. Then it's meds, and vitals, and other annoyances. Even if Mindy isn't asleep, there will be a lot of interruptions.

"We're going to be in the way for a while, Zack. Let's go."

With a last glance at the sleeping form inside the white-and-yellow room, he nods.

46

THE WRIGHTS' HOUSE

Zack's first impression of the Wrights' house is *big*. They aren't hurting in the financial department. The place looks like a ski lodge or a spread from a high-end mountain house magazine. In the dark of the night, warm lights line the drive and spill from the windows. He can only imagine the view in the daylight; the ride up the mountain has several hairpin switchbacks, and he feels as if they are on top of the world. Kat leans her head on his shoulder. He feels the soft fur of her muzzle against his ear and is glad he isn't alone.

Seeing Violet—no, Mindy, he needs to get used to calling her that, because it will be hard enough for her to have all these changes, and really, the Violet he's always imagined is dead now, replaced by this unknown waif, lying in the bed, so small, so sick—he feels a natural compassion, and has shoved away the rest of his feelings. He has no idea where the next few days are going to take him, and he wants to keep himself on an even keel. As much as possible, that is. Kat serves this purpose well. Her job is to keep him from diving off the end of the ship. She can ascertain his moods, knows when the memories are overwhelming him, when he is about to fall apart.

They are good together. Kat failed out of service school for being too frisky, not serious enough, as her trainer said. The trainer in question being his old Army buddy Chad Mishin, who now runs a charity that trains animals for both retired service members and autistic and spectrum children. Zack was there for a weekend retreat with Chad and a few others from his old platoon, on the grounds of Chad's farm in Southern Kentucky, just below Bowling Green.

They were getting the tour, Chad explaining how things worked in the service world. "The dogs need to have a certain temperament. For example, see the little Malinois bitch by the fence post? She's much too silly to work for us. We need more serious dogs. Ones with a little gravitas."

Zack watched the large puppy gamboling around and felt a huge smile break out on his face. She'd found a mole and was happily digging it up, throwing it in the air, and chasing it down, but gently. Playing, not hurting.

"Looks like she's being a dog to me," he said, laughing at her antics.

"She's a big goofball, is what she is. Showing off because she knows we're watching. Too much personality can be a problem, just as too little won't work, either. You gotta have the exact right temperament to work with kids or soldiers who are hurting. We're going to list her for regular adoption. She's purebred. I can get a pretty penny for her."

"I'll take her," Zack said before the words even registered in his brain.

"You kidding?"

"I'm not. This is the most I've laughed in years. Maybe a goofball dog is just what I need."

It turned out she wasn't as much of a goofball as they all thought. Kat grew into a wonderful companion, serious when necessary, but also happy and loving and always there for Zack when he needed bolstering, or when the bad dreams got out of control. Being betrayed, shot, and left for dead in an Afghan warehouse, then finding your wife murdered on the kitchen floor and your child kidnapped did that to a man.

Since Kat was already registered as a service animal, she came with all the attendant paperwork. Zack tried to give it all back, but his friend said, "Naw, you keep it. You may want to travel with her or take her places most dogs won't be able to go. Besides, Zack, I think this is a good call. I might have suggested it myself, had I known the state of your sorry ass. You're looking kinda rough, pal."

He debated punching his friend in the nose, but instead gathered up Kat's things and drove her to his house in Nashville without a glance back. That was four years ago, and since, he's only used the *Service Dog* signage one other time until today. He is grateful as hell he has her with him now, though. He feels unsteady and off-balance, and she knows it. She nuzzles him and licks his nose, her black mask looking serious, for once. She always anticipates when he is about to go off the edge.

"Is Jasper going to have a problem with Kat?"

"Oh, no. They had a dog when Mindy was little, and when she passed away, they didn't get another because of the travel schedule. They didn't think it was fair to board a dog all the time, especially on the extended trips to Europe and Canada. Mindy begged and pleaded, but they held firm. I'm sure he'll be happy to have a dog in the house again."

She brakes in front of the garage. "Go ahead and take her out. I think Jasper is home, I saw a shadow moving in the kitchen. I'll just run in and give him a heads-up. Come on up whenever you're ready."

"Is this a very bad idea?"

"No, it's not. I promise. We're all going to be one happy family, you just watch."

A family. Is that what this is going to be?

Honestly, he hasn't thought this through at all. The shock of finding out about Violet—Mindy—God, he doesn't even know what to call her. He doesn't want to get his hopes up, but he wants this, so much, so badly, so viscerally, that he can hardly breathe.

If she is his, though, what will he do? Take her home to Nash-ville with him, like he did Kat? Move to Colorado to be with her? Let her continue living with Jasper and Lauren? Will he get custody, will they switch weekends?

Technically, legally, if she is his, what are his rights? What are theirs? And what kind of asshole is he for even thinking about all of this?

Forcing away the sudden spurt of anxiety, he guides Kat to the edge of the driveway. She happily sniffs around the rocks. There is still snowpack here from a recent storm, fresh and un-touched down the hill except for a series of black dots near the scrub oak, breaks in the snow he assumes are from deer walk-ing through. He is glad it is still too cold for snakes. Kat loves anything that moves, but snakes are a personal favorite, and he knows the poisonous ones rule these large hills.

Kat does her business, then glues herself to his side, looking up at the house as if she, too, feels like she is about to walk into a den of vipers.

A door opens, and Juliet comes out onto the front deck. He smells roasting meat, *hamburgers*, and she shouts, "What's taking so long? Come on in. Jasper knew we had to skip dinner. He threw a few burgers on the grill. Are you hungry?"

"I am," he calls, and with a deep breath, heads up the stairs to the front door.

47

Jasper Wright looks every inch the weekend lawyer, from his pressed chinos to his white button-down polo to the floppy mass of sandy hair on his head. He shakes Zack's hand with re-strained warmth, gracious of him, considering, and invites him to have a seat at the table.

"Beer? Wine? And how do you like your burger?"

"Beer's fine, thanks. Well done on the meat, please."

"Huh, that's how Mindy likes it," Juliet says. "We've been playing a strange game this evening, Jasper, matching up some of the things Zack likes to what Mindy does, too."

"Yeah? That's cool." He plunks two bottles of Heineken on the table, sits in a chair opposite Zack. Takes a pull from his beer. "This is weird for me, man, and I know it is for you, too. I've thought Mindy's biological dad was dead all these years, and Lauren never disabused me of the notion. I guess we're going to have to muddle through this together, okay?"

He clinks Zack's bottle with his own and goes to flip the burgers. Juliet beams at Jasper's back, then at Zack, tips her bottle his direction. *See?* her looks says. *One big happy hamburger-grilling monster-alpine-house-living beer-drinking family.*

Everyone is treating him like the crazy neighbor down the street, solicitous and kind to the point of stifling. He can't help but wonder, *Don't these people ever lose their tempers? Do they walk around oozing kindness from their pores to everyone they meet, strangers and friends alike? Are they really this genuine?*

He doesn't trust them, he realizes with a start. He's gone along on this far-fetched trip on the basis of a couple of photographs and some coincidences, hoping he's found his lost daughter, hoping there will be answers to the questions that haunt him. They could be anyone. This could be a massive setup. Have his long-honed instincts failed him completely? This is too much for one day. Too much.

A wave of panic passes through him, and he feels suddenly odd, light-headed and achy.

"You okay?" Juliet asks. "You must be tired. I know I am."

For a moment, he thinks he might be ill. *Have they drugged me? Was there something in the beer?*

"Bathroom?"

"Oh, sure. Down the hall and to the right. First door."

He shuts the door and runs some cold water, splashes it on his face. It makes him feel better, but he still feels ill, like something is wrong. His stomach twists. Has he caught the stomach flu from the hospital? Would it show itself so quickly? Zack isn't the get sick type; he has a strong constitution bolstered by healthy living and exercise. He can't remember the last time he's come down with something worse than a winter cold.

He can hear their voices from the kitchen, muffled, speaking low. He cracks open the door.

"—typical Lauren, right?" Juliet's voice is clearer than Jasper's.

"She's the world's softest touch." This is said with sadness and something else, a hint of love, maybe, or confusion.

"You're being a champ about all of this."

"What choice do I have? I just want Mindy well, J. I'll deal with the emotions and the hurt of Lauren's lies later. It's just..."

"What?"

"I don't know. This feels wrong. It's all happening so fast. It almost feels like Lauren led us right to Armstrong. Do you think she meant for me to find his name? If I hadn't, do you think she would have told us at all?"

"I think if Mindy got much worse, yes, she would have. I hope, at least. I can't imagine her letting Mindy decline further without doing something. Besides, I ran the blood work and found the cold case. It was going to happen regardless."

"But why didn't she tell us the truth the moment we knew Mindy needed a transplant? She had to know none of us would be a match, and we'd need to go outside."

"I asked her the same thing. She said she didn't realize how it all worked, that the science was confusing. She thought her blood would be enough."

Juliet sounds contemplative. Zack can imagine her sitting there, her head tilted to the side, tapping her fingers along the shaft of the bottle, thinking.

"She says this to her DNA tech sister? God, how naïve is she? Or is she just in denial?"

"I vote for denial. But she never was the scientific type. Even when we were kids, her head was always in the clouds." Bemusement now, and Zack thinks about what they've said, and he too finds it odd.

He also realizes he isn't going to die. The strange feeling, while not gone, hasn't worsened. Not poisoned, then, or the flu. Exceptionally tired, and overwrought, definitely. Maybe he should get out there before they think he's wandering the house, looking in drawers.

He flushes and makes some extra noise coming back down the hall, to give them a moment.

"Altitude get you?" Jasper asks. He is slicing tomatoes casually as if they haven't just been discussing life and death and lies.

"Altitude," Zack groans. "Yes, that's it exactly." He remembers now the horrible feeling of crushing panic and sick stomach he got in the Hindu Kush mountains, high above Afghanistan.

"It's been a long time since I've been up this high. I totally forgot what it felt like."

"Water and ibuprofen," Juliet says, digging in her purse. "I have some here. It will help." She hands him the pills and pours a glass of water. "Drink it all, and let's get another couple in you as fast as we can. You're dehydrated, and you'll go downhill quickly if we don't get plenty of water and painkillers in you."

He lets her mother him, lets her cluck and fuss. It feels nice to have someone care, even if that someone is tangentially attached to the worst memories of his life.

"Better get Kat some extra water, too," Jasper says, pulling down a large stainless steel bowl. "It can affect animals just like it does people. And let's get some food in you. Burgers are ready, fries are done. You might not want to finish that beer."

"Thank you," Zack says. "You're right, I think I'll stick with the water. I feel like a total wuss."

"Don't. I've seen people laid low by altitude sickness so badly they had to be hospitalized. You'd be shocked, at the competitions, half the treatments the paramedics do are for altitude issues. No different than heatstroke at a hot beach."

"You're both very kind. I'm so glad Vi—Mindy has you."

Jasper stops. "What did you start to call her?"

"Sorry, I'm trying to reframe her name in my head, it's not easy. Violet. That was supposed to be her name."

"Violet." Jasper's face grows utterly blank, closed, but he watches Zack with a new appreciation as if the whole thing has just clicked. "It's a pretty name. I wonder what she'll think about it?"

Juliet puts the food on the table as if nothing's happened. "Dig in."

Jasper is still watching him closely, as if he might explode at any minute. The reality is sinking in, he guesses, by the way Jasper is now fidgeting with a spatula. Zack's lost daughter, lost life, lost possibilities. A girl named Violet, now known as Mindy. That Zack's little girl is *their* little girl.

"After we eat, I'll show you her room, if you'd like."

Zack meets Jasper's eyes. They are a shockingly light blue, he didn't notice before, and veiled, as if he is forcing himself to be kind, to be open, while inside, he is slowly dying. *He's losing his whole family, just like you did.* The realization hurts.

"I'd like that very much."

48

Mindy's room is not what he expects from a teenage girl. It is immaculate, sparse. There is a small statue of the Buddha in the corner, sitting on a short wooden table, with a bronze gong and a few sticks of Nag Champa incense, a yoga mat unfurled. The walls are a warm green, like the forest outside, and the dark wood floors are unadorned except for a white shag rug and the mat. A desk completes the space, with bookshelves above, books alphabetically ordered. Mostly fiction, he notices, a pleasant flush going through him. It looks like a yoga studio, like a designer's room.

"Like us, she has a very minimalist aesthetic," Jasper says. "I know it's somewhat odd, but she has never been attached to things like other kids. Over the years, she's given most of her stuff away, clothes to Goodwill, toys to Toys for Tots. She always asks us to make donations instead of giving her gifts on her birthday and Christmas. Very altruistic. Except for her ski equipment, which has its own room downstairs. That, she insists on the top of the line, though now that she's so successful, the manufacturers are breaking down our doors to sponsor her."

Juliet is standing in the doorway, watching Zack with a small smile on her face. "Weird, huh? My room was always completely torn apart, books and clothes everywhere, posters stuck all over the walls. But Lauren's was perfect, all the time. Bed made, clothes in the hamper, nothing lying around. She was my mother's dream child, completely OCD, while I was always the mess. Mindy takes after Lauren in a lot of ways. She has a little OCD, too. It's part of what keeps her focused on the prize. She just doesn't bother with the extraneous stuff."

Zack looks at the iMac computer on the perfectly neat desk, a small notebook next to it. "Where does she go to school?"

"Lauren homeschools her, for the most part," Jasper says. "For a while, we had her in a program that allowed her to ski all winter and do school in the summer, but when she got onto the national circuit, it was just easier to do it ourselves. She loves school, loves to read. She'll graduate at the end of the summer. College isn't really in the cards right now, she's…well, we have a lot of hurdles to overcome before we look into the future." He glances at his watch. "It's late. You have to be tired. Why don't we show you to your room and you can get some rest."

They are halfway down the hall when Juliet's phone rings. She listens for a minute, eyes darting over to Jasper, then to Zack, and then thanks the person and hangs up.

The men watch her. Her face is unreadable. Finally, she speaks, a small catch in her throat.

"Well, we have one hundred percent confirmation. Zack, you are Mindy's biological father."

Jasper looks at his watch again, lips thin, his face suddenly pale. Zack barely notices. He stands in shock for a few moments, trying to wrap his head around what his heart hasn't let him fully experience. His girl. He's found his girl. This is real. It's happening. He starts to smile.

"My God. I didn't even want to hope, I mean, I didn't think I'd ever find her. I don't know, what do we… God." He has no words for the emotions he is having. He looks at Jasper, who is not looking joyful. "I'm sorry."

"Don't apologize. This situation isn't of either of our making."

"You're her father as much as I am, Jasper. Lauren is her

mother as much as Vivian was. Don't think I'm not aware of this. It's hard for all of us, but we'll figure it out."

Jasper claps him on the shoulder but doesn't say anything. Kat wakes from her nap in front of the fire and woofs at them, as if she too is celebrating.

"We should call the Nashville cops, let them know. They'll want to get moving on this right away," Juliet says.

"No. We should call Lauren, tell her first." Jasper already has the phone in his hand.

Zack nods. "Yes, you're right. Lauren first. I think the cops can wait until morning."

And inside, all he can think is, *She's yours. She's yours. But who stole her away? Because whoever did killed Vivian.*

49

VAIL HEALTH HOSPITAL

Lauren hangs up the phone and stares out into the night.

She should be ecstatic. There is a good chance Zack will be enough of a match that they can at least do an initial stem cell transplant. Maybe he'll even be a perfect match, and Mindy will go into remission. This is the best news they've had in weeks.

But the pervasive dread stalking her edges closer, and she shivers in fear.

Mindy is, thankfully, still asleep. It seems the worst of the flu bug has passed and she is going to be okay. They need her as healthy and strong as possible before the transplant, because it's going to be hell on her. Isolation, heavy chemo to kill her immune system, then the transfusion itself, almost an afterthought, strange blood snaking into her body, into her very essence, possibly making her whole.

She dials Dr. Oliver's line without bothering to glance at the time. She knows it's late, but she also knows this is news he'll want to hear as quickly as possible.

He answers right away, knowing she'd only call him if there is an emergency. She's been very careful not to abuse the privilege of having his personal phone number.

"Lauren? Is everything okay with Mindy? I know she caught the gastro floating around, but I thought she was improving."

"She's been feeling badly, but I think we're past the worst of it. That's not what I'm calling about. I'm sorry to bother you so late, but I wanted to let you know right away. We've found Mindy's biological father."

His intake of breath is gratifying. "How'd you find him?"

"My sister ran a DNA search and discovered his wife in the system. It's a long story, but he's here, in Colorado. At my house, actually."

"Okay then. I'll have to send out my own tests, of course, and see if the cellular match will work, but this could be very good news, Lauren. Don't get your hopes up too high, though. Often siblings are a better match than parents. Does he have any other children we can test?"

"Not that I'm aware of. It's a rather...difficult situation, Dr. Oliver." She blows out a deep breath. "It seems the doctor who helped me adopt Mindy did so illegally, and Mindy was stolen from this couple. The mother was murdered. It's terrible, and we're all very upset to learn that we're going to be involved in a scandal, but right now, all of us are focused on the next steps for healing Mindy."

He whistles, long and low. "Goodness. Well, I'm sure we'll have time to discuss everything in detail tomorrow. I'll get on the phone right now, and we'll be ready to do the testing first thing in the morning. Can you have her father—biological father—at the hospital at 5:00 a.m.?"

"Of course. See you then."

"Lauren?"

"Yes?"

"This really is good news."

"I know it is. I'm just trying to temper my hopes."

"Understandable. Get some rest."

He clicks off and she shoves the phone in her back pocket, and thinks back to that first night, seventeen years ago, when she brought Mindy home.

Frantic. *That is the only word for this feeling. The baby won't stop screaming, no matter what she does. She gives it her breast, though she knows there will be no sustenance, but hopes the child's basic instincts will take over and then Lauren will slip the nipple of the bottle in her mouth, too. It doesn't work. She warms a fresh bottle, changes another diaper—there's been nothing but urine since she brought her home, but she doesn't know how much the baby should go, considering she hasn't eaten yet. Lauren walks and joggles and swaddles and sings, and still the child cries, pitifully, turning her insides out, and making Lauren's ears ring.*

"Shhh, baby, shhh. It's okay, Mommy is here."

Of course, Mommy isn't here, but Lauren can't think of that now, can't think of anything but the crying, the crying, the crying.

Lauren remembers these first few nights with such clarity: the fear, the sorrow, the knowledge her life will never be the same, that they are all changed. The abject horror of the child's screams, Lauren knowing somehow it is her own fault for wanting the child so much, though that is silly, it's no one's fault, but she had a moment where she thought the baby blamed her and was punishing her. She understood, she did. If you were inside of one woman for nine months, and suddenly, that familiarity and warmth was gone and in its place an inexperienced stranger who can't even feed you...yes, Lauren supposed she would have screamed her head off, too.

If something goes wrong, don't go near the hospital. Take her somewhere else. A clinic. A friend.

Two days into the crying, desperate, she'd gone to the emergency room. The baby was quickly diagnosed with jaundice and put under a lamp. After the first couple of bowel movements, the frantic crying ceased, and Lauren's world righted itself.

She should have known. She should have realized something was wrong. She was too wrapped up in her guilt, in the idea that she wasn't worthy, to recognize actual distress.

She hovered over the baby until Jasper came along, and he had a way with Mindy that Lauren envied. She always quieted for him, always ate for him, always napped for him. Their date nights consisted of wine and pizza and a movie from Blockbuster so they could be close if Mindy woke and needed them.

Lauren fell in love with Jasper, without a doubt, but that was after, when she realized she and Mindy couldn't function without him. Truly, love was a bonus on the back end of things. Yes, he was handsome, but truthfully, Jasper wasn't really her type—Lauren always went for the bad boys, and Jasper was the preppy boy next door, a former English major and active tennis player, with his floppy hair and crooked smile and law degree.

They met at the laundromat, him washing an oversized comforter, Lauren scrambling to get the baby's clothes clean and folded while she napped; the warm whirring of the machines always lulled her to sleep. Of course, some idiot came in with a boom box and the deep bass rumble woke Mindy, and she'd started to cry, and the cute guy next to her had offered to hold her while Lauren pulled her clothes out of the dryer, and the next thing she knew, they were eating at the pizza place next door, and she realized he'd been holding Mindy the whole time. When he asked her for her phone number, she felt something akin to relief, that maybe she didn't have to do this all by herself.

She'd been so young, so naïve. So lucky. He could have kidnapped the baby, stolen her away. He could have been a killer. Though she likes to think she would have sensed evil coming off of him.

Jasper could have had anyone, but he'd chosen them, and she didn't question it, just counted herself among the luckiest women on the planet. She always thought he considered himself lucky, too.

The love came in like a wave one afternoon. She was exhausted—nothing new, everyone with a newborn is exhausted—but it was worse because Mindy had started an early tooth. She hadn't cried so long and loud since the jaundice episode, and even Jasper's magical touch couldn't ease their little girl's pain. He was carrying her around, singing softly, and had looked up with an expression of bemusement, and Lauren had smiled at him, and something inside her had clicked, like a big light switch going on, and she had a single thought, which she said aloud. "I love you."

He stopped, and smiled, and stuck a finger in Mindy's mouth. "I love you, too. Now, fetch me the whisky, will you? I think a little on her gums will help."

"We can't give the child whisky. They'll arrest us."

"Then don't tell anyone." His eyes were sparkling; she'd pleased him with her unscheduled announcement. She got the bottle of Scotch, poured out a finger, and watched him dip the tip of his thumb in and swipe it on Mindy's sore, red gums.

It worked, like everything Jasper tried with the girl.

The crying ceased, and the two of them managed to get her down for a nap, then snuck off to the bedroom themselves. After, he'd told her she was a good mother, and she'd cried a little when she said no, it was he who was the good father.

And he'd kissed her, hard, and proposed, right then, the two of them tangled in the sheets, smelling of baby spit and whisky and love, and she hadn't thought she could be happier than she was at that very moment.

50

"Mom?"

Mindy's voice pulls her from her reverie.

Her little girl's eyes are sunk into her head, but they have some sparkle back in them, thank heavens. Lauren gently caresses her cheek.

"Hi, sweetie. You're awake. You've been out for hours. How do you feel?"

"Empty. Can I have some crackers?"

"Of course. Hang on. I'll go get some."

Should she tell her? Should she?

She grabs the crackers and some fresh ginger ale and goes back to the room. Mindy has adjusted the bed so she sits up and is looking decidedly better than before.

"Did you go home?"

"No, I've been here all night. I didn't want to leave when you were feeling so awful."

"You should go, get some sleep."

"I will. Let's see if you can keep any of this down, first."

She watches her daughter nibble and sip, a brow raised, one hand on the green plastic biologicals bag—so much better than the old plastic tubs—but it is clear the worst is over. They both sigh in relief.

The urge to confess is overwhelming.

"Honey, I have some news."

"What's that?"

"We think we've found him. Your biological father." Once she starts, she can't stop. "He's here in Vail, at the house, actually, with your dad and Aunt Juliet, and Dr. Oliver is going to test him first thing in the morning, and I met him, and I think you're going to like him, he's very quiet, and your dad said he was very polite and well-mannered. Oh, and he has a dog. A big dog, really pretty, she's named Kat. Isn't that funny, a dog named Kat?"

"Mom, you're babbling."

"Oh, I am, aren't I?" Lauren pushes her hair off her face. "I'm just excited, honey, and nervous. He seems like a good man."

"He could be an ax murderer for all I care if his blood's a match to mine."

"Melinda. How could you say such a thing? And don't you dare say anything like that to him, do you understand?"

"Because his wife was murdered?"

Lauren freezes. "How did you—"

"You guys are really bad at keeping your voices down. I have my phone." She shakes it at Lauren. "I looked him up. You're right, I do look like them. It's kind of weird, knowing that someone killed her right when I was born."

"It's tragic, sweetie. Such a tragedy."

"Are the police going to come talk to me? I was a witness, right? I mean, I know I was, like, ten seconds old and all, but maybe some regression therapy, and I'll be able to remember my birth."

The little idiot grins at her impishly, and Lauren huffs out a breath and shakes her head. "You are impossible, you know that? I don't know where you hear these things."

"Daytime television, Mother dear."

Mindy puts out a hand, and Lauren catches it. "Mom. Listen. I may still be upset with you, but you will always be my mother.

No matter what. Nothing that happens will change that. I love you and Daddy."

Lauren brushes the tears from her cheeks. "Oh, my sweet girl. If only that could be the case."

Mindy seems like she wants to ask something more, but Lauren puts a finger on her daughter's lips.

"I love you, peanut. I love you very, very much."

"I love you, too." She pauses, then blurts, "Mom, do you have a friend you call V?"

And Lauren feels the world shift under her feet.

"V? As in victory? No, I don't."

Mindy nods. "Oh. Okay. Well, if I'm going to meet my biological father—what should we call him, my biodad?—I need to get cleaned up."

"Your biodad. I like it. Yes, let's get you looking pretty, sweetheart."

Lauren ignores her pounding heart, helps her daughter out of bed, to the shower.

Why would she be asking about V now? Why?

Oh, God. Mindy found the letters.

51

August 1994

Dear Liesel,

My last few letters have come back unopened with a stamp that says Return to Sender. I suppose that means you've moved. Moved away, moved on. I know your mother is keeping you from me, the bitch. If I ever see her, I will do bad things to her. But not to you. Never to you. I miss you muchly, Liesel. Please write.

Love,

V

September 1994

Fuck you, Liesel. I can't believe you've abandoned me here like this. Stupid bitch. I'm mailing this even though I know you won't get it. That's Einstein's theory of crazy, right? Doing the same thing over and over expecting a different outcome? Next letter I get from you, I'll return to sender. How's that sound?

January 1995

My sweet V,

It's been so long since I heard from you, I figure you must be mad at me. Or maybe you've moved on from the hospital. I hope so. You don't need to be.

there, V. You are so strong. If that's not the case, I'm sorry for whatever I said to upset you, and I'm sorry I couldn't come visit you before I moved.

I love my new home, and my new school. The view of the mountains is incredible, and so far, the students are very nice. Mother likes her new job. We left behind most of our furniture~it increased the value of the house, Mother said, so we have all new things, and I talked her into a big queen bed for my room, which has been very nice to test out with my new boyfriend. He likes my tattoo, too.

I think of you often. I hope you write me back.

Love,

Liesel

March 1995

Dear Liesel,

I was hoping to send better news, but I am back in the hospital. I've done a six-month voluntary. And the answer to your question is yes, I did try again, and yes, I failed, and yes, Dr. Freakazoid and Ratchet and the chattering whack-jobs are still here. Nothing has changed. Nothing ever changes. It's the same bleak-as-shit hole in the ground smelly shitty nasty ward.

Don't you wish you were here?

I know you're disappointed in me. I'm sorry.

Love,

V

April 1995

Dear V,

I just received your letter, and I am so sorry to hear you're back in. But, V, I could never be disappointed in you. I'm disappointed for you, of course, because I know how much you hate it in there. I completely understand. But remember, V, there is no shame in getting help. You deserve to find happiness, to have a life filled with joy. If being in the ward, being counseled by Freakazoid and Ratchet, eating healthy food~okay, stop laughing, I know we can't exactly call mystery meat healthy, but it is regular food. You've always been too skinny. If these things will help you get better, that's a good thing, right?

Seriously, take their advice, and let them help you. I'm pulling for you from afar! Hang in there~ha ha, some gallows humor for you~ Don't you dare!

Love,

Liesel

52

NASHVILLE, TENNESSEE

It's late, second shift is well-underway, the detectives in the bullpen loud and raucous, waiting to be called out to a crime scene. Parks locks himself in the conference room and pulls the Armstrong files from their corrugated boxes. He needs to look deeper into the murder and kidnapping, get completely up to speed. He set Starr the task of coordinating with the CBI tech; she is more than capable of getting them organized and ready for the current investigation. The two of them are heading to Colorado tomorrow afternoon. Just enough time for him to get his head into this case.

Earlier, he'd swung by Gorman's house, and Andrea allowed him to take Gorman's personal files on the case with him. He hopes a deeper dive will reveal something he missed the first time around.

Parks knows there has to be a reason Gorman went to Colorado in the first place. It had to be more than a hunch that the young skier he was such a fan of looks like his cold-case victims. That is a leap even Parks has a hard time buying.

He starts at the beginning again, pulling out Gorman's full facsimile of the original murder book, with duplicates of all the crime scene photos and Vivian Armstrong's autopsy photos.

The facts are straightforward and somewhat lacking. Vivian Armstrong had the child two weeks early, at home, with a midwife from the University Hospital midwife program in attendance, called late in the labor process. The delivery was un-eventful and relatively quick and, according to the midwife, Vivian was in fine spirits when she left. She worried about leaving the young mother alone, offered to call her husband, but Vivian insisted she wanted private time to bond with the baby and promised to be at her follow-up appointment the next day.

The call to 911 came from the husband. He returned to find the front door unlocked and Vivian Armstrong on the kitchen floor. She'd been dead for at least a day, maybe more. The baby was nowhere to be found.

A large kitchen knife was found on the floor next to the deceased woman, the only fingerprints smudged, though one was lifted that belonged to Vivian Armstrong herself—nothing surprising there, it was her kitchen, and clearly, her knife.

No forced entry. No video of the assailant entering or exiting the house. The suspect was a ghost.

Or the husband.

Parks shakes his head as he reads the reports. Zachary Armstrong was in Alabama when his wife was murdered, standing over the grave of his mother. There were three messages from him on the answering machine—all increasingly worried. He didn't commit the act, on that, most of the professionals agree. Oh, there are a few speculative reports that the husband drove home, murdered his wife, then drove back for the funeral, but Gorman's assessment: Armstrong was telling the truth. He passed a lie detector, was open and forthright, and was, by all accounts, utterly devastated. There were no strange money trails in his bank records, no indications he hired someone to kill his wife, but the forensic accountant couldn't say that cash hadn't been saved up over time and all the contacts made in person.

Parks reads the heavily redacted military reports on Armstrong's shooting, gathering as much of the story as he can, gleaning from between the lines. Armstrong was meeting an informant who'd been providing solid information to him for several months. Without warning, instead of giving over the latest dispatches, the informant shot him. Armstrong was wearing Kevlar, but the shot came from the side, ricocheted inside the vest, and damn near killed him.

The Army patched up Armstrong and sent him home. A month later, Armstrong's wife was killed. Had she been targeted to send a message? Something about this theory feels wrong. There is no evidence at all to point to a foreign national as a suspect. Nothing. No demands, no calls, nothing to suggest the child was kidnapped by someone who was planning revenge on the Armstrongs. The case went dead as a doornail within a few weeks, as soon as Vivian Armstrong's tox screen came back negative for illegal substances.

He flips through the correspondence between husband and wife. There isn't much—email and a few physical letters—but what is there is kind and loving, excitement about the new baby, lovey-dovey words. Nothing at all to set off alarm bells. The Armstrongs missed each other, cared for each other. Armstrong didn't discuss his work, didn't even release where he was. And she didn't ask.

Typical military household, as far as Parks knows.

The autopsy report is much more interesting.

Vivian Armstrong died from heart failure caused by exsanguination from two stab wounds—one to her right cervical carotid artery, the other to her abdominal aorta. The neck wound was a three-inch slice, just deep enough to nick the artery; the stomach a full-on stab, the knife going so deep that it scraped the L3 vertebrae. It was then pulled straight out and tossed to the floor next to her. Based on the wound trajectory, the suspect was most likely right-handed. The victim bled out within four or five minutes. There was no indication Vivian Armstrong struggled or tried to drag herself to safety; the blood pool beneath her was undisturbed. The knife was identified as a Wüsthof Classic eight-inch chef's knife, part of a set. The slot for the knife was empty in the butcher block. There was a handwritten note from Gorman—*Confirmed set purchased in Germany at the PX and brought home by husband as gift.*

Everything he sees points to a crime of convenience. Possibly even of passion. The suspect used the closest available weapon instead of bringing their own to the scene.

He flips the pages until he gets to the dictated autopsy report. There is an amendment to the original, and Gorman has highlighted a line. Parks reads it, confused. This is something he hasn't known or seen before. He can't remember anyone ever talking about it—granted, he didn't work the original case, so there was no reason for him to know. But Gorman felt it important enough to highlight. After the fact?

Expanded toxicology panel finds nortriptyline in high doses. Liver test confirms.

Nortriptyline?

He looks it up. It's listed as a tricyclic antidepressant marketed under the brand name Pamelor. He digs a little deeper, curious. Pregnancy class C.

Vivian Armstrong had been taking an antidepression medication while pregnant. Interesting, but hardly earth-shattering. So why is it highlighted?

Parks speeds through the rest of the file, searching for any other information. He doesn't find anything, and this is odd. There should be something from the prescribing doctor, at the very least. But Gorman from the grave has nothing more to offer. There are no doctor's reports, no follow-ups, no more notes. And the evidence list does not show the bottle of medication.

There is a simple explanation—concerned with the immediate problem of finding the child, and the delay in the final toxicology report, a mental illness diagnosis wasn't followed up on. If they missed this, what else did they miss?

Gorman wasn't a flighty cop. If he's marked this, he must

have been concerned. It's worth looking into. In Parks's experience, psychiatrists keep excellent records.

Where would a military wife go for mental health treatment?

He looks at his watch. He's been at it all night, it's nearly 7:00 a.m. Starr should be in. He calls her cell, and she answers on the first ring.

"Are you here?"

"If by here you mean the squad, yes."

"Good. I'm in the conference room."

A few minutes later, she knocks and enters, a notebook in one hand and an apple in the other. "You've been here all night?"

He rubs his face with both hands. "Yeah. Listen, I just saw something in the autopsy report about Vivian Armstrong being treated for depression. Did anyone ever follow up on that?"

"I did see something, hold on." She disappears, then comes back with a red folder and a steaming cup of coffee, which she sets in front of him.

"Ah, thank you." He takes a deep gulp.

Starr flips open the folder. "Yes, she had an antidepressant in her system, but there's no record of her receiving treatment, no doctor's bills or anything, so no way to know who was treating her. I was surprised. Do you think this is something?"

"Anything that wasn't looked at back then is fair game for us now. Gorman highlighted it in his personal file. We should track it down before we leave."

"Flights a few hours off. You have time to follow this trail. I'm putting together all the files for the Colorado cops. Shout if you need me to run anything down for you."

"Copy that. Thanks, Breezy."

He picks up his phone. Vivian Armstrong lived near Vanderbilt— the closest ER to their house. Might as well start there.

53

THE WRIGHTS' HOUSE

Zack falls asleep without issue after their late dinner, a result of the altitude, he supposes, and is awakened, surprisingly refreshed, at 4:45 in the morning, by Juliet, who is shaking his shoulder.

"Hey, I'm sorry to wake you, but the doctors want to do some testing as soon as possible. Can you get up and come with me?"

"Sure." He's awake instantly. He's always been a morning person, likes the quiet before the dawn when nothing stirs but his memories. He jumps in the shower, dresses, and is downstairs in the kitchen five minutes later. Jasper is there making coffee, and Juliet is feeding Kat, who is gazing at this new goddess adoringly for both taking her for an early morning constitutional and giving her food without asking.

"Traitor," Zack says to her, rubbing her ears while she scarfs down her kibble.

"Did you sleep?" Jasper asks. He looks like he was up all night, his face puffy and hair standing up in the back.

"I did, thank you. Passed out is more like it. Yesterday was a bit exhausting." He continues petting Kat. "Do you have a good place for me to leave her? She's used to sleeping on the couch at my place, but I don't want her on your good furniture."

Juliet shakes her head. "No, bring her. Today is going to be rough for everyone, and she'll be a good buffer. Besides, Mindy won't forgive you if you show up without her. She loves dogs, and Lauren's already told her all about Kat."

"Right. Good plan."

"We should get going. Here's a thermos." Jasper hands him the coffee. He is quieter this morning, thoughtful. *So much at stake*, Zack thinks. *All of our lives are going to change today.*

Zack snaps on Kat's harness, and they troop to the garage. Jasper gets into a silver Audi Q7, and Juliet leads Zack and Kat to her black Xterra. Kat clambers in the back and settles right down. Zack climbs in the front next to Juliet, cracks open the thermos and takes a deep drink.

"Jasper makes great coffee, doesn't he? I wish he'd show up at my place every morning, carafe in hand."

"He does." He takes another sip. "You're all so very kind. I appreciate it."

"I don't know about that. Mindy has been all of our priority for a long time, and especially now. Trust me, once we know how things are going to shake out with her, there will be plenty of drama."

"I can do without the drama. I've had more than enough to last two lifetimes."

"I don't know if the media will allow that to happen, Zack. This is going to be a huge story once it gets out."

"I'd rather it not be. I'm a private person, and with my past… let's just try to keep things between us for now, okay?"

"I'm fine with that, and God knows Lauren will be, too, but the cops might have another plan. They're catching a flight this afternoon. I've set up an appointment for them later today with my people at the CBI. Now that Mindy's been found, they're going to have to look hard at Castillo and her partner, Fuentes, to see how they managed to get her here. Did they have people across the country supplying babies? Was Vivian a casualty of something bigger? We're going to have to look into everything, Zack. I'm sorry."

"I want her murder solved as much as everyone else, trust me. But it's been seventeen years. I don't see how a few more days will hurt. At least give Mindy and me some time to talk, to get to know each other a little, hopefully."

"That's understandable, and I'll do my best, okay? You'll be happy to know Lauren told her last night that you were going to be here today. She's excited to meet you."

"And I am excited to meet her, too. It feels very strange saying that, I mean that I'm only now meeting my own flesh and blood."

He stares out the window as they wind down the mountain and cross under the highway into the city of Vail, then take the turn for the hospital. He is surprised by how much he likes the architecture of the small city, the stone and timber buildings, the well-placed evergreens, the high-end shops and walking-only streets. There are already a few skiers strolling around in goggles and boots with skis on their shoulders. He assumes they're gearing up for breakfast before the lifts open, eager to get a jump on the day. A few cars move slowly around the base of the slopes, but they pass through the stoplight then wind around to the hospital without too much delay, arriving at ten after five.

She turns off the engine. "First things first. Let's go talk to Dr. Oliver and get your blood work done, then Mindy should be awake and ready to talk. She's an early bird, we won't be waking her."

He feels that odd twinge, another similarity. *Like me.* Vivian was the opposite, always wanting to linger in bed, read the paper, drink some coffee. Zack had usually taken a run, showered, eaten breakfast and started a book before she even woke up.

Of course, that's when he was home.

All in all, he figures that out of two years of dating and marriage, he'd actually been with Vivian for about four months over the course of that time.

He barely knew her.

She barely knew him.

But they created a brief life together, and once she got pregnant, he planned to ask for a transfer back to base so he could be home with his family. Then she died, and the baby was gone, and he felt like he'd failed her on every level. He'd loved her. But that hadn't been enough.

And now, half of the biggest mystery of his life is about to be solved. Silently, he asks her spirit for strength.

Kat woofs from the backseat as Juliet gets out of the car. Zack doesn't move. He is suddenly terrified. He's clung to the notion of Violet being out there somewhere for so long that the immediacy of knowing she is just inside the walls in front of him makes him want to run away screaming and rush inside and never let her go all at the same time.

What if she hates him? What if she looks at him with disdain, or worse, indifference?

What if, what if, what if?

"Grow a pair," he says to himself and gets out of the truck.

54

The sense that everyone is staring makes Zack uncomfortable, but then he realizes they are looking at the dog, not him, and he relaxes a bit. The doctor, Oliver, is kind and excited, watching his nurse take Zack's blood sample then writing the label himself.

"They're going to messenger this to the lab and get the test done immediately. We'll know in an hour at most if you're enough of a match. If you are, we start the process. It's going to take a couple of days to get everything straight, get Mindy prepped, so you guys will have plenty of time to visit. We've had her on a non-myeloablative regimen, so we'd be ready the moment a donor appeared. We're going to move to an intensive myeloablative regime for the next two days, then, with any luck, transfer the stem cells." He claps a hand on Zack's shoulder. "Congratulations, sir. I don't know what else to say."

"Could you say what you just said in English, maybe?"

"We're going to nuke all the bad cells to prepare her body to receive the clean ones."

"Copy that. I guess I have a lot of catching up to do on the lingo."

"Ask Mindy. She understands everything. She's been studying exactly what happens. That kid is a seriously smart cookie."

"How do you get the stem cells?"

"We'll hook you up to a machine that pulls out your blood, captures the blood cells we need, then returns your blood to you.

The second I see these results are positive, we'll start you on a drug called Filgrastim. It pumps up your blood cells. Normally it's a five-day process, but to be frank, I don't know that we have that long, so we're going to ramp it up and make it go faster."

He pushes up his glasses. "In other words, you're going to feel like crap for a couple of days, and Mindy will, too."

"You have to make her sicker to make her better?"

"Yes. That's the problem with these treatments. But, with a specifically coded DNA match, this will go a lot smoother for her than it would from someone who's a match but completely unrelated. At least, that's my hope. I have a great partner who's been making serious strides in this field, from Boston University. He was here and laid out the entire protocol last week. It's all set and ready to go, including a specific treatment designed for Mindy's DNA so she doesn't suffer graft-versus-host disease. We have been planning for this, as you can tell. We want to give her the best possible chance to kick the cancer and go into remission from our first round."

"Graft-versus-host—that's when an organ transplant is rejected, right? It can happen to blood?"

"Yes, it can. But with this new treatment, it shouldn't be as high a risk as it might have been with an outside allogeneic donor. You being her father, your DNA is much closer."

Juliet sits outside the glass door to the lab, in the waiting room, watching intently while holding Kat. He smiles at her, gives a little wave.

"Thank you, Dr. Oliver. I appreciate you explaining things to me."

"No, thank you, Mr. Armstrong. If you can help me save my favorite patient, I'll owe you one."

They shake hands, and Zack enters the waiting room.

"All set?" Juliet asks.

Zack adjusts the bandage around his elbow. "Yeah. Good thing I don't have to do needles often. That hurt."

"You're a baby. Even Kat thinks so. I swear I saw her shaking her head at the faces you were making."

He spits out a laugh. "You are a seriously mouthy woman."

She grins, and he realizes again how young she is. "I just like to have fun. Come on. Jasper and Lauren are already in Mindy's room, waiting for us."

Trepidation building in his stomach, Zack takes a close hold of Kat's lead and lets Juliet steer him down the hallway.

She knocks on the door, and three faces turn toward them. Zack seeks Mindy's eyes first. She is staring at him, then ducks her head shyly.

Juliet nudges him, and though Lauren is pale, she nods encouragingly, so he takes a few steps into the room.

"Hey there. I'm Zack."

Mindy looks up again, and he has a moment where he quite literally feels the world turning on its axis. He's afraid for a moment he'll faint again. His daughter—*my daughter*—says, "Melinda Wright." Her voice is Vivian's, and his breath hitches in his chest.

Lauren stands, takes Jasper's arm. "We're going to grab some breakfast, let you two talk. Juliet, would you care to join us?"

"Heck no, I want to stay here and watch the fireworks."

"You're coming with," Jasper says, exasperated. "Let's go."

Zack barely hears them. Mindy rolls her eyes at Juliet, her lip quirked on the left side, and he feels something break inside him. *My God, she looks like Vivian when she does that.*

The three leave, and they are alone. Mindy doesn't wait, jumps right in.

"Can I pet your dog?"

"Absolutely. Kat?" He gestures toward the bed. The dog pads forward, then gently puts her front legs on the bed and takes a couple of sniffs. Mindy sets her hand on the dog's neck, waiting for Kat to make the next move. The dog pushes into her hand immediately.

"You're a pretty girl, aren't you?"

Kat closes her eyes in ecstasy. She loves being scratched around the neck. A low rumble comes from her chest.

"Good grief, is she purring?"

"Sounds like it, doesn't it?" Zack answers, moving closer. "She rumbles like that sometimes when she's really happy. She was supposed to be a full-blown service dog for military PTSD or autistic kids, but she wasn't cut out for it, so I took her home with me. She's a goof."

"You're not a goof. You're a gorgeous girl. Look at your pretty ears."

Kat takes this as an invitation and hops up onto the bed, knocking aside the IV pole with a crash. Zack lunges for it, catches it before the whole apparatus topples.

Mindy starts to laugh and hugs the dog to her chest. "God, this is the most normal I've felt in a month."

"It's been hard on you, the treatment?"

"That, and being stuck in this stupid cast." She gestures to the leg in question, still covered by the blanket. "It's been a real bummer. I'm not used to being still. You look like you're in shape. What's your poison?"

"I run."

"Does Kat go with you?"

"Oh yes. She's a fan of the park near my house. There's a copse of woods on the far end, and she's allowed off the leash there. She tears around like a torpedo, chasing everything that moves."

"I'd like to see her run."

"We can arrange that. She's just a streak of black and tan when she gets going."

A small silence. He is trying not to stare, but Mindy is so beautiful. Under the paleness and black circles and bald head, he can see vestiges of the girl she was. *Please*, he prays to an invisible god. *Please let me have more time with her.*

He clears his throat. "You like dogs. What else do you like?"

"Skiing. Obviously. Snow makes me happy. Does it snow where you live?"

"Nashville? Not very much, though every once in a while, we get walloped. They close school if there's even a hint of snow in the forecast. Our buses just aren't equipped."

"That's ridiculous. You teach English, my dad said. Sorry, that was weird. I mean, I know you're my real dad. But it's going to take some adjusting to figure all this out, you know? And I'm… I'm sorry about Vivian. My mother."

He swallows hard, takes her hand.

"I don't want you to waste any energy worrying about this, Mindy. You have a battle ahead, and I want you to focus on that. We can sort out who I am to you after you kick the cancer's ass, okay?"

She smiles wider this time. "Oh, thank God. Mom and Dad, sorry, and even Juliet, they can't bring themselves to talk about it. Like uttering the words will make something happen. Yes, it's going to be a nasty few days, but you're here now, and it's all going to be okay. I can feel it. I'm intuitive that way."

"I like your attitude. Yes, I teach English. I like to help young men and women find their voices. I've had a couple of students go on to become novelists. It's very gratifying."

"Do you like to read? 'Cause that's the other thing I love."

"I do. I saw your bookshelves. You have good taste."

The smile is so genuine, so open, that he can't help himself. "Can I hug you?" he blurts.

She thinks about it for a second, her gnomish forehead wrinkling. "Yes. I think that would be appropriate, considering you've been looking for me for almost eighteen years. Just watch the IV, it gets in the way. Mom's always yanking the tubing out of the machine by accident."

He carefully sits on the edge of the bed, reaches over Kat, and gathers Mindy in his arms. Despite her height, she is so tiny, and smells like the hospital, and medicine, and oddly enough, the flowery scent he often catches in the woods behind his house. The feelings he has are utterly confusing, strong and intense. He wants to cry and shout for joy at the same time. Her arms slip around his neck, thin but strong, and he closes his eyes and finally, finally, begins to weep.

She holds him, patting him on the back and whispering, not at all put out by the large grown man weeping into her shoulder. He finally calms himself, and pulls back, wiping his eyes. Kat is nestled between them, and Mindy's eyes are shining, too.

"I'm so sorry you've had to go through all of this," she says. "It must be incredibly difficult to find me after all these years and to have lost your wife, too. I really am sorry. I would have liked to meet her."

He watches her for a moment, those eyes of his looking back, the feminine face, the chin so like Vivian's. "You're amazing, do you know that?"

The grin turns wicked. "You should see me ski."

55

Lauren stares at the small biscuit on her plate as if all the answers will come from breaking the piece of soft bread wide open. Next to her, Jasper fiddles with a straw, folding it around his finger then unrolling it, over and over. Juliet babbles, as she usually does, talking about the police investigation to come, and how she likes the detectives from Nashville, and what steps they should take next. Jasper nods and answers a few times, but Lauren doesn't hear, not really. She is consumed with thoughts of her daughter, her Mindy, upstairs, alone with the man who helped create her.

And…her daughter's innocent question that feels less and less innocent as the minutes tick by.

V.

Shit.

Mindy knows. She found the letters, and she knows.

This is all going south, she can feel it. Everything is wrong. She should be happy there is a chance for a match, a chance to save her daughter, but instead, she feels exposed. Like every bad decision she's made in her life is about to be revealed.

"Lauren, have you heard a word I said?"

Juliet is staring at her, head cocked like a dog, brows raised in question.

"Sorry, no. What was that?"

"We're going to have to get a formal statement from you

about the conversations you had with Castillo. Plus, I need to see your paperwork."

"There is no paperwork! I don't even have the birth certificate she gave me."

"Why not?"

"When Jasper adopted Mindy, we had it changed. There may be some record of that in the Colorado databases. I turned the old certificate in to them. They made me."

"Was Kyle Noonan listed on the original birth certificate as Mindy's father?"

"Of course. That was part of the fiction Castillo created, that he was the father. That's why I wanted Jasper's name on there. That asshole was never part of our lives. Thank God he died before I brought Mindy home."

"In Mexico."

"Baja. A diving accident. You already know all of this."

"I do. But once the police start asking questions, they're going to push for every detail. I'm trying to help you remember."

"Juliet, I think that's enough for now," Jasper says quietly. "It's a difficult enough day without dredging up bad memories from the past. Can we give it a rest, and eat our breakfast, please?"

"I'm sorry. I'm getting ahead of myself. We need to focus on Mindy and the transplant, and her reaction to Zack."

"Yes, we do, and speaking of that, I'd like to go back up now. They've been alone for nearly an hour." Lauren hears the edge in her tone, can't help it. She drops the uneaten biscuit on the tray and stands. Jasper puts down his straw and stands as well, gathering the two trays together. Juliet watches them, a small frown on her face.

"Are you coming?" Lauren asks.

"I'll be there in a minute. I need to make a couple of phone calls."

Lauren puts her hand on her sister's shoulder. "We'll see you up there. And, Juliet, I do appreciate you finding Zack. I do. It's just hard to know things will never be the same again."

* * *

They are laughing. Lauren can hear them from three doors away, both of them cawing, their laughs weirdly similar, brash and unforced. Jasper hears it too, and she sees his brow furrow. She stops and pulls him to her. "I'm so sorry," she whispers into his chest. "This was never supposed to happen."

He lets her hug him, though she notices he doesn't hug her back. Oh, he puts his arms around her and rests his chin on her head, but that's it, no squeezing, no holding on for dear life, like she's doing. It is a polite hug, nothing more.

"I know, Lauren. This is hard on all of us, so don't try to corner the market on feeling bad, okay?"

She pulls back. "Wow. That's awfully harsh."

"I'm not in a forgiving mood."

"Don't take it out on me. I'm trying to hold this family together."

"Our lives have been turned upside down, Lauren, all because you chose to hide the truth from me. I'm not feeling charitable about it. Sue me."

"Sue you? What sort of flippant remark is that?"

"The kind you get for lying about things for so long. You don't seem to understand how this is going to affect us. How the police investigation is going to tear our lives apart, how the media are going to want to interview us. We're not just the parents of a missing child. Her mother was murdered. Mindy doesn't even belong to us. Technically, we have no legal rights to her. Did you ever stop to think of that?"

"We don't know that, we don't know—"

"I've done some research. Zack can walk out of here with her today, and a judge will take his side. It will be like our family, and the past seventeen years, never existed. Until they start investigating us for her kidnapping. You've read the reports on this. You know what happened to his wife. You are the one who got us into this, Lauren. I don't know how you're going to get us out of it, so I'm going to have to find a path for us. This is hard enough on me without you being temperamental, so please just knock it off."

"*I'm* being temperamental? *Me?*"

"Yes, *you!*" They are yelling at each other now. Nurses are turning; the hallways are silent.

"You're being a complete and total ass, Jasper Wright. I can't believe you'd say that to me. All I've done is try to make things easier on our little girl, and you say I'm being a jerk? Go, just go. I don't want to see you anymore."

Zack is standing in the doorway now. Jasper sees him, gives his wife a *satisfied now?* look, then storms off. Juliet comes out of the elevator, and he brushes past her like a bullet.

Lauren fights back the tears. "I'm so sorry," she says to the nearest nurse. "We don't mean to disturb everyone. The pressure… it's getting to us both."

It is Zack who comes to her side and puts his arm around her. "Come with me," he says quietly and leads her down the hall to the private room, right past Juliet, who looks at them both in astonishment.

56

Inside the quiet room, Lauren sags against Zack and starts to cry in earnest. He holds her, lets her get it out. It feels like the kindest thing anyone has done for her in weeks, and it makes the tears come anew until she is sobbing.

After a while, she realizes he is patting her back, murmuring to her as if she were a child who's had a nightmare. She is having a nightmare. Her life has turned into one big, huge fucking nightmare.

"Hey, it's okay. You poor thing, you're worn out, aren't you? You've gotten no sleep. Mindy told me how you've been nursing her practically full-time since the accident. Why don't you go home, Lauren? Get some decent rest."

She pulls away from him stiffly. "Why, because you're here now? You're riding in on your white stallion to save us all?"

"I'm going to try," he says, and the quiet strength of it makes her feel even worse. Zack is a victim here, just as she is.

She doesn't want this man to be so solicitous. He isn't supposed to be the one comforting her, damn it.

But here he is, big and solid and concerned, where her own husband has stormed off. She and Jasper were overdue for the fight. Jasper has been ridiculously patient, and she's taken advantage of that, kicking the can down the road so she won't have to deal with the bad feelings, the hurt and betrayal. Having Zack here so quickly messed with everything, in ways no one can truly understand. But she needs everyone on her side. She needs her team together if they are going to face down a police investigation and a stem cell transplant at the same time.

She wipes her eyes and pushes her hair off her face.

"I'm sorry. You're right, I'm overtired and angry and upset. I'm going to go home and rest, like you said. That's a good idea. Thank you, Zack."

"You bet. Have a good nap."

She ignores Juliet, who is standing in the hall frowning at her phone, and steps into Mindy's room for a second. Mindy's eyes are wide, and the dog is lying next to her, ears cocked forward.

"Everything okay with you and Dad?"

"Of course it is. Sorry about that, sweetheart. I think my nerves are a bit frayed. I'm going to go home and take a nap, talk to your dad—" she winces as she says it, she can't help it. God, she has to get it together "—and we'll be back a little later. Okay? Is Zack nice? Do you like him?"

"Yes, Mom, he is. Very nice. He's going to get me some new books. I like Kat, too." The smile is genuine now, and Lauren takes a deep breath.

"Good. I'll see you later. You hang tight. I'm so glad you're feeling better. Yesterday was rough, I know." Lauren kisses Mindy on the forehead and marches out.

Her first instinct is a drink, but that isn't going to solve anything. She gets into her car and spills her purse out onto the seat. She scrabbles through the mess, notebooks and tissues and wallet and phone. There it is, the bottle of antianxiety pills that Dr. Oliver kindly prescribed. She tosses one in her mouth, chases it with the dregs of a week-old bottle of water sitting in the car's door.

She has to think. She has to breathe. She has to look at all the angles here. She can't lose Mindy. She just can't. She knows

Jasper is right about their legal ties to Mindy—no judge in the world will take their side once the truth comes out.

She pulls out of the parking garage, not sure where she's headed, consumed by memories.

57

UNIVERSITY HOSPITAL

NASHVILLE, TENNESSEE

1993

LIESEL

Have you ever felt blood on your hands?

I don't mean this metaphorically. I mean it quite literally.

I have. It is warm. Surprisingly silky, viscous, like a good lotion. Slippery, too, if there's enough of it.

There was a time when all I wanted was the fleeting sense of pain that came from seeing my flesh part. The blood that came out was luscious and red, and as it dripped into the bath, the pain went away. My pain went away. My control returned. My soul was filled.

I know, it sounds quite wrong. No one in their right mind slices themselves open. Oh, but it feels so good. You don't know how good until you try it.

Letting the blood of another person doesn't give the same sensation. It feels and smells wrong, like danger.

★ ★ ★

My arm hurts.

The lights are so bright. I just want to crawl into a hole and die, but no one will let me. They keep up a constant patter of conversation, bland nothings meant to keep me awake and focused, while they clean and numb and stitch. It feels like hours, days, have passed before they deem me ready to talk to the resident shrink.

He looks kind. He shuts the door behind him and sits on a stool with wheeled casters for feet. He watches me carefully, then spins around in a circle. *I am whimsical*, the spin says. *I am to be trusted.*

I trust no one. If you'd experienced what I have, you wouldn't, either.

I merely blink at him, his short hair too black, his cologne too strong, his smile too wide.

"Tough nut, eh. All righty then. Here's the deal. Legally, since you tried to hurt yourself, we have to admit you to our psychiatric ward. Your mom tells me you're supposed to be going to Middle Tennessee Mental Health tomorrow, but if you want, you can stay here. At least for the week. See if you think we will work for you."

I shrug. I truly don't care what happens to me now.

He touches my wrist carefully. "Why did you do this?"

I shrug again.

"You want me to think you don't care, but I know you do. This was more than a cry for help. Trust me, I see it too much, young men and women who try to kill themselves, but they aren't entirely serious. They think they are, but something holds them back. They don't swallow enough pills, they don't cut deep enough. Thankfully, they survive, and we treat them, and they find happiness and are so grateful that they failed. You, you were serious. If your sister hadn't found you, you would be gone. I just wonder why? Why did you want to die so badly?"

I look at the floor. "Don't you know who I am?"

"Why don't you tell me?"

"Give me a break. You've seen the news. My chart. You know why."

He sits back and watches me. Finally, he speaks again, and his voice has changed.

"Listen, Liesel. You've had a rough go of it. I won't even begin to say otherwise. But trust me, you have so much to live for. You're only sixteen. There is a life out there with your name on it, waiting to be claimed. You can be who you want. Live where you want. You don't have to stay here and be the girl they talk about behind their hands. Another year and you can leave. Change your name. Go to Europe, eat chocolate every day, live on a mountaintop. Sail around the world. A year from now, you will have absolutely no limits on your life. You do not have to let this experience define you."

"I don't think I have a choice. A man is dead. A horrible, terrible, awful man." I can't help myself, I begin to cry. I've tried to stay strong, but I am so fucked.

"I can give you a choice. Will you give me a year?"

He speaks such honeyed words.

"I don't even know you."

He sticks out his hand, which I don't take. "Dr. John Freeman. I would be your therapist. I will personally work with you, design a program to get you back on your feet. And I swear to you, Liesel, I can get you through this. But you're going to have to help, too."

"Whatever."

"No, not whatever. You were only sentenced to a year of psychiatric inpatient treatment because of your actions. A year may seem like a lifetime when you're sixteen, but trust me, it's not. But here you are instead, because last night, you gave up. Will you tell me why?"

Why? For a thousand reasons, and none. I shake my head. The pain is still too intense. Words won't do it justice.

He touches my wrist again. "You have to promise me you aren't going to try this again."

My voice is so soft I can barely hear myself. "What if I can't stand it anymore? What if I can't take it? The stares, the snickers. What I did. I can't stop thinking about it. How it felt. The blood…there was something…good about it. I don't want to be here. I want to leave."

My voice is building to a wail. Tears come unbidden. I am trapped. Trapped, like a bird. In a cage. I will never fly free again.

"You can't leave, honey. It's either upstairs here, with me and some pretty interesting characters, or it's MTMHI. Those folks out there are lifers. Most are never getting out. Trust me when I say this is the better gig."

"My sentence says I have to go to that hospital."

"Let me work on it. My friend upstairs is a cool chick. She knows Judge Gilbert. We already have a call in. I swear I can help you if you let me. Help you find a reason to live."

"Do you have to use my real name?"

"We do, hon. I'm sorry."

"Okay."

After that, I don't fight them. They do their intake tests—blood, urine, weight, height. The nurse helps me dress in some shapeless cotton things, looks at me knowingly. Dr. Freeman comes back in. Now he is kind, soft-spoken.

"Liesel. Are you aware that you're pregnant?"

"Yes."

"Who's the father?"

I stare at him, defiant, until he says, "Oh," with a sad little sigh that makes me want to scream. "We'll let the judge know."

"She already does. That's why I got the sentence I did."

"We'll talk about your options tomorrow, then. Once you're settled."

At this, I laugh. "I have no options. I keep telling you this, but you won't listen."

★ ★ ★

When they take me to the psychiatric ward, I walk meekly, head down, hands clasped in front of me. The lidocaine hasn't worn off entirely, my wrist and arm are still numb, wrapped in bandages from palm to elbow.

They lead me to a private intake room. A nurse takes my vitals again, logs my weight, gives me a pill. "It will help you sleep."

I take it, though it's morning. Sleep sounds good right now. I want to sleep forever.

They walk me down the long, white hall. The room has two beds. It is empty.

They're talking, but I can't understand what they're saying.

The room is spinning, and not in a good way.

It's the pill. It makes me feel strange, disembodied, like I'm not touching my skin even though I'm inside of it.

They leave me alone. A girl comes in. She has dark hair. She is staring at me. She leaves, and I hear arguing down the hall, then she returns. She walks around me like a wolf circling prey, and I'm helpless to do anything to stop her. She snaps her fingers under my face, and I am tempted to bite them off, but I can't move. I hear her taking apart my bag, but I just stare, stare, stare out the window.

I know I need to stand up for myself. For once, I need to try to own the situation. She is waiting, I can feel it. She wants me to talk to her. So I do. I spit out the words because my tongue is numb and dry.

"Touch my things again, and I'll kill you."

"Right." The disdain in her tone pisses me off. I manage to turn and look at her, really seeing her for the first time. She is pretty. Long black hair, eyes like sapphires. There must be something in my face because she startles and backs off. Good.

I look back to the parking lot.

Welcome to the next year of your life, Liesel.

I fucking hate this.

I hate being locked in this ward.

I hate this stupid roommate. I can tell how nervous I make

her. Even now, she is staring as if she expects me to leap across the bed and rip out her throat.

I hate the people, the smells, the indignity of being here. The lidocaine is wearing off; the bandage itches, my arm feels like it's on fire.

I shouldn't be here.

I slam my fists into the bed, again, and again, the rage building inside me, boiling over into a scream, and the frightened roommate gets the nurses. They give me a stinging shot, and as I drift away again, I have one last thought before everything shatters around me.

It wasn't my fault. It wasn't my fault he died.

58

VAIL HEALTH HOSPITAL
CURRENT DAY

Mindy lowers the bed as far as it will go, scoots down, and puts her head on Kat's flank. The dog's coat is so silky. She is a great pillow. Kat is sound asleep, snoring a little, and Mindy loves the feeling of the soft fur beneath her ear rising and falling as the dog breathes.

She is supposed to be taking a nap herself, though she is wide awake; she can't bear to fall asleep anymore. It is the curse of the cancer—she is scared that every time she closes her eyes, it might be the last. After yesterday's awful stomach bug, she definitely slept for a while, so she is awake enough.

Her eyes slitted, she looks at the new presence in her life. Zack Armstrong is sitting with his hands on his knees, staring at her. He is handsome. He is nice. She feels a weird connection because she can see the places where she looks like him. Her own eyes are staring at her, which is downright creepy, but comforting, too.

She is having a hard time wrapping her head around all of this. First, she's adopted, then she's the child of a murdered woman, now her biological dad is here and might be a match to save her life.

And her mother has lied to her. Flat. Out. Lied.

V.

Mindy is not stupid. It doesn't take a brain surgeon to tie the two strange situations together. She finds letters from a teenager, the mysterious V. Then she finds out her biological mother is named Vivian. The odds that these two people are not one and the same, and are tied to her mother, are ludicrous.

It all adds up to something terrible. And her mother lied to her, she knows it.

She can't think about it anymore. It's exhausting. Mindy wants everything to be over, to be healed, out of the damn itchy cast, to ski, to feel the wind on her face and have control over her body again.

Dying in increments is a seriously lame way to go.

It is hard on the whole family, too. As angry as she is at her mom—strange how every time she thinks or says the word a new face floats into position—she also hates seeing her stressed and upset, her dad—*there it is again, this is going to be so hard!*—angry and quiet. He is the family jokester, the fun one, and Mindy doesn't think she's seen him smile without regret for weeks. Mom and Dad, Vivian and Zack. She assigns the names to the faces mentally, reminds herself who raised her. No more dual meanings with the parental names. There's Dad, and there's Biodad. Zack.

Zack is best. She likes the name. That's what she'll call him. That's what feels right.

She hears a commotion in the hallway, opens her eyes fully. Zack is looking toward the door. Dr. Oliver rushes into Mindy's room with a huge grin on his face.

"Folks, we are a go! Mr. Armstrong, you're a damn fine match to our girl, here. Let's get you both prepped and ready to start your individual treatments. I'm sorry to say, missy, that dog's not going to be allowed to visit. We're going to move you to a sterile room for the next couple of days, because the treatment you're getting is going to kill off everything, including what's left of your immune system."

"Is it going to hurt her?" Zack asks, and Mindy gives him a grin.

"It all hurts. But I'm tough. I can handle it. Can you? Aunt J said you don't like needles."

Zack shrugs. "Not my favorite thing, no, but if you're going to be all sorts of brave, I guess I don't have a choice, do I?"

She beams at him.

"You better get over the fear, Mr. Armstrong, cause it's needle city for the next couple days," Oliver says. "Where's your mom, Mindy?"

"She took off. Dad, too. Aunt J is talking to the cops that are coming to interview us. It's just me and Zack. He pulled the Mindy-sitting straw."

"Well, we're going to have to proceed without them. Let's shake a leg here. I'll find someone to take the dog."

"I'll find Juliet," Zack says. "She's nearby."

Mindy looks over at him, curious. There is something possessive about the way he says her aunt's name. Juliet is his ally; she gets that. But Juliet is also cute, and single. And Zack is handsome, and single. What a perfect match they'd make. But then, would Juliet stop being her aunt and technically become her stepmom?

Mindy lets the joy of that idea fill her. She is going to live. She just knows it.

She hugs Zack again before he leaves. She thinks she can get used to having extra parental units around, considering.

59

Juliet comes back upstairs for the dog, and Zack and Mindy are taken to their respective sterile areas. Things are moving so quickly, Zack almost doesn't know what to think. The doctors are firing questions at him about drug interactions, allergies, taking a full history while getting him ready. He passes with flying colors—he's thankfully been very healthy his whole life and taken no medications outside of some Zyrtec for seasonal allergies, which he is currently not on.

They start the IV while he looks away, thinking of his daughter's beautiful face. If she can suck it up and handle all the needles, so can he. They are doubling the normal dosages of the cell-building drug, getting it into him fast, and warn him it might feel like he has the flu, aches and pains and headaches. He already feels crappy from the altitude. He can't imagine this will make him any worse. They are going to give him the extra dosage morning and evening for two days, and then they'll take the stem cells from his blood over a marathon eight-hour session. He tries not to think about what it will be like to have an iron spike in his arm for eight hours, reminding himself again that Mindy is a trooper, and if she can handle it, so can he.

After the first round of the drug, they encourage him to lie down for a few minutes in case it makes him too dizzy to walk. Juliet is allowed in to see him.

"For a tough guy, you really are a wimp. Half the time I see you, you're horizontal on the ground."

"You want to get shot up with this blood-building crap?"

"All right, true confession time. I'm not a big fan of needles, either."

"The great and powerful Juliet, DNA expert, CBI tough girl, has a weakness?"

She cocks her head to match the angle of his and winds Kat's lead around her wrist. "Tell anyone, and I'll make sure you never see the dog again."

"Threats, is it? You just try to keep Kat away. She's Super Dog. She'll find me no matter where I am."

Juliet rights herself, grinning. "The Nashville folks are on their way. My boss is giving them a lift up the mountain. He'll help them with the case from here on out."

"You won't be working on it?"

"I'm a DNA wonk, remember? I'm not an investigator. Besides, I'm personally involved, so I have to recuse myself. Company rules. I'm part of the investigation now. It's my sister who bought a hot baby."

"How much do you know about Lauren back then? You said you just found out about Mindy yourself, along with Jasper. Why would she keep this from you in the first place? You're her sister."

Juliet looks away, out to the parking lot, and up the mountain. "We've never been close. All I know for sure is in the summer of 2000, she miscarried but let everyone believe she was still pregnant. I'm rather upset with her for not telling me. I mean, I'm her sister. If anyone should have been filled in on all of the stuff happening, it's me."

"Lauren's husband died, the doctor who helped her get Mindy died, my wife died, and the detective who was investigating all these years also died. That's a heck of a trail of bodies."

She looks suddenly horrified. "What are you saying?"

"Whoa, whoa. I'm not saying anything. I was just ruminating about how many leads we can't follow. Why? What did you think I was saying?"

She glances away. "I thought you were blaming Lauren somehow. For Vivian."

He reaches out a hand, and Juliet takes it. "Listen to me. Your sister gave my daughter a life. She and Jasper have been incredible parents to her. I wasn't implying anything, outside of the fact that the cops have their work cut out for them."

"Okay. I'm sorry for overreacting. I guess I'm as tired as everyone else."

"You have every right to be. I think I'm ready to sit up. Why don't we go grab some coffee or something? I could use some energy."

"Are you allowed to drink caffeine? Does it affect your treatment?"

"They didn't tell me I couldn't. But I'll get decaf, just in case. Fair enough?"

She helps him sit up. She smells good, something he can't identify, roses maybe. It isn't intense, just a gentle scent. But he likes it, and then he berates himself silently. He is not allowed to find other women attractive. He hasn't allowed that over the years. He has fulfilled his basic needs, but that is it. He isn't ever *attracted*. Because *attracted* means *involved*, and he is an avowed bachelor. The last woman he loved was killed because of him, and he isn't about to put another woman in that kind of danger.

Juliet knows all the shortcuts to the cafeteria. Zack and Kat follow slowly; he is already feeling a little odd from the medicine. Inside, she pays for their coffees and leads him to a seat by the window. A light snow is beginning to fall, and he looks at it with the wonder of a southerner. Kat watches intently too; she loves snow.

Juliet hasn't even noticed it until she sees him staring outside.

"What are you looking at?"

"The snow. It's pretty."

"Pretty? It's cold and wet and is going to mean a ton of accidents at the tunnel. Hopefully Parks and Woody won't be too delayed."

"I get it. You lack a sense of wonder about something you see practically daily five months out of the year. For us southerners, this is magic."

She sips her coffee and looks out the window. She leans closer to the glass, suddenly on alert. "Is that Lauren out there? What in the world is she doing?"

It is Lauren. He recognizes the fluffy blond ponytail. "I don't know. She was supposed to be going home to take a nap. It looks like she's messing—"

"With my truck. What the hell?"

"Does she have keys?"

"No, but I keep a spare set under the wheel well, and she knows that. I better go see what she's looking for, she must have lost something from her purse. We went to lunch the other day. She could have just texted, for heaven's sake. I'll be right back."

He watches her go, then retrains his sight on Lauren, who is definitely searching for something. A few minutes later, Juliet appears. Lauren jumps away from the car, looking incredibly guilty. The two exchange words, which quickly becomes a heated argument. Lauren turns away first, and he watches Juliet get into the car, head disappearing as she looks for something. She holds it up, and Lauren scurries away.

What in the world just happened?

He finishes his coffee, gets up and grabs a Milky Way. He needs the sugar rush; he is starting to feel a little woozy.

He sits down, and Juliet comes in, clearly in a huff. She throws herself in the seat.

"What was all that about?"

"She lost a glove."

"Big fight for a lost glove."

"The lack of sleep has gone to her head. She's worried that

whoever killed Vivian will come back to finish the job on Mindy. Like we're in *Breaking Bad*, or you're mobbed up. I think she's delusional. I told her so, and she blew up at me. She's really in a mood today. I don't remember the last time I saw her yell at Jasper. Me, well, we yell at each other all the time, always have. What in the world is going on with her?"

He steeples his hands. "You know what I used to do, right?"

"You were military intelligence."

"Yes. Which means I was trained to be a paranoid motherfucker. Lauren just found out her daughter was stolen in the commission of a murder, and for all intents and purposes, that it was designed to send *me* a message. And now I'm here, and Lauren feels like she can't protect Mindy anymore, from anything. If she thinks she's in danger, in her mind, it's because of me. It stands to reason she might be a little freaked out. Considering that, maybe we cut her some slack. She's a civilian, through and through. She doesn't think logically about crime like you and me."

"You know her awfully well for someone who just met her."

"I'm an observer. She's completely freaked out, her husband is furious with her, her daughter is sick and bewildered, her sister is bringing down law enforcement and the media, and then there's me. Her whole world just blew up. I'm willing to see things from her side."

"I am too, don't worry. She's a basket case right now, I know. I'm curious why you aren't."

"Because I've been living with the reality of Mindy's disappearance and Vivian's loss for a long time. I've had seventeen years to wrap my head around this moment. She's had seventeen hours."

Juliet rubs her chin. "Well, if we're going to split hairs, she's known all along that Mindy wasn't her child."

"I think we don't split hairs, okay?" He covers her hand with his. "How was she supposed to know about this? The doctor deceived her. She's a grieving mother. And she's petrified she might lose Mindy. I think it's clouded her judgment all of Mindy's life, but it's especially bad now since Mindy is afflicted with something Lauren can't control."

"Are you sure you're an English teacher?" she asks, eyes narrowed. "You seem awful Dr. Phil-ish to me."

He laughs, he can't help it, a great boom that makes the people around them start and turn, and she smiles, trying hard not to join him, but finally starts giggling. Kat watches them like they're insane.

When they settle down, he answers, "Yes, I'm an English teacher. But I was a great many things before I chose that profession, so yes, I might be looking for insights to understand her motives and actions. Maybe I'm just trying to understand why she lied for so long."

Juliet stares out at the snow. "I'd like to know that myself."

60

Juliet's phone dings, and she glances at it, then stands up. "Woody is here, with Parks and Starr. They're probably done moving Mindy to the clean room by now. You want to hang out with her while I go do cop things?"

"I'd love to, and yes, I will, but can I do cop things with you for a little while? I'd like to talk to them, just so we're all on the same page."

"Hold our table, then. I'll go get them."

"Why don't I get a round of coffee for everyone?"

"Good idea. And water. Lots of water. We don't want anyone dropping out of the chase because the altitude gets to them."

"Yes, ma'am."

★ ★ ★

The cops are in the lobby looking totally conspicuous, as cops are wont to do, even without their guns on display. Juliet waves to them as she approaches.

"I see you made it in one piece." She shakes hands with Parks and Starr, gives her boss a punch on the shoulder. "Woody treating you all right? I know he drives like a bat out of hell over the pass."

Starr nods, and Juliet has to stifle a laugh—Parks looks positively green.

"This is a fine mess you've dragged us into, Ryder. Watch it." But Woody grins at her. He is in his forties, clean-cut, with light blond hair swept back from his forehead and a faint tan line from ski goggles on his cheeks. A Colorado native, he is a snowboarder in the winter, and a good one, sneaking to the mountains every day off he has, and in the summer, spends a lot of time biking the mountain trails. He is also a shrewd investigator, not prone to excitement, but steady and true, and Juliet trusts him implicitly.

"I've got us a spot in the cafeteria. Who wants coffee?"

Hands raise all around. She leads them down the hall, following the arrows to the cafeteria. Zack has moved to a larger table, but one still by the windows. Two carafes of coffee and several bottles of water sit on the table. He must have charmed the cashiers into giving him the carafes because she hasn't seen any floating around except for on the staff tables, when they are having meetings.

He is a charming man, Zack Armstrong. Unfailingly kind, polite, a true gentleman. She wonders what will happen when that solidly controlled veneer cracks. She imagines it will be pretty messy. She assumes that's what Kat is for, the moments when he lets the control slip and allows himself to fall apart. God knows he has every right to.

Once they are all assembled, Woody introduces himself to Zack, then invites Parks to start.

"To begin with, I appreciate you letting us join you here. This is a big cold case for our city, one of the legends, and it's wonderful to get a close, at least on one part."

"Hopefully, we can help you solve part two," Juliet says.

"Yes, well…I've learned a few things since we talked last, but nothing that speaks to the kidnapping. We're all ears about this Dr. Castillo. We're hoping we can work our way backward from Lauren to the doctor to the people who stole Mindy in the first place. We have to assume that person killed Vivian as well, though of course there could have been two players involved. Zack told you how the focus has always been on someone hell-bent for revenge against him, but the more I dive into this, the more it seems something else was at play."

"We agree," Woody says. "We are looking into Dr. Castillo right now. We've subpoenaed Swedish for all her records, and of course, we want to have a sit-down with her sidekick and see if he knows anything. Fuentes is a white-collar criminal, but he used to be a gangbanger, so he certainly knows the caliber of criminal who could murder a woman and steal her child. One thing we need to look at is whether Vivian was a target, or wrong place, wrong time, and the goal was simply to steal the child. If these people were in the business of stealing newborns, the murder might be incidental."

Zack makes a noise deep in the back of his throat at that, and Woody holds up his hands, palms out. "Hey, I know. But this is information about Castillo, no one's had it before now, so we need to look at all the angles. If your wife was killed in the commission of a kidnapping, it does change our focus slightly."

"Go on. I'm sorry to interrupt."

Woody nods. "Because the child crossed state lines, obviously the FBI will be joining us for this investigation, and since there are so many organizations involved, a task force is inevitable. For now, we're the leads. We've been looking at all the cases of infant snatching, and there are only a few outstanding that match this scenario. Usually, the kidnapper is caught quickly. Could be this was a one-time thing, and then again, could be you and your wife were targeted, Mr. Armstrong. It's just too early to tell."

Zack is shaking his head. "So you're working under the assumption that we've been wrong all these years, that I wasn't the target at all?"

"Like I said, too early to tell, but yes, it's entirely possible that Mindy herself was the target, and everything that happened to you and Vivian was simply coincidence. Thank you for your service, by the way."

Zack nods. "Sure. I did my part. Like you do yours."

"Right. Until we're able to dig up Dr. Castillo's records, we aren't going to be able to pin this down either way, so trust me when I say my mind is completely open."

"Fresh eyes on this will be good," Parks says, and Starr nods her agreement.

"I've updated the forensics from our end, too, just in case," she says. "Mr. Armstrong's DNA wasn't in the system for some reason. I've also brought all of our files, and all our documented evidence. I assumed you'd need to see all of it, so I made copies."

Woody casts a brief glance at Juliet. *He knows,* she thinks. *He knows I had Cam upload the DNA before it was officially our case. Crap.*

He calmly refills his coffee cup. "Juliet has recused herself from the investigation, which is unfortunate but necessary. I'll handle the new files, make sure they're disseminated among our people, and Juliet's second-in-command, Dr. Bai Ford, will go through all the DNA and run it again, just in case something was missed."

"Got it. Good idea. We were using the state lab for our DNA analysis when this case was going on. Now we have our own, in-house, and the evidentiary protocols are a bit tighter than they used to be. The backlog at TBI was insane back then." Starr hands over two manila folders, one thick, one thin. She looks over at Zack. "Sir, this is the time when you might want to stretch your legs. We need to discuss some details that might be disturbing."

"I'm staying, if you don't mind."

"Suit yourself," Starr says, flipping open the thick file. "The autopsy shows Vivian Armstrong was stabbed twice, one a slice across the neck, the other a penetrating wound to her stomach. There were no prints on the murder weapon outside of her own, and the blood pool indicated she died where and when she was stabbed. The ME put her time of death at approximately thirty hours before she was found. Whoever did this had a big jump as far as getting away with the kid. Also—" she glances at Zack for a second, then back to the page "—Vivian was being treated for depression."

"Depression?" Zack jerks upright in his seat. "What are you talking about? She wasn't depressed. She was about to have her first baby. She was overjoyed."

"She had high levels of an antidepressant in her system, sir. It was in the autopsy report." She looks over to Parks again, who nods his go-ahead. "You weren't aware your wife was being treated?"

"No. Not at all. I was with her all the time the last few weeks. I didn't see her take any drugs. I certainly didn't find any. Did you?" He asks Parks, who shakes his head.

"The evidence list doesn't have any nortriptyline on it, no. No one asked you about it when you were…"

Zack almost laughs. Parks is trying to be delicate. "When I was considered the prime and only suspect? No, no one asked me about antidepressants. I'd remember."

"Well, this was an addendum to the original autopsy report. The tissue tox screens take a long time, and like I said, we didn't have our own lab then. It came back months later. Do you know if your wife was seeing a psychiatrist before her death?"

"No. She was working with University's midwife program, saw their doc when she had to. But that's it. She never mentioned she wasn't feeling well or that there might be a problem. But I wasn't there the whole time." There is a mournful note to his voice and Juliet has to stop herself from reaching for his hand.

"We talked to the midwife program, and she didn't disclose it on her record. But we dug further. Mr. Armstrong, were you aware your wife spent time in a mental hospital when she was a teenager?"

61

"Excuse me?" Zack realizes his mouth is open, closes it. "A mental hospital?"

"That's right. From June 1993 to January 1998, Vivian was in and out of the inpatient program at University Hospital. We have a subpoena being served for the records today."

"I didn't know. She never told me. But why wouldn't Gorman tell me? Or ask me? Or investigate it?"

Juliet catches a glimmer of fury coming off of him. Either he really hasn't been told, or he is a fantastic actor.

Starr shakes her head. "We don't know. And we'll never know, as he's gone now, too."

"Which is another thread that we need to pull," Parks says. "I don't want to send anyone off on a wild goose chase, but it feels wrong to me that Gorman died a day after meeting Mindy. He'd been researching her for a very long time and finding the note that said *Colorado* in his files tells me he was of a mind that Mindy was the Armstrongs' lost child. He came to meet her—I think to see her in person to prove it to himself, maybe see if he could grab some DNA somehow. There was only a cursory autopsy done, his family requested no autopsy, and since he died of blunt force trauma from hitting the rocks as he went off the cliff and witnesses saw him falling, the ME agreed."

"It's something that happens out here a lot more than you'd realize," Woody interjects. "People go off-piste and run afoul of the mountains. Unfortunately, it happens several times every winter."

"Off-piste?" Parks asks.

"Off the approved trails."

"Gotcha. I'm sure it does happen. But I'm a cop, which means I have a suspicious mind. Everyone attached to this case is dead. The mother, the doctor, the investigator. I think it's all related."

Silence sets over the table and everyone takes that in. Juliet glances at Zack.

"Zack said the same thing," Juliet says finally. "He's right. Do you think this person is watching us? I mean, my sister freaked out a little while ago, convinced we were being tracked somehow. I think she sees this connection, too, and she is scared to death."

"We'll need to speak with her next, obviously," Woody says.

"Woody, I've interrogated her ten ways from Sunday, and she's at a loss. She doesn't know anything."

"Thing is, Juliet, she might know something but not know she knows it. You know?" Starr says. "Sorry to sound like Dr. Seuss there, but we'd definitely like to sit down with her and have a chat."

"Be my guest. She's as prickly as a rattlesnake these days, so don't be surprised if she comes across edgy when you're talking. She's been very disturbed by all this, and to have Mindy be so ill..."

"It's hard when secrets come to light," Zack says. "I'll testify to that firsthand. What I want to know is if all of this—" he waves a hand at the files, and the cops "—is going to find out who killed my wife. Because that's the focus for me. We've found my daughter. Now I expect you to find my wife's killer."

"It's a legitimate ask, and we are going to do our best," Parks replies.

"I want more than your best. I want answers. I want some justice for Vivian. I know we have a lot of dead people surrounding this case, but my wife…" His voice cracks, and this time, Juliet puts a hand on his arm. She notices him reach down with the other to fondle the dog's ears. He takes a deep breath. "I'm sorry. It's been a difficult couple of days."

Starr taps her fingers on the files. "We all want that, Zack. We do. That's why we're here, in Colorado, conducting this investigation, to find out who is responsible for tearing your life apart. And we will get to the truth. You focus on saving your daughter's life and let us focus on finding the suspect. Deal?"

Four strong faces stare at him expectantly.

"Deal."

"Good. Here's the other thing," Parks says. "We are going to need to release a statement to the media. We've taken the liberty and already prepared some verbiage."

He passes out the statement Dan Franklin, Nashville Metro's spokesperson, has drafted at Parks's behest. They all read it, and Juliet watches Zack's face as he takes in the reality he is about to be dumped into. The statement is short, and simply says new information has come to light in the Armstrong investigation, and more will be forthcoming when there is information to be released. It is just enough to pique the media's interest without turning them into baying wolves.

"This looks good to me," Woody says. "I'd just like to add that CBI is involved as well, if you don't mind."

"Not a problem."

Woody drains his coffee cup, sets it down with a plunk on the table. It feels so final, so real, all of a sudden. Juliet takes a deep breath, and he notices.

"Juliet, I know this is going to be hard, but the minute we start talking to witnesses, word's going to spread. Are Lauren and Jasper ready for this? Are you? And you, Zack?"

"We're all going to have to be, aren't we?" she replies. "I'll talk to them, let them know what's coming. We may want to handpick a few journalists we trust and plan a sit-down."

"People will pay for the story," Zack says. "Magazines, online gossip rags. They circled like hawks in the beginning, when the case was fresh. Almost all of them offered money. Can we make sure no one profits from this?"

"Of course," Woody assures him. "I will make a point of finding people who aren't going to try to exploit the story or turn it into a free-for-all."

Juliet sighs. "I don't know, Zack. Mindy's hospital bills are insanely huge. Maybe taking some money—"

"No. Not happening. I'm not letting the media exploit my daughter."

She hears the emphasis on *my*. "Okay. No problem." To Parks, "You're releasing this now?"

"The sooner the better," Parks says. "You never know what might pop up if the media's working the case, too." He rereads the statement. "I have to say, it would be a lot easier if we could just name all the parties and get it over with. Take some of the verve and sting out, you know? We don't want the media discovering the truth before we do."

Juliet nods her agreement. "We might as well. It's not like it's going to be quiet for long. We'll have to tell Lauren and Jasper, get their approval. Zack, you good with that?"

He nods too, clearly distracted.

"Okay then. Progress," Woody says, sticking the paper back into the file. "Let's go have a chat with Mr. and Mrs. Wright, so we can refine the message and get this in the hopper. We'll also get a car to stand watch so the media doesn't hound them, and we'll start looking for the folks we want to sit down with the family for a public plea. We'll see you two later. Juliet. A moment?"

Uh-oh.

She follows him to the edge of the cafeteria. "I saw the time stamp on the sample that was uploaded. If you ever pull a trick like this again, I will have your job. Do you understand?"

She nods. No sense trying to defend herself. She knew the risk.

"Good. You're suspended without pay for two weeks. We are never going to discuss this again. Am I clear?"

"Yes, sir. Thank you, sir."

Woody's face is full of reproach, his whisper harsh. "Don't you dare thank me, Juliet. You're damn lucky this turned so quickly, or else we'd be having a very different conversation. You've threatened everything we stand for, and I am so disappointed in you."

He signals to Parks and Starr, and they walk out together, Starr chatting animatedly.

Juliet, spine straight, walks back upstairs with a very quiet Zack. Being suspended is mortifying, but she deserves much worse. Woody will never trust her properly again, but at least Cameron wasn't caught up in this.

Zack has still said nothing.

"You okay? I know that was hard to hear. It's a shock that Vivian was depressed and taking medication, that she was institutionalized and didn't tell you."

"I missed so much," he says, so low she almost doesn't hear him. "If only I had been there, I could have—"

She pulls him to a stop. "Don't do that to yourself. Do not. You hear me?"

He gives her a sad smile. "You can't erase years of guilt in a moment, Juliet. Trust me on that. Listen, can you take Kat for a little while? I'd like to go sit with Mindy, and Oliver said she wouldn't be allowed in."

She feels dismissed but doesn't show it. "Of course. I'll take her to Lauren and Jasper's. I want to be there while they talk to Woody and the Nashville cops anyway. See you back here later, okay? You have my number. Shout if you need us."

"Will do," he says, but he is already walking away.

62

THE WRIGHTS' HOUSE

Lauren sits on the deck, watching the snow come down around her. She is freezing, shivering under a blanket, but she has no intention of moving. Jasper is inside, not speaking to her, which she finds terribly unfair. Juliet texted that the police are on their way to talk, and she'll be right behind them.

Lauren wants to go back to the hospital and hold Mindy's hand, but she knows she needs to get through all of this first. The idea that the police are going to be under her roof makes her uncomfortable. She can't shake the feeling that something horrible is coming, that she is being watched, that someone knows her secrets. That she is about to lose Mindy forever. The weight of this fear is too much to bear.

She's gone over it in her mind several times, bringing Mindy home, searching for anything, anything, that stands out. Nothing does, and that calms her a bit.

The door behind her opens and Jasper comes out with a cup of hot cocoa. He hands it to her, lips compressed in a thin line.

"Don't get yourself sick sitting out here. It's cold."

"I know it is. I'm just feeling claustrophobic inside. Like I don't have control of anything at all, and the walls are closing in on me."

"This is a lot to have happen in such a short period of time. And it's going to get worse. I've warned Coach about what's happening. The media is going to affect the team selection PR as well."

"Is he going to—"

"No, she still has her spot, but I don't know if anyone believes she's going to be able to compete at the level she was before. Not after the cancer, and not knowing if the transplant...her leg... They're prepping the alternate."

Lauren swears, and Jasper flinches.

"I wish you wouldn't use that kind of language."

"We're losing everything. It's not fair."

"What have we lost? If anything, we're gaining here. Zack is our savior. We need to make the man a crown."

She hears the bitterness in his tone. "You feel the same way I do. You're as scared as I am. We might lose her. She might die before the transplant takes hold. Why don't you just admit it?"

He sits next to her, and she is shocked by what she sees. He looks utterly ravaged. It scares her, the transformation. He has been her rock for so long, and now he looks like he is about to crumble into dust.

"The police are coming to discuss releasing a statement to the press. This story is no longer our own, Lauren. You need to be prepared because there are going to be a lot of questions and a lot of scrutiny."

"What are you saying? Are you accusing me of something?"

"Stop being paranoid. And stop attacking me. I'm your ally here. I'm trying to help you."

She trains her eyes on the driveway, where the glint of metal shines through the trees. They are here; the cars are snaking up the drive.

Oh, I'm not being paranoid, Jasper. I've been prepared her whole life.

He takes her hands, rubbing them to get some warmth started. His voice is low and kind. "Honey, listen. You have to let me help. I'll forgive you, you know that, but you have to tell me the truth. Is there anything else you've been keeping from me? Anything at all?"

"Like what?"

"I don't know. You tell me. You're acting strange all of a sudden."

The icy snow on the drive crunches beneath the tires, and she draws in a deep breath. She is in control. She has this. Their lives are going to be fodder for the news for a while, but she can handle it. Mindy is the only thing that matters.

She pulls her hands free, stands and says, "I'm going to brush my teeth and hair. We should make some coffee, don't you think?"

Jasper pulls away at her dismissive tone, straightens and looks down the drive at the cars as if they are coming to wreck his life. "I already did. Our manners are on full display." He leaves her on the deck and goes to greet their guests.

63

Lauren uses a single finger to push aside the curtain in her bathroom window and watches the Nashville cops take in the exterior of the house with narrowed eyes, assessing and judging. She recognizes them from Juliet's description. Brianna Starr: small, red hair, young—she seems barely old enough to be out of college, much less be a homicide detective; Bob Parks: older, with a dark mustache and salty hair, thick through the shoulders, like he works out. The way they're looking at the house makes her nervous. The Parks fellow is much too observant, and his sidekick is clearly cut from the same cloth.

A blond ski bum in a suit stands with them. Lauren knows this must be CBI's Woody Stockton. He is jawing, pointing out the various peaks, and now Juliet is coming up the drive, too. Fabulous. Lauren is being descended upon, and her heart beats harder in her chest.

With a final stroke of the brush through her hair, she sets it down and puts on some lipstick, a little mascara and a touch of eyeshadow. She hasn't put herself together much over the past month, and she needs as much armor as possible.

With a final glance in the mirror—yes, she looks fine, tired, but who wouldn't be, considering—she shuts off the light and heads to the living room.

Jasper has already welcomed the entourage and is busy passing out cups and directing people toward the dining room table.

Parks and Starr have stopped by the fireplace, first taking it in—the huge hearth, the large gray stones leading twenty feet up to the vaulted cedar ceiling, the foot-thick driftwood mantel—then moving slightly toward the windows and staring out at the view, the slopes and the mountain, both of their mouths open a little. Lauren feels the spark of pride she always does when her home is being showcased to strangers. It is lovely, they are lovely, their daughter is a world-famous skier, and their lives are more than enviable. She's built this world, and she fits perfectly within it.

Nothing to hide, nothing to hide, nothing to hide. See how beautiful we are? See how our lives matter?

With this knowledge secure in her heart, she pastes on a smile and sails down the stairs to greet her guests. After the introductions are made, Parks is the first to speak. He has a brisk southern accent.

"Ma'am, thank you for taking the time to talk with us. I know this is a rough day, what with your daughter's treatment, and you'll be wanting to get to the hospital as soon as possible. I promise we won't take much of your time. Your home is beautiful, by the way."

Jasper comes to stand beside her, his shoulder touching hers, and she lets herself be bolstered by his presence. She smiles as graciously as she can. "You're kind to acknowledge it. We've had a rough month, that's for sure. I'm just sick learning the truth about Mindy's parentage. I had no idea…well, you know that already. What can we do for you? We're happy to answer any questions you might have. Please, let's all sit down."

Once they are arrayed around the table, Woody leads the discussion. "First, we wanted to see if you would like to add anything to the statement we'll be releasing to the media." Woody hands her a piece of paper. She reads it, heart in her throat. Their names, the details, everything is here. At the look on her face, Jasper takes it from her hand and reads it, eyes moving rapidly across the page.

"Right now, we're only stating that a lead is being pursued, but we'd prefer to cut to the chase and announce that Mindy is the lost child. It will come out, there's no keeping her out of the story, but we have time, should you want."

"What kind of time?" Jasper asks.

"A day, maybe," Woody says. "We'll do our best, but there is about to be a ton of law enforcement personnel from several agencies diving into this case, and the minute they do, we're looking at leak city. I can control my people, but as I said, we're going to be talking to inmates, and we've already subpoenaed the hospital's records, and with the presence of the Nashville police...it's going to be hard to keep it quiet. I'd suggest we get it out of the way now, do a press conference this afternoon, and then retreat behind the hospital walls for a day or so."

Juliet catches her sister's eye. "Mindy's having the stem cell transplant in two days. It stands to reason you and Jasper will want to be there, anyway. We can keep you isolated, let the initial fervor die down."

With her eyes and the tilt of her head, Lauren sends a private message to Jasper, who nods. "It's time," he says quietly, and she swallows hard.

"Yes. We can release her name. But we will not participate in a press conference. We are a family dealing with a serious medical situation, that's all I want out there. We won't be meeting with reporters until the transplant is over, and even then, Mindy will not be interviewed. It will be Jasper and myself only, though I suppose Zack Armstrong will want to be part of it, too."

"That's the last thing he wants," Juliet says. "He's made it very clear he wants the media attention to be investigation-related only. He's even stipulated there will be no taking money from magazines for inside scoops."

"We'll have to do it eventually," Jasper says. "Something legitimate, like *People Magazine* or *Sports Illustrated*, and they can do some coverage of Mindy's skiing as well, help bolster her chances for staying in her Olympic spot. But not some paparazzi crap."

"I'll let you and Zack battle that out. He was quite adamant."

"She's *our* daughter," Jasper says. "Zack doesn't get to make decisions that affect this family, not when all of our reputations are on the line."

Lauren tries not to cheer at this proclamation, only squeezes his hand and nods. She sees a flash of something in her sister's eyes, wonders for a moment why Juliet is facing her and Jasper, instead of being faced down by the bevy of cops. Juliet is on the wrong side of the table.

She's with them, a little voice says. *No matter what, no matter that she's your sister and Mindy's aunt, she will always pick them first. The law, and science, her precious props.*

The realization scares her, and she blurts out, "I think we need a lawyer."

This catches the Nashville sergeant's attention. "For what?"

"Of course we do," Jasper says smoothly, as if this has already been discussed and decided between them. "We will be retaining the services of my firm to protect ourselves, and Mindy's interests."

64

"Whoa, whoa, whoa," Woody says. "Hold up. Let's not bring the lawyers into it."

"I am a lawyer, sir," Jasper says. "And it's the only course of action that makes sense. We are facing weeks of attention, and I want to be certain there is no question that Mindy's interests are paramount here. For our protection, and hers, we will retain counsel, and will not discuss the case with anyone going forth—media and police included—without him present."

Lauren is surprised but not shocked. Something in the police's attitudes must have set off Jasper's alarm bells too because he hasn't mentioned this to her, but he backed her up immediately. Her heart swells when he continues.

"We will also be petitioning for full custody of our daughter. I've already started drawing up the papers."

"That's your right," Woody says. "I understand the impulse to hold your family close right now. But I promise you, Mr. Wright, we are not interested in creating some sort of media spectacle. That hurts our chances to solve this case just as much as it disrupts your lives. We want to get to the bottom of this, find out who kidnapped Mindy, and who killed Vivian Armstrong. Please don't throw roadblocks in our way by dragging it into court."

"No roadblocks, and no court, only necessary protections that will allow us to make the proper decisions regarding our daughter. My daughter." Jasper straightens in his seat. "Though my wife does not have paperwork regarding her end of the adoption with Dr. Castillo, I do have the paperwork from my legal adoption of the child. I have rights, just as many, or more, than Mr. Armstrong. Custodial rights."

"I see." Woody sits back in his chair, coffee cup abandoned. His tone changes. Gone is the loose, easy manner. Now he is all cop, and Lauren can't help but wonder if Jasper has overplayed their hand.

"I hear you loud and clear, buddy. But that's not what we're here to decide right now. We're releasing the statement regardless of how comfy you are with it, and we would like to control the message from the get-go. We're trying to help you out here, get you prepared. No need to get prickly with us. We're your friends."

Jasper laughs, short and humorless. "Right. Friends. Got it."

Parks spreads his hands out on the table. "Seriously, let's not get adversarial. We're all in this together, and we're trying to help you be ready for the media storm that's going to roar through here the second this is announced."

"Yes, we are," Juliet seconds. "And we want to make sure that this is painless for Mindy. That's the goal here. She is the only focus for all of us. Right, Lauren?"

"Of course." The house phone begins to ring. "Excuse me a moment. I'll be right back."

Lauren is relieved to step away from the table to gather her thoughts. Her husband is white-faced, the CBI agent's eyes are hooded, the Nashville cops look like they are smelling something exceptionally tasty, and her little sister is smiling at her encouragingly, a fox to the chicken. She turns her back on them as she answers.

"Hello? Wright residence."

"Mrs. Wright?"

"Yes?"

"Ma'am, this is Jeremy Finley, from WSMV in Nashville, Tennessee. Is it true you're the adoptive mother of the missing child Violet Armstrong?"

"I—"

"And is it also true that Violet is now named Mindy Wright, and she lives with you in Vail, Colorado, and is a member of the United States World Cup ski team?"

Lauren slams down the phone with a gasp, making everyone turn. Her face says everything.

"Uh-oh," Juliet says. "Was that what I think it was?"

She nods, and Juliet can feel the distress coming off her in waves. "Some media person from Nashville. They know."

Lauren whirls to the table, the unholy cabal of parent and cops staring at her. "Who let it out? Someone leaked. It had to be someone in Nashville."

"It wasn't us," Parks says. "We've kept this super hush-hush."

"But we did pull all the files, and put Armstrong's DNA in the system, and talked to University Hospital," Starr says thoughtfully. "Entirely possible someone at the lab got interested and mentioned it to someone. Or saw we set up the flight here, or Andrea Austin said something—there's any number of ways this leaked. Two plus two…"

The phone rings again. "Oh, that's just great," Jasper says, standing. "So much for your help. We'll attend to things ourselves from here on out."

Woody stands as well. "Mr. Wright, I wouldn't recommend—"

Jasper gives Woody a glare that would knock down a horse. Even Juliet feels a qualm.

"Get out. Just…leave us alone. We've managed this long. We'll manage this, too."

"No problem, we all need to head out anyway. I'll walk you out," Juliet says, hoping to diffuse the tension. She's never seen Jasper quite so upset. Lauren is trembling, a fist to her mouth, eyes wide. She can sense her sister's thoughts—*This is a total disaster. What are we going to do now?*

"Go with them, Juliet," Jasper calls.

"What?"

"You heard me. Lauren and I need to talk, and it's best for you to join the rest of the detectives and give us some space. And we're needed back at the hospital." To Woody, "You can direct the rest of your inquiries to my lawyer, Bill Conrad."

Juliet's eyes shoot to Lauren's. She sees resolve and fear in them.

"Is this what you want?"

Her sister's voice is soft. "Yes. It's best. We'll talk later. Just… give us some time to wrap our heads around this."

The phone blurts again, and Jasper picks it up, slams it down, then unplugs it deliberately from the wall, watching Juliet all the while.

"Okay. I can take a hint." She clicks her tongue at Kat, who drags herself away from the fire with a longing backward glance. Juliet's last glimpse into the room shows her sister bursting into tears.

65

Standing by the cars, Woody stares at the front door. "What the hell just happened, Juliet? One minute we're having a nice conversation, the next..."

"I don't know. It's like a flip switched in Lauren, and when that call came, Jasper picked up on it and manifested. He's going to do everything he can to protect his family. I don't blame him for being mad at us. I wish he wasn't bringing in that jerk of a lawyer. Conrad's a heavy hitter at the firm, and I don't particularly like him. He'll make sure we dot every *i* and cross every *t*, and then go back and make us do it all again. He's a stickler."

"We should have controlled the message earlier," Parks says. "Trying to get a family on board is sometimes the more difficult approach, especially considering it's their world that's being blown up. We should have just gone ahead with our original plan instead of trying to coordinate. Now they have their backs up, and they won't ever trust us again."

"I'll get them to see reason. I think it was the money thing. I wasn't kidding about Mindy's medical bills. They are outrageous. They'd never admit it, but I know they're strapped trying to keep up with it. Mindy lost out on a couple of sponsorships because she wasn't able to do publicity right after Worlds, and that's big money. Jasper's doing well, but Lauren hasn't sold a painting in a year." She scuffs her foot against the gravel drive. "Let's give them a day to cool off, and we can go from there.

In the meantime, I'd like to get Bai moving on the DNA. If the media is on this, we all have to play our parts, and the faster we move, the better."

"Agreed," Woody says. "I'll take the files down the mountain to the lab and get started there."

"Good. I'll talk to Zack and see if he can help with Lauren and Jasper." She turns to Parks and Starr. "You're going with Woody, I imagine? Start in on the Castillo investigation?"

"Right," Parks says. "I know you're recused from this, but we'll keep you in the loop."

"I appreciate it. I think once the shock wears off, Lauren will want to know what's happening. Jasper, too. He's upset. I don't think I've seen him lose it since Mindy was hurt and diagnosed. He's been holding on so tight, trying to keep them all together. With Zack showing up, and the investigation being opened, and the media…the call was simply the straw that broke the camel's back. He'll come around. He needs some time to get used to his new life, that's all."

Parks stares back up at the house. "I hope you're right."

Juliet grins. "I am. Trust me. He's really angry at my sister for putting us in this situation. She didn't tell him about Mindy's true parentage, and he's stinging from that. This is him trying to get control of the situation. He blew up and took it out on us so he wouldn't take it out on her. He's a good guy like that. Plus, Mindy's transplant is in two days. The stress of what might happen is getting to them, and the idea of media attention on top of that… The last thing any of us want or need is media trying to get into the hospital and get snaps of Mindy ill, or being treated."

"Makes sense," Parks says. "I'm glad you know them so well because I saw something different."

"Oh? What did you see?"

"I saw a couple circling the wagons around a secret. But I could be completely wrong. As you say, this is a high-stress time.

So down the mountain we go. You have my number. Call me if anything changes, and I'll do the same."

They climb in the car, and Woody puts the window down. "Where are you headed?"

Juliet glances back at the house, can swear Lauren is looking out the bathroom window, watching them, but then the window is empty, the curtains falling back into place. She flips her keys in her hand.

"I'm going to go see Zack. He needs a warning that the hordes are about to descend."

66

VAIL HEALTH HOSPITAL

Juliet finds Zack outside the hospital, walking, talking on his cell phone. Kat sees her daddy and woofs excitedly. Juliet parks and lets her out. The Malinois makes a beeline for Zack's side and glues herself to his leg. He smiles down at her and finishes his call.

"How'd it go?"

Juliet rubs her forehead. "I have a headache the size of Manhattan. Listen, the Nashville media has the story. We're not sure how…"

"I talked to them. I have a friend at Channel 4. I gave him a call. If we're doing this, I want to do it my way."

She feels her mouth drop open unbecomingly, then forces it closed. "Could you have maybe given us a heads-up first? Lauren and Jasper were blindsided, and they didn't take it well."

"Sorry. But I don't know who to trust out here, and I know my friend. He's not going to screw us."

There is a bench by the front doors. He sits on it heavily.

"You okay?"

"Yeah. The medicine's making me feel weird. I have my second round in an hour. They say it will be worse than the first. If I'm going to be incapacitated, I wanted to be in control of the message first."

"Still, Zack. This is a family decision."

His gaze is unreadable.

"What did the reporter have to say?"

"He was thrilled to hear we found Mindy and promised to handle the story as carefully as he could. I take it someone from the station called Jasper and Lauren?"

"Yes. Jasper didn't react well. Seriously, Zack, you should have talked to us first. We're all in this together."

He glances toward the mountain before he looks at her. "See, that's the thing, Juliet. *You* are all in this together. I, on the other hand, am alone. I realized that when we were talking earlier and decided I want to be in control. I also talked to my former colleagues, and I have calls in to Vivian's doctors at University Hospital. The investigation will take its natural course, but I'm allowed to ask for answers, too."

"You've been busy."

"What am I supposed to do, sit back and wait? Mindy and I discussed it, and we decided it was the best course of action."

"You talked to Mindy?"

"Damn straight I did. This is *her* life we're talking about. Did everyone forget that? She is going to be the center of this maelstrom, yet no one stopped to think to talk to her. Well, I did. I wanted her to know exactly what was happening. Keeping her out of the loop isn't good."

"She's a sick little girl—"

"She's a strong, vibrant young woman who needs something to fight for. I will never keep secrets from her. Never. She deserves to be part of the decision-making process. It's her life. One she's had absolutely no control over for nearly a month."

Juliet opens her mouth to speak, then closes it, looking at Zack with new eyes. He ducks his head and puts a hand on Kat's muzzle.

"I don't mean to yell. I feel awful, I'm scared, and my daughter is dying before I have a chance to know her at all."

"Don't apologize. You're right. Mindy should be consulted. Lauren and Jasper are grappling with some serious fear right now. Remember, they've had the care of her for seventeen years. They love her."

"I love her, too," he says, teeth gritted.

"I know you do. We all do. This isn't a competition, damn it. We have to stick together, because the media—"

"Juliet, I think you forget that I've been dealing with the media for seventeen years. It was especially bad the first couple of years. They were at the funeral. Outside the police station. At my wife's grave. They lived on my front stoop. They had close-ups of every tear, every grimace, every scream in the night. It was a constant inundation. Of all of us, I'm the only one who knows what's to come, and how important it is to get out in front of it. You've only ever been on one side of a situation like this, doing DNA to help capture a criminal. You have no idea what it's like to be the sole focus of the media and police attention. I do."

Kat woofs and goes on alert. There is something in the trees to the side of the hospital. Deer? Squirrel? Could be anything. But her short bark seems to pull Zack together. He runs a hand over his face, scratches Kat's ears. She calms but keeps a watchful eye on the woods.

"We should go in and let you take a rest. You're looking pale."

"Yeah, well, I'm tough. I'll go in shortly. What else is happening? When will we have some answers?"

Juliet shrugs. "Unfortunately, I don't get to work on any of this, so I don't know. Woody will be back with us soon, I'm sure. My assistant is doing a double-check run of the evidence the Nashville cops brought. By the way, Jasper and Lauren lawyered up. Do you feel like you need legal representation? I know some people."

He sighs. "I figured that was coming. They've been too kind. It's one thing to acknowledge the man who fathered your child, but when push comes to shove, the reality of losing Mindy was always going to cloud their judgment. I have a lawyer in Nashville. I'll let her know what's happening, see if she wants to co-ordinate. But Mindy is the one who gets to make the decisions here. I've already told her I won't stand between her and her parents, but that I'd like to be a part of her life." A smile now, at last. "Silly kid said I should move out here, that I could get tenure at the University of Colorado in Boulder and we could all live together."

"It's not a terrible idea, you know. I mean, it's not like they have ski slopes in Nashville, and Mindy will never be separated from the mountains. They're as much a part of her as her hands. If you want to be near her, Colorado it is."

He plays with Kat's lead. "We'll see." His watch chimes. "We should probably go in. My next infusion is in fifteen minutes, and I'm not looking forward to it."

"Zack, wait. How is Mindy doing? Since she seems to be confiding in you…"

"Honestly? She's pissed. She wants the dog, but the doctor won't let her." They laugh together for a moment, easier with each other.

Over Zack's shoulder, Juliet sees a news truck glide into the parking lot.

"We better get inside. The hordes are arriving."

67

Mindy, stuck alone in the clean room while her immune system is crashed in preparation for the possible life-saving treatment, tries to wrap her head around her new normal. There has been so much to absorb, so many lightning-fast changes, that she hasn't had time to process any of it. Her biodad, her mom's weirdness, the letters…they are important. Why else would her mother have them stashed away?

Mindy didn't have a chance to get them back to their hiding spot. She'd spent hours in the bathroom, hiding from her mother, reading through them several times, practically committing them to memory.

Now, the more she knows about Zack, the more disturbing the letters become. She recalls the last few, worrying a nail.

August 1996

V,

Sorry it's been so long since I wrote. I've been having a long summer. Mood swings galore, and I've been pretty down. I have to go back on medication, or my mother threatened me with a weekend visit to the local nut ward, which I refuse to do. So back on the soul-sucking drugs go I. It's fine, though. I need to get myself together. Before I fell down the rabbit hole again, I was accepted to an art college here. I must have been high to apply, but I was trying to impress a current boyfriend, who was very insistent that I must have a "life plan." He didn't understand why I wasn't interested in the whole go to college, pledge a sorority, major in MRS thing. I'm dumping him before I leave, for sure.

But here's the deal. I'm concerned about my privacy at this new school. So if you write, can you please not mention anything about where we met? I'm not ashamed, I just don't feel like it's anyone's business what happened. Cool?

Love you,

Liesel

September 1996

Liesel,

You mean you want me not to mention we were both locked in school that taught us exceptional coping mechanisms and bitchin' art skills, with an emphasis on interpersonal relations so we had the best chance in life to succeed? Copy that, Starbuck! (wink wink)

In other news, Ratchet's having another kid. Still no ring. Mystery semen!!

Love,

V

January 1997

Hey V,

I have an email address!!! Now we can write immediately instead of waiting months between letters. My address is lieselt1@aol.com

Hope you're doing well~what's been happening lately? It's been a while~

Email me!

Love,

Liesel

January 1998

Liesel,

It's taken me a while to answer you because I AM OUT!!!!! For good this time.

I am living (sort of) on my own, in a halfway house near our old neighborhood, and I couldn't be happier. It's broken into apartments. I have a nice roommate, and I feel like I'm on solid ground for the first time in a very long time. One day soon, I hope to have enough money saved up to come visit you. You're so far away now! I hope life has been treating you well. I also have a part-time job at a restaurant near my house, just bussing tables, but the owner said once I'm fully trained he will promote me to hostess. Can you imagine, me, a hostess?

I also have a boyfriend, though I think I'm going to dump him. He's too maudlin for me. Hung like a horse, though. He likes my piercings. I didn't tell you, I added another to my belly button, it's super cool. You should do it, the double ring looks really sexy.

Love you, friend,

V

PS: Sorry about the email, I don't have a computer. Besides, letters are so much better. Email feels like too many people are watching.

May 1998

Dear V,

You're aren't going to believe this, but I've gotten married!

His name is Kyle Noonan, and he is a big shot lawyer here in town.
We eloped! My mom is so upset with me. Almost as mad as when I got
that tattoo right after I got out of "school," and she made me have it
removed. God, that hurt.

Anyway. Kyle's a great guy. I hope you understand why I didn't ask you to
be in the wedding. We decided to do it, and went and did it. Vegas, baby!
It was crazy, and I'm not sure it's the wedding I always dreamed about,
but he is handsome and kind, and this is going to be such an exciting ride.

We're going to try for a baby, too. I've always wanted to be a young
mother, as you well know.

I'll send pictures once they're developed!

Love,

Liesel

December 1998

My darling Liesel,

That's awesome! Big news here too: I've met someone. Like, the guy,
someone. He's amazing. Tall, and handsome, and smart. He came into the
restaurant, and I served him. I acted like an idiot, all fumble fingers, but he
left me a massive tip with his phone number!! We've been seeing each other
for a couple of months now, and I have to say, I don't think I have ever been
happier. Thing are moving fast, and he asked me to move into his apartment
on base. He said if I like it, we can stay there, and if I'm not happy, we can
get a little house together somewhere. I think he's amazing.

Since I will no longer be a single white female, I have a huge favor to ask. As you can see, I've enclosed all your letters in this package. I am scared to death he might find them during the move. Once we're settled, and he's deployed again, you can send them back. But for now, can you keep them safe for me? I treasure our correspondence. It's kept me going through dark times and through light.

You are going to love him, Liesel! Can't wait to meet Kyle, too!

Love,

V

January 1999

V,

Completely understand. Your secrets are safe with me. He sounds DIVINE!!! Send pictures soon! Oh, if you have access, you can always email me. We can talk there if it's easier for you. It's lieselt1@aol.com. Don't tell anyone yet, but I missed my period. Shhhh~

Love,

Liesel

April 1999

Liesel, my dear,

Oh wow, L. I am very happy for you. I apologize that the email isn't working out, as our internet connection sucks big time, and it takes as long to open my email as the Pony Express took to go cross country. Z deploys soon. You'll be able to mail back the letters, and I will find a safe place for them.

He says he wants to marry me when he gets back from this tour. Can you imagine? I will make sure you have a spot at my side and are wearing something gorgeous. Lavender, maybe. It would look so pretty with your dark hair.

Love,

V

May 1999

V,

Just a quick note to say I think it's fabulous that you're getting married!

Though not sure about lavender, as I'm no longer dark haired. I've been highlighting mine for a couple of years, now. It's all the rage here, and it looks pretty. I like being a blonde. It's like I'm a whole different person.

Now, the not so great news. I miscarried. Kyle said he wasn't sad about it, either, which sort of broke my heart. I am going to try again in two months like the doctor says. I'll have time to convince Kyle what a wonderful idea it is.

Are you going to have children?

Love,

Liesel

February 2000

Dear V,

I'm pregnant again! The doctor says this time it's going to stick. I am so excited I can hardly stand it. I'm going to wait to tell Kyle until I'm past the danger time. But I had to tell you. I am so excited!!!

What are you doing? How's your hot hubby?

Love,

Liesel

March 2000

Liesel,

Oh wow. Congratulations! I'm so excited for you!

And here's some news: I'm pregnant, too.

I can't begin to tell you how freaked out I am. Knowing you're incredibly excited for me is a help. I'm scared to death. But I'll figure it out. I have to stop taking my meds, they can interfere with the baby's growth. So it's talk talk talk therapy for me—joy! I've been seeing Dr. Freeman. Can you believe he's still at University? He made an exception since I am such an old patient.

Anyway, it's cool that we can experience this together. It will help me feel less alone. I'm due in August, by the way. Jesus, that's forever from now.

Love,

V

PS: As you can see, I've sent another batch of our letters for your safekeeping. I know you said I should just come clean to Zack, but I don't have the heart to tell him what I've been through. He's such a strong man. I don't want him to see me as anything less than his warrior wife.

★ ★ ★

There's no question in Mindy's mind who V is anymore. Mindy's heart is broken for her biological mother. For her illness. Her sadness.

And she is so very confused.

How did Mindy actually end up with Lauren and Jasper? And who killed Vivian?

She needs to talk to her mom. But she doesn't quite know what to say.

Maybe Zack can help her make sense of the letters. She'll ask him the next time she's allowed to see him.

In the meantime, she lies in the strange bed, mind spinning with possibilities, awaiting her fate.

PART THREE

68

VAIL HEALTH HOSPITAL

Twenty-four hours. That's all it takes for a world to fall apart.

Zack was right. Juliet *wasn't* prepared for the onslaught. She is astounded at the intensity of the media storm, even though she's seen them time and time again. Hospital security has to be doubled—reporters keep trying to sneak in and take photographs of Mindy and Zack, Lauren and Jasper. The Vail police have their hands full with the sudden inundation of news trucks from every Denver station as well as all the cable news vans.

The media legion brings out the lookie-loos. People are filming the front of the hospital like it is some sort of multi-vehicle car crash, hoping for blood to spill and people to run away screaming. Twitter and Facebook have blown up, the hashtags *#violetmindy* and *#violetisalive* are trending. There isn't a corner of the country, and probably the English-speaking world, that isn't now aware that the lost Armstrong baby has been found.

Jasper and Lauren put out a statement asking for privacy in the face of their daughter's medical emergency, but it doesn't matter. Mindy Wright, aka Violet Armstrong, is news everywhere.

The child in question is not unaware of the attention. Though vetoed by her parents, she has insisted on watching, and the television is on while Zack's plasma drips into her veins. She has very little energy, the last blast of chemo saw to that, but Juliet can see the life spark in her eyes while Mindy watches clips of herself shooting down the side of mountain after mountain, the small winces when the crash is replayed over and over, or when the photographs of a young, happy Vivian and Zack are shown. She can only imagine what is going through the kid's mind. Mindy has never shied away from the spotlight before—she is a damn good skier, takes pride in it. She isn't cocky, but confident, and totally capable of talking to reporters and handling herself. Part of her appeal to the ski world is how great she comes across in front of a camera and microphone.

But now, shrunken, casted, bald and gray, how will the world who loves the vibrant young skier feel about her? Juliet knows her niece well enough to believe she won't be comfortable with the world seeing her in her current state.

Which is fine, because the media has enough fodder to work with until Mindy grants them an interview. On cable news, videotape of the crash, of Mindy's skiing, is being shown on a loop. Her coach is interviewed, her teammates harassed. The press conference Woody held flashes every few minutes, Detective Starr and Sergeant Parks by his side, along with several other CBI folks and more she doesn't recognize, probably the feds who've attached themselves to the case. Child psychologists extrapolate Mindy is trying to make up for a lack of real maternal care by throwing herself into extreme sports. *If she'd only been breastfed,* Juliet hears one of them say, and bites back a laugh as Mindy rolls her eyes and flips the channel.

Her insta-celebrity as the missing Violet Armstrong is a surprising step up for an already famous kid known for her prowess and daring.

Piles of teddy bears and flowers and candles create a shrine outside the hospital doors. A couple of times a day, Juliet selects one or two of the cutest animals and brings them in, places them on the window ledge overlooking Mindy's room so that she can see them.

She'll be in isolation for a while, making sure the transplant takes. It is going to be a long few days.

Lauren and Jasper have been exceptionally quiet, leaning against one another, answering whatever questions are posed to them but not offering up anything themselves.

Everyone knows everything has changed. There is no going back in time, to when Mindy was simply a sick kid, and Lauren and Jasper were holding on for dear life to get her well.

Juliet stands outside Mindy's door, watching the process. It is amazing that something so benign looking can save a life. The cells, packed into a sterile bag, drip, drip, drip into Mindy's arm as she distractedly watches the television screen. Juliet sees Lauren's eyes watching the drips as well, intently, counting them, as if she can infuse the blood with strength.

She has to make things right with her sister. The need is so pressing, so intense, Juliet has to shut her eyes and ball her hands into fists to handle the surge of emotion. Love? Hate? Fear? All of the above, plus a healthy dose of anger. Juliet is hurt that Lauren didn't trust her, pushed her away. Hurt. That's it. She's been hurt by Lauren plenty of times in the past, blithely ignoring her sister's barbs or inattention, but this is different.

She can't help but feel something else is wrong, and she has no idea what that might be. But Juliet is an adult, and she needs to fix this. Emboldened, she reaches over and touches Lauren's hair, tucking a piece back behind her small, neat ear. Lauren twitches but doesn't pull away.

"Lauren. Can we talk?"

Jasper shoots her a glance. "Haven't you done enough?"

"I haven't done anything you didn't ask me to do. I just want to talk to my sister."

"It's okay, Jasper." Lauren lays a hand on his arm, smiling at him softly. "What is it, Juliet?"

"I'm sorry you feel like I'm responsible for all of this. I just wanted to help."

"I know you did. Don't worry. This isn't about you anymore."

There is something about the way she says it that makes Juliet want to slap her, but she resists, lets the urge pass.

"Listen, what do you need? I know you're going to stay here for the next couple of days. I can go to the house and bring back whatever you might have forgotten. Fresh clothes, toothbrushes, anything. I'm going stir crazy here, I gotta get out and stretch my legs."

"How will you get past the media? They're camped outside, and I bet a few are at the house waiting, just in case."

"I can do it. I can get a police escort if I have to. They won't be able to stop me. Seriously, do you need anything?"

It is Jasper who answers. "No. We don't. The house is locked up so none of the media can peer in, and we're fine. Thank you, Juliet." So dismissive, so hard. When did he become this person? She barely recognizes him.

"Are you sure?"

Lauren glances once at Jasper, then nods. "I think it's best that you don't go near the house." She's become an automaton, parroting Jasper. *She's given up*, Juliet realizes. *She thinks Zack is going to take Mindy away, and she's given up.*

"My clothes are in there, so I'm going to go get them. I'll find a hotel room. I'll get Zack's things, too. We wouldn't want to be an imposition on you."

"Maybe that's best," Lauren murmurs.

"I wish you'd stop blaming me. My God, all I did was find the man who's saving her life. Why am I suddenly the villain here?"

At the twin looks of anger on the faces of the only family she has, Juliet storms out of the room, not caring that Mindy has heard her outburst and is watching her retreat with concern.

She doesn't understand Jasper and Lauren, not one bit. And it pisses her off they are treating her like she is some sort of monster, like she's brought this hell down upon them.

She does have a plan mapped out for leaving the hospital grounds. There is a back door out into the lower parking lot from the floor below the ground-level cafeteria. She's already gone out there once to check, and no one of note was hanging around. This time, she goes full speed, not bothering to look as she crashes out the door.

She reaches her truck without incident. She unlocks the doors, and as she climbs in, a face appears on her passenger side, making her jump with fright until she realizes it is a familiar face. Jasper.

She presses the lever and the window whirs down.

"What is it?"

"You need to stop upsetting Lauren. She's very fragile right now."

"Why? What in the world has changed? I don't understand the attitude shift from you two."

"She feels like you're siding with Zack, that you're going to try to take Mindy away from her. Apparently Mindy made an offhand comment about you and Zack being a cute couple, and it upset her terribly. We're all under stress, Juliet. Lauren is a very private woman, and she's not at all comfortable with your open relationship with the people she thinks are trying to steal her child away from her. I've had to give her Ativan to calm her, she's been a complete wreck since Zack showed up. Her fears might not be rational, but she is legitimately afraid. I have to keep her calm, keep her focused."

"She hasn't seemed like that big of a wreck to me. When did this shift happen?"

"Trust me when I say she's been trying to keep a brave face on. She's been under so much pressure lately, and this scrutiny is making her a little anxious. We'll get through this, but I wanted to remind you to be careful who you talk to, and what you say. We don't want anything misinterpreted."

"Do you mean Zack? My God, Jasper, it's like you're mounting a campaign to make sure he doesn't have access to Mindy."

Jasper doesn't speak, and then it hits her. "That's exactly what you're trying to do. You're going to mount a legal defense that she's yours and not his?"

"We're going to try."

Juliet shuts her eyes and shakes her head. "Don't do it. You won't win. And Mindy wants him to be a part of her life."

"Mindy is a minor. We make the decisions."

"For a few more months. Jasper, you will lose her if you try to make unilateral decisions, trust me. She'll fight you, and so will he. You'd be much better off accepting that now and working with all of us instead of trying to drive a wedge."

"*All of us.* So Lauren's right. You have chosen a side."

"Jasper. There are no sides here. We're a family. We are getting Mindy through this trial, and we need to do it together."

"Hm. Do you really know Zack Armstrong, Juliet?"

"What do you mean?"

"What do you know about him? His time in the service is classified, but I know what he did. Has he told you?"

"He was military intelligence."

"Right. I have a friend in the Defense Department, and he told me the truth about our friend Zack. He killed people. He did it for the government, sanctioned assassinations. The whole incident where he was shot? He wasn't at a safe house meet like he claims. He was sent to murder the head of the Taliban, and he almost succeeded, but they caught wind of the plot and shot him first. He's not the hero you think he is, and he's certainly not the hero the country makes him out to be."

"Jasper, I know you're a pacifist, but what happens during a war…"

"There is what happens during a war, Juliet, and there are the black souls of men who are happy to do their government's bidding and murder anyone they're told. What kind of man does that make him? He's certainly not the kind of person I want around my child, and if he tries to take her, I will make sure the whole world knows just who Zack Armstrong really is. And I will let Mindy know who he is, too."

"Jasper, you aren't making any sense. Zack isn't trying to steal Mindy. He wants to co-parent. He's talking about moving here. He's willing to upend his life to accommodate you guys."

"The man is morally corrupt, and I will not have him near my child."

She is getting angry now. She wants to jump from the car, stamp her feet, scream and pull his hair, but she maintains her measured tone and grips the steering wheel harder.

"He's saving your child's life, you idiot. Have you stopped to think about that? His blood is saving her, the same blood you claim is so tainted. I don't know what world you're living in, Jasper, but it's not reality. The stress has gotten to your brain."

Juliet is so intent on Jasper she doesn't notice the cameraman who's snuck up and is filming the entire incident. Jasper moves slightly, and that's when she hears the whirring of the camera. "Oh, shit," she says.

But Jasper only smiles coldly and walks back into the hospital, waving off the rest of the reporters who are starting to gather.

She hears someone say, "Did you get that? We better go check it out." And realizes Jasper has planned the whole thing. He's made sure he was seen approaching her car so the media would follow to see what he was up to. The bastard. She would never, ever have thought him capable of such cruelty toward another person.

She watches the reporters scramble and spin, talking into their microphones. Jasper wasn't kidding when he said he was mounting a defense. But it is more than that. He wants to discredit Zack entirely.

She puts the truck in gear with a deep sigh and dials Zack's phone with her free hand.

He doesn't answer, so she leaves a voice mail. "We have a problem. Call me back when you get this."

★ ★ ★

Back in the hospital, Jasper takes his seat next to Lauren and grasps her hand.

"It's taken care of. There's no way any court in the land will give him custody now."

She gives him a beatific smile.

"Thank you, my love."

69

There is nothing more for Zack to do at the hospital, and he is feeling oppressed by the fluorescent lights and beeping machines and the nasty looks Jasper keeps shooting at him. What a difference a day makes. The tenor of all their conversations has changed; the Wrights have turned on him, closing ranks around Mindy. Juliet seems to have been left out in the cold, too.

Since Mindy will be parked inside the clean room for hours as her body accepts or rejects his blood, and he is feeling decidedly uncomfortable in the Wrights' presence, he decides to take a stroll. During a press conference, he manages to duck the knot of media out front by following a doctor out the secured back door to the bottom parking lot and walks down the hill into the resort.

Zack wanders around Vail Village, Kat by his side, looking in stores, enjoying being alone for the first time in days. So much to process, so much to decide on. So much to be suspicious of.

Now that he is away from the hospital, and his head is clearing, he can acknowledge what has been bothering him since he arrived in Vail. Something isn't right with Lauren. She is under duress, certainly—the situation with Mindy is trying and would stress out the Dalai Lama—but there is something more. The way she looks at Zack makes the hair on the back of his neck stand on end.

Why? Why does a loving suburban mom set his radar on fire?

Because she is too perfect? Outside of a few lies, told mostly to protect her loved ones, Lauren is absolutely, utterly perfect. Jasper, too, is perfect. They have a perfect home, a perfect life, a perfect daughter.

And Zack knows that no one, no one in the world, is perfect like this. It is almost as if Lauren is directing a play, moving the pieces around. I am a good mother: stage right, my accomplished daughter. I am a devoted wife: stage left, my handsome lawyer husband. Backdrop: our glitteringly perfect home, not a speck of dust in sight. I am creative, concerned, loving, and disciplined. I have money, I have purpose. Nothing fazes me, except the thought of losing my daughter. Spotlight off, and…curtain.

It is practically written to script—the idyllic American family, world-class athlete daughter, parents willing to do anything to help their child excel. A river of normalcy, flowing through the lives around them.

And just below the surface, the current eddies, and is growing in strength.

Zack finds a restaurant that looks good, The Red Lion, and takes a table on the deck. He gets a bowl of water for Kat from the curly-haired ski-bum server, a Guinness for himself, and sits, arms on the metal table, face turned up to the late winter sun for a few moments, before settling in to people watch. He is only thirty yards from the gondola, facing a steep set of moguls. Skiers coming down the hills are black specks in controlled turns, swooping back and forth until they slam to a stop with a rooster-tail splash of white.

It is unseasonably warm, and the skiers who've taken a break around him are dressed in light layers, jackets off, boots unsnapped. Others *clump* through the narrow streets heel-to-toe in their bulky boots, skis over shoulders, some intent on the parking garage, some looking for a place to relax for a while, happy to sit and have a drink, unwind, reward themselves for their heroics on the mountain. They shoulder their own loads, which surprises him. For such an expensive sport, he'd expect more Sherpas to run the heavy gear from the cars to the slopes and back.

Moving among the rust-colored awnings are women who aren't skiing but are here to shop, hair perfectly done and wide sunglasses on. Trophies. Children in designer clothes trail in their wake, looking longingly at the mountain.

The constant flow soothes him, makes him feel normal for the first time in days. All these people without a care in the world outside of where and when the next adrenaline high comes from. He is jealous of their carefree lives. And on this bright, warm day, the general atmosphere is jovial.

"Did you see that last run? My hair was on fire."

"I almost slammed into that pole."

"Gosh, it is such a gorgeous day."

It is. The sun gleams off last night's fresh white snow; the evergreens are tipped in blue. Christmas decorations are still up, though he wonders, since this is an alpine town, if it's like this all the time. The winter wonderland motif works. He imagines it's quite beautiful at night, the fairy lights tucked into the green swags, highlighting the red ribbons and bows.

The sky is sapphire blue, broken only by a few puffy white clouds and several hawks riding the thermals. He wonders what the birds think of the people swooping down the slopes—do they see them as prey?

Cream-colored buildings with dark timbers, brick-cobbled walkways, dogs—tons of dogs, Kat is quivering by his feet watching them stroll by.

The women next to him are on their second margaritas, the men sitting with them in their ski boots and sunglasses are cool and funny.

In his observations, he sees himself, sitting at the table, a beer in his hand, a dog at his feet. His clothes are Nashville North Face, but for the rest… He has one of those strange moments of dislocation—*Could I live here? Could I fit in? Would the people next to me be my friends, or would I find them, and they me, tedious and boring?*

With Mindy here, this is more than a rhetorical question. He will be near her no matter what, and that means moving to Colorado. This *will* be his new life.

Will he and Jasper find a way to be friends, or will they dance around one another, pretending to be civil for Mindy's sake? He thinks they could be friends; quiet and smart, Jasper seems like a good man. At least he did until he started protecting Lauren. And protecting he is, desperately.

As for that, would Lauren welcome him?

A small shudder goes through him, and he pushes it away. And finally, his mind lands on the one thing he's been desperately trying to avoid.

Vivian.

70

Vivian appears to him as if conjured from smoke. The curl of her dark hair. The violet of her eyes in the darkness of their bedroom. The curve of her stomach. Her assurances she will be fine if he goes to visit his mother, the last words he ever hears from her. *I'll be fine. I promise. The baby won't be here for two more weeks.*

Though he is no longer hungry, out of habit, he eats a plate of brisket and French fries, washes it down with beer, hands tidbits to Kat. The sun is warm, and he puts his head back to catch a few rays, trying to turn off his mind. Remembering Viv is like poking a sore tooth, something to be avoided, yet somehow, feeling for the pain is grounding.

There you are. You are not forgotten.

Her ghost has sidled through life with him, always there, always present. The scent of her hitting him unawares when he takes a walk with Kat; in his monkish bedroom, waking him from his dreams of her warm, soft body yielding beneath him. Her laugh, almost forgotten now, a whisper on the breeze.

Why wouldn't she tell him of her past? Was it simply because they didn't have enough time? When he met her, she was working at his favorite restaurant. She was a terrible waitress. Even now, remembering how flustered she got the first time he saw her, a smile cracks his face. She dropped his coffee cup practically in his lap. If he hadn't moved quickly, he'd have been scalded. Her apologies, her mortification, so sure he wouldn't leave a tip—when instead he left her twenty bucks and his phone number. He fell for her hard and fast, and let himself. A pretty girl, a kind woman, someone to try to keep himself alive for. Did they rush into living together, and marriage? Sure. But he adored her. All of her. He'd been over the moon when she got pregnant.

He never saw her depressed, though maybe he, the great intelligencer, simply didn't know the signs to look for. Yes, she got quiet every once in a while, but he was also gone so much that it was entirely possible she simply didn't tell him. She wouldn't have wanted to add to his burden.

They'd chosen to live in Nashville because she didn't like the scrutiny of being on base. He was deployed often enough the hour-long drive to Ft. Campbell was no big deal. Now he wonders if perhaps there was more to this than he originally thought. That she wanted to be in Nashville so she could get treatment outside of the prying eyes of his superiors, who didn't look kindly on such things.

"Oh, Viv. You could have told me. I could have helped."

His minds drifts to Lauren again. Being suspicious of her isn't helping matters. He's spent all his time with her dissecting her words and actions, looking, picking, trying to find the thing that makes him say, *Oh, that's why you give me the willies.* And now Jasper is acting weird, too.

He hasn't discovered why so far, but he knows the answer is there, lurking under the surface. All the people around Lauren can't be expected to see the strain in her; they are with her every day, this is their normal. But Zack, new on the scene, can feel it. The tension comes off her like sweat, and he can sense she's ready to spring.

What is up with that?

He finishes his lunch, tips his waiter well, and is just stepping off the restaurant's deck when his cell rings. Juliet's number shows on the screen.

"Hey, what's up?"

He can hear tears in her voice.

"We have a problem."

His heart begins to race immediately, his muscles tense. "Is it Mindy? What's wrong? Is she rejecting the transplant?"

"No. It's…oh God, Zack, I don't know what to do. I've been trying to track you down. I didn't realize you left the hospital."

"I needed some air. Take a breath. What's wrong?"

"Jasper let slip to the media you used to be a government assassin."

Zack feels a calm steal over him. So this is the play. "He let that *slip*, did he?"

"Were you?"

"Would it matter if I was?"

"I'd say so, especially considering Jasper is planning to use it to mount a court battle against you. At the very least, he's trying to turn the tide against you as far as the media is concerned. Public opinion can be very influential in these high-profile cases, you know that."

He blows out a breath. "Well, he can try to ruin me all he wants. I was not an assassin. Did I kill people? Yes. I was a soldier in an active war zone. But I never killed someone who wasn't trying to kill me or my troops. And the Army will confirm that."

"He claims…"

"Juliet, he's desperate. He's going to say anything right now."

"You're being too nice about this, Zack. He's trying to ruin your reputation."

"I think it's something else. I think he's trying to draw attention away from him and Lauren."

"What do you mean?" He hears the wariness in her voice. Wariness, but not surprise.

"I just mean… I don't know what I mean. I'm getting a weird vibe off your sister, that's all."

She floors him by saying, "You too, huh?"

"It's not just me? I was worried…"

Juliet coughs a laugh. "No. I've never seen her like this. Half the time she is so distracted she doesn't seem to be in the room, the rest of the time she's hovering over Mindy and Jasper like they're gold nuggets."

"I see that as well."

"And I'm a traitor for even thinking something negative about her. She's a damn saint. She always has been. And with Mindy… Zack, you don't understand. Mindy is her world, her life. Of course she's stressed and things are weird. She's half expecting her daughter to die. I think she's trying to distance herself a bit, thinking that might somehow lessen the blow if it does happen."

"Mindy's noticed it, too. We talked about how uncomfortable everyone is about her cancer. It's bothering her, not being treated normally."

"Mindy told you that?"

"Yes. She hates that everyone's being so optimistic and upbeat. She'd like, for once, and I quote—'someone to get pissed off and rail against God or something.'"

Juliet laughs for real this time. "She trusts you. That's good. She's complained to me as well over the past few weeks, especially about how her parents are pretending everything is going to be peaches and roses when there's a good chance she won't make it."

"Totally understandable. Are you sure Lauren isn't holding something else back? Maybe something she admitted to Jasper, and now he's trying to pull up the drawbridge and save her?"

"I don't know, Zack. I really don't. I told you before, we aren't close. I'm the last person she confides in, and then it's only out of sheer need, not a desire for comfort or even advice." The bitterness and hurt come through loud and clear.

"I'm sorry this has been so difficult on you, Juliet. Is there any news on the investigation?"

"No. I should probably reach out."

"I'll do it. I'm not recused."

"Yeah, that was a stupid thing for me to do. I should have fought to stay involved, at least with the DNA."

"You can't, and you know it. But I'm sure if you wanted to call, they'd talk to you."

"Thanks, Zack. You're a good guy. You're handling this better than the rest of us."

He sighs loudly. "It's not that I'm handling it better, Juliet. I've just had longer to come to terms with it."

71

THE WRIGHTS' HOUSE

Juliet hangs up with Zack feeling marginally better, but still edgy. Her next call is to Woody, whose voice mail comes on almost immediately. Ducking her calls? Maybe.

She speed dials Bai next. He answers, breathless.

"Shit is hitting the fan, chica. Where are you right now?"

"In my car, heading to my sister's house to grab my bags. I'm being evicted. Why?"

"I need you on a computer. On secure connection. As quickly as you can. And I'm serious when I say secure."

"Okay. I'm pulling in the driveway now. I'll use Lauren's computer. Why, what did you find?"

"You don't have your laptop?"

"It's back at the hospital. I sort of stormed out. What the heck, man?"

"I need your eyes on something. I know you're recused, but…"

"Give me five and I'll call you back."

"Juliet…"

"What?"

"Just…make sure the line is secure, okay? Really secure. I have to send you a case file."

"Jesus, Bai. What's going on?"

"Juliet, please."

"Give me five. I'll call you right back."

She lets herself in the front door and goes straight to the office. Lauren's pass code is Mindy's birthday—of course it is. Lauren isn't worried about people stealing things off her computer.

Juliet logs in and downloads a private VPN service. It won't make things completely secure, but it will help. Then she downloads a secure email server called Virtru, which will encrypt any messages sent between her and Bai, and creates a throwaway email that she can self-destruct when they are finished. It isn't perfect, but it's the best she can do on a moment's notice, and she will be able to erase all traces of herself on the computer after she is through.

She dials Bai, puts him on the speaker.

"Okay, I'm in and secure. Here's the email address." She listens while he types it in, then hears the whoosh of the mail server sending the message.

It pops up on her screen moments later.

She opens it to see a DNA profile.

"What's this?"

He is whispering, like someone is nearby, possibly listening. "This is a DNA profile from Vivian Armstrong's crime scene. According to the evidence, it's always been attributed to the midwife. Thing is, that's not at all whose it is. But I did find a match in the system."

"That's great news. Whoever it is might be the killer, and who took Mindy. Tell me."

She hears another whoosh. "Check the email I just sent."

This one contains two DNA profiles, side by side. It takes her all of ten seconds to see they are a perfect match. Just to be sure, she scans the ID—the bottom right corner of each profile holds the identification data, coded by number to maintain the privacy of the samples for the lab, and avoid any intrusion or personal bias by Juliet or her staff when they run the DNA. It's fail-safe. These numbers also match.

"Don't keep me in suspense any longer, Bai. Do you have a name or only a number match?"

"Juliet, you did not hear this from me, okay?"

"Bai. Spit it out."

"The profile belongs to Lauren. Your sister was at the Armstrong crime scene."

72

The shock of the words slams into her. It takes her a minute to catch her breath. When she can speak again, she says, "What are you talking about? There's no way Lauren was there. She was in Colorado. The baby...the doctor... Bai, there must be a mistake."

"I ran it four times. There's no mistake. The evidence team from Nashville has your sister's DNA, but they don't have the report yet. I had to let you know first."

"Have you told anyone else?"

"No. But there's no way I can keep this quiet."

"I know, I know." She holds her head in both hands. *Think, Juliet. Think.*

Zack's voice comes to her. *There's something off about your sister.* "Juliet? Are you there?"

"I am. Bai, can you give me an hour before you tell anyone?"

"Oh God, Juliet. I—"

"I know what I'm asking. I don't blame you if you say no. But one hour, Bai. Just enough for me to talk to Lauren and find out what the hell is going on. Please."

He is silent for a moment, then she hears a click. "I've set a timer. One hour, Juliet, and then I have to tell Woody. And you sure as hell better act surprised when he calls to tell you, because I refuse to lose my job over this."

"You're the best, Bai. Thank you so much."

She slams down the phone and prints out the email. If she is going to confront Lauren, she is going to need proof.

But what kind of proof is this? Other than somehow her sister's DNA is in Vivian Armstrong's house. That's all it is, right? It doesn't mean…

She cleans her tracks from the computer and shuts it down. Sits for a moment, at the perfect marble-topped desk, staring at the paper with the samples side-by-side, the match clear as day.

Oh, Lauren. You really have been lying to all of us.

She steps out onto the deck. The day is gorgeous, unseasonably warm, sunny with blue skies and a few white clouds. Another big storm is coming tomorrow, a blizzard, estimated to drop anywhere from a foot to two feet of snow. Good timing, it will chase off the reporters for a little while, make them hunker down in their hotel rooms. No one wants to stand outside in a blizzard hoping for a glimpse of a sick kid.

The sense of the world spinning, rushing toward her, is palpable. The stream next to the house gurgles in warning, as if it too knows it's going to be overwhelmed on the morrow. Her tears start to fall; she brushes them away angrily.

She needs to talk to Zack.

She dials his number with shaking hands. He answers right away.

"Hey, what's up?"

"Zack. I just got off the phone with my lab. I…they found Lauren's DNA at your house. It's a part of the evidence Starr brought from Nashville."

"What?"

"I know, it's kind of hard to believe." A branch starts to wave, scratching up against the deck. "I'm stunned. I don't know what this means, or how, or why, but I have to find out what's happening."

"You said you were from Murfreesboro. How old was Lauren when you moved?"

"Sixteen. Seventeen. I don't know."

"Did she ever get treatment for depression?"

"What? No. Not that I know of. I was a kid, Zack. Why?"

"Vivian hid her world from me. Lauren's been lying to you. I just wondered if they knew each other."

"I don't know, but I'm going to go back to the hospital. I'll talk to her, figure this out."

Juliet hears the whine of an engine, then the crunch of gravel.

"Never mind. She's here. I see the car. She's pulling in the drive."

There's a new urgency in his voice, and he's louder, more commanding. "I'm on my way. Do not confront her alone."

"Zack, it will be fine. This is my sister. There's an explanation, I know there is. She can't be responsible for this."

"Juliet. Wait for me to get there to talk to her."

"Gotta go. I'll talk to you shortly."

"Juliet, no. Wait for me. You're not—" But she hangs up as Lauren pulls to a stop and gets out of the car. Looks up at the deck. She seems dazed, exhausted, and despite herself, Juliet feels the urge to comfort her.

"You okay?" Juliet calls down. "I thought you were sticking close to the hospital."

"I wasn't feeling well. I came to get some medicine."

"I'm sorry. But I'm glad you're here. We need to talk. Come on up. I'll make you some peppermint tea."

Juliet goes back inside, closes the door to the deck firmly. She turns on the fireplace with a click of the remote, fills the electric kettle, pulls out the teapot, finds the honey she loves. A cup won't hurt her, either, her stomach is churning. Lauren in Nashville? Why? How? And what does it mean?

Worse, what did she do?

73

They sit face-to-face in the dining room, their elegant china cups in saucers on the thick wooden table. A tea party. Juliet has the page she's printed out facedown, one hand on top of it as if she can contain its truth if it stays hidden. Lauren sips her tea, quiet and still. She doesn't look ill. She looks…watchful. As if she knows what's to come.

Juliet sets her cup on the saucer with an audible *conk*. Her hands are shaking. She has never seen her sister's face so carefully blank, and it's freaking her out. But she must get to the bottom of this. Lauren knows more than she is saying.

Juliet takes a deep, steadying breath. She should let Woody and Parks do this. She knows this. But it's her sister. Her *sister*.

"I know you're stressed about Mindy, but we have a problem. And we don't have much time. You need to tell me the truth, Lauren. Your honesty is the only way I'm going to be able to help you."

"What are you talking about?"

Juliet flips the paper over. "Your DNA was found at the Vivian Armstrong crime scene."

"Impossible."

Juliet smiles grimly. "That's what I said. They ran it four times. I've looked at the results myself. There's no mistake, Lauren. You were there. The police are going to come for you, and they aren't going to be as open and willing to hear your story as I am."

Lauren sits back in her chair, regards her sister. She crosses her arms over her chest. "Is that a threat?"

"It's a fact. Lauren. For God's sake, how did your DNA get there? If you tell me the truth I might be able to help you, figure out a plausible story."

Lauren laughs, oddly hollow, plastic. It is a stranger's laugh, cruel and mocking. Fear skitters down Juliet's spine. When Lauren speaks, it is in a stranger's voice. No affect. No warmth. Unrecognizable.

"You're offering to help me lie to the police? Why, Juliet, I didn't know you had it in you. You're so straitlaced. So perfect." She spits out the last word, and Juliet hears the years of resentment. She has never understood why Lauren despises her so much.

"I am far from perfect, but, Lauren, you're my sister. Mindy is my niece. I'm trying to protect this family, what's left of it, anyway. Tell me the truth. Did you kill Vivian Armstrong?"

"You can't possibly think I'm going to fall to my knees and give you a grand confession." Lauren sighs and pushes back from the table. "I need more tea for this. You?" She doesn't wait for Juliet to answer, snags her cup and steps into the kitchen. Juliet lets her, knows she's gathering herself. She saw the lies beginning to form in Lauren's eyes moments before she stood up. *She's thinking. She's planning what she's going to say. How she's going to spin this vicious truth.*

The realization of this is worse than knowing her sister's DNA is at the scene of a violent crime. Juliet knows nothing that comes from Lauren's mouth from here on out will be the truth, and the realization creates a fissure inside of her. Her sister is a murderer. A kidnapper. And what else?

Lauren comes back like a hostess serving a party—teapot on

the tray, the two cups aligned, the local honey she knows Juliet loves, shortbread. Bribes, a tray of bribes.

"I didn't add any honey since you always say I short you. Here's the whole jar. Are you hungry? I'm famished." She takes her cookies and tea and strides to the fireplace.

Juliet watches her for a minute, then shrugs and puts a dollop of honey in her tea. Lauren never does sweeten it properly. Stirs, tastes. It is overly sweet, but she tops off the cup from the teapot and sips some more. Better, but not perfect.

"Lauren, I want to know what the hell happened in Nashville."

"Yes," Lauren says, almost to herself. "Knowing you, I have to tell you something, or you're going to go screw up everything I've spent my life building."

She comes back to the table, sits heavily across from Juliet. "It's time for you to know the truth. Yes, Vivian and I knew each other. We met years ago, in Nashville. We were friends in our teens, kept up with each other after we moved to Colorado. She helped me through the divorce, the miscarriage. She was pregnant too, at the time. We supported each other, and once she was the only one carrying a child, I supported her. And then she got sick. Sick enough that she knew she was going to die. She asked me to keep Mindy safe for her. She was afraid of what Zack would do to the girl."

"Afraid of Zack? He's the dad."

"He's a stone-cold killer. She told me time and again how afraid she was of him. How she hoped he'd die in combat and never come back because she never knew when he'd forget who she was in the middle of the night and slit her throat. She was terrified of him coming home permanently. She was scared to death what he would do to the baby, what—"

"We're talking about the same Zack Armstrong, right? My God, Lauren, he's one of the kindest, gentlest men I've ever met."

"You know nothing about him. And you would be well advised to cut off whatever little romance you're having with him because he is not safe. Not at all."

"Romance? I've known him less than a week."

"I see how he looks at you. And how you look at him. You think no one notices, but I've seen it all."

Juliet hears the bitterness in Lauren's voice, but presses onward.

"There is nothing going on. Now tell me what in the world you're saying about Vivian Armstrong being afraid of him."

"Drink your tea, it's getting cold."

Juliet takes a sip, even though the mint with the honey isn't a good combination.

"Knowing she was going to die at his hand, she asked me to see the baby safe. She couldn't risk him hurting the baby. He had another six months on his tour, but they usually give compassionate leave when a baby is due. She knew he was going to get leave when she was so close to her due date. So she researched ways to induce labor. She had to keep the baby safe."

"Induce labor?"

"Yes. When he was shot and was sent home from Afghanistan early, she had to move up the timetable. It was luck his mother got sick. She encouraged him to go to her, and the minute he left, Vivian took castor oil so she'd go into labor before he came home. She called me, said she was pulling the trigger. I got in the car and drove like a bat out of hell—you know that's normally a two-day trip, from Denver to Nashville? I made it in a little less than eighteen hours, straight through. She was lucky, she was able to get her labor going, had the baby without incident. She'd just gotten rid of the midwife when I arrived. I hugged my friend and took her child to be my own. It was what she wanted. For Mindy to be safe."

"Right. And then somehow she got herself stabbed to death at the same time?"

Lauren looks over at the mountains. "You'll have to talk to

Zack about that. Supposedly he was still out of town, but we all know how crafty he is. He could very easily have made the drive, killed her, then driven back to his mother's funeral. He got away with it, and he's been searching for me ever since."

"I am having a hard time believing this."

"He's violent, Juliet. He's a killer. He smothered her, wouldn't let her out of his sight when he was home. She was being abused. And now he's within a hands-breadth of my child, and God knows what he's going to do. That's why Jasper and I are keeping watch. That's why we're so afraid for her."

Juliet is so confused. The certainty in Lauren's voice is enough to convince anyone, but Juliet can't believe this of Zack. He is too good. He is too kind. She takes another sip of the tea, sets it down with a grimace.

"You asked me to find him. You wanted me to find Zack. You practically handed Jasper the name to give to me."

"I never thought you'd be able to locate him. The military scrapped his DNA from the system. Vivian told me they do that with all their intelligence operatives. God knows how many crimes he can be linked to. And he was supposed to be living off-grid, not easily findable. His career choices made him a target. And now we're all going to be a target. His target."

Juliet is hugging herself now, arms wrapped tightly around her waist. She can't believe the words she's hearing, can't understand them. Zack, a killer. Vivian, in danger from her own husband.

Has Juliet just signed their death warrants by finding the man who can save Mindy's life? But she doesn't have time to think it through; Lauren is on a roll now.

"And of course, super sleuth Juliet, our modern-day Nancy Drew, with your beakers and potions, you found him and brought that viper into our lives. And now what are we supposed to do? The media is watching, and he thinks he's safe. That the *grieving dad* will supersede the truth. Well, it won't.

If something happens to me, there's a letter ready to go to the press, explaining everything he's done."

"But the doctor, Castillo...why lie?"

"Don't you see? I was trying to keep us safe. I couldn't have any ties to Vivian. The Castillo story was the perfect cover. She was feeding babies into the system. It was the right timing, the right scenario. I saw the story in the paper, about that Graciela girl. I knew it was the perfect cover in case anyone—especially Zack—ever found out. There was no way anyone could prove I hadn't received one of those babies."

Juliet shakes her head, trying to absorb all of this. "Zack isn't a bad man—"

"Says you? He's charmed you to pieces. Him and his dog. Also a trained killer, mark my words. That beast is his weapon when he can't hold the gun in his hand. You can't see who he really is. You're blinded. But don't worry. Now that we have what we need from him, I'm going to take care of him. He won't hurt anyone in this family. Ever."

Lauren comes around the table to Juliet, sits next to her and takes her in her arms. Juliet is shaking, but Lauren is steady as a rock. "It's okay, honey. I forgive you. I knew you'd break all the rules to save Mindy's life. We both—all three of us—thank you for doing that. I'll make sure Woody knows you weren't responsible."

"What are you talking about?"

"I know you broke into the files, took Mindy's DNA, and put it into CODIS to look for a match. I'm so proud of you for breaking the rules. It must have been so difficult for you. I explain it all in the letter, because I didn't want you to get in trouble for doing something so unethical."

"That's not exactly what happened. And don't bother. He already knows. I'm on suspension." And then she really hears what Lauren is saying. "Wait, you threw me under the bus in your letter?"

Lauren smiles and puts a finger on her lips. "I'm trying to save you, sweetie. Zack Armstrong is very dangerous, and if something happens, we need to be covered. We need to protect our family. I will do whatever's necessary to protect us. Whatever it takes."

"The man's an English professor at Vanderbilt. He's a grieving widower. He's Mindy's father. You're wrong about him."

Lauren's chin rises. "I will not allow him to hurt my daughter."

"So you're going to discredit him? Or what, get rid of him? Dear God, Lauren, you've gone entirely insane. Has the lack of sleep made you psychotic? Does Jasper know how ill you are?"

"Jasper knows everything. I told him what Zack is, why he's such a danger to us. What you did. And now I've told you as well, not that I think it will matter."

"You can't be serious, Lauren. You can't just kill Zack. The police will be all over you in a heartbeat."

"I've handled threats to this family before."

Juliet stands up, the chair screeching back. "Like Vivian Armstrong? Did you kill her so you could steal her baby? Because that's a hell of a lot more plausible to me than this whopper of a story you've just told me. You're lying. Why are you lying about this?"

"You really don't remember. It's amazing." Lauren shakes her head with an uncanny smile, and the frisson reverberates through Juliet's spine. It is not Zack who is the problem. Her sister is a monster.

"Remember what?"

"Why we moved to Colorado. I know you were young, and Mom always said you blocked it out entirely."

"What are you talking about, Lauren?"

"Bennett Thompson."

"Our stepfather? He died when I was little. I don't remember him."

"Oh yes, he died. I took care of that for us. I paid the *price*. I lost a year of my life for *you*. You never even knew what I did for you."

Lauren's eyes are furious, and Juliet cringes.

"What do you mean?"

"He was molesting you."

"What? No, he wasn't. I would remember!"

"I found him in your bedroom, on top of you. I had to stop him. I cut his throat. Mom helped me. She made me swear never to talk to you about him."

"You're telling me you murdered our stepfather, and our mother helped?"

Lauren turns off as quickly as a switch flipped. She turns her head to the side, evaluating Juliet. "It doesn't matter. Not anymore."

"Of course it matters." A penny drops. "You didn't go away to school. You went to jail."

"I went to a fucking mental hospital with a bunch of criminally insane schizophrenics, so you could be safe and warm in mommy's arms. No one ever worried about me. I was the one who had to deal with him. I was the one who had to deal with the consequences."

Juliet's memory feels foggy, but she is having a hard time believing this story. She would remember if she'd been molested. She remembers everything—except the face of the man who was her stepfather.

Her gorge rises, and she chokes it down. "Why would Mom help you cover up a murder? That's wrong."

"She figured out he was diddling her kids. When she found out the truth, well, Mom was sorry she didn't cut his throat herself."

"I don't believe you."

"Haven't you ever wondered why you and Mom weren't close? She always resented you. I was her favorite, and I had to go to that place, and she was stuck with you. I was the one who suffered all his attention. I was the one who got pregnant. I was the one who sacrificed my life. All because we had to protect sweet, innocent little Juliet."

"Was there a trial? Were you convicted?" A connection forms. "Wait, you were pregnant?"

"I miscarried."

Juliet feels uncomfortably warm. Something is wrong. And at this point, she has no idea what to believe, whether this is plausible or not, when another, even more horrid thought hits her. *I've handled threats to this family before.*

And it all comes together for her. The rage, the sadness. Her infertile sister, already off balance, who would do anything to have a child to love.

"You met Vivian Armstrong in the hospital, didn't you? You stayed friends with her all those years, and when the time came, you murdered her and stole her child for your own. You sicken me."

Lauren waves her hand like a queen to a crowd. "You are nothing to me."

"Is that why Detective Gorman came out here, because you killed our stepfather, and he figured it out and tracked you down? He knew you were tied to Vivian. He knew about Mindy. He came to confront you, and you killed him."

The serene smile doesn't leave Lauren's face, though one edge of her lip quirks. There is pride in her face, in her smile. Pride at stopping the threat to her family.

"Oh, my God, Lauren. What have you done? Who are you?"

"Gorman was in the way. It was the most expedient thing to do. I've spent my life clearing a path for Mindy to have the world. Now that she's received the stem cells, she's going to be healed, and get back on her skis, and she's going to have an incredible life. Just as she should. And if anyone tries to hurt her, or stop her, I will make sure they are taken care of."

Juliet sits heavily.

"You're mad. You're absolutely insane."

"I'm the sanest person you'll ever talk to, little sister. I have my priority, and it's my daughter. It's always been Mindy. Everything I've done for the past seventeen years has been for her."

"What do you think Mindy will feel like when she finds out her mother is a murderer?"

"She will never know."

"No? How are you going to assure that? Kill everyone involved? Murder the CBI team and the Nashville detectives? It's too late, Lauren. The DNA proves it. They already know what you did."

Lauren's face doesn't change. She continues watching Juliet with her pasted-on *Mona Lisa* smile.

"This is ridiculous. I refuse to listen to any more lies. I'm leaving, right now."

"Are you?"

Juliet's heart is racing. The warmth she felt earlier is spreading. Her feet feel like lead. She can't lift them. Her knees are locked, her mouth dry. Spots swim in her vision. Her head feels so heavy.

"What have you done, Lauren?" Her voice is thick, her tongue too big for her mouth. Saliva begins to flow; she can't stop it, she's drowning. The room is spinning, spinning.

"As I said, I will do whatever is necessary to keep my daughter safe."

"So you're trying to kill me?"

The smile turns sad, and Lauren gestures to the cups on the table. Juliet turns to look at them, but the thoughts won't come. She barely hears Lauren's next words.

"Oh, sister. You're already dead."

Juliet crashes to the floor.

74

Zack hangs up with Juliet, a terrible feeling of dread spreading through him. Lauren at the crime scene is unfathomable. And yet…her attachment to Mindy, her fierce protectiveness, the lack of friends, the practical isolation of the child, the claustrophobia of their relationship—Lauren spending weeks refusing to leave her side until forced to do so and not allowing visitors—it all makes an obscene kind of sense, and leads him to a frightening conclusion.

Lauren murdered Vivian and stole their baby for her own.

This thought alone is enough to propel him straight to the Wrights' house, but he is on foot. He has no car, and there is no question of trying to make it up the mountain in anything but a vehicle.

He turns in circles, assessing, looking. There are people around. He can ask someone heading into the garage, pay them if necessary. And while he's doing it, he can call a cab or an Uber. See which reaches him first.

Bolting off the porch with Kat at his side, he notices a man with a long-focus lens camera standing down the brick-lined alley. Two steps later his mind registers what his eyes have just seen. The face is familiar, but it's the red baseball cap worn backward that identifies him. Zack saw him this morning in the parking lot, sitting in his car, taking shots of the hospital.

A reporter.

Zack about-faces, darts down the alley toward the man, who sees him charging and starts backing up, horror on his face, one hand out as if that will stop the onslaught of frantic man and angry dog.

"Hey. Hey! I need your help."

"Dude, I'm just here taking pictures. No harm, no foul."

"You're a reporter. I saw you at the hospital. I need a ride. It's an emergency."

"Is it Mindy?"

Zack starts to say no but realizes this may be the most expedient way of getting what he needs. "Yes, it's Mindy. Her mother is at the house, she just called and said there's a problem and can I meet her there. I don't have a ride. Can you get me up the mountain?"

"To the Wrights' place? Shit, dude, for a price, sure."

"What's the price?" Zack reaches for his wallet. There is no time to negotiate. He has to get to Juliet.

"I don't want money, man. Interview."

"Fine. Fine. It's a deal. Let's go." Zack starts toward the garage, but the photographer points down the alley.

"My car's right over here. I know the gate security agent, he let me park it by the village entrance."

They are in the car—a small green Subaru Impreza with a ski rack on top, the back full of equipment, technical and ski— and rolling away less than a minute later. Kat is perched in the backseat, legs at angles, balancing against the sharp, fast turns.

"Do you know where you're going?"

The reporter adjusts his Maui Jim sunglasses. "Actually, dude, yeah. I've been scoping the story for a while now, trying to get Mindy alone to talk to me." He seems unembarrassed by this blatant greed. Zack wants to punch him but has a feeling even violence won't stop the kid.

The car zooms around the circle, and they are climbing. Zack wants to jam the car into fifth and make it go faster. Whatever is happening, it's happening now, and he needs to get there.

"Could you hurry?"

"I'm going as fast as is smart, dude. The roads are still icy up high. I'd rather not plunge off the side of the mountain."

"Who are you even with? You don't exactly have the corporate vibe."

The kid grins, puts out a hand. "Bode Greer, at your service. I work for *Ski Magazine*. I did the profile on Mindy a couple of months ago. We got along. I figured I have as good a chance as anyone to get in to talk to her. I think she dug me."

The smug, knowing smile is enough to make Zack's blood pressure rise. He knows exactly what Greer means. He gives the boy—he is only a boy, in his early twenties, handsome, carefree—a long look. He is shocked to hear himself say, "You aren't getting anywhere near my daughter, young man."

If he wasn't so scared, so witlessly terrified, this sudden surge of protectiveness would make him laugh. But as it is, he knows only one thing. It is paramount that he protects Mindy. From the reporters. From Jasper. From Lauren. Hell, even from Juliet. He needs to get her separated from the entire world here, all the people who have been using her and riding her coattails and forcing her into the daily servitude of being a world-class athlete. She needs peace to heal, time to get to know her real family.

Vivian, help me. Help me save our girl.

He tries Juliet's cell phone, which goes to voice mail immediately. This is not good.

He realizes Bode is still talking. "—no offense, dude. I'm just saying she's a cool chick. She was a fun interview. I'm not trying to exploit her or anything. It's a huge story, whether she can keep her lead in the World Cup standings or whether she's going to miss it this year."

"The story is bigger than her World Cup standings, trust me."

"Tell me. And hey, there's a recorder in my pocket, mind reaching over and turning it on?"

"What?"

"Oh. Did I not mention we're on the record?"

"You manipulative little shit."

Bode smooths his cap. "Hey, man, I'm just trying to make a living. You'd do the same in my shoes."

They are flying up the mountain now, hitting the straightaway that leads to the final set of switchbacks that will bring them to the Wrights' drive. Zack's hands are balled into fists. He bites the inside of his lip, and the pain is sharp and intense. He relaxes his hands and takes a deep breath, the metallic tang of his blood on his tongue. His blood that will save her. His blood that flows through her veins. In his blood, the truth.

"Fine. On the record. An interview with Mindy and me. Now shut the fuck up and get me to that house."

★ ★ ★

It is quiet when he arrives. Juliet's truck is in its usual spot, off to the right in the guest slot. The garage doors are closed; the house feels empty. He doesn't know why he expected it to be any different than normal—maybe he imagined the two sisters tearing each other's hair out on the front deck, fighting to the death over him. The idea makes him snort, and Bode, who has just put the car into Park, glances over inquisitively.

"Never mind, it's nothing."

"Okay. Now what?"

"Stay here."

"Come on, man, you said—"

"Mindy isn't here, Bode. And we agreed—an interview with Mindy and me. Now, stay in the car. And no taking photos, all right? I'll be back in a minute. Kat, stay."

She whines but listens. He runs up the front stairs, dodging the icy corners, and rings the bell, but no one answers. He tries the knob, but it's locked. He doesn't have a key. What's he going to do, break down the door in front of the reporter? That will go over well.

He presses the doorbell, tries Juliet's cell phone again, too, knowing something is terribly, dreadfully wrong.

Bode is out of the car now, sensing the urgency. Kat's head is out the window. She begins to bark. The garage door goes up.

Lauren's car appears at the end of the driveway. The car stops, and Zack can imagine what this looks like—him on the front porch, looking ready to break down her door, a stranger's car blocking the garage doors. Zack waves and runs down the stairs. Lauren pulls up closer. She is alone. Where is Juliet?

He is standing by the car now. Lauren puts down the window.

"Where is she?"

"Who?"

"Juliet?"

Lauren points to her sister's car. "Isn't she inside?"

"I don't know. The door is locked, no one's answering. I thought she was meeting you here."

"She is. She called and said she had something to discuss. I was shopping, drove up here as quickly as I could. She called you, too, I see." Mild curiosity, or is it derision? He can't tell with her anymore. He wants to wring her neck. He wants to reach through the window and pull her hair, twist her head to the side, force her to admit what she's done. But his hands hang limp at his side, and she shakes her head impatiently as if he's simply an insect who's buzzing around her face. What sort of game is she playing? Has she really not talked to Juliet yet? She's not acting evasive or concerned.

"Yes, she did call me. We were talking when you came home. She hung up when you pulled in the driveway. She hasn't answered her phone since."

"She must have seen someone else, because I've been at the

grocery store and just got here. Could you get…whoever that is to move his ratty little car? I'd like to pull into the garage."

"I'm happy to. Hey, Bode? Move the car to the other side, will you? Mrs. Wright wants to pull in."

Bode salutes and jumps behind the wheel, and Zack steps out of the way. Lauren zooms past and into the garage, then comes out, keys jingling. She pops the trunk. "Can you grab the bags for me? I thought we could all eat here tonight. Since we can't eat with Mindy, a family dinner among the rest of us is a good thing, right? We have to get used to our new normal."

Either she is the coolest customer to ever live, or Juliet saw the wrong car and Lauren doesn't yet know she's been implicated in Vivian's murder. He grabs two brown bags of groceries and a zipped-up insulated freezer bag. Lauren has already gone inside. Bode signals and Zack nods. He opens the door, and Kat rushes out, straight past Zack, into the house, a streak of brown fur. Zack pushes the freezer bag into Bode's arms. "Listen, I don't know—"

Kat begins to bark, sharp and urgent, and Zack hears a long, high-pitched scream.

75

Zack bolts through the garage door and up the stairs, Bode tight on his heels. He enters into a nightmare.

It takes a moment for him to register everything. Lauren, on her knees, screaming. Kat, two feet away from Lauren, neck stretched taut with the ferocity of her barking.

Legs, clad in jeans and boots, akimbo on the carpet.

Three long strides and the face comes into view.

Juliet.

Her face is dusky purple, her eyes slivers of white, a thick foam on her lips. He drops to his knees by her side, dimly hears Bode yelling in the background.

"Call 911," he shouts, and Bode whips out his cell phone.

"Is she alive?" Lauren is calling to him, crying, grabbing at his arm. He shoves her away and sticks two fingers against Juliet's carotid. There is a slow bump, then another, but the intervals are too spaced, and he realizes she's very nearly dead.

He has no idea what's happened, no idea what is causing this, though the back of his mind is screaming, *Some kind of poison, some kind of overdose*; that foam is a dead giveaway.

"Is she on any medications?"

"I don't know. I think she takes an antidepressant. Oh, God, is she trying to commit suicide?"

They have no time to lose. Without another thought he starts chests compressions, hard and professional, a soldier's response, counting off as he does. He feels a rib give way. Lauren weeps by his side. Bode drops to his knees across from Zack. His face is white as bone.

"Ambulance is on its way. Can I do anything? Should I breathe for her?"

"No. Don't touch her, don't touch her mouth. Get Lauren out of here, and let the paramedics in the second they get here. Shout 'Narcan' at them as they come in."

He pumps on her chest, heels of his hands to her breastbone, feeling the strange intimacy of flesh to flesh, knowing this is the only chance he can give her.

He calls over his shoulder, "Lauren, look in her purse. Is there any medication in there? Do you know if she's ever taken illegal drugs?"

"I don't know," Lauren wails back. "She doesn't tell me anything like that."

He hears the sirens now, and a small spark of hope begins in his chest. Kat edges closer, then runs to the windows to watch the fire truck pulling into the driveway, the ambulance right behind.

And then they are surrounded, and a woman in a uniform is pulling him away, saying, "Sir, sir, let me take over now. What did she take?"

"We don't know. We found her this way." There are needles now, and tubes and an aspirator and oxygen, and within moments, they are administering the Narcan and strapping her to the gurney.

"We're losing her, we gotta go, now. The Narcan isn't working. She's not responding."

"The front door," Zack says to Bode, who is standing to his right, a hand over his mouth. He has never seen death up close and personal, Zack knows this from the horrified look on the boy's face.

Lauren is on the phone now, calling Jasper, he thinks. The

gurney begins to clatter down the stairs, and he rounds on her, the fury barely contained. He knows this is all wrong, she is all wrong. Juliet did not do this to herself.

But he can't read this mercurial woman standing before him. She is freaking out, falling apart, crying hard, and as they load her sister into the back of the ambulance, he has no choice but to whistle for Kat and grab Bode's arm. "Stay with her," he commands, and Bode nods, eyes wide. "Give me your card. I'll call you when I know more."

The kid fumbles a card into Zack's hand. "You're going with them?"

But Zack is already down the stairs and hopping in the back of the ambulance. The female paramedic starts to push him out, "Sir, the dog—" but he snaps, "Close the door," and she obeys immediately. The sudden quiet is unnerving. "Just get to work on her," he says, dialing his phone.

Parks answers on the first ring, and Zack doesn't hesitate. "We have a problem."

"Where the hell are you? I need—"

"Listen to me. I'm in an ambulance with Juliet. She's been poisoned. And I think Lauren did it."

"What?"

"Juliet called me, frantic, about thirty minutes ago. She said Lauren's DNA was found at the crime scene in Nashville."

"What—"

"I don't know where she got the information, or what the hell happened before I got there. She told me Lauren was coming up the driveway, and she would handle it, but I didn't like the idea of her confronting Lauren alone, so I headed right up the mountain. She didn't answer her phone again. When I arrived, Lauren wasn't there. She drove up a minute later with groceries in the car, and we found Juliet down in the dining room.

"She tossed out the idea that Juliet was trying to commit suicide, but I don't buy it for a second. Someone needs to find a time stamp on that grocery receipt because I have a terrible feeling Lauren hurt Juliet. I think she's been covering her tracks ever since I came into the picture."

"Let me make sure I'm hearing you right. Lauren Wright knew your wife?"

"I don't know if she knew her. But I'm pretty damn sure she killed her."

76

VAIL HEALTH HOSPITAL

The emergency room doors have been kept clear of the media, but they are still swarming over the parking lot near the hospital's main entrance. The ambulance screeches to a stop, the paramedic pushes him out of the way, and Juliet disappears inside before Zack is fully upright. Kat is glued to his leg, her lead trailing behind her. One of the reporters sees them—the dog is as distinctive as he is—and starts to shout. The scrum begins moving toward him, but Zack gathers Kat's lead and hurries into the hospital.

At the emergency desk, he gets the attention of a young nurse. "I'm with Juliet Ryder. They just brought her in by ambulance."

"Oh, the overdose? They took her back, they're working on her. You her husband?"

"Um… Yes, yes I am."

She narrows her eyes at him but nods. "Okay, come with me."

She leads him through the doors to a small triage cubicle, then shoves a stack of papers on a clipboard at him, thoughtfully providing a pen from her blue scrub pocket. "Fill these out. I'll let them know you're here."

"Can you check on her, please? I'm… I need…"

"I'll find out. You fill these out now. And get that dog out of here." She gives another curt nod and disappears down the hall.

He stares helplessly after her, then glances at the forms in his lap. There is nothing more for him to do.

He obviously can't fill out the forms, so he calls Parks again. "Where do we stand?"

"You're right about the DNA. Juliet's second in command, Dr. Ford, just confirmed it to Woody. Apparently, he told Juliet, and she asked him to wait for an hour. Which he did. I get the sense he's in hot water. And Juliet's been suspended. Did you know?"

"No. Why?"

"They didn't tell, and I didn't ask."

"Damn it, what was she thinking? What about Lauren? I left her under the supervision of a very young reporter who's clearly getting the scoop of his career right about now."

"I don't know. Vail police have been called to take Lauren in. We're coming up from Denver, should be there quick, they're using a chopper. What the hell happened to Juliet?"

Zack relays the scene, fighting to keep his composure. "It sure looks like Lauren wasn't there, arrived moments after I did, and she was a total wreck, crying and freaking out, but I'm telling you, something is wrong about that woman. I've felt it since I met her. Like there's a cold core inside of her, and all her actions are fake."

"You think she tried to kill her sister?"

"I think the odds of Juliet Ryder calling me to tell me Lauren's DNA was at my house, then committing suicide, are next to nil. So yeah. I think Lauren thought Juliet ran the tests and hadn't told anyone, and she could shut her up."

"That's a serious charge."

"The woman may have killed my wife! Who knows what she's capable of?"

"I hear you. Don't go anywhere near her, do you understand? Let the police handle this. Just stay where you are, don't talk to anyone. You're a monk on a fucking mountaintop until I get there, you hear me?"

"Loud and clear."

He hangs up the phone and starts to pace. Damn it, he doesn't want to wait here quietly. He wants to find Lauren and make her tell him the truth, by force, if necessary. He wants to rush down the hall and see if Juliet is going to live. He wants to hurry upstairs and hug his daughter.

Jasper isn't on his radar. But when he comes down the hall, walking quickly, his hiking boots squeaking on the linoleum floors, Zack has to stop himself from punching the man in the jaw.

"What the hell is going on?" Jasper demands. "Where is Lauren? Isn't she with you?"

"I have no idea where she is. I'm waiting to hear if Juliet is going to live or not."

"Lauren said she overdosed."

"Did Lauren also tell you—" he cuts himself off. Monk. Mountain. He tries again. "What did she say happened? I heard her call you when I was giving Juliet CPR."

"She was that bad?"

Zack sags back against the wall. "I'll be surprised if she makes it."

"Christ." Jasper runs his hand across his face. "Mindy will be devastated. She thinks Juliet walks on water. Lauren said she found her on the floor in the dining room. That she may have taken something and overdosed."

"Do you honestly think Juliet would commit suicide? Come on, Jasper."

His brows furrow. "What else could have happened? What are you saying?"

But Zack is saved by the nurse, who gestures for him to come with her. He doesn't look back, marches away with Kat by his side.

"I told you to get rid of that dog."

"She's a service animal." He pulls out the badge.

"Oh. Well, they aren't going to let her into the room. I guess I'll just hold on to her. Your wife is very sick. They did a blood gas trying to figure out what she took and found ethylene glycol in her system. They're giving her the treatment now and will be putting her on dialysis, too. That stuff is bad on the kidneys. She's intubated, she can't talk, her lungs are torched. I won't lie to you. She's in rough shape, sir."

"Ethylene glycol? Isn't that antifreeze?"

"A component of it, yes. My husband's a veterinarian, he sees it all the time in his practice. Not as common for people to drink it, but it happens."

Zack tries to wrap his head around this. How can a person accidentally drink antifreeze? A kid, maybe, he can see that. But an adult? Either they did it on purpose...or someone slipped it to them.

"The fomepizole, that's the treatment, it's super expensive. They are going to need to get some forms signed before they start, in case your insurance doesn't cover it. But there's no time to waste."

"Good God, give her the medicine already. Don't wait another second. If it will save her, do it."

"You'll have to sign—"

"It will be covered," he says. "She has excellent benefits, she's a CBI agent."

"No kidding? Wow. Do you have any idea why she'd try to hurt herself? They're going to want to do a psych consult..."

"She didn't hurt herself. Someone did this to her. I'm sure of it."

77

THE WRIGHTS' HOUSE

Lauren stands in her dining room, watching the ambulance shriek away. The mess the paramedics have made is incredible. The floor is littered with plastic wrappings, discarded needle caps, tubing. They should come with a disclaimer—yes, we'll save your life, but only if you clean up the mess.

"Watch out. Is that puke? Ugh, grody."

She has nearly forgotten the kid—who looks familiar—standing bug-eyed in her living room.

"Who are you, exactly?"

"Bode Greer. *Ski Magazine.* My man Zack promised an interview. What do you say we sit down, and you can tell me what the heck just happened? That was your sister, right?"

"I remember you. You interviewed Mindy."

"I did. Best single-issue sales we've had in years. I was hoping for a follow-up, now that we know who she really is."

Who she really is. The words are a knife to Lauren's already fragile heart.

"You want to know who she really is? I'll tell you. She's my daughter. And this situation is a private family matter. I don't know how or why you've insinuated yourself in at this particular moment, or what sort of bargain you and that Armstrong man made, but you're not welcome here. I have no comment for you, and there will be no interviews with my daughter. And I swear to you, if you write about this, I'll sue you and your magazine. Now, get out. You can see yourself to the door."

There is honey on the table. "Tsk," she murmurs. "Messy, messy, Juliet."

She picks up the teacup from where it's fallen on the floor.

"Hey, isn't this, like, a crime scene or something? Don't the cops need to see everything the way it is?"

She eyes him coldly. "I told you to leave, and I meant it. Get out, or I'll call the police and have you forcibly removed."

Bode puts up his hands and reverses his ball cap. "Fine, fine. I'm out."

She locks the door behind him. There is little time; she has to get everything cleaned up and get to Mindy.

Stupid Juliet. Just had to go sticking her nose in. Lauren could have handled all of this if her dumb little sister hadn't decided to solve the crime of the century.

She hums one of Mindy's favorite songs, something from a band called Imagine Dragons, as she thoroughly washes the cups and teapot, pours the honey down the drain, follows it with hot, hot water. It wouldn't do to have anyone else get ill, then she might be blamed, and she can't let that happen.

She washes the teapot and sets the kettle to boil. She leaves the groceries melting in their bags on the counter where Zack and the reporter left them; it seems appropriate that she would forget about them in the chaos.

She makes a fresh pot of tea, pulls a new cup and saucer from the cabinet and sets them on the table. She tries to think what color lipstick Juliet had on, but can't remember. It must have been something very subtle—probably that Burt's Bees Pomegranate lip balm she carts around everywhere. Mindy uses it, too.

Down the hall in Mindy's—*my daughter's*—room, she finds a tube on the night table. Back in the dining room, she pours some tea into the cup, carefully picks it up and kisses the edge, then runs her finger across the nude smear. Perfect. She throws the cup and its contents to the floor, making sure it lands where Juliet fell.

She takes in the scene. Yes, this works. All is as it was.

The letters…she moves quickly to her bedroom and slides the dresser away from the wall. Sure enough, the manila envelope of secrets is gone.

Mindy, Mindy, Mindy. You are so naughty. She should feel panic, but she is past that. Now, it's all about self-preservation.

She takes a quick look through her daughter's room, doesn't find them. The bathroom—ah, yes. Here they are. Under the sink, wedged against the wall. She takes the package and heads back to the living room.

One last thing…from under the kitchen sink, she takes the bottle of straight ethylene glycol that she borrowed from the garage. Jasper loves to save a dime here and there, and orders gallons of it online to make his own antifreeze, hating how much the brand names charge. She wipes it clean of her fingerprints, and sets it back in its proper place, making sure to coat it lightly in dust she swipes from the corner of the garage. A spider scuttles out of her way, frightened by the intrusion.

She watches its retreat. Normally she would rout it out immediately; she can't stand the idea it may drop onto her shoulders as she passes through to her car unawares, but a reprieve is given. She feels a strange kinship with the small creature, hiding fearfully in its dirty corner. It will do anything it can to survive. It is at the mercy of its environment, of the people it comes in contact with. Any moment could be its last.

Just like her.

★ ★ ★

Bode Greer waits until the car pulls out of the driveway, debating. What kind of woman takes fifteen minutes to follow her dying sister to the hospital? What has she been doing in there?

The Lauren Wright he remembers is not this woman. The interview had been fun. They'd been in the lodge at the top of Copper Mountain. Mindy had finished her last practice runs before the big events started, the interviews were standard at this point. He'd felt lucky to get one with her; everyone wanted to talk to the young phenom.

During the interview, Mindy's mother had been charming, self-deprecating, offering to buy hot chocolate for him and Mindy as they spoke. She'd hovered a bit, yes, but in a pleasantly protective way. Mindy hadn't seemed to mind at all. It was clear they were very close.

The woman he met upstairs is cold, calculating, awful. She makes his gonads shrivel. There is something very, very wrong with her. With all of this.

He's torn. Go back to the house, try to get in and see what she's just done, or follow her.

In the end, he thinks about what Zack Armstrong might want. Bode has a good feeling about the man. He seems like a straight shooter.

He puts the car in gear and follows her down the hill.

78

Parks packs up his bag for the chopper ride to Vail, shoving everything in without rhyme or reason. Starr is standing by the windows, looking out to the helipad, talking on her phone. He beckons to her, and she raises a finger. He taps his watch, and she nods.

The case is coming together. Lauren Wright's DNA at the crime scene is explainable by only a few scenarios. Parks, with the long-honed instincts of a veteran homicide detective, feels certain the link between the two women has something to do with Vivian Armstrong's incarceration at University Hospital.

The subpoena for Armstrong's records came in two hours ago, and Starr has been on the phone since the document was served, combing through the files from afar. The 1990s have already been scanned and archived, so it's not taking as long as it could to find the information they need.

Starr hangs up and rushes over. "Let's go. I'll brief you guys on the way."

They clamber into the chopper, put on their headsets, and are airborne moments later. Starr's voice comes over the headset, tinny against the whapping rotors.

"I'm going to cut to the chase. We know Vivian Armstrong—née Vivian Sato—did inpatient treatment for a depressive disorder at University Hospital. She was in and out from 1993–1998. She attempted suicide several times, both before her treatment and while she was there. When they let her out, she went to a halfway house and found a job in a restaurant. Soon after, she met Zack Armstrong and the rest of her story we know.

"Here's the new info: She roomed with another teenager named Liesel Thompson. Thompson came in after a suicide attempt. I got another subpoena and pulled her juvie records, which show she was charged with manslaughter and sentenced to no less than one year at Middle Tennessee Mental Health Institute."

Parks taps Woody on the knee. "That's our criminal psychiatric facility."

"Copy," Woody said. "Who did she kill?"

"A man named Bennett Thompson, thirty-six, worked at Nashville International as a baggage handler."

"Her dad? She killed her dad?"

"Her stepdad. He married Liesel's mother in 1990. Here's the thing. The judge noted there were extenuating circumstances, which is why the charge was manslaughter, and she was sent to a hospital instead of jail. The case was never adjudicated. She was sixteen at the time."

"What extenuating circumstances?"

"In November of 1993, while an inpatient at University Hospital, three months after she was admitted, Liesel Thompson suffered a miscarriage. She was five months pregnant. The baby was Bennett Thompson's."

"Her stepdad got her pregnant, so she killed him?" Woody asks.

"Yes, he got her pregnant. But that's not why she killed him. She had a little sister."

Parks is seeing the whole picture now. "He was abusing the sister, too?"

Starr nods. "It doesn't say that explicitly in the records, but it's a safe bet."

"I take it Lauren Ryder Wright's real name is Liesel Thompson?" Woody says.

"Yep. It was legally changed back in 1994, here in Colorado. Juliet was only six when they moved. Ryder is the mom's maiden name, she dropped Thompson, too. Once Liesel—Lauren—got out of the hospital, the mom sold everything and moved them west. They all got a fresh start. Lauren went to a pricey boarding school for her senior year, Juliet was enrolled in the local elementary school, and everyone proceeded on with their lives as if nothing happened."

"Is Juliet Ryder aware of all of this?" Parks asks.

Woody shakes his head. "I've never heard a whisper of this, not even during her background check. She hasn't ever spoken of it to me. Juvenile records of a family member wouldn't necessarily be opened, and the name change…well, we'll have to take a look at our files, see if there's anything in her jacket that talks about this. But as far as I know, there isn't anything." He rubs his chin. "God. Poor Juliet. Poor Lauren."

"Juliet was very young, and we have no idea the extent of the abuse. But if her sister tried to kill her today, could be Lauren wants the past to stay hidden. Honestly, without reopening the Vivian Armstrong case, no one would ever have looked into this. As far as we know, the two women don't intersect at all, outside of their months together in the hospital."

"They intersect again between 1995 and 2000," Parks says grimly. "We need to find out how."

"Let's step back for a moment," Starr says. "This woman killed her stepfather. She's allegedly tried to kill her sister. We think she killed Vivian Armstrong. Do you think…"

"She killed Gorman, too?" Parks says, nodding. "Possibly."

"That makes four victims. Her ex-husband is dead, too, and so is the doctor she claims to have worked with. What the hell are we dealing with here?"

"A psychopathic killer, who nearly got away with it," Starr says.

"Starr, let's not jump to conclusions."

"Yeah, Parks, tell that to Juliet," Woody replies, looking out the chopper window.

79

VAIL HEALTH HOSPITAL

Zack is allowed in to see Juliet after they administer the expensive antidote to the poison. Buried under tubing and ventilators, she is practically unrecognizable. The doctor, a young ER resident, stands at the foot of the bed, inputting his notes into the computer. He glances up when Zack enters the room.

"Will she live?" he asks the doctor.

"Are you the bastard who broke her ribs?"

"I am."

"Then yes, she will, and it's because of you. She would have died on the mountain before the ambulance arrived without your quick work. You have medical training?"

"Long time ago. Army."

"Gotcha." The doctor holds out a hand. "Flynn. Nice job. Don't know if she's going to be too happy when she wakes up. Broken ribs are a bitch, especially cracked off the sternum. You saved her life, though from what I'm hearing, she may not thank you for that. EMTs said she was a suicide. It's an awful way to go if you're trying to off yourself, I'll give you that."

"She didn't do this to herself. Someone fed her the antifreeze."

"You're sure?"

"I'm one hundred percent positive. There's no way she tried to hurt herself. No way. She called me thirty minutes before I found her like this. This is a long story, and the CBI will be here any minute. They can fill you in on all the gory details.

But I have to go check on my daughter, who is upstairs, and I'm afraid to leave Juliet alone without professional protection."

"Your daughter is in the hospital, too?"

"Mindy Wright."

"Oh, the skier. Let me call Dr. Oliver and get an update for you."

"Protection. She needs protection. They both do. Please." He points at Juliet, covered in leads, intubated, the machine breathing for her. She looks so weak and ethereal, so damaged. "This wasn't an accident. It was attempted murder."

"Okay, I hear you, Mr. Armstrong. Give me a few minutes to make arrangements, okay? Juliet has some rough hours ahead of her. She ingested a heck of a lot of ethylene glycol, plus a hefty dose of benzodiazepine. Her level was well above normal dosages, even for someone who was taking the drug consistently for weeks."

"What, like antianxiety medication?"

"Exactly. You're sure she wasn't trying to end things? Because this particular combination would have been very effective if she hadn't been attended to so quickly."

"I'm sure," Zack says, his voice firm.

"We have to reverse the damage the ethylene glycol did to her kidneys, watch for other organ failure, keep checking her levels, and the benzo overdose, well… She's stabilized for the moment but in very serious condition, and this is all touch and go for the next twenty-four hours. We're taking her to ICU for the duration of the treatment. I'm assuming she'll be in there for a couple of days at least. It's as secure an environment as this hospital has. Plus, we have decent security. We get celebrities in here sometimes. I'll get the guards up here right away, both to Juliet's room and to oncology. Okay?"

"Thank you."

Flynn leaves the room, but not before asking a nurse to step in. Zack is heartened by this action. It means that he's not stupid;

if someone has already tried to murder his patient, he's hardly going to leave her alone with a stranger.

The nurse fiddles with the IV, and Zack takes Juliet's hand. "Juliet," he whispers, and almost cries with joy when he feels a slight answering squeeze.

80

When Parks, Starr, and Woody arrive, they are greeted by a phalanx of police and hospital security. Dr. Flynn, true to his word, put out the call, and the hospital is now swarming with law enforcement. The reporters outside are in a dither—first Vail police show up, followed by the Eagle County Sheriff's deputies, then the CBI comes in on their helicopter with unidentified cops from Nashville. Everyone knows something major is up, and everyone is trying to find out what, exactly, is happening, all while going live to report this new development, though they aren't sure exactly what it is.

The downside to all of this attention: Zack has been deflecting questions from multiple people for the past ten minutes, and he is getting antsy. All he wants is to see Mindy, to tell her everything is going to be okay.

When Parks appears down the hallway, he waves him over gratefully.

"What the hell is going on?" Parks asks.

"These folks want to know the same thing," Zack says. "But I have to go see Mindy. I have to talk to her."

"Is she in any kind of shape to talk?"

"I don't know because no one will let me see her." He glares at the Vail policewoman who's been trying to take his statement about Lauren and Juliet.

Woody steps in, flashes his credentials. "CBI, Special Agent

Stockton. I'll take responsibility for Mr. Armstrong. I agree he should be allowed to see his daughter."

The gambit works. Zack is freed for the moment. Parks takes Kat's lead, which doesn't make her happy, but Zack kneels and says, "Hang in, sweet girl. I have to run upstairs to see Mindy."

She barks once as if saying *OK, fine, but hurry*, and he sprints toward the elevator with Woody on his heels.

Mindy is, of course, still in isolation after the treatment. Oliver, garbed in blue and wearing a mask, is in the room with her, and two sheriff's deputies stand guard. Mindy is clearly scared; he can see her straining to see out of the room's door from her bed.

The nurse hands him a phone. "Gotta talk to her on the room phone, we're not ready to let in anyone from the outside yet without you getting scrubbed down."

"Just patch me in."

He stands by the window to the room, and Mindy settles a bit when she sees him. Oliver puts a phone in her hand, and her tired, worn voice comes across the line.

Mindy has one question for him.

"Where's my mom?"

He shakes his head. "I don't know."

"What's going on?"

"Juliet is sick. She got into some poison. She's in the ICU right now. The doctors think she'll be okay, but it is a dangerous situation. Where's Jasper?"

"I don't know. All I know is no one is answering their phones, and there are cops everywhere, and the news is saying my mom did something wrong."

"They are?"

She points to the television. He recognizes the outside of the hospital, the curved sidewalk by the parking lot. The sun is setting; the scene is being lit by the many lights of the news trucks. Mindy's television is tuned to the local CBS affiliate out of Denver, and Zack realizes the story is out.

"Oh, God."

"What the hell is happening?" Mindy demands. "Can you ask Dad?"

Zack turns to see Jasper striding toward him. "Speak of the devil. I will, honey. Just hold on a second. How are you feeling?"

"I'm okay. I'm tired."

"That's normal. I know you can't sleep, but try to rest, okay? We're going to figure all of this out."

"Is Aunt J going to be okay? Tell me the truth."

"She squeezed my hand a little bit ago, so yes, I think she will be. I sure hope so."

"But is she going to wake up?"

Using two fingers, he traces an X on his chest, then holds them up next to his right ear. "She is. Scout's honor."

Mindy sags back against the pillows, and Jasper gestures for Zack to hand over the phone.

"Here's your dad."

"You're my dad, too," she says, her words broken by emotion, and he swallows down the lump in his own throat and gives her a blinding smile.

Jasper is in a fine fury, Zack can tell by the tightness in his voice. "Sweet pea, everything is going to be okay. We're going to find your mom and talk to her. Please turn off the television. You don't need to see any of this."

"No. I want to know exactly what's happening. Tell me what's going on. I'm not a child, Dad."

Jasper looks at Zack, beseeching, but Zack shrugs. "Might as well tell her what we know. It's better she hears it from us than the reporters."

Mindy nods vigorously.

Jasper swallows. "There's been a development from Nashville. We think your mom knew your biological mom. We don't know what that means, sweetheart, so—"

But Mindy isn't stupid. "You can't possibly be saying Mom

stole me from Zack and his wife. Because that's what the reporters are saying. That Mom murdered Vivian Armstrong and
stole me."

"Sweetheart, calm down—"

"Where. Is. Mom?" She is shouting now, half out of the bed.
Oliver puts a restraining hand on her shoulder.

Jasper's eyes close, and he whispers, "We don't know."

Zack watches Mindy's face collapse, the tears begin. He pulls
the phone from Jasper's hand.

"We're doing everything we can to find her, honey. You do
us a favor, okay? If she calls here, you let us know, all right? We
don't want her getting hurt, we all just need to talk to her."

Mindy's mouth forms a tiny O as she grasps the situation.
Her shoulders sag again, and when she speaks, she sounds like
a little girl.

"I'll tell if she calls. Promise. But I need to tell you something first."

"What's that?"

"Mom had letters taped to the back of her dresser. I was
snooping, and I read them. They were between a woman named
Liesel, and someone called V. The V person was writing from
someplace called University Hospital." She takes a deep breath.
"V is Vivian. And I think Liesel is Mom."

81

The furor grows. When the media find out Dr. Juliet Ryder, CBI, is in ICU clinging to life after being poisoned, the stories begin to coalesce. They are careful to use the word *allegedly* in front of everything to do with Lauren Wright.

Allegedly poisoned... Allegedly murdered... Allegedly stole...

Zack wanders the halls with Kat by his side, feeling utterly impotent. There is nothing he can do here except watch and wait. Pray for a quick and non-lethal outcome. Avoid the entrances and exits, where reporters lurk like starving wolves. The police are taking apart the Wrights' house, looking for the letters Mindy mentioned.

Online and on air, the sort of gleeful befuddlement that follows any great criminal unveiling is underway. Twitter and Facebook explode. Tips come pouring in. Sightings abound. Talking heads are pulled in. No one has any idea what they're talking about, but talk they do.

* * *

By 10:00 p.m., Lauren Wright is a household name.

And despite this myopic attention, nothing pans out.

No one has seen her. She has disappeared.

A statewide BOLO has been issued. The airports have been alerted. The CBI have added her to their Most Wanted list, which gains extra attention from law enforcement officials across the state.

Zack is disconcerted to see his own face, and Vivian's, flash on the screen every few minutes. The photo of him is from his Army days. He is in uniform, unsmiling, shoulders broad, a beret cocked over his right eyebrow, his jaw square.

He barely recognizes himself.

He barely recognizes Vivian, either. The photo is not one he remembers. She is very pregnant, hands cradling her belly, a smirk on her lovely face. Someone close to her took this, he is certain. But who? And where did the media find it?

The guilt he's stashed deep in his soul bombards him.

It is his fault. It's always been his fault.

Mindy has finally fallen into an exhausted sleep, with a little help from Dr. Oliver, whose latest check of her levels says everything looks good, but they need to keep her stress down, so he slipped her a Mickey in the form of a mild sedative. She might be mad tomorrow, but for now, everyone's tension has gone down a notch. Her body needs rest to heal. Without her, none of this matters anymore.

Juliet continues to hang on. She is still unconscious, now purposely so, but her blood gases are returning to normal levels, her blood chemistry's getting back into line. The fomepizole is working. The dialysis will continue until morning, and she'll stay intubated until they see the extent of the damage to her lungs. Tomorrow, they'll talk about taking out the breathing tube. Letting her wake up. Getting the whole story. The patience needed for the next twelve hours seems impossible to bear.

Jasper has been slumped in a chair outside Mindy's room, staring at the ground, his hands between his legs, for the past few hours, refusing comfort or conversation. He is utterly, completely defeated.

The police report in frequently about their finds at the house. Bottles of ethylene glycol have been found in the garage. One in particular has his wife's fingerprints on it. A teacup in the dishwasher has traces of the chemical in it. There is a bottle of Ativan in the bathroom cabinet, prescribed by Dr. Oliver to Lauren Wright, only last week. The count was thirty, there are now only three left. No letters are found. Lauren must have taken them with her, afraid to have any tangible links to her past discovered.

Jasper is clearly a man who can't believe what's happening, but the story that's emerging from the evidence is clear. Lauren is in possession of every aspect of a capital murder charge against her sister.

Motive. Means. Opportunity. And the worst—premeditation.

Parks and Starr have briefed Zack in detail about both crime scenes—his old home in Nashville, and the Wrights' house on the mountain. Despite the evidence, despite the assumptions, nothing fits. Lauren's DNA at the Nashville crime scene means only one thing, and everyone knows it, but it makes no sense. Or it makes a perverse kind of sense, which is what the media has latched onto.

Only two people have any answers. One who might be able to shed any light on where Lauren was and what she was doing seventeen years ago lies intubated in a hospital bed, fighting for her life. The other has disappeared.

Zack has to admire Lauren, in a way. How she managed to orchestrate stealing his daughter and kept it a secret from everyone around her for seventeen years is nothing short of miraculous. And when she's found out, instead of trying to deny it outright or play dumb, she simply, cold-bloodedly, removes the obstacles in her path.

Gorman, for one. His accidental death is being reopened as a possible homicide.

Juliet, for another. Attempted homicide is a nasty charge.

What's confusing to everyone—why she didn't just try to kill Zack, too? The answer is beyond him, and he's not the only one interested. Everyone is fascinated by how a loner suburban wife can hide herself so thoroughly. At least every ten minutes, the question comes up from one of the law enforcement people: *Where is she?* And the even grimmer news people: *Is she still alive?* People tend to kill themselves when their more horrifying secrets come out, and many of them do so in a show of strength and fury, taking out people around them. The news warns people again and again not to approach Wright if she's spotted. They don't know if she is armed, but she is undoubtedly dangerous.

It seems everyone in the state, hell, in the nation, is looking for her. But she has disappeared.

Poof.

The suddenly famous suburban criminal is gone.

82

It is past midnight, and Zack's phone won't stop ringing. He wants to turn it off, but Parks won't let him. They keep hoping Lauren will call Zack, or Jasper, or Mindy, but so far, it's only been a bevy of reporters wanting comments.

But Park's admonishments to suck it up and get his thumbs some exercise turns out to be the best advice of the day because as Zack is about to decline yet another call, he sees a familiar name pop up on the screen.

Bode Greer.

God, in the melee, he's forgotten all about the kid. The cops are going to want to talk to him. Zack answers with a grateful, "Bode. I'm glad you called."

"Dude, listen. I heard on the news they're searching for Mrs. Wright."

"They are, she's disappeared and—"

"No, dude, listen to me. She's in Denver. I'm sitting a block away from her car right now."

★ ★ ★

The mobilization is immediate. Even Zack, a retired military man, is impressed. Woody is as good a manager as they come; he has everyone hopping in the correct directions within five minutes. Denver police are rolling up on Bode's location—which turns out to be half a block from Juliet's town house. It seems Lauren has gone to her sister's place to hide out and has been stashed there during the evening's melee.

It's not the smartest plan. Then again, Zack reminds himself, despite her luck over the years, Lauren isn't a criminal mastermind. She's simply a mother whose child is being threatened.

This is what Jasper wants everyone to believe. Since Bode's call, Jasper has been spewing messages in Lauren's defense every ten seconds like an automaton, but no one's really listening.

"She's not capable of this…"

"She's the kind of woman who says thank you when a stranger sneezes, for Christ's sake. She's not a murderer…"

"You don't understand, she would never…"

"How can you possibly believe Lauren could be responsible…"

"You've scared her off, that's why she's run…"

Zack finally tells him to go for a walk and get out of the way. He isn't unkind, but Jasper's sudden jazzy energy is making it difficult to think. He can't help but feel like Jasper is a part of this, that he's responsible in some way. His rational mind tells him he's being unfair, but the small shrieking child in his soul who's been torn asunder since Vivian's death wants answers.

How could Jasper not have known?

How could he have been lied to all these years?

How can he defend a woman who's clearly dangerous as hell?

Zack knows he's not getting anywhere with these questions. Truthfully, he wants to get Jasper up against the wall and interrogate him personally, leading with his fists, but the case is in the CBI's hands now. Parks and Starr and Woody are in charge, not Zack.

So he gets coffee for the crew, tries to listen in on their status briefings. Stares through the glass at Mindy's sleeping form. Thinks about Vivian in ways he hasn't allowed himself to in more than a decade. About what she would think of all this. About her eyes. About the sweet kiss of her breath on his neck, and the gentle roundness of her belly with Mindy inside. For so long, he's only been able to see the crime scene, her neck and stomach gashed open, her eyes milky and slitted, the black stain beneath her bloated, maggot-covered body.

Now, he lets himself see some of the good things. That picture being flashed on the screen, for one. Her smile when they first met. But without any word, he is getting more and more frustrated.

He spends fifteen minutes downstairs with Juliet. If she wakes up, if her mind isn't permanently damaged and she's able to understand, he intends to ask her to dinner. He is tired of not living his life. It makes him sad, the idea of everything he's lost. But what else was he supposed to do? He's been grieving for so long he doesn't know how to exist any other way. It took Juliet, and Mindy, to crack through the hard shell he encased himself in. And now he might lose them both.

If she survives becomes the mantra that takes his feet from the second floor up the stairs to the third. He alternates between Juliet's room and Mindy's, the prayers different, but no less emphatic.

The idea that he's come so far, that he's found himself again in this mess—it is too much to bear losing anything more.

It is his turn to have a family. It is his turn to have someone to love.

Hours are spent in this loop. Hours wondering what the police are saying to Lauren Wright inside Juliet's home. Hours wondering how he could have let all of this happen. Hours berating himself for not trusting his instincts. He knew something was wrong with Lauren the moment he met her.

As dawn breaks, he bangs through the doors onto the oncology floor. A fine ripple of tension is moving from person to person as some sort of news spreads.

Parks sees him and starts down the hall. It is clear he has something to say. Zack glances at the television screen, immediately assuming something has changed. He is right.

The blinding flashes of light from a hovering helicopter turn the scene into a strobe. It's like a movie set, and he knows by the stiffness in Parks's stride that they are hitting Juliet's town house hard, with Lauren inside. Negotiations have failed. They have decided to breach, and things rarely down go well when the SWAT team starts throwing smoke grenades into homes.

There is a television with the volume raised in the alcove outside the nurses' station. He stops to watch, Kat glued to his side, trembling as if she, too, is under attack.

Men in SWAT gear run toward the town house. A small fire starts in the corner of the screen, almost like a flame inside a trashcan. The flames grow, he can see them rising behind the glass, the curtains catching.

Juliet's home is on fire.

When Parks is five feet away, a long, low alarm starts going off. For a second Zack thinks it's coming from the television until the fire alarms on the floor start to flash, a sharp white strobe, eerily similar to what he's just been watching. Parks stops and looks over his shoulder, mouth agape. Zack tries to process what he's seeing with what he's hearing.

Fire on the screen.

Fire here?

Doctors and nurses appear, pushing people out of the way, and suddenly people are running, making phone calls. Some seem panicked. Some are calm.

And over the loudspeakers, a robotic voice tells everyone to evacuate the building immediately.

83

The wig is black, a sharp bob, one Lauren used for Halloween the year they went to the costume party, she and Jasper, dressed as Mia Wallace and Vince Vega from *Pulp Fiction*. Juliet borrowed it, bless her. It was in the town house's garage, in the big box that held things from their mother's house that Lauren hadn't wanted and Juliet couldn't—or wouldn't—part with. Their mother's box. Their mother's car. Juliet always keeps things in top-notch running order. She jokes she takes the car out on Sundays like a little old lady.

Convenient, finding these things in the clean darkness.

Dressed as she is, in the wig and a bit of bright makeup, Lauren walks directly into the hospital. No one gives her a second glance. She is just another person with a cross to bear—a woman on her way to visit a sick friend, or perhaps a nurse starting a shift after a date, her scrubs in her locker.

Once she's past the first-floor gift shop, she ducks into the stairwell and runs up the two flights to the oncology floor. She stops for a moment, catches her breath. She has one chance at this. One chance to say goodbye.

Her life as she knows it is over. There is no going back.

She is furious with Juliet. Why couldn't she have died at the house? This would be so much easier. Lauren would be the only voice people would hear. And her story was one she was certain would elicit sympathy.

More importantly now, what state is Juliet in? Lauren will find out soon enough. Juliet knows more than she realizes. Silencing her is the only choice. Yes, Lauren is guilty. Yes, she might even get arrested and go to jail, if this goes wrong.

But there are secrets no one knows, no one but Juliet. They can't come out.

Mitigate the circumstances, as her ex-husband used to say.

Until Mindy got sick, she hadn't thought of Kyle Noonan in a very long time. Better off without him, the fucking bastard.

Kyle's leering face—oh, how many times has she pictured him dead? Bloated from the water, red-faced from the carbon monoxide that backed up and poisoned his lungs. His death was deserved, more so than all the rest combined.

These thoughts lead her to an image of Jasper's kind, loving face, smiling down at her, Mindy in his arms, and she chokes back what might have become a sob in a lesser woman. He will be hurt in this, there's no way he won't. She must mitigate the circumstances for him as well. Protect him.

What's most important is to protect Mindy. Mindy is the only thing that matters. The truth, and the lies, the slights and the secrets, the long shadows of Bennett Thompson and Kyle Noonan and Vivian Armstrong—everything that's happened over the years is irrelevant now. The sacrifices she's made for her daughter are worth it.

Lauren is prepared for the worst, but is hoping for the best. This is how she's lived her whole life. How she's managed to get this far.

Another seventeen minutes won't change anything. She really should make sure there are no loose ends.

Breath caught, she thinks it through. Her moment of weakness, confessing to her sister… Yes. This is the right way. The only way.

Her hand leaves the door, and she retreats silently back down the stairs.

★ ★ ★

There are police in front of Juliet's door.

Which means Lauren needs yet another a distraction.

She has the gun, but shooting it will bring all the attention her way, and she isn't quite ready for that. The gun is small, a Saturday night special, .38 caliber, normally stashed under the front seat of Juliet's truck, just in case she's carjacked, or attacked by an animal. Juliet is so stupid. Believing Lauren was looking for her glove. She certainly hadn't looked to see if her gun was missing. Naïve, stupid little girl.

Lauren takes a deep breath and steps out of the stairwell. The fire alarm is right next to the door. She pulls the red bar. The screaming begins. Confusion sets in. A robotic voice can be heard telling everyone on the floor to evacuate immediately.

The two cops move toward the nurses' station to get their orders, and she slips into her sister's room right behind their backs. Lauren clings to the wall, assessing the situation.

Juliet has a tube going into her mouth, and it takes Lauren a moment to register the thought—*the machine is breathing for her*—before she steps to the wall and pulls the plug. Juliet jerks immediately, then her body relaxes. Lauren leaves the room without a backward glance.

That's Juliet, handled.

She steps into the crowd heading toward the stairwell, blending in with the people being evacuated. There is no klaxon wail from the machine in Juliet's room, but instead, it comes from the nurses' station. Damn it, she forgot the nurses' station. The beeping is nearly drowned out by the fire alarm, but she's not that lucky. Behind her, a nurse and the cops rush back to Juliet's room. One of the cops breaks off and heads toward the stairwell. Lauren glances over her shoulder to see the man's face distorted, his finger pointing, his mouth open in a yell that's being drowned out by the noise, and she slips into the stairwell as he starts toward her.

They are on alert now. She must move quickly.

She runs two steps at a time against the stream of people up to the third floor. She ignores the warning shouts, bursts out onto the third-floor hallway and heads directly to Mindy's room.

The evacuation is going smoothly, but Jasper and Zack are standing by the door with the two Nashville cops. Damn it. She needs them to move away. She has to get inside. She has to talk to Mindy.

She edges along the wall, knowing this is her last chance. The door is shut; Mindy is still in isolation.

As suddenly as it began, the fire alarm shuts off. People stop in their tracks, looking confused. The small crowd by Mindy's room take a few steps away. Zack is pointing out the window at something, she has no idea what, but their collective gaze is averted, and she bolts for her daughter's room.

Five feet, three, two, they're still looking away, and she reaches for the handle. She flings open the door and slips inside. But as she does, she trips, and something knocks her off her feet, and she goes down, hard, her shoulder smacking into the door, which swings closed as if caught in a draft. It slams behind her, loudly. She scrambles to her feet and turns the lock just as Zack and Jasper and the cops turn to see her, their mouths open, calling. Hands go to waists to pull weapons, the door handle starts to rattle, but Lauren is already looking toward her daughter. She rips off the wig.

Mindy is groggy and bleary-eyed in the bed. Lauren feels a rush of love; she recognizes this state. Her daughter has just woken up. Must have been the fire alarm.

"Mom? Is that you?"

"Sweetie, yes, it's me. I am so sorry, darling. I know you're scared, and there is so much to explain—"

A low growl starts near her leg. Lauren looks down in horror to realize that somehow, Zack's dog has gotten into the room.

84

The Malinois moves like lightning, putting herself between Mindy and Lauren, hackles raised, teeth glistening. Angered as she is, she looks more like a wolf than a dog, and Lauren is afraid to look away. Maintain eye contact but don't try to stare them down? No, with dogs, no eye contact, so it's the same when you're about to be attacked by a wolf. It will be seen as aggression. Make yourself bigger. Wave your arms and shout. Throw things at them. Or so the literature says. They live in the woods; Lauren knows what to do if faced with all sorts of wild animal attacks.

But there is nothing to protect herself with. This room is cleared of all extraneous blankets and pillows. The IV pole is on the other side of the bed.

"Mindy, darling, call off the dog. I know she'll listen to you."

"Mom, what have you done? Tell me the truth, what did you do to Aunt Juliet? Is it true? Did you kill Vivian Armstrong and steal me? I saw your letters. I know you were in the hospital with her. I know you tried to kill yourself. Those scars on your arm aren't from a car crash. Why did you lie to me?"

The plaintive note breaks Lauren's heart. This isn't how things were supposed to go. Mindy is accusing her of something that she can't answer fully without a long talk. It upsets her, she who has become so touchy, so feral, in these last few days.

Sensing the change in Lauren's demeanor, the dog growls, low and mean, crouching down on her front legs. There is banging now—Zack is pounding on the door, Jasper on the window—but Lauren ignores everyone but the dog. And Mindy, of course. *She read the letters; she knows everything.*

Kat inches forward, lips trembling with her growls, and Lauren stamps her foot and raises her arms.

"Bad dog. Bad!"

Kat growls louder, showing her teeth.

"Mom. Stop! She'll attack you if you don't stop. Kat, stop. Stop!"

Kat's growling ceases but her teeth are still bared. Lauren feels a moment of pride—even a stranger's dog recognizes how important it is to protect Mindy—but she must get the dog to calm down. She takes two steps to the left, and the dog follows with her head but doesn't move. Her teeth glisten in the fluorescent lights.

"Mindy, sweetie, don't fret. Mommy's here. I won't let anything happen to you."

"Mom, what are you doing? Open the door. Let them in."

"I need to talk to you, sweetheart."

"Then talk! They're calling you a murderer."

"I am not a murderer, honey. There's an explanation for all of this, I swear. I need to tell you the truth myself. I want you to hear it from me."

The room phone begins to ring. Lauren glances up to see the row of furious faces at the window, and Dr. Oliver at the door. He has a key, he has it open, and then the guns step in.

Kat is not distracted by the shouting of all the cops. She has been trained for this. She doesn't like the guns, though, backs up a few feet, growling heavily.

"Kat, Kat, come here," Mindy calls, but the dog takes a step toward Lauren, who is caught between the weapons of three officers and the wall.

Lauren has no recourse. With an almost audible sigh, she

pulls the weapon from her waistband. The gun is small, perfect for her hand, and she raises it. The calls are immediate, and the tension in the room rises.

"Don't do it!"

"Put it down!"

"Put your hands up, set the weapon on the floor!"

But Lauren's hand doesn't waver. She speaks to Mindy, not losing eye contact with the cops. "I didn't do what they've said, I swear to you. None of this is what it looks like. I've only ever wanted to protect you. You're the only person who's ever mattered to me. Mindy, darling, you have to know everything I've ever done is for you."

"Mom, stop moving. Put the gun down."

"I can't do that, darling. But I want you to know you are everything to me. I love you. Everything I have ever done is because I love you so, so much."

"Mom, please." Mindy is crying now, and Lauren risks a glance at her only daughter.

"Honey, don't cry. It's all going to be okay. It's what Vivian wanted. I swear it. You are everything, to both of us."

"Stop moving, Mrs. Wright."

Lauren edges closer to the bed.

"Last warning. Stop!"

"You leave, now," Lauren says to the cops. "If you don't shut the door, I will hurt her."

A deeper voice now, calm and assured. "Let me talk to her." Zack Armstrong strides to the door, looking every inch the grieving widower. "Put down the guns. Let me talk to her. Trust me," he adds in a tone that makes the cops take notice. They lower their guns. Lauren takes a deep breath, shoulders dropping an inch, but doesn't lower hers.

Zack steps through the door. Mindy cries out for him, but he ignores her, takes another step forward, a hand out as if he could stop a bullet if she tries to shoot.

"She loved you," Lauren says. "Until the end. You and Mindy were her last thoughts."

"I know she loved me. I know she loved Mindy. I know you do, too. Put the gun down, Lauren, before someone gets hurt."

"I only wanted what was best for Mindy. Even Vivian knew this was the best way."

He edges farther into the room, signaling with his hand for the cops to back away.

"Lauren, you don't want things to end this way. We can all sit down together and talk, but you have to put the gun down. If you put it down, I will pull the door closed, and we'll talk."

She is trapped, she knows it, but she still wants to find a way out, a way to make this right. "Don't you dare tell me what I want. You leave me alone with my daughter, let me talk to her, and then I'll talk to you."

"Not going to happen."

"Leave. Us. Alone!" Lauren spits out the words, and the hate in her voice is enough to make Zack take a step back.

"You're scaring Mindy," he says quietly.

Mindy *is* scared, Lauren can sense this without even looking at her daughter. But it can't be helped. She has to talk to her. She has to make her understand. The words keep playing in her head, *Help her understand, let her love me again.*

"Don't make me do this. You have to leave now so I can talk to Mindy by myself."

"Talk, Mom. Just...talk. But don't do this."

Lauren turns to her daughter, her joy, her life. Her gun arm is still raised, and with her turn, the nose of the weapon points at her daughter's head. Mindy gasps and scrambles backward, but there is no place for her to go. She falls off the edge of the bed, and from outside the room, there is a flurry of motion.

As Mindy falls, and Zack dives to catch her, the dog sails into the air and latches onto Lauren's gun arm, her sharp teeth puncturing the fragile flesh. The weight of the dog takes them both down.

Lauren screams her frustration, tries to pull free, but the strong jaws are clamped tight. The pain helps her focus on the unjustness of the situation. Mindy's eyes are huge, staring at her from under the bed like she's a monster, and the small parts of Lauren that are still hidden crack.

"Mindy," she chokes out. "It was the only way. I want you to understand. I love you, honey."

Zack is standing over them, shouting at the dog. He kicks the gun away, and whatever he's saying makes Kat release her prey and back away. Lauren is hurt, stunned, bleeding heavily, and doesn't make a move when the cops rush in and handcuff her.

She lost. She's lost it all.

Zack steps between her and Mindy, and she is grateful. She doesn't want Mindy to see all of this blood. Mindy can't see the carnage. Mindy must be protected, still.

"Mom? Mom!"

"Mindy. It's okay, baby. Mommy loves you."

But she knows that finally, finally, it is over.

85

The shouts, the confusion, the look of naked longing on her mother's face, it's all too much. Zack lifts Mindy from the floor and gently places her back on the bed, and she immediately ducks her head under the blankets. Kat jumps up to cuddle beside her and barks once, sharp. She slips the blanket down and sees her mother's blood staining Kat's muzzle.

She has to look. She has to be brave.

Fingers twined in the dog's fur, Mindy lifts her head. She will never forget the sight before her: her mother, bleeding profusely on the linoleum floor, the flesh of her arm torn apart. Zack, the avenging angel, standing over her, glowering. Two people she assumes are cops wrestling her mother into handcuffs. Her father is standing motionless outside the window as if he's been frozen to stone.

Dr. Oliver is by her side now, shushing her, holding her head away, looking at her with a doctor's practiced eye, shushing her again. She doesn't understand why he keeps trying to quiet her; she isn't saying anything. But she makes an effort to close her mouth, and the sudden silence is deafening; she has been screaming, she realizes, screaming one word over and over and over.

"No no no no no no..."

She says it one last time, a whimper, her voice hoarse. The crowd parts as Lauren is dragged to her feet. Mindy sees her mother's eyes watching her, limpid and ice-cold at the same time.

"It's okay, baby. It's all going to be okay."

The man with the skier's tan is talking. "Lauren Wright, you're under arrest for the attempted murder of Juliet Ryder—"

Her mom ignores him, her eyes latched on Mindy's, her voice a mantra now: "It's okay, sweetie. Don't worry about anything. I'll fix it all. Love you. Love you so much, baby."

Dr. Oliver yells at them all to leave. Mindy's head begins to swim, and she has a second to wonder how contaminated she is now—*all these people*—before the medicine Dr. Oliver has just shot into her veins takes her away.

86

VAIL HEALTH HOSPITAL

CURRENT DAY

LIESEL

I can't help but think about the last time I was in handcuffs.

I haven't thought about that night in a very long time. I never want to think about it again. But my daughter is staring at me as if I'm an animal, and the handcuffs are sharp on my bones, and there is no way I can go back there, to try to explain, to try to make it right for her.

I told the police what I'm telling you.

I had just finished a bath. Sated and calm, I was carrying the razor blade I'd been using to cut myself in the warm, embryonic water to its hiding spot—taped to the back of my dresser— where my mother would never find it.

My sister's door was closed. I heard a noise. Sounds of a scuffle.

When I entered my sister's bedroom and saw what he was doing, I didn't think. I didn't hesitate. I yelled, "Stop!" He didn't. So I ran the razor blade across his neck to get his attention. My sister's eyes were closed tight. Blood splashed across her face.

He went down so quickly, blood spurting everywhere—on me, my sister, the rug, the walls. There was no way to hide what I'd done, no way to pretend something hadn't happened. I recall the queasy nausea brought on by the coppery tang of his blood, the initial sense of despair coupled with triumph. I had stopped him. He would never hurt her—us—again.

I didn't tell them everything.

I didn't tell them that after I slit his nasty throat, I stood over him, his tainted blood purling on the crappy carpet, his mouth opening and closing like a fish gasping for water, and felt nothing but joy, a deep well of happiness that I'd never felt before, as I watched him die.

I didn't tell them Juliet watched with me, eyes wide as an owl, blood dripping down her chin. Fifteen glorious minutes of watching him suffer, the best sister time we've ever had.

When it was over, I wiped Juliet's face, gave her a dose of Benadryl, and put her to bed in my room. I washed my hands, which were covered in red, and my own face. I wrapped my arm in gauze, the cuts were very deep, and put on a long-sleeved shirt.

Then, I went back to Juliet's room. His eyes were glazed. One lifeless palm cupped his chin, the other was on the floor. He'd moved since I left. I didn't want to touch him so I kicked the bastard in the ribs to make sure he was well and truly dead. When he didn't move, I watched him for a few more minutes, and then I went to wake my mother.

I didn't tell the police that my mother stared at her husband for a full five minutes before taking me to the kitchen. That she sat me down at the kitchen table and poured a glass of brandy down my throat because I'd started to shake. Nor that we spent an hour talking about what to do.

My mother was in shock. She had no idea Bennett had turned his affections to her daughters. She was glad he was dead. She told me that. And bless her heart, she decided to take the fall. She decided to tell the police she killed Bennett Thompson, that she had caught him molesting Juliet and flew into a rage.

She wept when I told her what I suspected. My period was late. He was responsible.

Knowing that last truth, though, allowed her to be clear-eyed about the situation.

That beautiful woman was willing to go to jail for me.

I decided to let her.

She called 911. The ambulance came, and the police.

She told them what she'd done. That she'd caught her husband trying to rape her youngest daughter. That she'd grabbed the closest available weapon—a razor from the bathroom—and in a rage, cut his throat.

They believed her, too. She was good. She didn't embellish; she didn't flinch.

It was Juliet who ruined things.

Juliet, who stood in the door of the kitchen, splashes of blood on her, drunk on Benadryl, weaving, nearly. I guess I gave her too much.

Juliet, who offered up the truth to the kind EMT. A single sentence that condemned me forever.

"Mama was in her room, and Liesel came to save me. Liesel cut him."

My mother looked on helplessly as the police found the bastard's blood under my fingernails.

An hour later, the police took me away, the metal sharp and cold on my wrists.

★ ★ ★

The courtroom was closed, no reporters, no witnesses, just my mother, the psychologist, the lawyers and the judge.

The judge felt badly, you could tell. Her reading glasses on a cord around her neck reminded me of my stepfather's last red grin. I managed to keep that to myself. She droned on and on, tapping a pen on her blotter. She was pretty. Her forehead furrowed when she talked.

It all boiled down to this: There was nothing she could do. A man was dead by my hand. I had to be punished.

When she'd seen the row of cuts on my forearm, the psychologist who'd examined me figured out pretty damn quick why I had a razor blade in my hand when I'd happened upon my stepfather trying to rape my little sister. On the psychologist's recommendation, the pretty judge sentenced me to inpatient treatment at Middle Tennessee Mental Health Institute for a period of no less than twelve months, to both punish my sins and help me right my ship.

For reasons unknown to us all, the pretty judge allowed me to spend one last night at home. I took advantage of the situation, slit my left wrist. This time, I used a kitchen paring knife. Better blade.

Do you blame me? I mean, I would much rather be dead than incarcerated with a batch of psychos.

My sister found me. The irony is not lost. She screamed for my mom, who was in the kitchen, alone, drinking Chardonnay from a large glass. Mom rushed me to the hospital though she shouldn't have been driving, and the folks in the Emergency Room stitched me up, cooing softly all the while. The things I remember from that night are so strange. The pain of the blade; the cries of my mother, the gentle voice of the nurse; the flat, sharp eyes of the psychiatric resident, his no-nonsense, dispassionate shrug when I screamed.

Without a second chance to pack my things, I was admitted to the psychiatric ward. The hospital was informed of my upcoming incarceration, and my delicate condition, and it was determined I would serve my term there in University Hospital instead since I was already on site. There were people my age, and the intake nurse knew the judge well and put in a word for herself as a guardian of sorts.

I remember so little about those first few days.

The sting of the needle injecting me with liquid calm.

The roommate.

But the rest… I remember it all.

And I know all the letters by heart.

Especially the last one.

I hadn't heard from her in a long while. V always got quiet and disappeared; it was just her MO. Then she'd pop back up.

I didn't encourage her to stay in touch. It wasn't that I didn't want to be friends anymore. She just reminded me of the worst time of my life, a time I wanted to forget, to bury. I didn't want my sordid past affecting my life anymore.

But when she wrote me that last time, I had to help.

She was so disturbed. Depressed and unhappy and desperate to be free from this world. She wanted Mindy to have a chance at life, though. She wanted Mindy and Zack to be happy. I tried to help her. Truly.

I suggested she check back into University Hospital STAT. She refused. "I will never go back there. Never. But you can help me. You can help me go, and make sure the baby is all right until Zack comes back."

It took some convincing, but I agreed to help.

Who could walk away from their child? No one in their right mind, certainly.

She didn't deserve Mindy. I did.

87

July 2000

Dear Liesel,

I need to talk to you. I'm having a really rough time. I don't know what's wrong with me. Or, I do, but I don't understand. This is supposed to be the happiest time of my life, but it's like I'm sinking, drowning in a deep lake of black. No matter what I do, I can't get my head above the water, and I'm gulping down mouthfuls of hate and sorrow. I don't know how to handle this. I am so tired of the blackness, of the sadness, of the horror of pretending to be a happy wife, a happy mother-to-be. I just want it all over. I'm alone. I am so tired. I need the baby out of me. I can't take being pregnant another minute. I can't take any of it. I don't want this. I don't want this life. Getting pregnant was such a mistake.

And Zack... I can't stop thinking that there is always a chance he'll ship off and never come back, that something awful will happen to him. He's already been shot once. He says he's going to resign his commission, but he's an intelligencer through and through. I bet he won't be able to. And if he dies, then I'll be alone with a baby.

The medicines don't work. The doctors care, but all the talk and compassion in the world can't change me. It is my genetic makeup, not my fault. I stopped taking the meds when I found out I was pregnant, and I've been sinking deeper and deeper. I've tried using them the past few weeks, but it's too late. They've never worked right anyway. They're pointless.

The baby kicks inside me, letting me know she doesn't care whether I live or die, just so long as she can be born.

She should have that privilege. Me, I just want to get her out of me. I want to move on, at last.

Please, can you call me? I need your help.

Love,

V

88

VAIL HEALTH HOSPITAL

It is embarrassing to Lauren, being handcuffed to the gurney like she is a common criminal. The sting of the lidocaine injection makes her flinch, but she sits, stoically silent, as the ER doctor cleans and stitches her arm. Thirty-five stitches on top and bottom from the fucking dog bite, more from where she'd fallen, catching her shoulder on the counter when the dog attacked. She hadn't even felt the blow; she was completely focused on Mindy's forlorn, frightened face.

She didn't mean to point the gun at Mindy.

God, she really didn't.

In a life defined by impetuous moments and accidental actions, this will haunt her forever. The gun was meant for her, and her alone.

Thirty-five new stitches, to go along with the forty she'd received when she was a girl. She'd told everyone in her life her scar was from a car accident, from her arm plunging through the windshield. Looking at it now, under the glare of the hospital lights, the thin, pale line, straight as an arrow from wrist to elbow, the edges only slightly raised, she is thrown back in time again.

The knife, running through her flesh like butter, the skin parting, the moment of emptiness before the cut fills with blood, the light, airy feeling of her blood pressure dropping, the happiness that she isn't going to be humiliated any further. The inky darkness, full of peace. The ride to the ER, the siren, the lights. The wrenching horror when she wakes, bandaged. The long walk to the ward.

Vivian.

All roads lead to Vivian. All memories, all love, all hate, rise from the specter of their combined past. Why can't the bitch stay dead?

Two Vail police officers stand watch over her; their CBI fellow is in front of the door talking animatedly to the Nashville cops. Jasper has joined the group outside in the hall; she can hear his voice demanding to see her. At least Jasper won't desert her. Jasper will never desert her.

The silent doctor gives her a pill to swallow—"For the pain"— and she takes it gladly. Even with the lidocaine numbing her tender, torn flesh, the dog bite itself hurts like hell. Deep in her body, her soul hurts worse.

When she finishes gulping down the tiny cup of water, she says, "I need to speak to the police. Let them in, please."

The doctor looks at her in surprise. "You're sure? Most people in your situation would rather me run interference."

"I want them, now."

"Okay."

He flings back the privacy curtain and disappears into the hallway. The group comes in immediately, clearly curious as to why she's asking to see them.

"Who will be in charge of prosecuting me?" Lauren asks.

"You have the right to an attorney," the ski bum starts to say, but she cuts him off.

"I am waiving my rights. There are witnesses. I need to talk to the person in charge."

"Then that's me. But I ain't talking to you without giving you a Miranda warning."

Jasper immediately goes red with fear and fury. "Lauren, shut your mouth right now. You can't talk to them until the lawyers—"

"I am going to talk to them. You can stay, or you can go, but I'm going to talk to the police now. I waive my rights."

"Lauren, the drugs they've given you are messing with your mind. I will represent you…"

She shakes her head slightly and smiles sadly. "No, you won't. I have to do this, Jasper. Please." And to the cop standing at the foot of the gurney—"Sir, mister… I'm sorry, I've forgotten your name."

"Special Agent Stockton. CBI."

"Agent Stockton, I would like to confess to the murder of Vivian Armstrong."

Jasper starts to shout. "Do not say another word, Lauren. Not a word. I want it on the record my wife has been given painkillers, that extenuating circumstances exist, she hasn't been Mirandized, that this confession is illegitimate—"

"That sounded pretty legitimate to me, sir. Please, step back, or I'll have someone do it for you," Stockton says.

Jasper's mouth opens and closes a few times, but Lauren catches his eye and nods. She knows what she's doing. She's always known what she's doing.

"Honey, it's okay. I've been holding on to these secrets for too long. It's time. I need to come clean. I can't carry this with me anymore."

"Lauren, please, don't—" His voice cracks.

Stockton steps between Jasper and Lauren. "What about your sister, Juliet Ryder? Do you admit trying to kill her?"

Trying? She's not dead? Shit. Shit!

She shuts her eyes for a moment, mind whirling. What difference does it make at this point? "Yes. I tried to kill my sister."

A low moan starts from the corner of the room. Jasper, crooning, begging.

But Lauren ignores him. Stockton is speaking, the Miranda warning this time, so he won't have to throw out her confession, then makes her say it all again while he writes everything down, looking around the room as if making sure everyone there is hearing her confession. This is gold, she knows. This is going to make his career. Not only has he caught Lauren Wright, but he is also getting her to confess. Without a lawyer present, on painkillers, any decent lawyer could have a shot at getting it thrown out, but still. She offers to sign the confession.

"Lauren, stop, I'm begging you." The plaintive cry from Jasper almost breaks her resolve, but she shuts out his pleas. It is time for all the truths to come to light. They can only put her to death once, after all. She takes a deep breath. The room quiets in anticipation.

"And I would also like to confess to murdering Detective Gorman. He threatened my family, threatened my daughter, threatened to put me in jail, and I pushed him off the side of a mountain."

89

THREE DAYS LATER

"Tell me. Do you think she's telling the truth?"

Zack Armstrong is sitting by Juliet's hospital bed, absently stroking her hand. Parks is standing by the window, leaning back against the windowsill, his legs crossed at the ankles. He is tired. It has been a long three days since Lauren's confession, full of paperwork and interviews. Cases to close. Widows, and widowers, to speak with.

"Why would she confess to something if she didn't do it?"

"I don't know." Zack runs a hand over his face. He looks as tired as Parks feels. Parks knows he's been here nonstop for the past three days, cycling between floors, spending time with Mindy, then Juliet, then Mindy, then Juliet. It is the latter's turn now, which means Mindy is asleep upstairs.

"You need to get some sleep," Parks says, and Armstrong nods, though it's clear he isn't going to try to remedy the situation right now. "How's Mindy?"

"She's doing well. Dr. Oliver is very optimistic. Her numbers aren't getting worse. But with all the chaos…"

He drifts off, and Parks shifts gears.

"Listen, I know this is early to discuss, but are you going to be okay testifying? Lauren won't be going to trial, not with her confessions, but the sentencing hearing will be in another month, and they are going to want you on the stand. And that means digging into your past."

"I have nothing to hide."

"Are you sure, Zack? Nothing at all?"

Zack's hand stills.

"Everyone has something to hide," Parks continues. "And Lauren, while she's not exactly defending herself, has said a few things."

"A few things like what?" Armstrong's dark eyes are on fire, and Parks is reminded yet again that this man was, at one time, a professional killer.

"She claims you were abusive to Vivian. That Vivian asked her to take the baby because she was afraid for her safety."

"And you believe this?"

Parks holds up his hands. "Hey, don't shoot the messenger. If her lawyer has any moxie whatsoever, they'll get an insanity defense started, and if they do, all kinds of weird shit might come out. I'm just saying, if there is anything you aren't comfy with the world knowing, I'd be prepared to decline testimony."

He glances at the bed, where Juliet lies, silent as the grave, the machine pumping air into her lungs.

"I have nothing to hide. I did my duty for my country. And I was not abusive to my wife. I loved that woman completely. I'm just sorry she didn't trust me enough to explain her past to me. I would never hold her diagnosis against her. Then, or now."

Parks pauses a beat. "Lauren Wright is asking to speak to you."

"Hell no. She is the last person I want to talk to."

Parks shoves off from the wall. "Okay. I'll let them know. I'll see you back in Nashville. Starr and I are heading home on the late flight tonight. Our job here is done, for now. We have a bunch of threads to pull together back in Nashville, especially with the Gorman investigation. I have to tell his wife what happened. Ain't going to be a fun visit. She's a nice lady."

He is halfway out the door when Armstrong calls out, "Hey, did Lauren say what she wanted to talk about?"

Parks stops, rubs his thumb and forefinger across his mustache. It needs a trim.

"She says she has something important to tell you. That you'll want to hear what she has to say. And she won't tell anyone but you, directly."

Armstrong nods once, twice, as if he's making up his mind.

"I'll see her. Do I go to the jail, or what?"

"Yep. I can carry you down there if you want. I admit, I'm rather curious what she has to say, and I have a couple of hours to kill. I'm sure one of Woody's folks can get you back up here."

"Okay." Zack stands and turns, and as he does, Parks sees a flash of movement behind him.

"Armstrong," he says with a grin.

"What?"

"Turn around."

Juliet Ryder's golden eyes are open.

★ ★ ★

The doctors have left, and Parks stands outside Ryder's room, listening to Armstrong recount the events of the past few days, his voice soft and gentle. He wonders how many times Armstrong has told this story. So far, the man has refused all on-air interviews, has only talked to the police, but with Ryder, he's as animated as Parks has ever seen him. It does his heart good to see the connection between them.

Of course, Ryder is a captive audience. She is still intubated, though the doctors are planning to remove the breathing tube in a few hours. Armstrong isn't going anywhere right now, and sadly, Parks needs to get to the airport. There are more cases on his desk in Nashville; he can't wait around any longer.

"It was chaos. Kat was barking," Armstrong is saying, bending down to rub the dog's ears. "Your sister was screaming, Mindy was screaming, Jasper was shouting. It was absolute mayhem for a while there. Where the hell did she get a gun? I know, I know, you can't answer, I shouldn't be asking questions. But you don't need to worry, honey. She is in jail now. She can't hurt you, ever again. Kat here will make sure of it."

Parks clears his throat, and Armstrong looks up. He salutes him, then walks away.

A shame. He would have loved to hear what Lauren Wright has to say in person.

90

DENVER WOMEN'S CORRECTIONAL FACILITY

The morning sun sends a shaft of light through the waiting area. The windows are placed high, so there is no chance of looking out, of dreaming, of seeing sunsets and sunrises, or the world passing you by. There are simply mean little thick-glassed windows there to allow extra light into the room so the overheads can be kept off at certain times of the day to save money.

Lauren is wearing the tan jumpsuit the prison issues, with slip-on sneakers. Because Jasper told them she was at risk for hurting herself, she has been kept away from the rest of the prisoners, under a suicide watch. *All part of your defense*, her lawyers tell her. *Just stop talking, for God's sake.*

Her hair is lank, she hasn't had a shower yet, and she is lonely. So lonely.

But this is what she deserves. She knows this, in her heart. She's always known she was on borrowed time. For a sweet moment, her life was perfect. For almost eighteen years, she had it all. A family. A daughter. A life. That's more than so many have. If asked, she will say it again and again: It was worth it.

The guards haven't been kind, but they haven't been cruel, yet, either. Indifferent. They are indifferent to her suffering, her pain, her desires. She is just another cog in their overflowing machine, another idiot who chose to break the law. Her value to them is yet to be determined—she is famous, after all. There is plenty of time ahead to assess these things.

They come to get her at noon. She is escorted from her cell to the receiving room and left there to sit on the dirty metal stool. Everything here is dirty; though it's been cleaned, again and again, the stink of raw bleach hangs on every corner like a blanket. Bleach and fear, the prison olfactory. Plus the dirt of a thousand people, grimed into the history of the place.

There is a phone on her side of the Plexiglas, and a phone on the other side as well.

She doesn't know who is coming to see her. The visit isn't scheduled, isn't on the books. Her lawyers usually send word ahead, and they've informed her they will come on Tuesdays and Thursdays to discuss her upcoming hearings. The guards tell her when someone else will be coming; she keeps hoping for Jasper, but he's steered clear. She doesn't blame him; there is still so much at stake. Sometimes the CBI agents come to accuse her of awful things. This time, there was no forewarning, and she is vaguely curious, but happy for the unscheduled alteration of her day.

She hopes for a moment that it's Mindy. She's torn; she desperately wants to see her daughter—yes, daughter, still; she will always think of Mindy as her own—but hates the idea of her seeing her mother behind bars like this.

Those hopes are dashed when the door opens, and a tall, dark, handsome man steps through.

Zack Armstrong has finally come to call.

He sits and stares for a moment, as if unsure what to do, then picks up the phone. She picks up on her end.

"Hello, Zack."

"Lauren."

"How's Mindy?"

He doesn't answer, and she sighs. "Please, Zack."

"She's better. The transplant worked. She has another round of chemo to go, but Oliver is very hopeful. It's too early to say she's in remission, but the cancer has stopped growing."

For a brief moment, she shuts her eyes and raises her head skyward. *Thank you.*

"Is she still refusing to see me?"

"Yes. Do you blame her?"

"I blame myself. If I hadn't stopped off to pull Juliet's plug I would have had time to talk to her properly."

Zack stares at her. "Are you really crazy, or are you just playing another long con?"

"What do you think?"

She is enjoying the cat and mouse. Everything here has been so dull and gray. She's not one for torture, but it's rather fun to watch him squirm.

Not healthy, though. She needs to keep him in check for a little while longer.

"I'm sorry. I shouldn't say things like that. The prison psychiatrist says I'm too impulsive. That I blurt things out without thinking of the effect they might have on other people."

"I'll say."

"Why didn't you come sooner?"

"Lauren, just cut to the chase, okay? I don't want to play your games anymore."

"Fine. Quid pro quo, my friend. I will help you if you help me."

"I don't need your help."

"No? You don't want to know what really happened? Then what do you want? If it's within my power, I'll make it happen."

"You're in jail, Lauren. Haven't you figured out yet that you have no power?"

"Suit yourself. When you're ready to deal, you come on back. You know where to find me."

She stands, smiling, and begins to put down the phone.

"Wait."

Predictable. So predictable, Zack Armstrong. Such easy prey.

"Sit down. I want to hear it. I want to hear it all."

"No cops, no lawyers. Just us."

"Just us."

She leans closer to the Plexiglas. "Just us, Zack. This is going to be our little secret. No pillow talk with Juliet, no late-night confessions to Mindy. I tell you exactly what happened, and you do me a favor. Deal?"

Zack stares at her, calculating the cost.

"Deal."

"I swore to Vivian I wouldn't ever tell you this. But considering the circumstances…I suppose she might forgive me now."

"Are you playing a trick? Trying to get off? Is this some sort of technicality, some plan by your lawyers to prove how insane you really are? If you tell me the truth…"

"I will. I won't ever say this outside of this room. I will never repeat it, do you hear me? It's not going to come up at sentencing. I'm willing to pay the price for my actions. This is just for us, to cement the strange tie we've always had."

"How do you know they aren't listening?"

She leans back, looking around. She has considered this. Are there microphones in the telephones? It's possible. She will have to be extra careful.

"They aren't," Zack says quickly as if he's afraid he's chased her away. "I asked. There's no way for them to record these conversations."

She lets her shoulders relax. "Good. Thank you for checking. You always were a smart one."

"Would you stop playing with me and tell me, for God's sake?"

"All right. Vivian asked me to kill her."

"Bullshit. Give me a break."

He stands, and she shouts into the phone, "I swear it. And I have proof."

"What do you mean, you have proof?"

"She wrote you a letter explaining everything."

"I know all about the letters."

"Not this one. No one's ever seen it. Even me."

"And you've been keeping it safe all this time?"

"Yes, I have. Along with copies of our conversations. In case this ever happened—" she waves vaguely at the room around her "—I needed something to help mitigate the circumstances."

"I don't know what to believe anymore, Lauren."

"Read the letters. You'll understand everything. I promise."

"I want to hear it from you."

She looks at the ground coyly, and then she begins to talk.

91

VIVIAN

Vivian sits at the table with a cup of tea, watching Liesel bustle around the house. She has already packed the baby's things, and really, there is nothing left to do but wait until darkness falls.

It feels strange, counting down the moments until you die.

Of course, she's been doing it since Zack pulled away. She'd sat on the couch, consumed with a single thought: *I need the baby out of me. I can't take being pregnant another minute. And once she's out…*

The bottle of castor oil was decidedly unpleasant. It, and a few other little tricks, worked to start her labor. She spent the next several long, painful hours running everything through her head, so weary of the blackness, of the sadness.

When her water finally broke, she called her midwife, who hustled on over. She was surprised by the early delivery but winked when she saw the castor oil bottle on the counter. She's the one who told Vivian to try it when she was to term, after all. She cleaned it all up. Put the house in order while Vivian grunted and moaned.

It was the longest night. The blackest. Vivian feared it would never end. And when it was over, when she was empty, devoid of child, cleaned and stitched and assured the child was healthy, she breathed a sigh of relief. *Not much longer.*

Liesel, too, now moves about the house, setting it to rights. As she does, they discuss it at length, what would be the easiest way to go, discarding suffocation, shooting, and strangulation. Stabbing is on the table briefly, but Vivian demurs. There is something so awful about the idea of metal entering her body. She already feels violated from the birth; she didn't want anything else stuck inside her.

Pills, then. Liesel, always exceptionally resourceful, has shown up with a full bottle of Talacen. It is a painkiller, she says, to help control her migraines. Liesel industriously grinds up half of the pills into a pile of death. They save some in case they need more, later. In case it doesn't work properly.

The plan is set, and breathtakingly simple. Vivian will drink tea laced with the Talacen. It won't take much to make her stop breathing. Liesel will ransack the house and do something to Vivian's body so it is clear she's died in the commission of a burglary. Vivian doesn't want to know what is coming. It is easier to think she is simply going to go to sleep. Liesel will leave for half an hour, then come to the house to "discover" Vivian's body, murdered. She will call the police, and they will take the baby into protective custody until Zack can be informed. It won't take more than a half a day for him to return from Gulf Shores. He'll come home to the adorable young infant and get on with his life.

What a good friend Liesel is. Helping her plan this.

Only that's not the way it happens at all.

★ ★ ★

"It's time. Are you ready?"

Vivian nods. Kissing Violet one last time, she hands her sleeping infant to her best friend, who lays her in the crib.

Liesel places the cup in front of her. Pours the tea ceremoniously. It is Earl Grey, her favorite. The pain medicine is already ground up at the bottom, waiting.

Once the liquid is in, Liesel pours honey on top, lots of honey, to mask what they both assume will be a horribly bitter brew. She stirs it, adds more honey, then stirs it again.

"I should put some Scotch in, have a hot toddy. There's a way to go."

Liesel laughs absently. "Are you known for drinking?"

"Not really."

"Then we better not. We don't want to draw any attention away from what the scene is telling the police. We don't want them asking questions."

"How did you learn all of this?"

"I just have a logical mind. Are you ready?"

The baby squawks. She's been so quiet for the past few hours. As if she doesn't want to disturb her mother's final moments.

"If the baby starts to cry..."

Liesel gets up and puts the pacifier back into the baby's mouth.

"She's probably hungry. We should feed her first. So she doesn't wake up."

Liesel puts her hand on Vivian's. It's cool, cold, really. Vivian shivers.

"I've fed her, and changed her. She's going to be fine. It's all going to be fine. I promise. I'm here for you. I'm here for her. I will make sure she is safe in Zack's arms before I go home."

"Okay."

But Vivian's hand will not raise the cup. The baby squeaks again, higher pitched this time. Vivian feels her breasts begin to leak in reply.

"I should feed her again."

"That will taste ten times worse if it gets cold. I'll get her a bottle as soon as you're gone."

Liesel's eyes are strangely bright. Vivian puts the sheen down to unshed tears.

She starts to raise the cup, and Liesel smiles encouragingly. "That's it. It will all be over soon."

The baby lets out a low howl. She sounds so confused, as if she knows what's happening, and is begging Vivian to stop, to be with her, even if it's only for a few weeks. Fear starts, and with it, regret.

Oh, God. I can't do this. I can't.

Vivian puts the cup down. "I have to—"

The knife catches her in the neck. Her head jerks to the side. She feels the warm spill of blood begin. She tries to talk, but words won't come. Liesel fills the empty space between them. Her eyes are still bright, and there's something in them Vivian hasn't seen since the first day they met, and Liesel threatened to kill her.

"I knew you were going to freak out and bail on the plan. Would you just die already?"

Vivian sees the flash of silver this time, but she can't move, it comes too quickly. The knife plunges into her stomach. It hurts. Dear God, it hurts. It burns. The pain is incredible.

Vivian collapses onto the kitchen floor. Panic fills her. What has Liesel done? This isn't what they agreed on.

"Help." Her breath won't come, something is wrong, so wrong. "Me," Vivian manages to get the second word out, starts to move. Liesel places a foot on her chest, between the two wounds.

Now Vivian can't rise. She can't do anything. She feels soaking wet and cold, so cold. The edges around her are blackening. The baby is crying lustily, and Vivian can't do anything to help her because she's dying. What a mistake she's made.

And the last thing she hears before the world goes black is the singsong voice of her best friend in the entire world, her only true friend, as she says, "Thanks for the baby. I'll take good care of her."

92

"...So Vivian asked me to make sure it was clear someone at-tacked her. I didn't like doing it, Zack. It broke my heart. I re-fused. She wanted to die by the blade—it was something she said to me a few times. It meant something to her, I'm not sure what. But there was no way I was going to stab her. I'd brought a bottle of painkillers, and I begged her, pleaded, that it would be so much easier to just drink something with them crushed up, and she'd go to sleep. She insisted the insurance company could rule that a suicide instead, that it had to be absolutely clear it was murder. She'd done all the research." She shuddered. "I still couldn't do it. I couldn't. And she knew that. She pulled the knife across her own throat."

Lauren is crying now.

"She started to bleed, and went down, but she wasn't dying. She hadn't cut deep enough, she was just drowning. There was nothing I could do. She kept pointing at her stomach, slapping it, so I jammed the knife in. It was over quickly after that."

She wipes her eyes, pulls herself together.

"You have no idea how hard it was, Zack. I hated to do it. I hated every minute. She begged me to take Mindy, to make sure she was safe and cared for. She was afraid that without her at the helm, you'd give the baby up. You didn't even know her, she was practically a stranger. She told me how distant you were those last few months. That you had been fighting. She was worried you might not want the baby after all of that. She begged me, begged me, to save the baby. To protect Mindy."

This last bit is enough to shake Zack from his horrified stupor. He's been listening in disbelief to Lauren talk. Her words make an obscene kind of sense. There had been a major insurance payout. Vivian had increased the policies on their life insurance as soon as she'd gotten pregnant, that he knew. What he didn't know was how much she'd increased them, nor that she'd gone back when she was seven months pregnant and doubled hers. When she died, he got a payout of almost half a million dollars.

It was information he hadn't shared with anyone. He'd put the money in a high yield interest-accruing bank account for Violet, should she ever be found. Statements came, but he never opened them. He assumed it was worth quite a bit now.

It all makes a sick kind of sense. Why Vivian wouldn't tell him about her severe depression. Why there were no records of her seeing a psychiatrist. Why no one knew she'd been suffering.

She was trying to take care of him. Of them.

"It was only in the end that she agreed to take the antidepressants. I told her she had to. She didn't want to hurt Mindy, even before she was born, but being off the meds dragged her into the abyss.

"You do see now, don't you, Zack? All I've ever wanted to do is help you. First Vivian, then Mindy. Now you. I'm giving you the last piece of the puzzle because I am going to die in here. Either they'll kill me, or I'll grow old and gray, or someone will knife me in the shower, but however you cut it, I am a dead woman. And now it's your turn to take care of our girl."

Zack sets the phone down on the counter. He sits back in the chair and crosses his arms. Processes. Watches Lauren get antsy. There's something more happening, but he doesn't know what it is.

Finally, he picks up the phone again.

"I don't believe for a moment my wife asked you to keep my daughter from me."

"Well, she did. She wanted Mindy to have a happy life, a carefree life, and she knew you'd be all thumbs at fatherhood."

The words strike deep in his soul. Vivian said that to him once, when they were arguing, but it was in exasperation, not anger. *"You're going to be all thumbs at this, so why even bother to learn how to change a diaper? You'll get shipped off somewhere and I'll end up doing it all anyway."*

"What do you want, Lauren? I listened to your story. What's your quid pro quo?"

"She left you a letter. It's in a safety deposit box. The key is in my closet, taped to the top of the door frame. Everything is ready for you. Her letter, and the letters we shared between us. I want Mindy to know that I only did this for her. That I would never have killed my best friend unless she begged me to do it, and even then, I had many reservations. But I wanted Mindy to be safe. That's all I've ever wanted. Yes, maybe I shouldn't have taken her, should have known Vivian wasn't entirely in her right mind. But I fell in love with that child, Zack. Surely you understand that. And I've given her a good life. A happy life. A solid family. Encouraged all her talents. Sacrificed everything for her. She adores Jasper, and he adores her. Please don't take that away from them."

"She could have had that with me," he snaps, standing. "Does Jasper know?"

"No. I've never told him. And that's your part of the bargain. You need to get him to go with you to open the safety deposit box. You have to tell him about Vivian, you have to explain for me. He won't come see me."

She is pouting. She is actually pouting.

"Tell him yourself."

He ignores the cries he hears through the phone, the fact that Lauren has gone white, that she's banging on the glass. He ignores it all, slams down the receiver, and signals for the guard waiting outside to let him out of this hellhole.

93

THE WRIGHTS' HOUSE

Zack rings the Wrights' bell. After a few moments' wait, Jasper opens the door, lets Kat out, and shoves it closed behind him with a bang.

Zack knocks. "Jasper, let me in. I saw Lauren. I need to talk to you."

Crickets.

It takes ten minutes of alternately banging and shouting, but Jasper finally reopens the door.

"What do you want? Haven't you ruined enough?"

"I need to tell you something."

Jasper listens, incredulous at the story Zack is telling him, and finally lets Zack into the house.

It is clear Jasper is still furious, and for good reason. In his mind, Lauren wouldn't be in jail if Zack hadn't pressed them so hard. But he's taken care of Kat since Zack took off down the mountain to see Lauren, and Zack knows he's going to cool off eventually.

Honestly, Zack doesn't care if Jasper likes him. All he's worried about is Mindy's safety and security. He has already filed for full custody. His lawyer thinks he might get it, considering. He hasn't gone so far as to ban Jasper from seeing her, if only because he knows she won't want that, but it's been tempting. He and Jasper are never going to see eye-to-eye on the situation.

But now that Zack knows why Lauren killed Vivian, he is

more relaxed. Still livid, still torn to shreds at her stupidity and callousness, but something is settled in his mind. He knows what happened to his wife now, and the idea that she was so sick, and tried to save them financially, that she was trying to be noble and make her suicide as painless as possible, well, it doesn't make him feel better, but it gives him some closure.

The key is where Lauren promised it would be.

"What the hell?" Jasper says, seeing it.

"Believe me now?"

He nods, still clearly in shock. "She really did it?"

"It looks like she did. I need to get the rest of the letters to verify her story. Do you know where this bank is?"

He flashes the small white-and-green envelope that contains the key.

"Yeah. First Bank on Vail Road. I'll take you."

The drive is short. Kat sticks her head out the window joyfully, the innocent who saved a child. Zack tries desperately not to think, not to cloud his mind with suppositions. *Read the letter. Then you'll know.*

Ten minutes later, Jasper parks in the bank's lot. They leave the windows cracked despite Kat's reproachful whine.

"Relax, sweetie. I'll be right back."

Inside the bank, he and Jasper approach the first open teller. Zack slides the little white envelope that holds the key to box 615 in it. *Strange*, he thinks, *that's the area code for Nashville. Another dig? Or a way to remember easily?*

"I need to get into my safety deposit box."

"I'll need some ID, sir."

He hands over his driver's license. A few moments later, the teller hands back his ID and steps from the counter to the cage. He and Jasper follow mutely.

Inside, the teller says, "Mr. Armstrong, I'll need you to sign the signature card."

He notices the deposit box is in his name. Clever Lauren. So very clever.

"How long has this box been open?"

She pulls it from the small index file. "Looks like...2005."

"That's when we bought the house," Jasper says.

The teller uses her key, inserts Zack's into the second slot, then turns them both and opens the small door. She steps away, pulls the door, saying, "Just let me know when you're done."

When they are alone, Zack lifts the lid.

The box is empty except for three things. A sheaf of papers, folded into thirds, a passport, and underneath them both, a sealed envelope, addressed to Zack, in his dead wife's familiar script.

Zack opens the passport first, sees Jasper's photo.

"Wait, is that *my* passport?"

Zack hands it to him. He opens it incredulously. Flips through a few pages. A tiny piece of paper flutters to the ground. He picks it up, reads it, then shuts his eyes and swallows, hard, like he's trying not to be sick.

"What?" Zack asks.

Jasper hands over the piece of paper. It is handwritten in a script Zack isn't familiar with.

It says: *I know your secret.*

94

Jasper is white, and Zack almost feels sorry for him. The passport is obviously a shock and the meaning of the message clear to him.

"You want to tell me what's going on?"

"Lauren specifically asked you to make sure I was here when you opened the box?"

"She did. I assume she wants me to know everything, too?"

Jasper glances up at the corner of the room, where the camera hangs, a single eye watching them.

"Can we go somewhere else? Please?"

"Of course." Zack is dying to read the letter from Vivian, but also afraid to open it, afraid of what he might find, what truths might be revealed. What if Lauren is lying again? What if, what if, what if?

Zack sees Jasper's hands are shaking, offers to drive. Jasper gets into the car without a word. Zack climbs behind the wheel. Kat is happy to see them; she hates being left alone in the back of the car. Both men get licks on the ear.

"Where to?"

"Let's... I don't care. Just drive."

Zack only knows a few places in Vail—the restaurant, the hospital, the Wrights' house on the hill. But he remembers there was a scenic overlook on the way down the mountain. He heads there. The day is fine, the snow holding off, the sun shining, the skies blue again. He pulls into the overlook, and they climb out. Kat is thrilled for the excursion, and Zack sets her lead to the longest setting.

They lean against the stone wall. Finally, Zack takes off his sunglasses.

"You want to tell me what's going on?"

★ ★ ★

"There were five of us. All lawyers. All experienced divers. We were off the coast of Baja, on a day trip. There's a reef out there."

He goes silent until Zack prompts him. "And?"

"We went out with five and came back in with four."

"That's not good."

Jasper half laughs. "No. Not good at all. We were all hungover. Had no business going on the dive. I was buddied up with a guy I'd just met that week. We were working on a case, had partnered with a firm out in San Diego. He was a decent enough lawyer, but a blustery asshole of a man, all hat, and no cattle, as they say. A talker, a major talker. He'd been talking my ear off all week. Mostly about how his divorce was final, and that was a good thing, because his stupid ex-wife had managed to get herself knocked up, and he hated kids, wasn't ready to settle down, so he'd *bailed on the bitch*, quote unquote."

"I take it his name was Kyle Noonan?"

"Yeah." Jasper rubs a hand over his face. "You know how guys like that are. They don't like to be told what to do. We were setting everything up on the boat, and we were all goofing around, getting ready for our last dive of the day, and I must have misread his tank. I remember thinking it might have been a little low, but nothing dangerous. Either way, I should have warned him he needed to stay close to the boat in case he needed to rise up quickly, but I got caught up in another conversation, and before I could tell him, he went down, and the tank mal-functioned. He couldn't get back to the surface in time.

"It was my fault. I was his partner on the dive. We shouldn't have been geared up at all, we had all been drinking pretty heavily the night before, but that's no excuse. He was my partner. I screwed up, and a man died."

"Sounds like all of you were to blame. Did anyone know? Any of the others?"

Jasper shakes his head. "Everyone thought it was an accident, we all agreed I'd warned him of the low air. It was an accident, and shit happens, right?"

"Right."

"Hey, don't judge me, asshole."

"I'm not. I've screwed up, and it cost lives, too. Get off your high horse, I'm not saying anything."

"Sorry."

They are quiet for the moment, watching two hawks soar the thermals. "I guess that's not the end of the story?"

"No. I came back to Denver and looked up the ex-wife. I was going to say something, I guess to apologize in some way. As-suage my guilt. Make it right for her, offer some cash to cover things while she got set with the kid. Noonan made it clear he'd gotten out of the marriage scot-free, and she was left with nothing. Marital deception, some arcane ruling he managed to talk a judge into. And here she is, with this perfect little baby, and she seemed so lost and overwhelmed, and I couldn't help myself. I stepped right into the void and never looked back."

"Did you love her?"

"Yeah. I did."

"Did you tell her? The note, the passport—she figured some-thing out."

"Early on in our marriage, I got drunk one night, and we had a big fight. I hinted I knew that Lauren's ex was a total douche from personal experience. My passport went missing right after that. She figured it out. She is so smart."

"She's cunning. Do you think she was trying to protect you, or putting it aside to dangle it over you at the right time if she needed to?"

"I don't know. I don't know anything about her anymore."

★ ★ ★

They agree, in the way of men who have carried guilt for much of their lives, that no one will benefit from hearing the whole story except for those directly affected—in other words, Mindy.

They agree to call a truce between them, to focus their energies on helping Mindy heal, and to helping Mindy move on.

They agree, standing on the windswept hillside, to share the girl between them. To always stand by her, to be there for her, to make up for the losses of both of her mothers.

They shake on it, then drive back to the hospital to visit their daughter.

Later that night, in the cool air of the Wrights' guest room, Kat cuddled next to him on the bed, Zack reads the letters between the two women, and the letter to him from his dead wife.

Thirty minutes later, in shock, he whispers, "Oh, my love." His heart is breaking for what could have been, for what he was too stupid to see. "Oh, V."

He reads the letter again, the tears welling. Revels in the words from his dead wife, hearing her voice, smiling and laughing and crying. Is angry at himself all over again.

He could have saved her if she'd just told him the truth.

95

July 2000

Zachary, my darling,

I miss you. I miss you so much it hurts. The baby is kicking up a storm, I really can't wait for you to meet her.

I have some bad news. I don't know how to tell you this, so I am going to write it down, and then... I can't tell you over the phone. This is news that should be shared in person, but I'm not strong enough.

First, let me say you have been the greatest gift of my life. I love you very much.

True confession time: I have a long and storied history with severe depression, and with suicide. And now, it's time for me to end things properly.

I know this means I will not live to see our baby grow up. That makes me sad, it does. But every time I go down, it's worse than the last. I just can't take the blackness anymore.

I've asked a friend to help, to make sure there are no mistakes. I'm going to give her this letter and make sure it gets to you after I'm gone. Liesel will tell you about how we met, and the shape I was in then. I'm worse now. And I know it will never get better. The years I've spent sliding up and down—this kind of life, it's not fair to you, or Violet.

I hope you'll forgive me someday. I hope you'll understand just how weak I am. I want to be strong, for once. I want to die a soldier's death, clean and sudden, instead of lingering in pain and black.

I will always love you and watch over you. Raise our girl right. Don't let her do anything reckless.

I've taken care of everything from my end. Now it's your turn. Find someone to love, who will love our girl like she's her own. Be happy. Be wonderful.

With all my heart,

V

96

THE WRIGHTS' HOUSE
SIX WEEKS LATER

Mindy wakes from a delicious dream. Her mother—Vivian, walking through a green park, a book in her hand, toward a light. The air is scented with roses, and Vivian looks so happy, so carefree. She looks back over her shoulder and smiles at Mindy, waves, blows a kiss, and then she is gone.

This dream should make her sad, but instead, she feels good. Right. Strong.

The transplant worked. She can feel Zack's energy flowing through her. The cancer was stopped in its tracks. Dr. Oliver and Dr. Berger fixed her. Zack saved her.

She slides out of the bed. The cast came off yesterday, and today she is allowed to begin light training again. She stretches her long arms to the ceiling, feels the pleasant pops and cracks that allow her spine to lengthen.

Jasper has left the breakfast makings on the counter for her. Breakfast of champions, cornflakes with strawberries and coconut milk. As she settles in, there is a knock on the door, then it opens and her aunt Juliet walks through.

"Are you ready?"

"Almost."

"Nervous?"

Mindy smiles. "Maybe a little. I don't want them to stare at me, you know?"

"They won't. No one blames you for any of this. Finish your cereal. The Jeep is warm."

Mindy puts her bowl in the sink, walking slowly on her hurt leg, using a cane for balance. It will be weeks before she can get back on her skis, but for now, a strengthening program is in place.

She's managed to stay out of the muck of Lauren's sentencing and incarceration. The psychologist tells her she doesn't have to forgive her mother for being a murderer. From before Mindy's birth, Lauren was a killer. It freaks her out to think about the lengths Lauren went to in order to protect her. Freaks her out that Lauren killed three and tried to kill a fourth. Freaks her out that her mother has gone from a beloved influence to a stranger who will be in jail for the rest of her life.

Stop thinking about her. You have your whole life to come to terms with her.

Today you train.

Mindy knows she has to stay focused. Extreme, myopic focus is the only way she will overcome this setback. She is going to get back into shape, back in her boots, and conquer the shit out of the mountain.

Juliet holds the door for her. She too moves a little slower than before. The two of them are a pair. The sun greets her as she gets in the shiny black Jeep. Her dads gave it to her as a *you beat the cancer* gift, though she's not allowed to drive it yet. As they head down the mountain, Mindy watches her aunt from under her lashes. Finally, she screws up her courage.

"Aunt J? How's your therapy going? Are you getting better?"

Juliet's grip on the wheel tightens. "It's going," she says quietly. When Mindy doesn't reply, Juliet continues. "Honestly, the physical therapy isn't a big deal. It's the damn psychologist that sucks. I don't like trying to resurrect the past."

"I don't, either. I hate having to talk to the woman at the hospital. She's all over the fact that I didn't make the Olympics this year." She adopts a deep voice with a slight Germanic accent. "And how does that make you feel, Mindy?"

Juliet laughs at her imitation. "It's weird trying to dissect your life for a stranger. You know you can always talk to me, Mindy. Anything you ever want to know, you can ask. I know how hard this has been on you. You're being a total stud."

Mindy smiles. "Yeah. I'm a total stud. Speaking of studs… when do you leave for Nashville?"

Juliet glances over at her niece, fluffs her hair. "Tomorrow."

"Excited?"

A grin blossoms on her aunt's face. "Maybe."

"I think you two are really cute together. Are you going to get married?"

Juliet laughs. "It's a little soon for marriage, kiddo. He's a nice guy, and I like him an awful lot."

"He likes you, too. Why else would he be moving to Colorado?"

"Uh, I don't know, maybe because his kid lives here?"

"I don't think that's the only reason," Mindy says, grinning now. "Seriously, I'm glad you found each other. Glad there's something positive out of all this mess."

"You're better, kiddo. That's the only positive we all need." But Juliet is grinning too, a soft blush on her cheeks.

The drive is only ten minutes. Juliet parks. "I'll be back for you at noon. Don't get too crazy."

Mindy nods. She is feeling uncharacteristically nervous.

The smell of the gym is so familiar, so much a part of her, she stops and breathes it in, eyes closed. When she opens them, she realizes everyone inside has stopped what they're doing and are watching her.

She gives them a little bow, and the whole place breaks into applause.

Her smile lights up the room. The sunny girl is home.

EPILOGUE

DENVER WOMEN'S CORRECTIONAL FACILITY

FOUR YEARS LATER

Lauren has barely slept and wakes in the middle of the night to the sound of her door being unlocked. The excitement of this occasion turns her stomach to jelly.

She is already dressed; she didn't want to waste any time when they came for her.

She has been granted a television pass because of her good behavior. Because of all the work she's done to help other prisoners. She's started an art program and has found some peace in the daily routines. She is a popular prisoner, among the inmates and the guards. After the first few months, through the hearings and the sentencing, she was kept in solitary, and she enjoyed the silence. But today, she wants to shake off the last twenty-one years. She's been hiding inside the memories for so long she's almost forgotten what it's like to live out loud, to be present. To have something to live for.

They walk her to the television room. No one else is there—it's the middle of the night in Denver, but morning halfway across the world in Beijing. The downhill race starts in fifteen minutes.

She is allowed a glass of water and has the television privileges for an hour.

One race.

One time.

Winner takes all.

The papers have had a field day with Mindy's triumphant return to Team USA. The story of her birth, her cancer, the risky transplant, her mothers and fathers, has been fodder for weeks leading up to the 2022 Olympic games. A young reporter named Bode Greer even won a Pulitzer a few years ago for his coverage of the story. Granted, he was the only reporter who seemed to get the full, inside scoop, but he wrote with great passion and style, and the world loved it.

The trumpets blare, and the coverage starts. Lauren watches and listens intently, leaning forward in her chair. This is the moment she's waited for. That they've all been waiting for.

The announcers go immediately to the story everyone is excited to hear. The package runs—tiny Mindy on short skis, hands in the air, whipping past the camera; the crash; Lauren in a prison jumpsuit; the photo of square-jawed Zack Armstrong; a grainy photo of Vivian; Vail Health Hospital. Quotes on Mindy's perseverance and courage from Dr. Oliver, from the coaches, from her teammates. No one has ever seen such determination. No one has ever seen someone who loves to ski more. Her incredible successes over the past couple of years on the World Cup circuit. It is all there. The whole story unfolded in a three-minute clip.

The third racer flies down the hill to the clanging cowbells. Her split is excellent; the course is fast. Mindy has pulled the fifth slot. Which is great. The field of thirty, the deteriorating conditions; she's caught a huge break drawing an early lot.

Lauren is breathless by the time Mindy is called to the gate. Lauren imagines she can feel the icy snow under her own skis, can feel the hard plastic grips of the poles.

The buzzer rings three times, and Mindy is off with a *thwack!*

It is a good start. She poles into her tuck almost immediately, sailing over the first jump without losing her balance. Lauren is amazed at the strength in Mindy's thighs as she makes minute adjustments to her legs and knees, allowing her to take the cleanest line.

There is no windmilling, no showboating. She is silver, she is gold. She is fast. So fast.

The microseconds tick off, and she's suddenly done, spraying a huge rooster tail of snow into the hay at the bottom.

Lauren stares in disbelief at the screen, at the bright green banner next to her daughter's time.

She is nearly three seconds faster than the previous skiers. It will take a miracle for someone to beat her.

The world holds its collective breath as skier after skier follows. No one even comes close.

Mindy Wright has won the gold.

The camera pans to the family. Jasper is screaming, howling to the sky with joy. Zack is jumping up and down, an arm around Juliet, who is flinging her hands up over her head in glee. Mindy, skis in hand, gives the crowd the tiniest curtsey, and then they are on her, mobbing her, the teammates and the family.

Mindy is screaming now, too. The cameras have gone up close to her teary face. She smacks her chest three times and looks to the sky, pointing two fingers in the air. And then, Mindy looks directly into the camera and mouths the words, "Thank you."

Lauren bursts into tears. A hand to her heart, she says to the television, in the empty room, "I am so proud of you, baby, I am so proud."

The salty lines flowing unchecked down her face, Lauren too looks heavenward.

"Oh, Vivian. She's done it. I think we did okay, considering."

And the television flickers off.

★ ★ ★ ★ ★

Author's Note

This book was many years and several iterations in the making. I couldn't shake the idea of a young mother sacrificing herself so her family could have the best chance at a happy life, of a young father trying to raise their dynamic, driven, elite athlete daughter alone. In early drafts, Violet was an ice-skater—but she only existed in her father's dreams, as he'd never met her. I knew Vivian had taken her own life, but why would a young mother in a happy marriage do such a thing? The very thought tore at my soul, but wouldn't leave me alone.

As stories tend to do, this one morphed into what you've just read. It's taken me years to be brave enough to tackle a main character's suicide. It is a sad, disturbing topic, one that has deeply affected my family. I wanted to do it justice, to show the proper respect and compassion for what is a heartbreaking decision for all involved.

I also want to use this book to raise awareness for Project Semicolon. When I learned of its existence, I was very touched by the movement, by the message of inclusion and strength, and the idea that most suicides can be prevented. Many followers tattoo themselves with a semicolon to signify their support of a friend, family member or themselves. While each bit of flesh marked with a semicolon breaks my heart, it also makes me shout for joy that light is being shed on the issue of self-harm.

Sadly, when I began this note, I learned Amy Bleuel, the founder of Project Semicolon, had herself succumbed to suicide. Her loss is tragic and a harsh reminder how very brutal depression can be. Oddly, moments after I saw the news, a Twitter friend began a series of posts honoring the death anniversary of a luminary writer, Sylvia Plath. In this note from *Letters Home: Correspondence 1950–1963*, Plath's mother, Aurelia, talking about her daughter's demise was especially poignant:

Her physical energies had been depleted by illness, anxiety and overwork, and although she had for so long managed to be gallant and equal to the life-experience, some darker day than usual had temporarily made it seem impossible to pursue.

Some darker day than usual. It is this I want you to remember, should you ever find yourself in the darkness. This feeling is temporary, no matter how cruel and pervasive it feels. It will get better. There is hope.

I hope this book will allow us to have more open dialogues about mental illness. There is no shame in a diagnosis of depression, or bipolar disorder, or severe anxiety, or any other mental illness. On the contrary, a diagnosis should be celebrated, because you, or your friend, or your family member has been brave enough to seek help. A wonderful doctor once told us there is no difference in these diagnoses than discovering you have diabetes—your body simply doesn't process the same way another's does. It's something to remember, and with that mentality, perhaps we can erase the stigma altogether.

But if the darkness becomes too great, if you need to talk, or think someone close to you might be in trouble, please, please reach out. Silence and solitude are not helpful when you're feeling low. Tell your friends and family how you're feeling.

Call the suicide hotline. Reach out to a mental health professional. Email me.

Remember, you are glorious. And you are not alone.

National Suicide Prevention Lifeline
Call 1-800-273-8255
www.projectsemicolon.com

J.T. Ellison
March 2018

Acknowledgments

A book that's been in the making for so many years will obviously have a lot of people to thank, so here we go.

First, I need to send major props to skiing phenom Lindsey Vonn, who inspired me to create Mindy Wright. So much courage, grace, dedication and sheer, raw talent in a single being should be outlawed; I'm so glad it's not. Thanks, Lindsey. You rule.

Three wonderful individuals bid on character names for various charity fund-raisers. Sandra McMahon won a name and asked me to surprise her niece, Brianna Starr, better known as Breezy. Andrea Austin, unfailing supporter and friend, finally got her due, and Cameron Longer from the UK lent his name to the mix. It was a joy to think of their selfless contributions every time I typed their names.

When I was having my "all is lost" moment, friend and fellow author Victoria Schwab swooped in and suggested I change the tense. It fixed the book, and I am most grateful for both the advice and her excellent taste in tea and bacon.

The divine Laura Benedict, first reader, best friend and unflagging cheerleader, promised me the opening worked. I would also be lost without her guidance and great friendship.

Ariel Lawhon and Paige Crutcher, without whom I would be lost, provided regular comfort, suppers, wine, enthusiasm and relentless faith to this effort, which is most appreciated.

Helen Ellis, who never ceases to amuse and amuse, and is the most gracious hostess I know.

Catherine Coulter, my cowriter extraordinaire, keeps me in stitches on email daily. Thank you for teaching me so much.

Jeff Abbott was always there when I needed to vent, to be challenged or simply wanted a good movie recommendation.

Sherrie Saint has been a steady hand on pretty much every book I've written in the past several years, and having her love and strength, and wicked brain, sustains me. Thanks for the research!

Amy Kerr, who helped get this book into shape and managed me well, too.

My wonderful agent, Scott Miller, friend and confidant, who knew the story wasn't ready way back in 2011 but never let me forget to revisit it, for plotting and planning and guiding me through the mayhem that is publishing.

Many thanks to my awesome film agent, Holly Frederick, whose wise counsel and steady hand are so appreciated.

My editor, Nicole Brebner, needs three cheers and then some. She coached and cheered and coddled, helped develop the story in so many ways, read this book three (four, five?) times and found ways to improve it with every pass. This, my friends, is the hallmark of an excellent editor. I really couldn't have done this without her. Authors say that all the time, but I mean it. Also, Kat is no longer eating people food thanks to her.

Margaret Marbury sat across many tables, lunches, dinners, meetings, glasses of wine and pushed me to go deeper, helped me find the darkness that this book needed. Never fear, she is the brightest, sunniest person I know.

My entire publishing family at MIRA Books needs pages upon pages of acknowledgments for their untiring work and support getting my work into your hands. Craig Swinwood, Loriana Sacilotto, Brent Lewis, Amy Jones, Randy Chan, Heather Foy, Stefanie Buszynski, Emer Flounders, Shara Alexander, Margot

Mallinson, Catherine Makk, Miranda Indrigo, Malle Vallik, Susan Swinwood, Monika Rola, Olivia Gissing, Larissa Walker, Sean Kapitain, Kristen Salciccia, and everyone else—you are the most amazing group to work with, and I adore and appreciate you all.

All the amazing librarians and booksellers and book clubs and bookstagrammers and social media folks who recommend my books to patrons, friends and followers—thank you so, so much!

My lovely parents, Jerome and Joan, who are the best first readers a girl could hope for and pretty amazing parents, to boot. Also have to send some love to my awesome brothers, who keep me grounded.

And to the love of my life, my darling husband, Randy. Without you, these books would be mere shadows of themselves, dreams unfulfilled, as would I.